M000208085

A NEWFOUND LAND

On a muggy August day in 2002, Alexandra Lind was unexpectedly thrown backwards in time, landing in the year of Our Lord 1658. Catapulted into an unfamiliar and frightening new existence, Alex could do nothing but adapt. After all, while time travelling itself is a most rare occurrence, time travelling with a return ticket is even rarer.

This is the fourth book about Alex, her husband Matthew and their continued adventures in the second half of the seventeenth century.

Previously published titles in The Graham Saga:

A Rip in the Veil

Like Chaff in the Wind

The Prodigal Son

ANNA BELFRAGE

A Newfound Land

SilverWood

Published in 2013 by the author
using SilverWood Books Empowered Publishing®

SilverWood Books
30 Queen Charlotte Street, Bristol, BS1 4HJ
www.silverwoodbooks.co.uk

Copyright © Anna Belfrage 2013

The right of Anna Belfrage to be identified as the author of this work
has been asserted by her in accordance with the
Copyright, Designs and Patents Act 1988.

All rights reserved. No part of this publication may be reproduced,
stored in a retrieval system, or transmitted in any form or by any means,
electronic, mechanical, photocopying, recording or otherwise,
without prior permission of the copyright holder.

This is a work of fiction. Names, characters, places and incidents either are
products of the author's imagination or are used fictitiously. Any resemblance
to actual events or locales or persons, living or dead, is entirely coincidental.

ISBN 978-1-78132-135-5 (paperback)
ISBN 978-1-78132-136-2 (ebook)

British Library Cataloguing in Publication Data
A CIP catalogue record for this book is available from the British Library

Set in Bembo by SilverWood Books
Printed on responsibly sourced paper

This book is dedicated to my four children,
a constant source of joy and pride

Chapter 1

The household was still asleep when Alex Graham snuck out of bed. Matthew grumbled, half opened an eye, and subsided back into sleep. On tiptoe, Alex traversed the room, stepping over one sleeping shape after the other. No more, she sang inside, throwing a look at the furthest wall and the as yet boarded up doorways. Matthew had promised he'd finish the extension today, and tonight they'd sleep in their new bedroom, an oasis of privacy after years living as cramped as salted herrings in a barrel.

Alex stuck her feet into her clogs, grabbed the little basket that contained her soap and oils, and stepped outside. The sun was no more than a promise on the eastern rim, the stands of grasses to her right sparkled with dew, and just by the door her precious rose was setting buds. This was their new home, a small pocket of domesticity in a wilderness that at times she found most intimidating. Not that she felt particularly threatened by the miles and miles of uninterrupted forest that surrounded her, but should anything happen they were very alone, their closest neighbours well over an hour's ride away.

When they had first arrived in 1668, not yet four years ago, this had been virgin forest, a gently sloping clearing with man-high grass and not much else. Now they had managed to carve out several sizeable fields and pastures, a respectable kitchen garden, as well as the yard she was now crossing on her way to the river. She turned to look back at the small house. The elongated wooden building with its shingled roof was already beginning to grey, acquiring an air of permanence that Alex found comforting. It spoke of roots – as yet shallow, even extremely shallow – but still, roots.

The water numbed her toes in a matter of minutes, but Alex didn't mind. She enjoyed these early morning outings, moments when she was alone with only her thoughts for company. A brisk wash, a couple of muttered curses at just how bloody cold the water was, and she was back on the bank, dressing quickly before settling down to comb her wet hair.

In the nearby shrubs, a couple of thrushes squabbled. The sun had risen enough to send a ray or two her way, and on the opposite bank a couple of deer came down to drink. So peaceful – until she became aware of the eyes. Strange that: there were eyes all over the place, but somehow one knew when another human being was gawking at you – in this case someone who was doing his or her best to stay hidden.

She returned her comb to the basket and groped until she found the knife. A sidelong glance revealed someone sitting just behind the closest stand of trees. Alex loitered, humming casually while straining her ears. Someone whispered, was hushed. She did a double take: women, not men. Without stopping to think overmuch – one of her major faults according to Matthew – she rushed for the trees.

One of the women squeaked. The other tried to run, slipped and fell.

"Sit," Alex said, waving her knife at them. They complied, huddling together under the oak. They looked bedraggled, caps askew, one with tears in her apron, both quite dirty. Escaped bond servants, Alex guessed, and she recognised the monogram on one of the aprons.

"You've run away," she said.

"Please, mistress, please don't tell." The eldest – or at least the biggest – of the girls placed a protective arm round her companion, a thin little thing with tendrils of red hair peeking from under her dirty cap.

Hmm. Alex was no major fan of indentured servants, but her Leslie neighbours had paid good money for these two, and would be pissed off if they weren't returned.

"He hit us," the girl continued. "Belted us, he did."

"He did? For what?"

The younger girl hunched over, dark eyes never leaving Alex. "We stole."

"Stole?" The other girl sniffed. "I didn't steal. I took payment."

"Payment?" Alex echoed.

The girl gave her a condescending look. "He helped himself."

"Ah." Alex was somewhat taken aback. She'd never have taken Peter Leslie for the lecherous type. "And now you're planning to do what?"

"Walk." The girl shrugged, sounding confident. Her red-haired friend nodded.

"To Providence?" Alex shook her head. That was well over a week's walk, and the two girls seemed to have no sense of direction as they'd walked north from the Leslie settlement, rather than south.

"No, to St Mary's City," the younger girl said. Good luck to them. That was almost twice as far.

"You're Catholic," Alex said. No other reason to go that far – unless they'd done more than steal.

The elder girl glared at her. "And what if we are?"

"I couldn't care less," Alex told her with a little smile. "But it's a very long walk – that way." She pointed south. "How are you to survive, all on your own?"

"I have a knife."

"Whoopee," Alex muttered. She should send them straight back to the Leslies', but she already knew she wouldn't. Matthew wouldn't like it, but on the other hand, why tell him? She gnawed her lip. "I'll see what I can find. You'll need food and a blanket or two."

The youngest girl burst into tears and clutched at Alex's skirts.

"Yes, yes," Alex said, rather embarrassed by all this. She gestured into the deeper forest to their right. "Hide in there, somewhere. You'll have to stay put until you hear me whistle for you." She shooed them off, admonishing them to keep well out of sight, and set off up the incline.

★

9

She was almost back at the house when her three youngest children ambushed her.

"Ouff!" Alex said when Sarah barrelled into her. Her daughter grabbed at Alex's legs and rubbed her head against Alex's skirts, dislodging what little remained of her night braid. The fair hair fell in soft waves around Sarah's face, making her look like a sweet angel – which she definitely was not.

"Where have you been?" Matthew said from behind her.

"I went for a swim."

"A swim?" Sarah's reproachful blue eyes stared up at her. "Without us?"

"Aye, why didn't you say?" Ruth asked.

Because I wanted to go alone, Alex thought, smiling at her little redhead. Ruth smiled back, the hazel eyes she shared with her father and most of her siblings shifting into a light greyish green.

"We can go later," Alex said. "I probably need to give all three of you a proper scrub."

"Not me," Daniel muttered, shoving his dark hair off his brow. "I'm clean, very clean."

Alex looked at the trio; three children in three years, but since then Matthew and she had been very careful, even if at times both of them were left extremely frustrated by this. Her eyes slid over to rest on her man. Alex fluffed at her hair, catching Matthew's interested look. As far as she was concerned, five children – six, counting Ian, her stepson – were quite enough, but she wasn't sure Matthew agreed. What the hell; she wanted to have wild and uninhibited sex with him, and damn the consequences. She saw his mouth curve and felt the blood rush up her cheeks, making him smile even wider.

"Right, you," she said to her children. "You all have chores to do."

Daniel made a face but at Matthew's nod he and Ruth hurried off. Sarah loitered, throwing Alex a hopeful look. You wish, Alex thought, handing her three-year-old the egg basket.

"You look thoroughly," she said. "Now that they're back to laying properly, I want them all."

Sarah set her mouth in a sulk and dragged her feet on her way to the stables.

Matthew took Alex's hand and squeezed it. She knew exactly what he was thinking: that their youngest daughter was in many ways a throwback to their eldest girl, Rachel, and both of them were very relieved that in looks Sarah did not take after their dead daughter – that would have been a bit too much.

"She'll drive her future husband to the edge of despair," Matthew said in an undertone.

She chortled. "Let's hope she calms down a bit."

They walked across the yard, him shortening his stride to match hers.

"I don't like it, that you go about alone," he said.

"I was just down there." Alex gestured in the direction of the river.

"Still, I don't like it."

Alex chose not to reply, studying her house – well, cabin – instead. Two chimneys, one sticking up from the new extension, and several windows, four with horribly expensive glass panes that Matthew had transported up here piece by careful piece, swaddled as if they were priceless porcelain.

According to dear Elizabeth Leslie, window glass was an unnecessary luxury, but Alex didn't care about her opinion, thrilled to have light streaming into her kitchen and front room, and now into her bedroom as well. Elizabeth... Alex threw Matthew a look. She should tell him about the girls; he didn't like it when she kept things from him. On the other hand, it made her shudder just to imagine how Elizabeth would punish her two servants for running away. Bread and water for a month, and no doubt a severe beating with that cane Elizabeth always kept close at hand.

"What is it?" Matthew said, placing a hand on her arm to draw her to a stop when they reached the house.

"Nothing."

He turned her to face him. "What?"

Alex sighed. This man of hers read her like an open book, no matter how much she tried to dissimulate. Briefly, she told him of her encounter with the girls, shifting on her feet under his eyes.

"But I don't want to force them to go back," she finished. "Can you imagine how angry the Leslies will be?"

"Escaped servants must be returned. You know I don't much hold with it," he said, swinging her hand as they covered the last few yards to the door. "It sticks in my craw, it does, to hold a fellow man as a slave, however temporarily. But that's how things are ordained here, and Peter Leslie paid good money for them. Besides, two lasses on their own in all that…" He waved a hand at the woods.

"So what do we do?"

Matthew opened the door for her and gave Fiona, their maid, a curt nod before replying. "For now we do nowt." He leaned close enough that his breath tickled her ear. "But if they come looking, we tell them."

Alex nodded; a fair compromise and hopefully Peter would expend his efforts to the south.

The small kitchen filled with people: Mark and Jacob came from the direction of the stable, Sarah danced in to show them just how many eggs she'd found, and Daniel and Ruth were sent off to wash when they appeared dirty at the door. Eggs, ham, porridge and thick slices of rye bread were set down on the table. From the yard came Jonah, their second indenture, and after a hastily said grace everyone threw themselves at the food.

"And Ian?" Alex looked at Mark.

"I don't know," Mark said. "He may have gone hunting."

"Or fishing," Jacob suggested through his full mouth. Alex smoothed at his thick, blond hair.

"Maybe." She shrugged. Ian was old enough to take care of himself.

No sooner was the table cleared than Fiona begged to be excused, whispering something about her monthlies. Alex just nodded. The last few weeks, Fiona was forever begging to be let off for one reason or the other, and this latest excuse was wearing a bit thin. Still; mostly she did what she was told to do, and if Fiona found some sort of relief by wandering the nearby woods, so be it.

Matthew sat for a while longer at the table, conversing with her as Alex went about the dinner preparations. She still had days when it shocked her just how much time she spent on something as simple as cooking. In the here and now, there were no electric cookers, no microwaves; it was all open fire and heavy pots. Alex wiped her hands on her apron and leaned against the workbench.

She rarely thought about the life she'd left behind – given the circumstances, she preferred not to – but every now and then she was swept with a wave of longing for her people, lost somewhere in the future. Isaac, her son, he'd be sixteen by now, and she wondered if he'd be taller than her and if he still wore his hair short. And Magnus, now pushing seventy...she couldn't quite see her father as old – to her he was an eternally middle-aged, tall, blond man with eyes as blue as hers.

She counted in her head: it was 2016 there in the future. Almost fourteen years ago since fate and a gigantic bolt of lightning combined to throw her more than three hundred years backwards to land stunned at Matthew's feet. Alex twisted at her wedding ring. Should she ever be yanked back she was certain she'd die, of something as hackneyed as a broken heart.

She started when Matthew covered her hands with his.

"Alright?" he asked, kissing her brow.

"Yeah, I'm fine. I just had one of those flashbacks."

"Ah."

She eyed him from under her lashes. Matthew was never comfortable discussing her strange – impossible – fall from one time to the other. Heck, neither was she. It made her hair bristle. Just as she'd expected, he changed the subject.

"This afternoon I'll finish the house. Tomorrow I start with the barn," Matthew said in a resigned tone, looking at what was presently a roof on stilts. He studied his calloused hands and muttered that he was always one step behind, whether in the building or in the tilling. But at least there was a stable, and an assorted number of small sheds, including a well sized laundry shed with a large wooden bathtub.

"No hurry, is there? After all, there's nothing to fill it with as yet."

"There will be. This year the crops will be good." With that very confident statement, Matthew grabbed his hat and went outside, telling Alex that he'd be taking Mark and Jacob with him to clear the new field.

The boys came rushing when he called for them. Mark was already shooting up in height while eight-year-old Jacob was still very much a child, all downy cheeks and knobbly knees. So young, Alex reflected, watching her sons fall into step beside their father, and already most of their days were spent working side by side with Matthew. Not that they seemed to mind, both of them inflating with pride when Matthew praised them for their hard work – which he did quite often.

Alex packed her basket with some food, found a blanket in the laundry shed, draped it over her arm and made for the woods. Late April in Maryland was like a warm summer day in Scotland, and Alex adjusted her straw hat as she went, before beginning her customary scanning of the ground for anything green and edible. She was sick to death of the few sad onions in the root cellar. She wanted huge salads, ripe tomatoes, and while she was at it, why not a chocolate bar or two... Boy, was she in a maudlin mood! She slowed her pace and ducked into the shade of the closest trees.

It was strange that the few times she was truly homesick it wasn't for her life in the twenty-first century: it was for Hillview, the small manor in Ayrshire that they'd left one cold and drizzly March day four years ago. She'd spent weeks saying goodbye, walking for hours through the woods, standing silent by the edge of the moss. Worst of all had been the last time she and Matthew had stood together in front of Rachel's grave, bowing with the pain of forever leaving behind this one tangible reminder of their daughter's brief time on Earth.

"Rachel," she said out loud. She did that sometimes: she called her dead daughter, and just by saying her name she was making sure she wasn't forgotten. Now she closed her eyes and Rachel sprang to the forefront of her mind, her hair a messy tangle down her back – just like she'd been the last day of her life, her little face contorted with fury as she flew to the defence of her beloved Da.

"Mama?" Ian materialised beside her and Alex turned away. "Are you alright?"

Alex nodded, wiping her eyes with the back of her hand before facing him.

"One of those moments." She suspected Ian had quite a few such moments himself, but he chose to keep them to himself. Alex stood on her toes and pulled out a couple of cockleburs from his hair.

"You're too tall," she grumbled, and Ian grinned and sat down, crossing his legs. Alex knelt behind him and extracted her comb from her apron pocket to comb his hair free of debris. "Where have you been? Chasing deer through the undergrowth?"

Ian mumbled something unintelligible in reply.

Alex smiled down at the back of his head and went on with what she was doing. They sank into a companionable silence, broken every now and then by the loud calling of a bird or the rustling of something moving through the forest that surrounded them.

"There." Alex sank back on her heels and returned her comb to its keeping place. "You're so like him," she said, studying her teenaged stepson, who had now gotten to his feet. A younger version of her Matthew, tall and well-built with the same hazel eyes, the same dark hair that went chestnut under the summer sun, and the same generous mouth.

"Is that good or bad?" Ian teased, helping her to stand.

"Good, obviously." She bent to pick up her basket. A flurry of movement made her rear back as something mid-size and grey rushed by her.

15

"A wolf?" she asked tremulously.

Ian laughed, shaking his head. "Raccoon. Curious as to what's in yon basket."

"Nettle shoots – will make us all a very nice soup." She was very happy with her find, thinking that she'd poach some eggs to go with it.

Ian eyed the contents with a decided lack of enthusiasm. "Eat nettles? Won't it blister our mouths?"

"Of course it will. It will make all of you shut up for days and days." Alex elbowed him hard. "Idiot," she added, making him laugh.

"What happened to your promise to fix the hen coop?" Alex took hold of Ian's hand when they clambered over a mossy trunk.

"I'll do it now," he said, his cheeks staining a suspicious red.

Alex studied him narrowly: grasses and leaves all over his clothes, all that stuff he'd had in his hair... She smiled and hefted her basket higher onto her arm. Apparently young master Graham was discovering the pleasures of the opposite sex. She wondered if it was Jenny he'd met up in the woods – she sincerely hoped it was Jenny Leslie, given that Matthew and the girl's father were very much in agreement regarding the desirability of such a match.

Ian turned towards the house. Alex dithered; she had to find the girls.

"Are you coming?" he asked.

"Soon, I...well, I need some more nettles."

"I'll come with you."

"I'll be fine on my own."

He shook his head. "I'll come, aye?" Great, absolutely marvellous. Those protective genes so prominent in his father had made it down to the next generation unscathed. From the way Ian's mouth set into a line, she knew there was no point in arguing and, anyway, what did it matter if he saw the girls – he'd never tell.

"Da said you'll be staying with the Leslies when we ride down to Providence," Ian said.

Alex made a face. She was fond of both Thomas and Peter Leslie – although she should probably revise her opinion of Peter given what those girls had told her – but Mary Leslie, Thomas' wife, had the intellect of a dormouse, and as to Elizabeth...

"Aye," Ian said, following the train of her thoughts. "She is a bit much at times."

"Very," Alex agreed, thinking that Elizabeth Leslie must be an awful cross to carry for a man as mild-tempered as Peter.

A high wail had Alex almost jumping out of her skin. "What was that?" She stooped to pick up the nettles she'd scattered all over the ground.

"I don't know." Ian frowned.

Yet another shriek, and now there was no doubt – this was a human voice, raised in fear and pain. The girls! Oh my God, and now they were being eaten alive by a bear, or were surrounded by wolves, or... Alex flew down the slope, making for the terrified sounds. Another voice: low, male. Someone laughed, harness jangled, and Alex faltered. Could it be one of the Leslie brothers?

"No, please! No—" The sound was cut short.

Ian's hand closed on Alex's arm, bringing her to a halt. They crouched behind a screen of bushes, silent spectators to what was happening in the small clearing. Three men, unrecognisable in broad-brimmed hats, and then there were the two girls, one of them fighting like a hellcat, while the other was gagged and hogtied, squirming like a caterpillar where she'd been thrown across a horse. To the side stood yet another man, eyes trained on the surrounding woods and musket held at the ready. Alex did a double take; she knew this man from somewhere. Thinning hair, a long narrow face with a rather prominent mouth, and dark eyes sunk into deep hollows. Yes, she had definitely seen him before, but when? Where?

"We must do something. Those poor girls!" She made as if to stand but was arrested by Ian's hold on her hand.

"Nay," he whispered, "there's nothing we can do – not the two of us against them."

However much she hated admitting it, Ian was right.

In the clearing, the screaming girl was slapped – repeatedly. The last slap was so hard her head snapped back. The man who had hit her laughed, watching as his companions wrenched her hands behind her back and tied them, before sauntering over to the sentry, saying something in a low voice. He took off his hat, releasing black hair to fall like overlong bangs over one side of his face. A handsome man, his face a collection of sharp planes and angles, complemented by a square chin and a chiselled mouth. A cruel face, Alex decided – or maybe that had more to do with what she'd just witnessed. His eyes wandered over the closest bushes and Alex had never before seen eyes so disconcerting. Irises so light as to look almost white, the pupils like black, miniature well shafts. For some reason, Alex knotted her hands together and held her breath – anything to make sure he wouldn't discover her.

The man took a step or two to the side, unlaced himself and pissed, talking with his companions over his shoulder. It was evident he was the leader, the sentry nodding at whatever it was he was saying. Alex caught the word *Virginia* a couple of times and focused her attention on the sentry. Why did he seem so familiar, all the way from his obsequious grin to how he stood, slightly pigeon-toed? There was a flurry of movement, the men sat up, and then they were gone, horses whipped into a canter as they set off towards the south.

Chapter 2

Matthew didn't like this: four men, riding through his lands, and on top of that they had the temerity to abduct two lasses. Thank the Lord Ian had been with Alex, because God knows what his temperamental wife might have done had she been alone – attempted to intercede, no doubt.

Even more, it concerned him that Alex insisted she'd recognised one of them, although she could put neither name nor place to him. He set his jaw. Peter Leslie would be most upset, and as to the two lasses, there'd be days when they wished themselves back under Elizabeth's stern care.

He dispatched Ian to ride with the news to the Leslies, and walked over to inspect the small clearing but gleaned nothing from the trampled ground. What would those men be doing here in the first place? He backtracked them and concluded that they'd ridden in from a north-westerly direction. Traders or trappers, mayhap the kind of white men that dealt regularly with the Indians. But still, to ride through claimed land and not come by the main house. And it wasn't as if they wouldn't have noticed this was settled land, because through the screen of trees the house was visible, however distant.

"What will happen to them, do you think?" Alex asked later that afternoon, trailing Matthew on his way to the river.

"No major change: they'll sell them as labour to someone else." He shed his clothes and, with a few hissed expletives, submerged himself in the cold water.

Alex threw him the pot of soap and sat on the bank to watch him. "Do you think they'll be back?"

"Who? The men? Nay, I think them opportunists, no

more. They recognised the lasses for what they were – bond servants – and stole them."

"Will the girls mind?"

"Mind? Of course they will, and I dare say they've been badly frightened." And hurt, and probably raped, but he didn't tell her that.

She moved over to him as he came out of the chilly waters, laughing when he grabbed her by the waist and gathered her close.

"Nice," she murmured when he released her lips, her hands moving down his back to give his buttocks an appreciative squeeze.

"But now you're all wet, far too wet to walk back like that. You might catch a cold."

"And I won't if you undress me here?" she said, trying to help him with her laces. He batted away her hands, took his time undoing knots, sliding fabric down her hips, off her arms.

"Nay, I'll warm you up soon enough."

Matthew enjoyed loving his wife outdoors, finding more privacy here than in the house. A stand of shrubs afforded some protection against prying eyes – not that they needed it, because his elder sons knew better than to disturb them when Matthew took their mother with him down to the river.

He ran a finger over Alex's lips, over her cheek to circle her ear, and up to draw the high arc of her brows. He kissed her, one hand drifting down to stroke her breast through the damp material of her shift, and she stretched like a cat, a low, humming noise deep in her throat. His arms were full of her, of warm flesh and soft curves, of strong muscles and soft skin.

"Here." He spread her skirts as a makeshift blanket and eased her down on her back. She was right bonny, his wife, all pink skin and a cloud of curling hair. Matthew sat back on his heels to properly savour the sight of her, sprawled half-naked on the ground. "Beautiful," he murmured, walking his fingers up her legs. Her toes curled and she held out her arms, making him smile; impatient as always, his Alex.

She moaned when he entered her, her legs coming up to cradle him. He pushed deeper, and she tilted her hips so that their pubic bones pressed together. Again, and she breathed his name, her lips kissing his neck. His woman… This time she was going to conceive, or at the very least they were going to begin trying for yet another child. One, perhaps two more bairns, he thought fuzzily, concentrating on the sensations that settled round his cock.

He slid a hand in under her bottom and lifted her closer. She made a breathless noise and for an instant was absolutely still, eyes the colour of budding bluebells locked into his. Matthew brushed his nose against hers and began to move, a steady coming and going that increased in pace and intensity until he voided himself inside of her. He didn't move for some time, relishing being where he was. Under his hand he could feel the beating of her heart.

He lifted his head and met her eyes. There was a slight frown on her face, something dark shading the bottom of her eyes.

"It's not a safe day," she said.

He almost smiled. He knew that – he always knew. He rolled off her, lying naked on his back beside her. He fumbled for her hand and raised it to his lips. "Do you mind?"

"A bit late to ask."

"It's just…" He picked at her hair, curling and uncurling a long lock round his finger. "I like it when you grow all rosy and round, and it's with my seed, my bairn…" He felt terribly embarrassed admitting this, but it was clearly the right thing to say.

His wife smiled and kissed his cheek. "Well, if we're going to go for yet another kid, we might just as well enjoy the making. And personally I hope it takes months."

"I always enjoy it." He tightened his hold on her hand.

"So do I," she replied, just as solemnly.

Next morning Alex was returning from inspecting her potato patch when Mark's voice made her come to an abrupt stop behind an overgrown bramble.

"Do you think it will be the same?" Mark said.

"Will what be the same?" Ian's voice said.

"For you, with Jenny."

There was an irritated snort from Ian. "The same like what?"

Mark sighed loudly. "Like with Da and Mama."

Alex sank down on her haunches. This was a conversation she intended to eavesdrop on.

"I want my wife to be like Mama," Mark went on. "I want her to smile at me like she does at Da."

Ian made a sound of grousing agreement.

"So?" Mark asked again. "Will it, do you think? Be the same for you and Jenny?"

"No," Ian snapped, "on account of me not loving her. Or her me."

A stone whistled through the air and landed with a soft thud at Alex's feet.

"Come on then," Ian said. "Da's waiting."

Alex remained where she was, thinking: first of all of how to tell Matthew Jenny might not be an adequate match for Ian, and secondly about who the girl might be Ian was meeting in secret in the woods.

She didn't have much time to think about this girl over the coming days, her waking time spent preparing for Matthew's trip to Providence. Pelts were packed in neat rolls; smoked trout were wrapped and stacked in the pannier baskets; Alex wrote list after list of things she wanted, crossed them out and wrote lists of things she needed instead. Spices and salt, some precious sugar, perhaps some tea – but only if the money was enough – bolts of linen and serge, needles and thread... On top of that, she packed clothes for Matthew, Mark and Ian, prepared food for them to take along, and worried about Fiona and Jonah: would they cope all alone? Matthew assured her that they would, helped her with the last of the packing, and one early morning they set off, one long caravan making for the Leslie home.

A couple of hours later, Alex and her younger children were installed at Leslie's Crossing. She trailed Matthew out to the yard, at present a somewhat chaotic place what with all the horses and the loaded mules. Ian and Mark were already astride, eager to be off.

"Will you be alright?" Matthew kissed Alex on her brow.

"I'm not entirely sure," she stage-whispered. "Ten days with Elizabeth may impair my mental capacities."

He laughed into her hair. "Behave. Be sure you're a credit to your husband – meek and demure."

"When pigs fly. And whatever you may call Elizabeth, paragon of womanly virtues that she is, it is neither meek nor demure."

"Nay," Matthew whispered into her ear. "She's a right dragon."

"Yeah, the fire breathing kind." Alex took a step back. "Like mother, like daughter, Matthew," she said, seeing his brow crease in confusion.

She watched him ride off, flanked by his sons and Thomas Leslie, before turning to smile at her hostess.

"So, aren't you going to show me your new dairy shed?" If she didn't ask, she'd be dragged there anyway. Since they'd gotten here, Elizabeth hadn't stopped talking about it. To be fair, Elizabeth was an excellent cheese maker and had sent off several rounds of well-aged, pale yellow cheese with Thomas to be sold at the market.

"It brings in money," Elizabeth said as they walked across the yard. "God knows very little else does." She broke off to offer a hasty apology for using the Lord's name in vain before ushering Alex into her little kingdom.

Three girls were working in the dairy. One of them was cutting up the stomach of a recently slaughtered calf and putting it to soak to make rennet, while the two others were busy cutting the latest batch of curd into small cubes.

"I haven't seen two of those girls before," Alex commented on their way back to the main house.

"They came in on the first ship this season." Elizabeth went on to add that her husband had acquired not only two maids but three field hands, and had in the process also received a further five hundred acres in headright – as yet uncleared land, but all in all Peter Leslie had a sizeable tract of land under his name, coming close to eight thousand acres.

"Ah." Alex tried to look suitably impressed. Matthew had bought two thousand acres at a nominal price upon arriving and had since then acquired three hundred acres more, for Fiona, Jonah and Paul, who drowned the same winter he came out. More land than he could have dreamt of back home, he said to Alex, but he wasn't comfortable with taking indentures, no matter that both Jonah and Fiona were voluntary bondsmen, escaping from hardship back home.

"But now we'll need more, what with those two silly girls letting themselves be abducted. No great loss, either of them, and one of them was pregnant." Elizabeth rolled her eyes. "These Catholic girls, brought up without strong moral values."

Alex eyed her with dislike. "She may have been abused."

Elizabeth snorted. "Not she. I saw the way she looked at my Nathan, all doe's eyes and pouting mouth." She threw a fond look at her eldest son, reclining in the shade of an impressive chestnut tree. "Fortunately we've found him a wife, a sweet girl from a good Puritan family."

"How nice," Alex said. "And do they like each other?"

"They haven't met. How can they, when she's down south? Peter and Nathan will be riding down for her sometime in June."

"They're getting married now?" Alex swung to look at Nathan.

"He's eighteen, an adequate age."

"And the girl?"

"Of an age," Elizabeth replied with a shrug, and rushed over with surprising speed to stop her youngest, James, from throwing himself in the trough. Ten live children, Alex thought with a slight shudder as Elizabeth bundled James into a firm grip and carried him off in the direction of the house. Ten ranging in age from twenty-nine to three, and as she understood it there had been five others as well.

It always made Alex grin to see Peter and Elizabeth Leslie together. When Peter strode into the kitchen, she surreptitiously studied them both. Elizabeth was a broad, strong woman, of a height with Alex and with hips the width of a cow's according to Matthew. And that he meant as a compliment... Her grey hair was wound into a tight bun and covered by a cap, and in her face a plump and soft mouth was disconcertingly offset by a rather bulbous nose.

Peter, on the other hand, was tall and willowy, with an impressive head of curling blond hair and a receding chin that gave him a false air of malleability. In reality, Peter was as hard-headed and stubborn as his wife, and together they made an impressive couple with an eye out for any opportunity of advancement for their children, which was why Jenny Leslie was proposed as a wife for Ian, the match ensuring Jenny would in time be mistress over a sizeable property as well as staying close to home.

"Alex." Peter Leslie smiled a bit too widely, making Elizabeth glower.

"Peter." Alex twisted her face to receive his kiss on the cheek, not on the mouth as intended.

"Have you seen the new dairy?" Peter said.

"Yes, quite impressive, and the cheese is delicious." She nodded in greeting at Jenny, who had trailed her father into the kitchen, and received a quick curtsey in reply before the girl set down the basket of folded linen on the table.

"It's hot," Jenny said.

"Yes, most unseasonal." Peter smiled at his wife, accepting a brimming mug of beer. "Somewhat of a shock for the new men. One of them just sat down and refused to work during the midday hours, complaining that the sun was making him ill." He shook his head. "I don't much like it, but I fear that one will need to be punished."

"Which one is that?" Jenny asked with a gleam of

interest in her pale blue eyes. "The one with the dark hair, the fair one, or the one with no hair at all?"

"They have names, I assume," Alex cut in, making all three turn to look at her.

"They do," Peter said, "but I won't have my daughters on first-name basis with them. The less they see of each other the better."

Well, that clearly wasn't working, Alex thought, giving Jenny a curious look. The girl met her eyes for an instant and went over to sit by her mother.

Jenny was a pretty enough girl, with the complexion of a dewy rose. Her dark hair was mostly covered by her cap, but here and there a strand had escaped to hang in a soft curl. As Alex recalled she was nineteen, two years older than Ian. Maybe that was why she was more interested in her father's indentures than in Ian. The girl leaned closer to her mother and murmured something which made Elizabeth nod, one capped head very close to the other.

"So when will you hold the wedding?" Alex asked over supper.

"The contracts have already been signed, and there will be a wedding at her home when we come for her." Peter grinned slyly at his son. "And a wedding night."

Nathan nodded, looking rather unenthusiastic, and served himself a large helping of stew.

"And will you live here?" Alex asked Nathan.

"There's plenty of room," Elizabeth said, "so of course they will. And I can do with an extra pair of hands to help in the household now that Amy and Martha have both been wed. Besides, all this will one day come to Nathan. It's important his wife learns to run it properly."

Poor unknown girl; she was going to be at the beck and call of her domineering mother-in-law.

The evening was spent in the front room. Three times the size of Alex's own little parlour, it was furnished with an odd assortment of chairs, a desk and a couple of tables. There was a lute that was so dusty Alex concluded it was more for show than use, and a beautiful tapestry that had come from Elizabeth's mother hung on one of the walls. In pride of place stood Peter's armchair, a throne-like thing in dark wood, with carved lion paws decorating its feet and armrests. With a happy little grunt, Peter subsided to sit and closed his eyes. Elizabeth worked on her accounts, while Alex and Mary busied themselves with their sewing.

After a while, Elizabeth closed the heavy ledger and stood up, sauntering over to Alex and Mary.

"You did this?" Elizabeth inspected the embroidered flowers that decorated the pillowcase.

"Yes," Alex said, "to remind me of summer in winter."

Elizabeth ran a hand over it. "You should embroider and sell."

"Do you think anyone would want to buy?"

"Oh yes," Elizabeth said, "there is always a market for frippery."

Bitch. Alex met the cool look in Elizabeth's eyes with a glacial one of her own. Elizabeth broke eye contact first, muttering something about putting more wood on the fire.

"She's just jealous," Mary whispered after ascertaining Elizabeth was out of range. "She can't do much more than hem herself."

"No, I see that," Alex murmured, holding up a small boy's shirt. They shared a smile, in Mary's case quickly suppressed when Elizabeth came over to join them, sinking down with a sigh.

"Is she pretty?" Alex asked to break the silence.

"Who?" Elizabeth enquired.

"The girl – Nathan's bride-to-be."

"I have no idea," Elizabeth replied. "I haven't met her. Peter says she's comely and quiet."

"Maybe it would be easier for her if she got to know Nathan before they were wed," Alex said. "It must be a daunting experience to meet your husband on the day of your wedding and be expected to bed with him that same night."

Elizabeth raised her brows. "She might just as well get

used to it. I'm sure she'll do her duty."

"Her duty?" Alex gave her a surprised look.

Elizabeth shrugged. "I've taught all my girls that in bed they must be submissive and do as their husband wishes. It's quicker that way."

Alex swallowed down on an urge to guffaw. Elizabeth submissive? It was a mind-boggling concept.

"So you don't...err...you don't like bedding with Peter?"

Elizabeth looked at her as if she were insane. "I can bide with it. The good Lord has made it that way: that the woman must subject herself and procreate as her husband wishes. It's not precisely unpleasant, but it's somewhat of a relief now that I'm of a certain age to have left that part of my life behind."

Alex looked over to where Peter was fast asleep in his armchair, snoring loudly.

"Left that part of your life behind?" she echoed.

Elizabeth eyed her askance. "It isn't seemly, for a wife to display inappropriate affection for her husband – particularly after a certain age."

"Really? Well, I don't agree with you," Alex said, "and my husband rather enjoys my inappropriate affection."

Elizabeth acquired the hue of a ripe plum. "Man and woman are made husband and wife to procreate. Anything else is sin."

"And your husband?" Alex asked. "What about him? His needs?"

Elizabeth waved her hand dismissively. "I'm not sure I want to know."

But if an indentured maid gets pregnant because your husband has urges, all you do is extend the poor girl's contract and call her a whore, Alex thought angrily.

"And you?" Alex said to Mary, who had sat silent throughout the exchange, her concentration on the shirt she was making for her husband.

"Me what?" Mary dimpled, looking much younger than her fifty-two years. In fact, it was difficult to believe that Mary was the elder of the sisters-in-law, just as Thomas was the eldest of the Leslie brothers, even if only by a year.

"Do you...you know?"

Mary blushed a delicate pink and bent her head to her sewing. "On occasion, he still wants to, and so do I."

Elizabeth produced a sound that conveyed just how close to the brink of eternal damnation Mary hovered and left the room.

Chapter 3

The room was stuffy and dark, inadequately lit by a number of lanterns that hung from the beams. It was also crowded, every table occupied by men who drank and ate – well, mostly drank. The taproom smelled of spilled beer and spicy stews, of lavender perfume and of tobacco.

Matthew shoved his cleaned plate to the side and burped discreetly into the crook of his arm. The lamb shank had been delicious, cooked to the point where the meat fell off the bone, and a mug or two of beer had him in a mellow enough mood, an interested spectator to the steady flow of business in the little inn. The stairs to his left led to the upper floor and, as the evening progressed, one man after the other trooped off with one of the bonny whores, was gone for a half-hour or so before reappearing at the top of the stairs. The whores rarely lost times between customers; no sooner were they done with one but they were leading the next one up the stairs.

Matthew called for some more beer and let his eyes wander the room. Many of the men he knew; a few of them were even elders. The door opened, there was a rush of cold air, and for some moments Matthew was convinced his heart had stopped. He blinked, settled back on the bench and stared at the man who'd just entered the busy room.

Jones! Dominic Jones, here! Matthew was surprised to hear his own harsh breathing and wiped a sweaty hand down his breeches. He leaned further into the protective shadow of his corner, throwing an irritated look up the stairs. Where was Thomas? How long could it take to conclude his business with the little whore?

Where before his heart had come to a standstill, now his pulse was thundering, leaving him weak-kneed and covered with a cold sweat. He gripped his dirk, unsheathed it. To sink it into Jones... He snuck another look at the hulk of a man, now standing only some feet away, demanding beer and company. As big as ever, Jones was also very well off, at least to judge from the resplendent coat and matching waistcoat. The hands were as huge as Matthew remembered them, but otherwise Jones had aged badly. The light from one of the lanterns illuminated his face, revealing skin that was criss-crossed by a network of broken veins, and his small, displeased mouth had all but disappeared into his heavy jowls.

Jones turned in the direction of the proprietress and crossed the floor in a couple of strides – still as graceful as a lethal serpent, moving that mountain of flesh effortlessly and swiftly. Matthew shrank back, watching as Jones pulled off his wig, scratched at his bald pate and replaced the curling hairpiece, all the while in an intense discussion with Mrs Malone.

Matthew was drowning in hatred, in remembered pain and humiliation. Oh God! Their first meeting: him being forced to stand straight while Jones, overseer at the plantation Suffolk Rose, walked round him, using his short riding crop to prod Matthew as he inspected his latest human beast of burden. The beating administered when Matthew refused to take his clothes off, the other time when Jones whipped him until Matthew brokenly admitted he was a slave... He still bore the scars on his skin. Until his dying day, he'd carry the reminders of those terrible months when he was nothing but an expendable resource to be worked until he died.

Jones laughed, draped an arm around Mrs Malone and inspected the paraded girls. A respected and valuable customer, Matthew concluded, irritated by how the whores were fawning on Jones. The large man had by now made his choice: a pretty lass with red hair and a neckline that left very little to the imagination. Jones patted the girl on her behind and steered her towards the stairs.

Halfway across the floor, Jones saw Matthew and came

to an abrupt standstill. His small eyes narrowed and he stood staring for some moments before he paled, taking a few stumbling steps backwards. After a couple of heartbeats, he nodded, once. Matthew just stared him in the eyes, and then Thomas was there, clapping him on the shoulder and asking him if he wanted yet another beer. Matthew shook his head in a no. All he wanted was to leave Providence – but he couldn't do that, what with the market tomorrow.

Matthew was almost at the door when Jones stepped forward to block his path. As if by chance, the meaty hand dropped to rest on the hilt of the dirk he was carrying.

"Move, Graham," Jones said.

"I think not. You stood to block my way; you move." Matthew met Jones' eyes and took another step towards him, rising on his feet to stare the somewhat taller man straight in the eyes.

"Dominic?" The red-headed girl popped up beside them. "Who's this?" She smiled at Matthew, both arms wound tight round Jones' arm.

"No one, a nobody, my dear." Jones smirked at Matthew and brushed at his waistcoat, straining over an impressive gut. He took a step towards Matthew, stopped when Matthew stood still as a rock, not about to give an inch.

"Dominic!" The girl pouted, tugging at his arm. With one last look at Matthew, Jones allowed the whore to drag him off.

"Who's that?" Thomas asked.

"An old acquaintance," Matthew said.

"Not a cordial relation, I take it," Thomas said.

"Nay, rather the reverse."

Thomas ran his eyes up and down Jones a couple of times, did the same with Matthew. "My money's on you should it come to a fight."

"Why thank you," Matthew said, "but I think it best for both of us if it never comes to an open confrontation."

Matthew weighed his pouch, thinking that the pelts had brought in much more than he'd expected. He left Ian to oversee the sale of the smoked trout and spent the following hour wandering the market, now and then making a purchase or two. The marketplace was crowded, the stalls set up in makeshift narrow rows that left thoroughfares at most three feet across. People thronged; there was a pleasant smell of barbecued meat and mulled wine, and from the livestock pens came a constant cackling, now and then interspersed with an indignant squeal. In a big stall standing by itself, old Mrs Redit was peddling spices – peppercorn, nutmeg and ginger, cinnamon sticks and cloves. She even had limes, and a few minutes later Matthew had concluded his business with her.

He was running late for his meeting with the new minister and extended his stride, but when he turned into the alley that led to the main street he came to an abrupt stop. The alley was short, steep and dank. Coming the other way was Jones, accompanied by three men who effectively blocked the whole passage. There was no way round him, and damned if Matthew intended to retreat.

"Mr Graham." Jones inclined his head. He was as resplendent as yesterday, his linen newly changed, his black broadcloth breeches and matching coat of an elegant cut.

"Mr Jones."

They both fell silent. Jones regarded Matthew, eyes resting for an instant on Matthew's various parcels.

"I must be on my way." Matthew tried to sidle past one of Jones' men. An arm shot out, hindering him.

"Now, now, Mr Graham, why the hurry?" Jones nodded at his men, and in a matter of seconds Matthew was surrounded. Matthew wet his lips. He was only yards away from the main street, bustling with people, and should he need to he'd yell.

"It's a pity you didn't die back in Virginia," Jones said. "As it is, I am not much pleased to find you here, in my new home."

"Mine before it was yours," Matthew said. "And I had hoped that by now someone would have rid the world of you, scavenging bastard that you are."

"Tut-tut, Graham, I am not impervious to insult. You'd best be careful; I might feel obliged to defend my honour."

"Honour? You?" Matthew took a step towards him, having the distinct pleasure of seeing Jones back off. "I could beat you with one hand tied behind my back."

Jones chuckled. "Maybe you could, Mr Graham. But I would never be fool enough to challenge you outright, would I?" He leaned forward. "I rid my life of enemies discreetly – best you remember that."

"A threat, Mr Jones? I wonder what the elders will say when I recount this to them."

"I will deny it." Jones tugged at his waistcoat, his fat hand caressing the wooden butt of the pistol that he carried stuck in his belt. "Stay away from me and mine, Graham. Let things lie, as they say, and I will do the same for you."

"And if I don't?"

Jones smiled – a nasty, cold grimace. "You have sons. Who knows what might happen to them, eh?"

Matthew dropped his purchases, grabbed Jones by the collar and shoved him back against the nearby wooden wall. "How dare you," he hissed.

"Take your hands off me," Jones said. "Do it now, or I swear I'll have my men gut you like a fish."

Something prodded Matthew's side and, reluctantly, he released his hold. Jones smoothed his collar back into place and bent to retrieve his hat.

"This is my town now." Jones straightened up. "Keep that in mind, Graham."

For the few remaining days in Providence, Matthew was constantly on his guard. Twice he saw Jones, twice he turned and hurried away, sons in tow.

"Da?" Ian said. "What's the matter?"

"Nothing," Matthew replied, yet again casting a look in the direction of where Dominic was standing, surrounded by a group of other merchants.

Ian followed his eyes. "Is it that man?"

"Aye." Matthew did not want to discuss this.

"Why?"

"It's just..." Matthew shook his head. "Salt," he said instead, "we must buy salt, aye? And if they have it, buy a half-pound of tea – that will make your mama happy."

It was drizzling the day they were to set off for home, but no matter that Thomas suggested they remain one more day, hoping for better weather, Matthew refused. He was leaving now, his horses were saddled, the panniers packed, and he had no intention of biding one more night here. Ian gave him an odd look, Mark grimaced at the rain but said nothing, and Thomas sighed, muttering something about the stubbornness of Scotsmen.

Matthew was astride the ugly gelding, leading the cavalcade out of town, when someone hailed him in a loud voice that even now, a decade and more since his days as indentured labour, made his insides clench. Out of the rain loomed Jones, four men at his heels. One of them Matthew recognised as Sykes – a much older Sykes, but unmistakeably him, narrow-faced like a horse and with dark, sunken eyes. Sykes smirked and sketched Matthew a bow. Matthew suppressed the urge to spit this constant shadow to Jones in the face.

"Leaving?" Jones asked.

Matthew saw no reason to reply, or even halt his horse.

Jones laughed. "Please convey my regards to Mrs Graham. Is she still as...?" He mimed a swelling chest.

Matthew wheeled his mount, sword at the ready.

"No, he's just trying to provoke you." Thomas spurred his horse forward, blocking Matthew. "Ride on."

Matthew sheathed his sword and kicked his horse into a gallop, leaving sons and friend to follow as best they could.

Late in the afternoon a couple of days later, they rode into Leslie's Crossing.

"Thank heavens!" Alex threw her arms round Matthew's neck. "One more night and I might have buried a knife in her back."

Matthew set her back on her feet, smiling at the way her

greeting had unfastened her hair, spilling curls from under her cap. "That bad?"

"Well, no, except for when she gets started on my moral lassitude."

"Moral lassitude?" He nodded seriously. "It's a bit of a concern. You're somewhat remiss when it comes to matters spiritual."

"Oh, really? And would you prefer it if I prayed instead of joining you in bed? That's what she does apparently."

"You can pray in bed – before and after." He grinned.

"Huh," Alex snorted and moved aside to allow his children to rush him.

"What's the matter?" she said a bit later, hoisting Sarah up to sit in front of him. Ruth was already perched behind him.

"Later," he mouthed, ducking his head to evade her eyes.

Homecoming was a bustling, noisy affair, and it was well after dark before Matthew and Alex retired to their bedchamber. Around them, the house was going silent, even if Fiona could still be heard in the kitchen, laughing at something Ian was saying.

"Did you know Providence has a new establishment?" Matthew sat down on the bed. "A brothel, no less."

"A whorehouse? No!" Alex sounded sarcastic. "In a place so full of moral rectitude?" She sat at the wee table he'd made her, busying herself with her face and her teeth.

"Where there's a town, there are whores." He peeled off his dirty stockings and, after a tentative sniff, decided the shirt was ripe for laundry as well.

"Must be a tough business climate, in view of it only being Catholics and amoral Anglicans who fall for the carnal itch."

"Alex! Do you want me to tell you or not?" He shoved a pillow under his head and suppressed a yawn.

"By all means do." She braided her hair and came over to join him in bed.

"It's a discreet establishment, standing somewhat south of the town proper but close to the docks."

"Ah," Alex nodded, "sailors…"

"...and the odd God-fearing merchant, an assortment of clerks and tradesmen, even Mr Farrell."

"Mr Farrell? In a brothel?" She shook her head. "But he's an elder of the congregation!" Her eyes narrowed. "Anyhow, how would you know?"

"Thomas suggested we go there on account of the food being particularly good."

"The food?" It came out very clipped.

"Aye. Mrs Malone is a canny businesswoman. Men come there for food and beer — excellent beer, she's Irish — and stay to partake of other pleasures."

"But you didn't," she stated in a dangerous tone.

Matthew was hugely offended. "Of course not! I have no need to."

"And if you did? If your wife was sickly or denied you her bed or just generally disliked having sex?"

Matthew smiled. "But that isn't the case, is it?" He slid his hand up and down her thigh, over her hip. "Should I find myself entirely alone, then I might. After all, I have done so before — in my wild youth..."

"And the boys? Did they come along?"

Matthew sat up and stared down at her. "My sons? In a bawdy house? What do you take me for?"

Alex grinned up at him. "Well, Ian is in his wild youth by now, right?"

Matthew sank back down with a muttered comment that such things were best handled by the young man in question on his own.

"Oh, I'm sure it is." Alex's brow furrowed for an instant.

"Will you let me get to the point of my tale?" Matthew said, somewhat irritated.

Alex nodded.

"Thomas didn't go there for the food alone." He sighed and shook his head. "She's a pretty enough lass, and she knew him from before."

"Poor Mary, she's still in love with him."

"Aye well, it isn't that Thomas doesn't love his wife. It's just..."

"That he thinks her too old," Alex finished. "It's not as if he's God's gift to womankind, is it?"

Matthew chuckled. Thomas was a nondescript man, leaving behind a vague impression of grey and more grey. Grey eyes, grey hair, grey clothes and grey stockings, Thomas very much melted into the background unless he set out on purpose not to. Always had, he reflected, recalling the first time he saw him, back in 1659 in Scotland.

"But I didn't tell you this to have you revise your impression of poor Thomas," Matthew continued. "I told you because, as I sat waiting, I happened to see a former acquaintance." He almost spat out the words. "Jones, Dominic Jones."

"Ah." Alex scooted closer to him. "That must have been difficult."

Matthew stretched out one arm and clenched and unclenched his fist repeatedly. Difficult? Aye, that it had been.

"Did he recognise you?" Alex fiddled with his chest hair.

"Aye," Matthew replied with a short laugh. "When he stood to go upstairs he saw me sitting in the corner, and it took some time for him to make the connection, but finally he did." It still pleased him that Jones had looked as aghast as Matthew felt.

He shifted in bed. All of him was drowning in remembered blackness and despair, and with a strangled moan he turned to face her. He wouldn't be here if it hadn't been for Alex and her determination to find him and take him home, saving him from an existence that would have ended far too quickly in an anonymous grave on a Virginia plantation.

"That was a long time ago," Alex soothed. "Ten years ago, more or less."

Aye, very long ago and since then they'd had five bairns, lost one, been forced to leave their home and cross the sea once again to come here, to Maryland. And yet it could have been yesterday when he woke to find himself in chains, sold by his damned brother Luke into indentured labour on a Virginia tobacco farm.

"I'd totally forgotten about him." Alex stroked Matthew's hair. "I wonder if people here know he left Virginia under something of a cloud."

"Nay, I would think not. Being suspected of murdering your employer is not something you would share with all and sundry, is it? I must be a very unwelcome reminder of his past." He frowned at that. "He recently moved up from the south of the colony; I found that out the next day. He has a plantation just outside of Providence. Numerous children, I heard. And slaves. He trades in them – well, it would seem he trades in everything." Matthew pillowed his head as close as he could to her heart, closing his eyes to concentrate on the steady thudding of her pulse. In through his ear, down through his spine, into his bloodstream and up to his heart... Her rhythm wove itself tight around his own strong beat, a familiar sound that lulled him to sleep.

Next afternoon Alex went to find Ian, and as they worked in the root cellar she gave him a brief recap of Matthew's time in Virginia.

"We think – well, Matthew insists he knows – that Jones killed Fairfax, the plantation owner down in Virginia. Remember I told you about that? How your father almost was hanged for a crime he hadn't committed? Strangely enough, Jones inherited Fairfax's estate – as per a will dated the day Fairfax died." Alex shook her head. "Too much of a coincidence, according to your sleuth of a father."

Ian held out his hand for yet another plank, hammering it into place with a couple of strokes.

"He was very upset." Ian stood back to admire his handiwork: a much improved door to the root cellar. "He kept on scanning the crowds for him. Difficult to miss, yon Jones, what with him being the size of an ox."

"He has reason not to trust Jones," Alex said.

"But they won't run into each other much, will they?"

"No, I suppose not – a three-day ride makes it highly unlikely. Still, it's good that you know, just in case." She almost smiled at how Ian puffed up, chest expanding with pride at her confidence in him.

He tucked the hammer into his belt, grabbed the wooden spade and turned to her with a smile. "Shall we plant your bitty trees, then?"

Alex jumped up. "You dig and I'll fetch water. And maybe come autumn we can bake one apple pie."

"I don't think so." Ian laughed, prodding the little saplings.

An hour later, Alex sat back on her heels. "There." She patted the slender little trunk. "Grow and grow quickly, okay?" She sighed, her shoulders falling together. "Pathetic," she muttered, running a finger up and down the smooth dark grey bark. "It'll take years and years before they come even close to the trees back home."

"But someday they will." Ian dropped to one knee beside her. "And your grandchildren will bake pies and thank the Lord they had a grandmama wise enough to plant a tree – for them."

"It's always the worst this time of the year." Alex craned her head back to look at the sky. "I miss the twilights, those long, blue hours where nothing is either light or dark, but something just in between."

"We have twilights here," Ian said. "This is twilight."

"But it isn't the same. They're never as long, never as magical as they were up there, in the north. For him, the worst part comes later." She crumbled a clod of earth between her fingers.

"Aye, for Da it's harvest time."

"And you? Do you miss it?"

"Not as much as I thought I would; this is home now. All of this is home." He opened his arms wide, indicating their surroundings. "It is easier for us bairns: we have you to make us a home, wherever we go." He kissed her brow. "It's enough to have someone who kisses you and wishes you goodnight and know she loves you."

"Most of the time," she said in a dry tone, trying to disguise how touched she was.

"All the time," he contradicted her with conviction.

Alex laughed. "Yes, you're right; all of the time. But I don't always like you." As if on cue, an angry shriek flew through the air, followed by some heavy thumps, and suddenly there were two voices shrieking in unison.

"Sisterly love." Alex got to her feet, tilted her head in the direction of the noise, listened for some time, and shrugged. "They're too small to kill each other – yet. Let's go and see if Matthew and the boys have caught any fish.

"Was there a letter from your mother?" Alex asked as they made their way down to the river.

"Aye. She's breeding again. It's all she seems to do, lie in bed and rest her way through pregnancy after pregnancy."

"Well, five pregnancies in six years is pretty impressive," Alex said. Luke and Margaret were definitely making up for lost time. Quite the strain on Margaret, and the late miscarriage last year must have been a painful experience. "Is she alright?"

Ian dug into his breeches and produced the letter. "You can read it yourself."

Alex unfolded it and looked down at the spidery, unformed handwriting that crawled its way across the thick paper. Margaret spent a lot of time describing her three babies, two boys named Charles and James respectively after their father's royal patrons, and one girl named Marie – and now mayhap yet another son, but it was early days yet; the babe was not due until early October. Luke was mentioned in passing, the odd dropped hint that he was continuing to do very well, how he had commissioned their portraits from Peter Lely himself, and how Margaret had spent hours choosing what to wear for the sitting.

"Well, of course she would," Alex muttered, inundated by that childish jealousy she always felt when thinking about Margaret – Ian's mother, Matthew's first wife. The wife who had cuckolded him with his own brother, lied to retain custody of Matthew's son, Ian, and stood by and allowed Luke to falsely accuse Matthew of treason. Not – in brief – Alex's favourite person, and it didn't exactly help that she was startlingly good-looking to boot.

"I suppose Luke must be very proud." Alex refolded the letter and handed it back to Ian. Right at the end there was a cramped effort trying to put into words how much Margaret missed her firstborn, but otherwise the letter was one long gushing exposé over a life that no longer included Ian.

"Aye." Ian came to a halt and turned towards her, eyes shining with unshed tears.

"Her loss, Ian, her very big loss, and our gain. Our eldest son, and look at you. What parents wouldn't be proud of a boy – no, man – like you?" She grinned at him. "Even if you can't hold a tune and still complain when I serve you vegetables."

Ian burst out laughing and gave her a quick hug.

"All of us complain. Even Da complains. If we were meant to eat so much green..."

"I know, I know, you would've been born a cow."

After supper, the younger bairns were sent to bed. Ian took Mark with him to see to the beasts, and Matthew and Alex retired to the parlour.

"Have you read the letter from Simon?" Matthew caressed Alex's cheek in passing and went to sit in his chair, facing hers in front of the fire.

"Yes, although I'm not entirely sure if I understood it all. Simon's handwriting is at times atrocious."

"It seems all is well with them, even though Simon does complain that life is a trifle difficult."

Alex shook out Sarah's mended smock. "What was it he said? Thousands of Highlander soldiers let loose on Ayrshire?"

"Aye, and they have no reason to love us, do they?" He pursed his lips, washed by a wave of concern for his sister, Joan, and Simon, his brother-in-law.

"Well no, given the way the Covenanter armies acted in the Highlands. Bloody religion," she said, making Matthew raise a disapproving brow. "Well, it is, isn't it? Making Scots turn upon Scots, English upon English...and at the end of the day for what? For the right to proclaim your own interpretation of the Bible as being the valid one? God must roll His eyes in desperation at times."

"Aye," Matthew sighed. "He must. But it isn't His fault, and as for the Bible, it's all there. You don't need an interpretation; you must but read it and reflect on it."

"Not according to some of the ministers. Some ministers are of the firm opinion that it is them that can interpret, and we must but listen and obey — especially us featherbrained women."

Matthew laughed and raised his foot to rest in her lap. "Obedience is an attractive quality in a woman, one unfortunately very lacking in you."

"Watch it," she mumbled, brandishing her needle. "You don't want me to run this through your toe, do you?"

He laughed again and sat back with his pewter mug of whisky in his hands to look at her. In the glow from the fire and the light of the candle by her side, all of her was haloed, her dark hair throwing off glints of bronze and even gold. Not much grey in it, just the odd hair here and there and the little patch just off her right temple, creating an interesting streak of light in all that dark.

For almost fourteen years she had been in his life, and there were still days when he would give silent and fervent thanks for having her with him, for that random and miraculous occurrence a day in August that had thrown her from her time into his. 1658, he mused, on a Scottish moor, and he had found her after a terrifying thunderstorm, badly burnt and concussed, wearing the strangest garments he had ever seen. Breeches on a woman... And what breeches, narrow and blue they hugged her so close it had been like seeing her naked, her rounded arse straining against the tight cloth.

Now her bottom was hidden beneath modest skirts, her hair was no longer a wild short cap but fell to well below her shoulder blades. And only he saw her fully; she was for his eyes only when the hair tumbled in wild disarray, when her limbs were uncovered to lie pale against the sheets. Only his... He stood up and waited until she met his eyes. A small movement of his head, and she folded her work together and doused the candle with her fingers before moving in the direction of their bedchamber. He banked the fire and followed, his bare feet silent on the wooden boards.

Chapter 4

"It's a bit sad." Alex ran her hand down one of the ring-barked saplings. "All these beautiful trees and we kill them."

"Aye, well," Matthew said, wiping the sweat off his face, "it's trees or fields. And we can't eat the leaves, however bonny they may be." He swept the area with his eyes and sat down in the long grass. "In a year it will all be wheat, a large field of golden wheat." But first it would cost him weeks of toil – as had every square yard presently under the plough. At times he felt like yon Sisyphus, constantly rolling a boulder uphill.

Alex came to sit beside him. "Wheat, hey? No tobacco?"

"Never, not on my land." He drew the sodden shirt over his head and threw it to lie on the ground.

"Oh." Alex stretched out beside him, her head pillowed on her arms.

Matthew swigged at the beer bottle, set it down and stuffed a boiled egg into his mouth, chewing methodically while he studied his surroundings.

Alex raised her hand to his bare back, running a light finger over his scarred skin. "Tobacco is a good cash crop."

"I don't care if it grows with gold foil leaves; I won't touch it." And especially not after having run into Dominic Jones again; not after having all those memories of his months on Suffolk Rose prodded back into uncomfortable life by laying eyes on his former tormentor. It would be best for all if he never met the man again, but he couldn't help feeling a niggling curiosity about Kate, Dominic's wife. Would she have aged as badly as her husband? Surely not, not pretty Kate with her honey-coloured hair and soft brown eyes. Not Kate, who had held him and loved him and thereby saved his life.

"What are you thinking?" Alex asked.

Matthew drained the beer flask and fitted the last piece of bread into his mouth, making it impossible to answer.

"It's sometime since you bled," he said as they made their way back home, the June sun warm on their shoulders despite it being late in the afternoon.

"Yes, about two months ago. It didn't take us very long, did it?"

Matthew slipped an arm round her waist and drew her close, forcing her to do a series of small skips before her stride was aligned with his.

"A lad." He smiled down at her, proud of his own virility and his wife's fertility.

"And I suppose you already have a name for him?" she teased.

"Aye, I do."

"So, what is it?"

"Ah no, you don't find out until you've birthed him."

"Unfair," she muttered, "and, anyway, maybe I have an opinion."

Matthew hitched his shoulders. The naming was his to do, and they both knew it.

They balanced their way over a couple of fallen trees, and Alex accepted Matthew's hand to help her up a particularly steep bank.

"Fiona's been in a vile mood all day," she said, "what with it being laundry day tomorrow. Not her favourite chore – not my favourite day of the month either."

"Fiona's always in a bad temper when it comes to work."

"Not always, and just the other day I actually heard her singing up beyond the kitchen garden."

"Was she working?"

"No, she was taking a walk." She frowned. "A lot of that lately, if you ask me."

"You need to put your foot down. You're allowing her to shirk work, and that's not right."

"I know," Alex sighed. "But, frankly, at times I prefer to do things myself than have her sulking for a whole day."

They walked in companionable silence, hands as always braided together. His thumb drew a circle over her skin; Alex returned the caress. She wiggled a finger insinuatingly where it was trapped between his larger digits, and Matthew tightened his hold, suppressing a smile.

Alex slowed her pace and gave him a blue look. "It's nice here, don't you think?" She sank down to sit in the grass. The birch leaves overhead rustled in the evening breeze; shadow and sun streaked the ground; and when Alex tugged at his hand, Matthew kneeled beside her. "I have to make you a new shirt," she said as she undid his lacings.

"Do you now?" He leaned forward to kiss her, his tongue darting out to follow the contour of her lips. Alex kissed him back, her arms encircling his neck.

"Not right now, I don't," she murmured, rubbing her cheek against his chest. "Right now, I have other things to do."

"Wanton," he whispered in her hair, tightening his hold on her.

She kissed him between the clavicles. "It's not as if you mind, is it?"

"Nay, not as such."

She stretched out on her back, caught his eyes and winked as she pulled her skirts up, inch by delightful inch.

"Go on, uncover yourself for me." He caressed her bare shin with his fingers.

"All of me?"

"All." He cleared his throat, eyes never leaving his wife as she struggled up to sit up, impatient fingers working at the lacing on her bodice. It fell discarded to the ground. Through the sheer linen of her shift, he could see her breasts, and he couldn't resist the temptation to brush his hand across her bosom.

"More?" She rose on her knees to undo her skirt.

"All of it." He extended a hand to help her.

From somewhere to his right, there came a muted sound, somewhere between a sob and a honk.

"What was that?" Alex crossed her arms over her chest.

"I'm not sure." He scanned the surrounding woods. A twig snapped, the resulting sound loud like a musket shot in the drowsy stillness of the forest.

"Indians?" Alex whispered.

Matthew peered into the shadows of the nearest shrub. Something light caught his eyes: a man, the shirt hanging untucked as he flitted away.

"Hey!" Matthew picked up his axe and rushed after. There was a loud crash, a brace of birds rose screeching towards the sky, and the white blob picked up amazing speed, darting off like a wild stag down the incline.

"Matthew! Wait for me!" Alex came charging after, still half undressed, her hair falling to her shoulders.

Matthew had by now reached the wee stream that burbled its way across the valley's floor. In the mud was a clear imprint of a hobnailed boot.

"Not an Indian." Alex stared at the huge footprint.

"Nay." Most definitely not an Indian, but why would a white man rush off like that?

"Could it be Jones?" Alex asked, head swivelling as if she expected Jones to appear from behind the nearest stand of trees.

"Jones? Yon fat bastard could never move as fast as this one did." He studied the imprint. "And this is too big to be Sykes."

"Sykes? Oh my God, Sykes!" She turned to face him. "It was him, the man I saw."

"You saw him? Where?"

"I told you. How I recognised one of the men who abducted those two girls. It was him, Sykes."

"Are you sure?"

"Of course I'm sure! Men that ugly don't exactly grow on trees, do they?"

It made him laugh; it shouldn't, but it did, because she was right. Sykes was a right ugly character and, as he recalled it, equipped with balls the size of peas unless Jones was nearby to back him up. He was tempted to set off at a run after the trespasser – should it be Sykes, it would bring him the greatest enjoyment to bash his head in with the axe. But it wasn't; he knew that. He frowned, staring in the direction in which the man had disappeared.

"A trapper, mayhap," he said out loud. Aye, that was probably it, although why a trapper should flee instead of requesting bed and board was beyond him. He waved away this disturbing thought, took Alex's hand and led them back home.

As expected, Fiona looked most put out next morning, muttering that never had she lived in a home where linens were changed as often as they were here. Alex ignored her grumbling, concentrating instead on keeping the lye at a safe distance from her body.

"I saw one of the girls up at the Leslies' the other week," she said. "Her whole arm was badly blistered on account of having the lye spill over her."

Fiona shrugged; such things happened. "Are they English, the new lasses?"

Alex had no idea. None of them had opened their mouth. "One of them is pregnant. She must've been with child before she boarded, and her contract's been extended with a full year. She didn't seem too happy about that."

"Nay, she wouldn't be. Five years is quite enough."

"Only two left for you." Alex found this difficult to talk about, even knowing that Fiona had chosen this as the only way she could start a new life for herself. A brave young woman, Alex thought, to cross the world all on her own. Brave or desperate, and despite having lived at close quarters with Fiona for three years, she still didn't know which.

She studied Fiona as she lifted the steaming linen from the cauldron into the rinsing trough: black hair pulled back in a strict braid, eyes a warm chocolate brown, and a nice figure. Fiona had no idea how old she was, but thought she might be twenty-five or thereabouts, insisting she had recollections of the uneasy times back in the War of the Three Kingdoms, fragmented images of hiding from the Commonwealth army that rode into Scotland in pursuit of Charles Stuart.

"What will you do?"

"Do?" Fiona gave Alex a blank look.

"You know, once your term of indenture is up. Will you stay up here or will you go south to the towns?"

"The towns, I think." Fiona wrung the shirt in her hands, shook it out and hung it on the clothes line. "I'm not a country lass." She threw a disgusted look at the woods that stood thick and dark around them. "I miss the sound of people. And I miss the sea." She turned to Alex. "And you, mistress? Are you happy here, up in the wild?"

Alex surveyed her home, a fragile man-made clearing in the encroaching forest. This was a safe haven, a new start far away from a country where her man was constantly persecuted on account of his faith.

"Yes I am, even if it's a bit far away from everything. A town half a day's ride away wouldn't have come amiss."

"You have the Chisholm place, and on account of them being so many, that's like a wee village in itself."

Alex laughed. Fiona was right: their neighbours were numerous, three brothers who'd come out twenty years ago, and now with their sons and daughters a small community numbering fourteen families or so. She liked the Chisholms, but they tended to keep themselves to themselves, an enclave of Catholicism in an area mostly settled by Protestants.

"A man," Fiona said out of the blue a few moments later.

"A man?"

"A husband," Fiona clarified. "Most of all I'd like a husband."

"That won't be too hard, will it? Not here, where unwed women are as rare as sweet water pearls."

Something flitted over Fiona's face, a smugness quickly suppressed that made Alex throw her a long look.

"Mayhap not," Fiona said, and there it was again, a satisfied little smirk.

As a treat after an entire morning hanging over the laundry cauldron, Alex succeeded in wheedling Matthew's permission to visit their new neighbours – as long as she took Jonah and his musket along. She was curious about the Waltons, the wife and children having come but recently from the east to join the husband who'd been here since spring. Not that she'd met him either, being far too busy at home to do more than send along the odd pie with Matthew on those few occasions when he'd ridden over to help.

"You think it's safe, mistress?" Fiona sounded nervous.

"As safe as it was yesterday. Anyway," Alex grinned, "it's you the Indians will go for, not me." That made Fiona wipe her palms on the dark cloth of her skirts. Jonah chuckled and made a show of brandishing the musket he was carrying.

Alex swept the forest with her eyes; four years here, and they'd never seen an Indian. A couple of years ago, she and Matthew had come upon a sizeable clearing, with overgrown mounds showing where buildings had stood. Among the weeds, Alex had found shards of pottery and, growing in a corner, a few stands of maize, apparently the result of spontaneous germination in seeds left behind when the inhabitants moved away. The maize she'd taken care of, and now there were several rows of Indian corn growing in her kitchen garden.

Fiona gripped Ruth harder and hurried them on, muttering that this was a fool's errand in times when Indians were abroad, but Alex turned a deaf ear. She wasn't unduly worried by the news that Indians had been sighted, and so far all they'd done was steal a horse or two off Andrew Chisholm. No, she was made far more uncomfortable by the humid heat that made clothes stick to damp skin and brought out small beads of sweat along the bridge of Alex's nose. She tilted her straw hat so that it shaded her face, and examined her new skirts. Matthew had brought back several bolts of fabric from Providence, and this time he had spontaneously added yards of pale green cotton to the standard linen and dark wool, for which she was very grateful – especially on a day as hot as today.

Alex adjusted Sarah's cap and called Daniel back from his brutal inspection of an ant hill.

"Remember," she said, "they might not speak English."

51

Fiona looked at her with incredulous eyes. "Not speak English?"

"Quite a lot of people don't." Alex bit back a little smile.

"Da says only very few speak English," Ruth piped up, skipping by Fiona's side. "It is too bad, on account of them not being able to read the Bible."

"Of course they can," Alex said. "The Bible was written in several old languages, and it's been translated into English, just as it's been translated into Swedish or German or Spanish."

"But it's only us that have the true Bible," Fiona said to Ruth. "Only us of the Scottish Kirk, aye? Ask your da," she added with a triumphant look in Alex's direction.

For a moment Alex considered throwing herself into a religious debate with Fiona, but instead she smiled at her children and told them that she wasn't a Presbyterian, and yet she was quite convinced that she had access to just as valid a Bible as any member of the redoubtable Scottish Reformed Church.

"Is it much further?" Sarah whined. "I'm hot and hungry."

"I'm not quite sure," Alex said. The riding trail meandered in a rough westerly direction, but all around the woods stood thick, gigantic chestnuts, sycamores and oaks, and here and there stands of dark pines. The air hummed with insects, and from the surrounding undergrowth came the chirping and rustling of birds. Alex smiled at the bright orange of the orioles, darting from one shrub to the other.

"Here." Fiona pointed at where a new trail cut into the woods. "This must be it."

They walked Indian file down the narrow trail that opened up into a small clearing.

"Hello?" Alex called. "Hello?" she repeated taking a further step towards the log cabin. How had they managed to build something that permanent in such a short time? The door swung open and a young woman stepped outside, smiling at her visitors.

"Good day," she said in accented English. "Welcome to Forest Spring."

"Forest Spring?" Alex looked about. "Is there a spring somewhere close?"

The young woman tilted her head in the direction of a mossy hollow in the ground.

"There," she said. "I'm Kristin," she added, curtseying.

"Alex Graham. I'm your closest neighbour, and these are my three youngest children, Daniel, Ruth and Sarah. And this is Fiona."

From behind their mother, three white blond heads appeared, all of them with pale blue eyes; three boys, the youngest still in smocks, holding on to his mother's apron.

"Per, Erik and Johan," Kristin introduced, nudging her boys forward.

"Swedish names!" Alex said.

Kristin regarded her with some caution. "*Ja*. We come from New Sweden." In a matter of minutes, she explained how her parents had immigrated in the early 1640s, homesteading high up on the Delaware River in the recently established county of Upland. "Sweden lost the colony in 1655, and in 1664 the English came." Kristin blushed prettily. "And my husband, Henry Walton."

"Why did you decide to move here?" Alex smiled at the youngest of Kristin's boys.

Kristin looked away. "It was for the best."

From the half-built stables came Henry Walton, a narrow-shouldered man with hair as fair as that of his sons, and once again Alex wondered how he'd managed to get something as solid as the cabin into place in less than four months.

The answer appeared from behind the privy, adjusting his breeches. Fiona inhaled, her mouth falling open. Alex swallowed back on a gasp. This had to be Kristin's brother, sharing with her rye-coloured hair, blue eyes and lightly freckled skin. Not only was he big, he was possibly the most beautiful man Alex had ever seen, and to her embarrassment her eyes glued themselves to him as he came towards them. He surveyed them with a blank face, and looked questioningly at his sister.

"This is Lars." Kristin placed a light hand on the man

beside her. She said something in what Alex supposed was antiquated Swedish, making Lars turn all of his six feet and four of gorgeous manhood towards them. Fiona moaned, and Alex could but agree with the sentiment; the broad chest, the slim hips, the long, long legs...mouth-watering, all of him. Except for his eyes: flat and indifferent, they showed no animation when he nodded in her direction.

"Lars," Alex said, receiving a weak smile in return. The large man's gaze was riveted on Fiona, who gawked at him, her hands clasped tight. From the corner of her eye, Alex saw Kristin and Henry share a look, a swift locking together of eyes that was quickly smoothed over into a smile.

"It was sort of amusing," Alex said to Matthew later that evening, walking hand in hand with him down to the river. "She's comfortable in the woods, and so is that strange brother of hers, but poor Henry looks totally out of place."

"Aye, he's dependent on his wife and yon giant of a brother-in-law."

"I wonder why they left New Sweden. It seems sort of desperate to start all over again."

"Mayhap there wasn't enough land."

Alex raised disbelieving brows. "Here? Come off it. They should have been able to find something closer to home." She laughed and shook her head. "Listen to me; I sound like a veritable gossip, don't I? I suppose they had good enough reasons. Maybe Kristin's father couldn't stand Henry's guts or something." She dipped her foot into the river and looked back at her husband. "Race?" She drew off her shift and plunged into the water.

A quick bath and they were back on the shore, Alex donning a clean shift before spreading a blanket on the grass and motioning for Matthew to lie down. He made happy sounds as she worked her way up and down his back, now and then protesting when she dug her fingers into a particularly tense muscle.

"Are you asleep?" Alex whispered in Matthew's ear some time later.

"Almost." He stretched to his full length. The skin on his back and buttocks was red in patches after her massage, and all of him smelled quite nicely of lavender.

"Supper soon," she said, busy with her clothes. She handed him a clean shirt, collected the towels and her small stone flasks, and sat down on a felled log to wait for him. "It's beautiful, isn't it?" She took in their surroundings. "But so huge, miles and miles and more miles. Unbroken expanses of forests, deserts, mountains and more forests..."

"Aye." Matthew sat down beside her and pulled the comb through his damp hair. "It is enough to make a man feel most humble, and very small." He froze with the comb halfway through his hair and hissed a warning.

Alex followed his eyes to the other shore. One by one, a group of Indians were coming out of the forest. Matthew stood up, raised his hand in a silent greeting and bowed. The men facing them returned the greeting, filled their water skins and melted back into the surrounding woods as silently as they had come.

"Indians?" Ian sounded jealous. "What did they look like?"

"Like men do in general," Alex replied, earning herself six – nay, eight if one included Fiona and Jonah – disbelieving looks. "They did, right?" she said, turning to Matthew.

Matthew concentrated on his food, drank and wiped his mouth before sitting back to answer. "They did. Less clothes, most of them only in leather breeches, but aye, much like men in general."

Two of them had carried muskets and that worried him, as did the fact that he now had a band of a dozen or so Susquehannock braves close to his home, on his land. Should they choose to attack, there was nothing he could do to defend his family – they would easily overrun whatever defences he, Ian and Jonah could offer. He swallowed noisily, disguising it as a cough attack. Occasionally, there were stories of Indians attacking homesteads such as theirs, but they were rare, he reminded himself, and anyway the Susquehannock were allies, a tribe that traded with white men.

Just in case, Matthew insisted on leading the livestock into the stable for the night and took an extra round to ensure all his doors were safely fastened. He gave Ian one of his muskets, placed a loaded pistol within reach on Alex's side of the bed, and leaned a musket against the wall on his own.

Alex didn't say anything, but he could see in her eyes that she was disconcerted by his behaviour, and she spent far longer than usual in their bairns' rooms before joining him in their bed.

"Do you really think they might attack us?" she said in a small voice.

"Nay, not really." He kicked off the quilts. It was hot in their little room, and with the shutters closed it was worse than usual. "It doesn't hurt to be prepared."

The Indians came into their yard next morning: twelve silent men that stood waiting until Matthew went out to greet them. It took some effort to stand at ease in the half-circle of braves that surrounded him. His hands itched for the weight of a musket or a sword, but he'd decided that to go out armed was too much of a provocation, keeping only the dirk that always hung on his belt.

He stood still under the leader's appraising inspection, meeting the dark eyes of a man of an age with himself. The man's hair was streaked with grey, his face the deep brown of a ripe hazelnut, as was his lean torso, the strong arms and long fingered hands. The supple leather of his leggings clung to him, and round his waist was wrapped a decorated band from which hung an axe and a long, evil-looking knife. He radiated no overt animosity, more a wary curiosity towards these strangers who were encroaching on lands that had for generations belonged to his people, his tribe. The Indian adjusted his quiver and plucked at his bowstring, eyes straying towards the river.

"I was born here." The Indian spoke good English, surprising Matthew.

"Here?" Matthew indicated the ground at his feet.

"No, over there, in the ruined village."

"Ah." Matthew nodded. "I'm Matthew, Matthew Graham."

"I am Qaachow – of the Susquehannock." The Indian bowed; Matthew followed suit.

"What happened?" Matthew asked. "To the village."

"Smallpox." Qaachow grimaced. "They all died – including my wife and my little daughter."

"I'm sorry. It's a terrible thing to lose a child." He met Qaachow's eyes and smiled ruefully. "My daughter died in Scotland, five years ago, and not a day goes by that I don't think of her." My lass, my Rachel. He raised his eyes to the sky like he always did when he thought of her, hoping for a glimpse of his angel child, somewhere way up high.

He shook himself, recalled his duties as a host, and invited Qaachow and his men to share his table. He was somewhat relieved when Qaachow declined, saying they preferred to stay outside.

"Alex!" Matthew called. "Will you be so kind and bring our guests some food?"

His wife appeared so quickly she must have been waiting behind the door with the heaped platters and jugs of beer that were now carried outside. Once the food had been distributed, Alex served the beer, curtseying in the direction of Qaachow before handing him a mug.

"You can go back inside now," Matthew said.

"I'll stay," she replied, pouring him some beer. "What do they want?"

"We speak your tongue," Qaachow said, making Alex go so bright red Matthew smiled.

"I'm sorry," she mumbled, "that was impolite of me. I'm Alex." She extended her hand.

Qaachow backed away, staring at her hand. "I am Qaachow." He gave her a little bow. "We must be on our way," he added, directing himself to Matthew. "We have a long way to travel." He inclined his head, swivelled on his heel and led his men due south.

"What did they want?" Alex slipped her arms around Matthew's waist.

"He grew up here," Matthew said into her hair. "In the abandoned village. He wishes us to respect his dead, I reckon."

"His dead?" Alex reared back to see Matthew's face.

"His people – they died of the smallpox." He uttered a quick prayer and looked down at her. "We'll not to disturb them: his wee daughter and his wife – we'll leave them to rest in peace, aye?"

"Of course," Alex said. "His daughter?"

"Aye, a wee lass. Like our Rachel."

Chapter 5

Edinburgh, 2016

Magnus Lind rarely talked about his daughter anymore. Not at all, actually, except with Isaac, his grandson. But not speaking didn't mean not thinking, and not a day passed without Magnus throwing at least one thought in the direction of his lost girl, gone now for almost fourteen years.

He poured himself a cup of coffee, grabbed a bun hot from the oven, and stepped outside into the garden. June twilights were purple moments of time perfumed with lavender and honeysuckle, roses and the heady scent of the mock-orange that grew by the garden shed.

He sank down into his rickety garden chair and stretched out his legs. He felt lonely and abandoned, with his woman, Eva, in London and Isaac away for the weekend with some of his friends. Even more abandoned after his late afternoon appointment with his doctor, but that was his own fault – he hadn't told either of them about his resurfacing headaches.

"It's back," his doctor had told him straight on. He liked that about her: she never prevaricated. He'd nodded, not at all surprised. Almost five years since last time, a long period of grace for a man diagnosed with brain cancer.

"So what do we do?"

"Three this time," the doctor informed him. "At least one of them sits so deeply imbedded it will be impossible to operate. So we'll start you on chemo next week."

Magnus hadn't said anything then, but now in his garden he made up his mind. No chemo, no radiation, no months of constant nausea, of seeing his hair fall out...This time he was going to refuse all that – he had another plan. He bit into the bun, but it grew in his mouth, swelling into something that threatened to choke him, so he spat it out, drawing a shaking hand across his mouth. His little idea obviously scared the shit out of him, he thought sarcastically.

A few minutes later, he was standing in the studio at the top of the house. Once a place full of Spanish music, cigarette smoke and his mysterious Spanish wife, nowadays this was the territory of his grandson, seemingly as talented as Mercedes. On a nail hung the cardigan Mercedes would wear when she was cold, a paint-spattered black wool that smelled of her, even now, seventeen years since she'd last used it.

Magnus did what he always did when he entered the studio: he prowled through cupboards and the stacked canvases, ensuring there were none of Mercedes' magical pictures lying about. More out of rote than necessity, because by now he'd gone through the room so often he knew there weren't any postcard-size canvases heaving in greens and blues, horrible little maelstroms of paint that swallowed you and spat you out elsewhere.

"*Vilken djävla underlig familj,*" he said, once he was done. What a strange family! Understatement really; his family was more than strange, it was bloody weird. His wife some sort of repetitive time traveller, born into a family of magically gifted painters in medieval Seville. His daughter yanked through a time funnel, and his grandson... Magnus grimaced, looking over to where he kept the special picture Isaac had painted for him last time he was ill.

"A return ticket," Isaac had said at the time, holding up two small canvases. "One to go and see her; one to come back to me." Except that now there was only a single, seeing as John, Isaac's dad, had since then destroyed one of them.

It frightened the daylights out of Magnus to realise that Isaac had inherited Mercedes' magical gifts. People shouldn't be able to paint holes through time! Thankfully, it scared Isaac as well, the boy going pale around the gills whenever they discussed it – well, he would. Isaac had twice experienced what it was like to be sucked through one of Mercedes' time portals, and had no wish whatsoever to repeat the experience.

Magnus looked about the room. Everywhere were Isaac's paintings, fantastic paintings, but all of them normal.

Normal? Magnus swelled with pride. These were the works of a budding genius, canvas after canvas of non-figurative art. Whatever; the important thing was that there was no magic in them, no sensation of vertigo if one got too close, which was not the case with the miniature painting that Magnus now extracted from its hiding place. He peeked at it. The picture hummed, vibrating in his hands. Hastily, he stuffed it back out of sight. Not yet; he had things to do first.

"But you can't do something like that! It's suicide!" Eva looked at him with an expression of absolute shock.

"No, it isn't, I'm going to hang on for as long as I can, but not with all of me disintegrating." Magnus wasn't quite sure how to tell her this, so he went over to where she was sitting on the sofa and laid down, pillowing his aching head in her lap. "I was thinking of trying..."

Eva stiffened under him. "No, Magnus, please no."

He twisted round onto his back and lifted one hand to cup her face.

"My little Eva, have I ever told you how glad I am that I went on that cruise all those years ago and met you?"

She smiled, covering his hand with her own. "Not as such. But I know."

"I'll die pretty soon," Magnus went on, closing his eyes to avoid her pleading look. "If I'm with you one month or six months doesn't really make that much of a difference, does it?"

"Yes, it does, that's another 150 days."

He smiled at her preciseness. "But they might be rather awful days." He sat up beside her and took her hands in his. "I might have a chance to see her again. I've no idea if it will work – and anyone with a mind as rational as yours will of course scoff and say it won't work – but I'm going to try."

She disengaged her hands and hugged him. "How will I ever cope without you?" she whispered into his neck.

"You'll have to learn, sweetheart. I'm going to be gone anyway." He swallowed back on an urge to cry and hugged her back. They sat like that for a long time.

★

"I promised you several years ago that I'd tell you the truth." Magnus bent down to extract the roasted chicken from the oven. "Breast or leg?"

"Leg," Isaac said, "and more potatoes than carrots.

"So it's back," Isaac stated once they were both seated.

Magnus nodded. "Three. The size of walnuts. And if nothing's done I'll be dead within two to six months."

"And if you do something?" Isaac's voice wobbled.

"They don't know. A year? Two years?" Magnus waved his chicken bone at him. "But I don't want to. I hated it last time, and this time I've decided not to."

Isaac shoved his plate away from him. "But that means you die."

"I die anyway. It's just a question of how quickly." Magnus took a deep breath. "Last time I almost fell through one of your paintings by accident, remember?" He'd just been looking at it, holding the delicate canvas in his big hands, when it had begun to hum, to whisper and cajole. Moments later, he'd been sucked into a vortex of bright light, and even now, so many years later, Magnus had to fist his hands to stop them from trembling at the recollection of that horrible sensation of falling down an endless, narrow chute.

Isaac nodded, eyes wary.

Magnus gave him a lopsided smile. Yes, this was terrible stuff to talk about.

"Dad pulled you back. He says all he could see were your legs..."

Magnus shuddered. John had pulled him back in the nick of time, after which he'd demolished the canvas with a knife.

"Shit, it hurt! My head felt like it was about to explode with pressure. And next time I went to the doctor the tumour had disappeared." He met his grandson's dark eyes and pursed his lips. "This time I'm going to try and fall all the way."

"No," Isaac groaned, "no, Offa."

"I have to, I..." He exhaled loudly. "I miss her so much. And if I'm going to die anyway, then why not? Who knows, the tumours might be zapped into oblivion this time as well."

"Or not, and then what? No hospitals, no doctors..."

"I'm prepared to take that chance."

"And what about me?" Isaac sounded much younger than he was.

Ah, shit.

Magnus leaned forward and tousled the dark mop of hair. "You? You'll do fine. You have to. And you've got John and Diane and even Eva to help you out."

"But not you," Isaac said accusingly.

"I'll be dead shortly anyway. But somehow I'll be around. In your dreams and in your thoughts, I'll still be there."

Isaac didn't reply. He just took hold of Magnus' hand.

Over the coming weeks, Magnus said silent farewells to everything: his garden and his home, his family and friends. His favourite pub just off the Castle Rock, the bench he liked to sit on in the Botanical Gardens, the long walk up to Arthur's Seat where he stood for a long time looking in the general direction of the north-east, towards his birthplace in Stockholm. Most of all, he spent his time with Isaac and with Eva – the days with his grandson, the nights with his woman.

Magnus had decided on a day in July, and when the final countdown began, he was unable to sleep. Instead, he sat through the nights in his study, taking down his leather tomes to study them for one last time. The last night he stood in the passageway between the kitchen and the front door, looking at the photographs that lined the walls. Alex, Alex, Alex – everywhere Alex; twenty-six years documented in fading colour prints. He stood before each and every one of them and wondered if he was totally insane to contemplate an attempted leap through time on the faint hope that he would find her again. Probably. He dragged a hand through his short hair and, for the last time, switched off the lights downstairs.

He had decided long ago that he would say no goodbyes – for his own sake. But he did, lying on his side while Eva slept to engrave all of her in his mind. She snored, she always did, and he brushed her hair off her face to see her better. In the grey predawn he kissed Eva tenderly on her cheek, stood for some minutes looking down at her sleeping shape, and tiptoed out of the room. On the nightstand he left two letters, one for Eva and one for Isaac.

He hesitated on the upper landing before entering the studio. Jesus! What on earth was he doing? On the easel he had already placed Isaac's little painting, and he hurried towards it before he should lose his nerve.

He was drowning in second thoughts, his brain buzzing with apprehension. What if Isaac's painting didn't work or, even worse, what if it did work but only partly, leaving him hanging in the in between? He was exhausted and, behind his brows, the ubiquitous headache swelled into an unbearable dissonance, with swirling, concentric circles dominating his vision. He squinted and shook his head. This was the way it was going to be; even the doctor more or less admitted that there was nothing much to do.

"Right." He tightened the belt around the unfamiliar clothes he was wearing: scratchy breeches, woollen stockings and an old-fashioned linen shirt. "Magnus Lind, this is it."

He stepped up to the easel, took a big breath and looked deep into the swirling blues and greens – a magical painting, a captured funnel through time, expertly executed by his grandson. He heard the painting whisper, and he wasn't sure what he wanted anymore. He heard it sing, a soft humming that wrapped itself around his head. Where was she? Isaac said he had to actually *see* Alex to be able to go to her, and he couldn't see anything but blue. He felt as if he was drowning and closed his eyes, gulping precious air when the pressure that banded his chest eased. Maybe this was a stupid thing to do... Yes, maybe he should go back to bed instead.

The picture sang, high sweet tones that made him open his eyes. Green; everything was green, spinning round him. And look... There! Haloed in a glowing light he saw her, a dark silhouette in long skirts. Was it really her? He heard her laugh, and there was the sound of a child as well. He leaned forward, his eyes on the elusive shapes. He stretched out his hand and the funnel closed like a vice around him.

Herre Gud! Magnus tried to rear back because something was tearing at his insides, clawing viciously through his head. He didn't want to do this anymore, God it hurt, and what were all those terrible, terrible sounds? In his head, a chainsaw was digging into his brain, and he could swear he was on fire. He opened his mouth to scream for help but it was far too late, and with a final, painful wrench his body was sucked into the maelstrom.

Chapter 6

"Come on." Alex shooed her daughters in front of her. "And don't forget your baskets. The more we bring home, the more jam we have for the winter."

Ruth and Sarah followed her up the slope behind their home and on, walking for about half a mile before they stopped. Alex studied the small red strawberries that covered the ground. It had been one of her more pleasant discoveries some years back, and this was the second time she harvested this particular place this summer.

"Can we take some jam to Per and Erik?" Ruth asked through her crammed mouth.

"If you eat them all, there won't be any jam, will there?" Alex said.

"Can we?" Ruth insisted.

"Yes, of course we can." Alex sighed. From the moment they woke up, her children were on about the Waltons, fascinated by these new playmates. Alex wasn't quite as enthusiastic, not so much because of the boys whom she found charming and polite, but Lars... There was something seriously wrong with that man, however gorgeous he might be. Taciturn to the point of rudeness, eyes that studied everyone but his immediate family with absolute blankness, and then there was his disconcerting tendency to pop up out of nowhere, a silent presence that would gawk and slide away. The more she thought about it, the more Alex was certain it had been Lars who'd been spying on her and Matthew a few weeks ago.

She filled her first basket and began filling the second one, picking her way over the ground. A soft rustle made her look up. On the other side of the clearing, Fiona appeared from behind a large oak, smoothing down her clothing. At the sight of her, Fiona dropped a curtsey and fled, making Alex shake her head. She sincerely hoped Fiona was being careful, because neither Jonah nor Fiona had the means to support a child. Still, who was she to deny two adults what little fun they could find? She made a mental note to talk to Matthew about this, even if she suspected he would be less than pleased.

"Ruth?" Alex frowned in the direction of where she had last seen her daughter. "Ruth? Where are you?"

"Over here!" came the floating reply.

"Don't stray too far." Alex went back to her picking, listening with half an ear to Sarah's story about one of the hens.

The shriek had Alex off her knees and rushing madly in the direction of Ruth's voice. A snake, or a bear, please not a bear...not a snake either. She slipped and landed on her rump, skidding at surprising speed through the damp grass to end up only a foot or so away from her daughter.

"Ruth?" Alex struggled to her feet. "Are you alright, sweetheart?" She inspected her child, hands running over limbs and head to make sure she was undamaged.

"Mama," Ruth moaned, raising her hand to point behind Alex. Shit, Alex thought, it was a bear, or perhaps a mountain lion. Sarah plummeted down the incline and leeched onto Alex's leg, and it was with a wildly thudding heart that Alex turned to face whatever it was that had Ruth standing immobilised.

The man lay thrown into a thorny thicket, impaled face downwards. He uttered a low howl and tried to pull himself free. His head was crowned by greying blond hair, and his hands hung white and soft, helpless in the brambles. Where had he come from? Alex looked about, trying to understand from where he had fallen to land where he was.

"Stay here," Alex said to her girls and took a tentative step towards him.

"Mama?" Ian materialised by her side. "Who's that?"

"I have no idea, but he needs some help." She glanced

at Ian, taking in the leaves in his hair and down the back of his breeches. "Aren't you supposed to be helping your father with the new clearings?" she asked, a niggling suspicion nudging at her brain.

"I heard Ruth."

"Supersonic hearing," Alex muttered. "Come on then, let's see if we can get him out of there without leaving him a permanent pincushion."

"How in God's name…" Ian huffed, standing on his toes. "It would seem he dropped from the skies."

Alex nodded with a fluttering tendril of unease uncoiling in her belly. "Or he was riding an uncommonly large horse that threw him."

Ian made a derisive sound. "Aye, about ten feet at the withers and now gone up in smoke." He cursed when one of the evil thorns tore a gash into his forearm. "There is nothing to do but pull him free."

"Okay." Alex took hold of the closest extremity. "It's going to hurt," she said to the trapped man. "I'm sorry, but we can't get you out of here otherwise." There was an inarticulate sound that Alex decided to interpret as a yes and, with a nod to Ian, she heaved backwards, dragging the stranger free.

"*Herre Gud!*" the stranger said. "Holy fucking Matilda!"

Alex thought she was going to die on the spot. It couldn't be!

"Go and fetch help," she told Ian, succeeding in keeping her voice calm. "He's in no fit state to walk. And take the girls with you. Ruth, take the baskets."

Her children hurried off, leaving Alex alone with the man lying face down on the ground. She rolled him over, ignoring his winced protests, and stared down into a face she'd never expected to see again.

"*Pappa*?" Oh my God, it was Magnus, his blue eyes burning into hers. "Bloody hell, Magnus," Alex said through her tears. "What are you doing here?"

"Oh, just dropping by for a cup of tea," he wheezed, making her laugh. And then she was crying, because he was here, the one person she still missed from that other time, but how could that be, that he had dropped like a kamikaze pilot from the skies?

Magnus tried to shush her, patting at her leg, at her arm, but he was crying too.

When she threw herself onto his chest he groaned. "Shit! What did I land in?"

"I have no idea, but it's huge and has thorns." Alex wiped at her eyes and attempted a smile.

"Really? I would never have guessed." He studied the trees surrounding him. "Plane trees, huge bloody *platanus occidentalis*. Oh my God, we're not in Scotland! We're in North America somewhere."

"Sherlock Holmes in person, I presume." Alex sat back on her heels and looked at him. He looked awful. Apart from all the scratches and gashes that covered him, he had a sunken look to him, and there was a distinct smell of singeing emanating from him.

"It's excruciating to fall through time." He squirmed under her scrutiny. "At one point I think my shirt took fire."

Alex inspected his sleeves: yes, the right-hand cuff was bordered by a sooty line of burnt cloth, and his skin was blistered. His breeches had ridden up, revealing a knee that was swollen and blue, badly sprained from the look of things, and his foot lay at an awkward angle.

"What are you wearing?" She pinched the cloth of his breeches.

"I couldn't show up in jeans and an oxford shirt, could I?"

"Show up? What, you planned this?"

Magnus broke eye contact and admitted that he had, explaining how he'd used a magic painting in a last bid to see her before he died of his aggressive brain cancer.

"Die? You came here to die? You show up here, in a time where there's nothing I can do to help you – not even with a simple infection, even less with pain – and you tell me you have a brain tumour and expect to die within a year or so?"

Magnus shifted on the ground. "I think it helps – the falling through time. It did last time."

69

"Last time? You've had this before?" Alex frowned in recollection of the dreams she'd had several years ago – dreams in which she'd been convinced Magnus was dying or dead.

Magnus nodded. "Six years ago or so, the first time. They operated and had me on chemo, and for some time it all looked okay and then the headaches came back, and I was pretty sure I was going to die... I didn't want to."

"In general you don't." Alex clasped his hand.

"Anyway, I had this little painting," Magnus went on, nodding at her astounded expression. "And one day I thought I saw you in it, so I looked too deeply and fell towards you. It was like being twisted through a keyhole, one long agony, and even more when John yanked me back. And when I went to the doctor, the tumour was gone. *Puts väck.* Wiped out. A miracle, according to medical science."

"Well, they do happen – miracles, I mean." She gnawed at her lip. "The painting, was that one of Mercedes'?" As always, her mother's name shrivelled her throat into a narrow chute. There were some aspects of her life she preferred not to dwell on: first and foremost, her own inexplicable drop through time, and secondly, the fact that she had a witch for a mother, a person who could paint portals through time.

Magnus shook his head. "Isaac. But he's only ever painted two and he has promised me never to paint another."

Isaac? Alex stared at him, thinking – hoping – that she'd misheard. Magnus just nodded, verifying that Isaac had inherited Mercedes' gifts.

"Ah," Alex squeaked. "And you think he'll hold to that promise?"

"Yes, I do. He has no particular wish to fall through time again, and he definitely doesn't want a random someone doing it just because they stumble over one of his paintings."

"No, I imagine not." Alex hugged herself in an effort to calm down. Isaac; last she'd seen him – after his unfortunate drop through time courtesy of one of Mercedes' pictures – he'd been seven and already an accomplished painter. And now... Bloody hell! One witch in the family was quite enough, thank you very much.

Magnus tried to sit up, but gave up with a low exclamation. He yawned, showing off a complete set of white teeth.

"I'm so tired," he mumbled, "so very tired..."

Alex sat by his side and tried to bring some order to the turmoil inside of her. She stretched out a hand, placed it on his cheek, and he didn't vanish; he was solid and warm under her touch. Her father, here... A small glow bloomed inside of her, sheer unadulterated joy at seeing him again, but just as quickly that feeling was replaced by fear tinged with anger. What was he playing at, taking a dive through time when he knew he was terminally ill? And how was she to cope, first having him back and then watching him die away from her?

When Matthew showed up with Ian and a makeshift pallet, Magnus was sleeping, Alex's hand held in his.

Matthew looked at him with widening eyes and turned to Alex. "Magnus?" he mouthed.

She nodded, thinking that she must have talked very much about her father for Matthew to recognise him immediately. Alex undid her hand from her father's hold and stood back to allow the men to lift Magnus onto the pallet.

"You know him?" Ian had noticed the hand holding and gave her a suspicious look.

Alex nodded. "He's my father, and no, I have no idea how he comes to be here."

"But..." Ian looked from Alex to Magnus and back again. "He died. In a thunderstorm, just before Da found you on the moor."

"I never said that. I said he disappeared, and now it seems he has reappeared." She frowned at the thicket and shook her head. "But I have no idea how. We'll have to ask him once he's feeling better." And until then she hoped they could come up with a credible explanation, because otherwise it might all become quite difficult.

Chapter 7

"Look what I've found." Matthew blew her in the ear..

"Surprise, surprise," she mumbled. "It just fell into your bed overnight, did it?"

"Aye." Matthew spooned himself around her. "I wonder what you do with this?"

"Let it sleep?" She yawned, pushing her bottom against him.

"Nay, I don't think so." He smiled, turning her towards him. Before he was done, her fingers had locked themselves in his hair, and in his ear he heard her repeat his name over and over again, her hot breath tickling his cheek. He collapsed on top of her.

"Every morning," he said, rolling off. "This is how every day should start."

Alex twirled a strand of his hair round her finger and yanked. "I'm ready whenever you are."

"Well, of course you are; you're my wife." He laughed at her face and kissed her on her nose. "My wee wife, always obedient and dutiful, just as she should be."

"Huh," Alex grunted, trying to shift away from him, but held still by his tightening grip. "We'll see about that, shall we?"

Matthew laughed again. "Now?"

Magnus twisted on his pallet bed and covered his ears in an attempt to stop hearing the intimate sounds that were coming from his daughter's bedchamber. The rhythmic creaking of the bedstead, his daughter's voice lowered to a seductive whisper – he resented her for it. No wonder they had so many children, with them being at it like rabbits!

The sounds ceased, and Magnus relaxed against his

72

pillow, closing his eyes. Any moment Alex would tiptoe across the parlour on her way to the kitchen, with Matthew following her a few minutes later, and then the whole household would swing into the business of yet another day.

Two weeks here, and he was still hobbling about in a permanent state of astonishment at the sheer quantity of work necessary to keep the family up and running. Not in his wildest imagination had he been able to comprehend how hard life was here. Just to make a cup of tea required someone to fetch water, blow life into the fire, and wait until the water boiled before preparing the teapot. Fat chance of a cup of tea anyway, as Alex was all out of tea leaves, and the next opportunity to buy more would be when Matthew made the long trip down to Providence come autumn.

The bedroom door creaked open and Alex moved by swiftly, whispering a good morning to Ian, who slept on the other side of the room. Mark and Jacob rushed by, headed for the stables and their morning chores. Magnus heard Ian and Alex converse in the kitchen, and then Matthew's heavier foot treads crossed the floor, followed by the patter of small feet when the two girls shadowed their father in the direction of breakfast. Ten minutes later, it was impossible to even pretend to sleep, and anyway he had to pee before his bladder burst.

Magnus rolled off the pallet bed and managed to get himself upright, the shirt flapping round his bare legs. It was still an unfamiliar feeling to walk about without underwear, but Alex had confiscated that particular item of clothing immediately, telling him silk boxers were an absolute no-no and he'd best get used to going about commando.

He pulled on his breeches, using the wall as a prop, and stood for some moments regaining his balance before hobbling over to where he had left his crutches, cursing under his breath whenever his damaged leg hit the floor. It was a small, bare room: two armchairs, one of which out of deference was offered to him, a small writing desk, an even smaller table with a chess set on it, a couple of stools, a shelf holding a few books as well as three small baskets containing

73

wools and threads and all the other things Alex needed for her continuous sewing. All the rooms were the same, utilitarian and bare, but whoever had made the furniture had taken his time, allowing his knife to carve surprising shapes into bedposts and armrests. Magnus caressed the exquisitely carved roses that decorated Alex's chair, thinking that Matthew had quite the artistic flair – very much at odds with the stern and demanding patriarch Magnus perceived him to be. He adjusted the crutches under his arms and hobbled towards the door.

"Good morning," Magnus said to the kitchen at large, made his way outside and hurried off as well as he could in the direction of the privy.

"Mayhap you should offer him a chamber pot," Matthew suggested to Alex, watching his father-in-law's unsteady progress.

"Oh, believe me, I have. He's just uncommonly stubborn." Alex set down a heaped pewter plate in front of her husband.

"Ah, a family trait." Matthew winked in the direction of Mark.

"Then that's one thing we have in common," Alex bit back, setting down bread and butter and a stone jar of strawberry jam on the table. She handed Mark the milk, poured herself some hot water with honey in it and sat down.

"Sometimes it brings to mind the plagues of Egypt," she commented to Magnus later, shaking her head at the razed plates. "More specifically the locusts."

Her father laughed and bit into his slice of bread. "Well, what can you expect with six kids?" He regarded the children through the open door, looking from Daniel to Ruth to Sarah, and frowned at Matthew's receding back. "Very close in age."

"It wasn't his fault. Sarah sort of just happened." In a small cramped cabin somewhere in the mid-Atlantic... Alex smiled at the memory, even if at the time it had been more about assuaging grief than making love. Nights in which she'd held Matthew as he mourned the loss of his home, nights in which she gave him all of herself instead, assuring him that

74

it would be alright; somehow it would all work out, and he needn't worry; she'd be fine – she was still breastfeeding Ruth. And so she'd arrived here with five live children and a sixth unborn one in her womb. Well, if she was going to be precise, one of those children was her stepson, even if she never thought of Ian as anything but her own.

"It's still something of an open wound." Alex looked in the direction of where her husband had dropped out of sight. "Even now, four years on, when he's achieved so much here, it's Hillview he means when he says home." She used her nail to scrape splattered tallow off the table and frowned down at her hands. The Waltons had been here less than six months and their place already had a name, while they had been here for four years without even attempting to name their new home.

Magnus patted her hand. "It's not only Matthew that misses it, I hear."

Alex sighed. "Every morning when I wake I have this nanosecond in which I think I'm back there."

"And us? Don't you ever wish yourself back in your time, with us, your real family?" It came out very harsh.

Alex met his eyes. "Never. This is my time, *Pappa*. This is where I live and die."

"Not yet, I hope."

"No, not yet. Now," she said in an effort to change the subject, "how about you finally teach me how to make those famous cinnamon buns of yours?"

Elizabeth Leslie rode in late next afternoon with Jenny in tow. Ian muttered something, but at Elizabeth's heavy-handed suggestions that he might want to show Jenny around, he nodded and set off towards the stables.

From what Alex could see, the two young people weren't speaking, but Elizabeth beamed in their direction, voicing that they were well matched, for all that Ian was younger than Jenny.

"Mmm." Alex led her guest over to sit in the shade, detouring by the kitchen for something to drink.

"I haven't told you, have I?" Elizabeth said once they were settled on the bench.

"Told me what?"

"About those men."

"Men?"

Elizabeth rolled her eyes. "You know, the men you saw making off with our maids."

"Oh, no, you haven't."

"Peter has been quite busy. Most irate he is – and rightly so. Anyway, he heard how there's this band of men who procure wives for the colonists. Sells them at a premium price, according to Peter."

"Procure wives?" Sell them? It sounded just like a business venture Jones might be involved in, which would explain Sykes' presence in the clearing.

"Yes." Elizabeth scrunched her brows together. "Burley, I think he said. Yes, that's his name, the rogue who leads them, Burley."

"But where does he find these wives?"

"Mostly by stealing away an Indian woman or two, but now and then they resort to abducting bond servants." Elizabeth's face set into a scowl. "We can't have that, can we?"

"Oh, so that's worse, is it?"

"Of course it is! We paid good money for those girls! The Indians, well, they're just heathen."

"Just heathen!" Alex choked.

"They live like savages in the woods. Mark my words, over time those Indian women will be grateful."

"You think?"

"Well yes; they'll be married off to Christian men."

Alex made a face, but Elizabeth didn't see, concentrated as she was on Magnus, who was sitting on the bench under the huge white oak, surrounded by his grandchildren.

"Your father, you say?"

With an effort Alex left the infected subject of Indians, nodded and handed Elizabeth a pitcher of barley water.

Elizabeth poured herself a mug and drank it down. "Cinnamon?"

"Yes, and ginger and lemons." Alex sat back in the shade.

"He looks battered," Elizabeth said. "How did he make his way all the way up here on foot?"

"I have no idea, but he says he hurt his leg on the last stretch. He insists he saw a huge bear and turned to run..." She peeked at Elizabeth to see how this went down.

"A bear?" Elizabeth threw a worried look over her shoulder.

"That's what he says, but he isn't familiar with the local wildlife. It could have been a mountain lion, or a large raccoon."

"A raccoon? Surely no one would mistake a raccoon for a bear?"

"On its hind legs in the dark of the woods and when you've never seen one before?" Alex grinned at Elizabeth. "But for a man to admit being frightened of something the size of a dog is difficult. A certain embroidering is to be expected."

Elizabeth laughed and shook her head.

"Will we see you at the harvest dance?" Elizabeth asked, looking down at Matthew from where she sat astride her horse.

"Of course," Matthew helped Jenny up to sit behind her mother and smiled at the young lass. Very pleasing to the eye, she was, and he hoped Ian thought the same.

"It may be there will be other business to discuss." Elizabeth nodded in the direction of Ian.

"Mayhap," Matthew said, aware of Alex's disapproving stance beside him. "You'd best make haste." He indicated the dark clouds that were forming across the skies. "We'll have rain before the evening."

"We will." Elizabeth wheeled her horse, followed by her silent escort, a large man on a mule.

Matthew took Alex's hand and led her in the direction of where Magnus was sitting. Having her father here was disconcerting, and Matthew had to work hard to suppress the urge to say a prayer whenever he was close to Magnus.

Magic; ungodly magic that no one should tamper with – that was how Magnus got here, and it was wrong. It was different with his Alex: she'd been yanked unawares out of her existence to land at his feet. He tightened his hold on her hand, thanking the dear Lord yet again for the gift of his wife.

"Did she believe your story regarding your father?" he asked, studying his lanky father-in-law. It irked him to find himself overtopped by Magnus, accustomed to always being the tallest, what with him being well over six feet.

"She didn't seem to care one way or the other," Alex said. "At least she didn't laugh outright."

"Well, that's good." He smiled at her preoccupied expression. "What are you thinking of?"

"Two things: firstly I am wondering why we haven't named our home yet, and secondly I have these strange vibes regarding Ian."

"Vibes?"

"Feelings, concerns," she clarified. "He doesn't want to marry Jenny."

Matthew grunted. This wasn't something he wanted to discuss with Ian well within hearing distance.

"Later," he admonished, receiving a nod in return. "As to the name, you're right. We should give our home a name." He looked across the yard to the sheltered house and its surrounding buildings. Just by the main door grew Alex's rose, carried over the seas all the way from Scotland and now in its fourth year here an impressive bush, dripping with sweet-scented white blossoms. "Graham's Garden," he suggested.

Alex laughed. "Garden?" She gestured at the wilderness around them.

"Garden," he insisted, "it will be. Over time..." Never quite the same slice of paradise Hillview had always seemed to him, but all the same his little piece of Eden, his small corner of the world.

"Graham's Garden," Alex repeated and opened her fingers to braid them into his.

"And behold the chief gardener," Matthew murmured in her ear with a quick nod towards Magnus.

Alex groaned. "Not quite three weeks here and he's already driving me crazy with all his ideas about how to improve my vegetable beds."

Magnus watched them approach and was struck yet again by how seamlessly his daughter and her husband fitted together, how fluidly she leaned into him and he into her. Without being aware of it, they adapted their movements to each other, he shortening his stride, she extending hers until they moved in perfect synchronisation over the grass. He'd never seen anything like it, although he supposed that at times he and Mercedes would have appeared the same way to an objective beholder.

As their parents drew near, the children stopped what they were doing and gravitated towards them, Sarah clinging to her father, while Jacob said something to Alex, receiving an approving nod and a quick tousle in return. Ruth walked backwards in front of them and whatever she was saying made Matthew laugh, and then Daniel was at Matthew's side, tugging at his shirt, while Mark lifted a squealing Sarah to sit on his shoulders. And there came Ian, and the way Alex looked at him had Magnus drowning in jealous rage. She loved this young man much more than she loved her own son, Isaac. She had chosen to remain here when she could have followed Isaac back all those years ago, and in choosing to stay in this time she'd forsaken her original family. It hurt. It hurt even more to see how right the choice had been – for her.

Chapter 8

Magnus was gratified by how impressed his grandsons looked as he recited the healing qualities of the herbs they'd just planted. He smiled at Jacob and Daniel – one boy with his fair hair, the other with his blue eyes – and with a little grunt got back to his feet, limping over to sit beside them on the rustic bench.

"Are you a physician?" Jacob asked.

"No, not as such. I work with plants."

"A healer." Daniel nodded.

"Yes, I suppose I am, at least when it comes to the plant part."

Jacob shifted on his seat and threw Magnus a dubious look. "Are you a Christian healer?"

Magnus was taken aback. "Why do you ask?"

Jacob hunched together, muttering that everyone knew that some healers were in pact with Satan and witchcraft was a mighty evil that had to be fought diligently.

"Witches don't exist." Well, with the exception of his own dear departed wife, his Mercedes.

Both boys stared at him with an expression of disbelief.

Magnus cleared his throat and infused his voice with as much authority as he could muster. "People who believe in witches are people who have limited education and hold superstitious beliefs."

"Your grandda's right – to a point," Matthew said from behind them. He came over and stood looking down at them, his eyes guarded whenever they met Magnus'. "Most of those condemned to die for witchcraft are innocent of anything other but being different, and it's only by examining the evidence with an open mind that a correct judgement can be made. Unfortunately, often superstition rules – not common sense. Now, you have chores to do, and then your mama said something about cake."

Daniel shone up and leapt to his feet, followed by a somewhat less enthusiastic Jacob.

"They work quite a lot for boys their age." Magnus loaded his voice with an element of reproof. The boys were already halfway to the stables, racing each other down the slope.

"All farm lads do – especially now, during the harvest."

"They're quite bright, even if uneducated."

Matthew frowned at him. "Uneducated? They know their Bible well enough, they know of lands and people far away, they all know their letters and how to cipher, and all the lads write passably."

"But still, much less than they would know had they gone to school – real school," Magnus said, ignoring the warning lights in Matthew's eyes.

"They're taught as well as we can. Alex and I raise our children to be God-fearing and industrious, and that is no bad thing, is it?"

"God-fearing?" Magnus made a disparaging sound. "Is that the same as narrow-minded? Like believing some people actually consort with the devil?"

"Nay, it's not. But it is acknowledging his greatness and understanding our own insignificance. I assume you agree with that, being Christian."

"Christian?" Magnus laughed. "Nominally, I suppose I am. But do I believe in God? I don't think so."

Matthew studied him from under a furrowed brow. "In my home you won't voice such doubts. I'll not condone it, aye?" He held Magnus' eyes, and after some moments Magnus nodded.

"Good." Matthew helped Magnus up onto his feet, handed him his crutches, and set off in the direction of the forest.

"If you see Ian, tell him I'm looking for him," he called over his shoulder. "I'm at the barley field."

"Touchy, touchy," Magnus grumbled to Alex a bit later, having recounted the incident. Alex sat down beside him, clasping her hands round her mug of chamomile tea.

"Maybe it's you coming over high and mighty. It's quite rude to insinuate that Matthew is narrow-minded."

"I did no such thing!"

"You think? As you tell it, you more or less laughed at his faith. Our faith," she added, irritated by the supercilious look on his face.

"Your faith?" Magnus broke out in loud laughter. "Come off it, Alex," he said once he had calmed down. "You're not sitting here telling me you've developed a belief in God, are you? What happened to my super-rational daughter?"

She gave him a cold look, stood up and moved away from him, crossing her arms over her chest.

"Alex, you can't believe all that stuff."

"I can't? How would you know? You have no idea what my life has been like these last fourteen years or what events have shaped me, do you?" She looked out into the yard where Ruth and Sarah were playing a game of tag, and then turned to face her father. "In this life, God is a constant. Sometimes He's all we have. So when I say our faith, that's exactly what I mean: our faith. I may not be quite as much of a Bible reader as Matthew, and there are aspects of his beliefs I don't agree with, but I've learnt the hard way to put my trust in God and hope He'll keep me and mine safe. And so far He has."

She fell silent, remembering those awful months ten years and more in the past when she prayed and prayed to God to keep her abducted husband alive, and how she'd known, all the time, that her prayers were being heard and answered.

"You've really changed," Magnus said, breaking into her reverie.

She swept together the crumbs on the table and threw them into the hearth.

"Of course I've changed! It's called adapting to your circumstances, and if you don't do that you die. Survival of the fittest and all that..." She gave him a direct look. "And I resent your comments regarding our children's education. We do as well as we can, striving to ensure they all have as good a start as we can give them. In this day and age, education is a prerogative of the higher classes, and that we are not. We're farmers, and we can't afford to keep a tutor to educate our children, nor would there be one to find – not in this little corner of the world." She collected plates and mugs and set them to soak in the battered pewter basin, pouring hot water from the kettle over them.

"Fiona!" She set the empty kettle down on the hearth. "Fiona!" No reply and Alex made an irritated noise. Where was she? She'd been gone for hours, and this was not a day off, definitely not.

"Daniel will be sent off soon enough anyway." She sighed, returning to her discussion with Magnus.

"Sent off?"

"Matthew wants him to be a minister, so he'll be sent to study elsewhere when he's around ten or twelve." To Massachusetts, which to Alex was like sending her boy to a different country, to live among people she knew absolutely nothing about.

"And what does Daniel think about all this?" Magnus asked with a disapproving edge.

"Daniel will do as his father bids him. I just hope he finds some happiness along the way."

"And Mark? Jacob?"

"Mark is needed here, on the land. Matthew will ensure there's enough land to support two or three of his sons. And Jacob, well for now he's also needed here, but Matthew has spoken of apprenticing him down in Providence."

Jacob was the one with the real aptitude for books, and just the other day Alex had found Matthew deep in thought, his eyes staring straight through Jacob, who was busy reading at the little desk. Mayhap a lawyer, Matthew had confided to Alex, who agreed.

"How can you let him take all these decisions?" Magnus looked at her as if he had no idea who this strange woman might be.

"How?" Alex rolled her eyes at him. "They're his to take. The children are his, not mine; he has sole say in what they do or don't do. Don't get me wrong; Matthew and I discuss this, and he does take my opinion into consideration. But ultimately it's he that decides." She flashed him a look. "I'm not a pushover, and I'm fortunate to have a husband who sets great value on my advice. But legally I'm without rights. I don't exist as a separate entity; I'm only an extension of Matthew. Fun, isn't it? Especially for a girl raised after Women's Lib..."

"Then why did you stay here?" Magnus said. "Why didn't you take the opportunity to go back with Isaac?"

"Yeah, that would really have made things easy, wouldn't it? Isaac torn between me and John; John torn between Diane and me." Alex shook her head. "I couldn't. Not once since I met Matthew has there been any doubt in my mind that I belong with him. It would shred me to pieces to be without him." She averted her eyes from his condescending look and moved over to the door. "Where the hell is she?" she muttered. "It's time to start supper and the cows have to be milked..." She yanked her straw hat off its hook and pressed it down on her head. "Will you keep an eye on the kids? If Matthew asks, I'm off looking for Fiona – in the direction of the Waltons."

It was a relief to escape the kitchen and the strained conversation with Magnus. In her head, she'd held long debates with her father throughout the years, but Magnus in reality was very different from how he was in her head. And it didn't help that Matthew and Magnus had not exactly taken to each other.

Belatedly, it struck her that it might not be the best of ideas to rush off alone and unarmed in search of Fiona, but by now she was well on her way and reluctant to turn back. She exhaled and picked up her pace, keeping just off the trail.

"Fiona?" Kristin said. "No, I haven't seen her. Did you send her here?"

"No, but she's been gone most afternoon, and...err...well, I think she's somewhat taken with your brother."

"My brother?" Kristin repeated, bringing her fair brows together into a frown. "How do you mean: taken with my brother?"

"She fancies him which, given how good-looking he is, isn't exactly strange, is it?"

Kristin's freckles stood stark against her paling skin. "He has a betrothed, so your maid must look elsewhere."

"I'll be sure to tell her, but it would probably have better effect if he told her that – instead of kissing her in the woods."

"Kissing her? *Nej, ni ljuger!*"

"Lie? Why would I lie? Well, seeing as she isn't here, I'll just go and look somewhere else, shall I?" Alex inclined her head in a quick greeting at Henry, who appeared from the stables, smiled down at little Johan and set off down the track.

"If I see her I'll send her home," Kristin called after her.

"Do that!" Alex replied without turning her head. "And if she isn't home before me, I might actually be tempted to belt her," she muttered.

On the way back, Alex slipped off the path to relieve herself behind a bush. As she sat crouched, she heard the unmistakable sounds of a man and woman making love, and a quick peek revealed Fiona and Lars in a compromising situation further in under the trees. Alex ducked back down and made her way back to the trail as quietly as possible. So Lars was betrothed elsewhere, hey? Alex snickered and increased her pace.

She heard Matthew before she saw him and came to a halt. Why was he standing in the forest telling someone off like that? Then she recognised Ian's voice, and when she rounded the sycamore that indicated she was now entering Graham land, she found them face to face on the trail, both of them with knotted fists and lowered heads, staring off like rutting bucks.

"Where have you been?" Matthew barked at the sight of her. "Have I not told you not to venture out on your own in the forest? And—"

"Later, okay?" Alex held up her hand. "What's the matter?"

"What?" Matthew's voice creaked. "Ask him."

"Fine," Alex said. "I will. What is it, Ian?"

"What is it?" Matthew interrupted before Ian got

85

a word out. "I'll tell you what it is. I did as you said and went to speak to my son about Jenny, on account of you not being certain the lad wished to marry the lass, comely though she may be."

"And I don't!" Ian replied. "I told you so."

"Aye, you did, blathering on about how you didn't love her, and how you wanted it to be like it is with us, with Alex and myself."

"Is that wrong?" Ian asked. "Don't you want that for me?"

"Of course it isn't wrong, Ian. That's why your father went to talk to you in the first place, to ensure that you were comfortable with marrying Jenny before he signed anything with Mr Leslie. And now we know: you don't want to marry Jenny."

"Hah!" Matthew snorted. "But that isn't all. You see, the lad has found the lass he wishes to wed."

"He has?" Alex sorted through the very short list of girls Ian's age in the district and came up with a blank. Unless... She narrowed her eyes at him, recalling several recent incidents when Ian had showed up in some disarray.

"Aye, I have." Ian's chin came up in a defiant expression. "And she loves me."

"Well, that's good." Alex placed a restraining hand on Matthew's sleeve. "So, who is it?"

"Fiona," Ian mumbled, dropping his eyes to the sun-dappled ground.

"Fiona?" Alex succeeded in sounding more surprised than she was. She was going to flay that young woman. How dare she seduce a boy of seventeen!

"And have you known you love her for long?" she asked, maintaining a level tone.

"Some months." Ian eyed her warily.

"Ah," Alex said. "Have you bedded her?"

"Alex!" Matthew hissed. "Of course he hasn't!"

"He hasn't?" Alex sank her eyes into Ian. "Have you?"

Ian squirmed under their combined eyes. "Aye."

"When?" Alex tightened her grip on Matthew's arm to the point that he actually uttered a muted 'ow'. But at least he understood and held his tongue.

"When what?" Ian hedged.

"When was the first time you slept with her?" Alex said.

Ian was a mortified red, the blush mottling his neck, his face, his ears. "Sometime in April."

"And have there been many times since?"

No, he told her, not more than a couple but it had been enough to know she was the woman for him. He threw her a challenging look, and Alex didn't know whether to laugh or cry. Poor boy...

"Any time recently?" Alex asked.

Ian shook his head. "Not since the day Magnus landed in yon thicket." No, because since then Fiona had been sneaking off towards Forest Spring whenever she could.

"You can't marry her," Alex said. "She's well over seven years your senior, and has at the most rudimentary education and skills."

"I love her!" Ian said. "And you said that you didn't want us forced into marriage against our will."

"No one is going to force you into marriage, not us, and definitely not Fiona." Alex could see she'd struck a raw nerve. "What has she told you? That she's pregnant?"

Ian nodded unhappily. "And it's my bairn."

"It is?" Alex asked. "How do you know?"

Ian flashed her a green look. "She loves me, only me..."

Alex sighed, let go of Matthew and placed her hand on Ian's arm. "I just saw her in the woods – with Lars. And they weren't talking about the weather."

Ian blinked and looked at her in confusion for some seconds, before comprehension dawned on him.

"No." He shook his head. "You're just saying that!"

"Are you calling your mama a liar?" Matthew said in a dark voice.

"My mama?" Ian's voice squeaked up a register. "She's not my mother; she's your wife!"

Alex couldn't help the sound of absolute hurt that escaped her lips.

Ian wheeled and ran.

Chapter 9

Ian came back very late that night, sneaking into the darkened kitchen. Matthew rose from his chair and, in a voice that brooked no discussion, bid his son to sit. Alex served Ian beer and food, and then they sat in silence while he ate.

Once Ian was done, Matthew got up, opened the door to the little lean-to where Fiona slept and told her to join them. Fiona came into the kitchen hesitantly, eyes darting from Alex to Matthew to Ian and back to Matthew. She licked her lips, clasped her hands in front of her and stood silent.

"Ian here has expressed a wish to marry you," Matthew began in a neutral tone.

Fiona lowered her eyes, peeking flirtingly at Ian from below her lashes. Alex had to close her hands round the urge to slap her, hussy that she was.

"Aye well," Fiona said, "Ian is a fine man."

The man in question squirmed, keeping his eyes on his plate.

"Hmm," Matthew replied, "man or lad, I don't know at the moment. We don't like it. I don't consider you a suitable wife for my son. You're far too old."

"Only twenty-five or thereabouts," Fiona protested.

"Yes, and Ian is seventeen. A boy you've known since he was fourteen," Alex put in with an icy edge.

"Not a boy." Fiona smirked. "Most certainly a man."

Matthew brought his hand down on the table, making Fiona jump. "You have seduced my lad, and you stand here and laugh my wife in the face?"

Fiona backed away from his anger, moving crabwise in the direction of Ian, who shifted further away on the bench, keeping his eyes on anything but her.

"I'm with child." She rested her hand on her stomach.

"Aye, Ian told us," Matthew said. "And he also told us you're sure he is the father, despite only having bedded with him a couple of times."

"It only takes the once," Fiona said.

Matthew raised his brows. "You've been sleeping with other men as well."

"No!" Fiona shook her head. "I've only bedded with him, with Ian – I love him."

"Ah, yes? And what were you doing off the path to the Waltons today?" Matthew asked.

"The Waltons?" Fiona blushed. "I was nowhere close to Forest Spring."

"Nay, you were swiving the brother in the forest."

"Nay!" Fiona twisted her hands together. "That's not true, Ian, I wasn't—"

Matthew held up his hand. "You were seen – by your mistress."

Fiona opened her mouth, closed it again. Ian uttered a strangled sound from the corner into which he had retreated.

"But it isn't only him, is it?" Matthew continued. "Do you want me to fetch Jonah?"

Fiona shook her head, looking from Alex to Matthew with beseeching eyes. "It's Ian's child. Your grandchild."

"I doubt that," Alex said. "I don't think you're pregnant at all. And if you are, it happened sometime after my father arrived, seeing as you had your courses the first week he was here."

Ian's head snapped up. "She bled?"

"Definitely," Alex said, looking askance at Fiona.

An hour or so later and the kitchen was empty of anyone but her and Matthew. Ian had given Alex a long hug before retiring, a wordless apology for his little outburst earlier, and Alex drifted over to sit in Matthew's lap. In the hearth, a piece of wood burst into fire, illuminating the large table, the benches, the scrubbed pots and pans that Alex had arranged according to size on the wall closest to the fire. With a hiss the flame collapsed into a glowing red and the enclosed space grew dark, the single source of light the fluttering flame from the tallow candle on the table.

"What will you do about Fiona?" She yawned and snuggled up against him.

"I'll sell her contract. I'll set out with her on the morrow." He threw an irritated look in the direction of Fiona's room. "I don't have time for this, not now, not during harvest."

"We could let her stay; give her one more chance."

"Would you be comfortable with that?"

"No, and I suppose it would be awful for Ian, but she can at least stay until you ride down for the Michaelmas market. It's only a month." She nestled closer. "Do you think I could go with you?" She'd only be four months along at the most, so the ride as such should not be a problem.

"Would you want to?"

Alex nodded, suppressing a yawn. "It's ages since I was away from here."

"Well, then you come with me and Ian stays behind to mind his siblings and the farm." He hugged her close, resting his chin on her shoulder. "And your father," he added in a tone that indicated he was only half joking.

Next morning, Alex stood arms akimbo and laid down the law to a red-eyed Fiona.

"...understood?" she finished, rather disliking herself.

Fiona eyed her with resentment but bobbed her head in assent.

"And let's hope you're not pregnant, shall we?" Alex continued, ignoring Fiona's sullen face. "It will make it that much harder to place your contract."

Fiona paled, making Alex suspect the stupid girl had been negligent on purpose, so certain she'd snared poor Ian.

"I'm not sure I understand," Magnus said, his eyes following Fiona's dejected shape as she crossed the yard. "She's under contract?"

"Fiona is a bonded servant, which means we've bought a number of years of service in return for having reimbursed the captain for her passage. In her case five years, at the end of which she receives a certain amount of money, a set or two of clothes and is free to go."

"Like a temporary slave," Magnus said.

"More or less. Matthew is responsible for her during her years of service, and that includes her moral and spiritual welfare, so you can imagine he isn't thrilled at having her sleeping around – particularly not with his eldest son."

"As if Ian minded," Magnus snorted.

"That isn't the point. What if she'd gotten pregnant? He'd have to marry her then – which she was probably hoping for."

"Yeah," Magnus muttered, "how terrible; the fallen woman and the precious eldest son."

Alex chose not to talk to him for the rest of the day.

Two days later, Alex was plucking a hen when several horses came down the lane.

"Jacob? Go and fetch your father," she said, wondering what Andrew Chisholm and his sons were doing here at this time of the morning. One of the horses had something slung over its back. Alex peered short-sightedly at it as she walked over to greet their neighbours. Was it a girl?

"Oh my God!" Alex reared back. "She's dead."

"We know." Andrew Chisholm's square features compressed into a scowl. "We've been looking for her all night; found her a few miles from here."

Alex approached the body. Long chestnut hair fell like a curtain towards the ground, baring a narrow little nape. How old could she be? Twelve? Thirteen?

"She's my miller's daughter." Andrew dismounted with a little groan. His sons followed suit.

"Soft in the head, she was," the eldest Chisholm son, Robert, said. "Wandered the woods on her own whenever she could." He rested his hand on the thin back and sighed, muttering a greeting to Magnus, who came hobbling over from the stables.

Alex invited them all inside. "We..." She looked at the dead girl. "We can't leave her like that. It's irreverent somehow."

91

"I'll take her." Magnus lifted the girl gently off the horse, for all the world as if she still were alive.

"Put her in the work shed," Alex said.

"Indians," Andrew said a while later, wiping his mouth with the back of his sleeve before serving himself yet another plate of eggs and bread. "Mark my words, this is the work of those accursed savages – no doubt the same band of braves that robbed me and Robert here some months ago."

"You think?" Alex produced more ham.

"Who else?" Robert snorted.

"As I hear it, they went south," Matthew said from the doorway, nodding a greeting. "I'm sorry for the lass."

"Yes, well, perhaps it's better she's dead, poor mite." Andrew belched, poured himself some more beer and sat back. "Damn heathens."

"Indians?" Magnus entered the kitchen. "No, this was no Indian."

There was an interruption in the conversation as Magnus was properly introduced, the Chisholm men giving him several curious looks and just as many questions as to how he'd travelled from Sweden to here. Magnus was adequately vague, admitting to having hit his head hard when he fell down the hillside, and so...

"Why do you say it wasn't an Indian?" Robert asked.

"Unless Indians wear belt buckles and hobnailed shoes... Someone has beaten that poor child to her death – and enjoyed it." Magnus made a disgusted sound. "Pervert."

The men trooped off to inspect the body, and when they returned they looked grimmer than before, as if the fact that this was the work of a white man, one of them, somehow made it worse. Not for the girl, Alex sighed. She was as dead as a doornail anyway.

"Could it be..." She broke off. For some reason an image of Lars flitted through her head. You're being unfair, she chided herself. He's weird, that's all.

"Who?" Andrew asked.

"I was just thinking, those four men that I saw abducting the Leslie servants, could it be them?"

"They carry off lasses to sell them, not kill them," Matthew said. Well, he had a point there, Alex conceded.

"Don't let her mother see her," Alex said as the Chisholms made ready to leave. She took hold of Robert's stirrup. "She doesn't need to see her like this." The girl was a patchwork of bruises, here and there with clear imprints of the booted feet that had done this to her.

"No," Robert said, "and neither does her father."

"Nay." Matthew came to stand beside Alex. "No parent should see their bairn like that." He draped an arm over Alex's shoulders, holding her to him as the sad little caravan rode off.

"Who would do something like that?" Alex asked.

"A very sick person," Magnus said from behind them.

"Amen to that." Alex shivered and pressed closer to Matthew. "Is he still around, do you think?"

"I don't know, but as of now you'll not walk about alone." No discussion, his tone indicated.

Chapter 10

Matthew offloaded his numerous family, bowed in the direction of Elizabeth, and offered Alex his arm. Leslie's Crossing teemed with people, and in a matter of minutes he'd lost sight of his bairns, his daughters rushing off in one direction, his sons wandering over to inspect Peter Leslie's latest pride and joy, a right fine stallion.

He looked down at his wife and smiled, thinking she looked quite the picture in her green bodice which was a wee bit too snug over her chest, therefore lifting her breasts in a way that detracted from her overall demureness. Demure? He stifled a chuckle. His Alex had no notion of what that meant. He pressed her hand harder to his side, caught her eyes and winked, liking it how her cheeks and ears went pink.

Thomas intercepted them on their way to the house, and for a couple of minutes they discussed the terrible events surrounding the miller's daughter. Thomas looked most concerned, eyes travelling over to where his three lasses were standing in a cluster round their mother.

"Twelve, you say?" he said.

"Aye, at most." Matthew sighed. "A bairn, Thomas, left ravaged and beaten to a pulp."

Thomas shook his head, muttered something about finding some more cider, and hurried off.

"Here comes Peter." Alex nodded in the direction of their host.

"Well, it's best to get it over with." Matthew wasn't looking forward to this conversation and was relieved he'd left Ian at home, not wanting to antagonise more than necessary.

"Do you want me to come along and hold your hand?" she murmured.

Matthew laughed and shoved her lightly towards Elizabeth. "You take care of her, aye?"

"Not fair; she's much worse than he is." Still, she did as he bid her, adjusting her hat and clothes as she went.

As he'd expected, Peter wasn't pleased, frowning for a long time at Matthew, who sat facing him in his office.

"But why? Jenny is a well brought up and handsome girl, is she not?"

"I already told you. Ian feels it would not be a happy match."

"Hmph!" Peter downed his whisky and banged the tin cup back down on his desk. "What does he know? He's not yet eighteen! Jenny would make him a dutiful and obedient wife."

"Aye, I'm sure she would, but he isn't of the same opinion." Matthew sipped at his whisky. "I won't force the lad."

Peter pulled at his lip. "Jenny will take it badly."

Matthew wasn't quite as convinced. From what little Ian had told him, it seemed young Miss Leslie had developed a fancy for her father's overseer, a German with very little English.

"Surely it can't be difficult to find a husband for such a pleasant lass," he said, receiving a black look in return.

"There aren't that many eligible young men in the vicinity."

Matthew pretended to think. "But what about Jochum?" he asked, working hard to look as if this was an inspired thought.

"Jochum?" Peter blinked. "He's my overseer!"

"But unwed." Matthew slapped his neighbour on the shoulder and exited the room. Some ideas were best left to germinate on their own.

"I understand you know Dominic Jones." Peter caught up with Matthew halfway across the yard.

"Know him? I had the unfortunate experience of working for him ten years ago, but since then I haven't seen him – until recently." And if he had his wishes come true, he'd never see him again.

"He's asking around about you."

"He is?" Matthew came to a stop. "And what is it he wants to know?"

"Oh, you know, where you live, how long you've been here." Peter threw him a perceptive look. "It doesn't please you, this interest."

"Nay, I can't say it does." It made him itch all over, his body hair rising in alarm.

"He's rich; rich and powerful. You'd best tread carefully around him."

"And he around me." Matthew inflected his voice with menace. He mustered a smile, said something about having promised to dance with his wife, and walked off towards the sound of music coming from the barn.

"Was it a good party?" Magnus asked the next day.

"Party is not exactly the word I would use; more like a parade ground for the dutiful daughter-in-law." Alex made a face. "Poor Celia seems totally terrified; of her husband, her new home and her mother-in-law, although not necessarily in that order. And Nathan spent most of the evening avoiding his happily pregnant wife."

"Pregnant? Already?" Magnus said. "But they've only been married what? Two months?"

"Three actually, and as Fiona so helpfully informed us, it generally only takes once."

Magnus frowned. "And it might come as a huge surprise to you that one can actually have unprotected sex and still avoid pregnancies."

"Oh, you can? And you would know, having extensive experience of this?"

"Not as such," he admitted grumpily.

"No, I didn't think so. Speaking of which, where is our Fiona?"

"Out back." Magnus waved his hand in the general direction of the privy. "She looked kind of nauseous if you ask me." The implication of what he was saying struck him the moment he uttered the words. "Oh shit, she's been looking ill for days."

"Great. Wait until Matthew finds out."

Matthew acted with such speed that Magnus realised he'd spent substantial time planning for this eventuality. In less than an hour, he had Fiona agreeing to do as he said, overseeing while Jonah and Fiona signed a marriage contract before assuring them he would make sure their union was registered when he was in Providence come next week.

Magnus stared as Fiona packed her few belongings and followed Jonah out to his room by the stables. Even worse, Fiona was pathetically grateful to Matthew for having sorted out her life, thanking him repeatedly for not throwing her out.

"Throw her out?" Magnus said. "Would he have done that?"

"No." Alex smiled in the direction of her husband. "But she doesn't know that."

"And him? Why does he want to marry her?"

"Jonah? Oh, Jonah's had his eye on Fiona for well over two years. And they've slept together, so the child could be his. Besides, unmarried women are quite the commodity here – and Jonah isn't the most attractive of men."

Rather the opposite in Magnus' opinion – overlarge teeth in a small mouth, narrow shoulders, long arms and a mousy thatch of hair. But he had nice eyes and a beautiful voice, and according to Alex he was hardworking and diligent.

"And now what happens? They live happily ever after?"

Alex looked doubtful. "I'd say Fiona has very little capacity for happiness. But maybe she can learn to be content – at least once in a blue moon." She stretched, bracing her back against her hands. "Matthew's promised them a cabin of their own, and even a patch of land for a garden."

Magnus didn't reply. His eyes were glued to the unmistakable bulge of her belly. Without a word, he stormed out of the kitchen, making a beeline for Matthew, who was down by the half-finished barn.

"How many more children do you expect her to give you?" Magnus was so angry he had spittle flying in the air.

"I don't think that's your business."

"She's my daughter! And this is what, your seventh child?"

"She is first and foremost my wife, and it's not as if I force myself upon her, is it? Not that that is your business either – what happens in the privacy of the bedchamber is between man and wife alone."

"Privacy? The whole bloody house hears your goings-on." Magnus was deeply satisfied by the dark flush that crept up Matthew's cheeks.

"Oh, aye? Well then, we'd best move you to sleep elsewhere. I'll have you installed in Fiona's old room before nightfall." With that Matthew stalked off.

"You didn't answer my question," Magnus called after him. To his surprise, Matthew lifted his hand in the air and gave him the finger.

"He's right. It's none of your business," Alex told him once Magnus had cornered her in the kitchen garden. She looked the picture of health, her cheeks pink with exertion, her eyes clear and bright.

"Oh, for God's sake, Alex, you can't want another child!"

"I said it's none of your business." She went back to her digging.

"But you've just turned forty! You might be fertile for another ten years!"

"You think I don't know that?" Alex sat back on her heels. She brushed at an escaped lock of hair, streaking her face with dirt. "There's not much I can do about it, is there?"

"Safe sex, abstain, coitus interruptus, oral sex—"

"Oh, shut up!" Alex straightened up and threw her trowel to the ground. "For your information we do a lot of that, okay? But this child is a wanted child – all our children have been wanted children." She left him where he was and strode over in the direction of where her husband was harnessing the mule.

Matthew saw her coming and turned in her direction.

"Kiss me," she said once she was close enough.

"Here? Now?" Matthew wasn't the most demonstrative of men in public.

"Now."

He gave an embarrassed laugh and tilted his head in the direction of Magnus. "To show him?"

"No," she said, making him smile at her lie. "Because I want you to."

"Oh, do you?" He hooked one finger into her apron to pull her closer, brushed his lips across her brow, and placed a finger on her mouth. "I'll kiss you later, but I won't kiss you for the sake of an audience."

"Stupid man," she grumbled, leaning her head against his chest. "How many men your age have women coming on to them, and tell them no?"

He tenderly put his arms around her and rested his cheek against her uncovered hair. "Not many I imagine, but then I'm an uncommonly fortunate man." Over her head, he met Magnus' eyes and grinned.

Magnus was beginning to regret coming here. In his head, he'd pictured a happy reunion scene complete with a huge chocolate cake, champagne and a 'Welcome Home Magnus' banderol fluttering in the wind. He had dreamed of spending hours in deep discussions with Alex, recouping on all these lost years, and instead she was constantly rushing from one task to another, a harried expression appearing on her face when he suggested they sit and talk, take it easy for some hours.

And he hadn't counted with the children...so many and a constant source of interruption whenever he managed to steal some moments alone with her. Their loud voices made his head ache, their lack of education made him long passionately for Isaac, and now there was another on its way, another source of distraction when he needed her to concentrate on him, goddamn it, because he was dying. He had brain cancer, for God's sake!

He grimaced in disgust at the tender little scene by the stable door. Another aspect he hadn't taken into consideration. Alex didn't need him; all she needed was the tall man with dark hair who was presently holding her to his chest and challenging Magnus with his glinting eyes.

Magnus gouged a hole into the rich, dark earth with his cane. Yet another misconception – he'd imagined all this would be in Scotland, not in bloody humid Maryland, at a time when colonists were scrabbling for a foothold on a continent teeming with woods, dangerous creatures and Indians. He exhaled and limped in the general direction of the house, keeping his eyes on the ground to avoid his son-in-law's gloating expression.

He came to an abrupt stop at the unfamiliar sight of several pairs of feet, all of them in soft leather moccasins. Bloody hell, real-life Indians!

Chapter 11

"I can't do more," Alex said to Qaachow, looking at the wounded man lying on her kitchen table. She'd stitched up the wound as well as she could and packed crushed yarrow and comfrey around it. "Now all we can do is hope it doesn't become infected – again."

She looked down at her hands. She'd never done anything like this before, and she'd fervently wished Mrs Parson had been here to help her as she'd heated the blade and sliced up the badly healed sword gash that ran all the way down the man's right side. Fat chance of that; she hadn't seen Mrs Parson for over ten years but assumed her to be hale and hearty down in Virginia. The man hadn't uttered as much as a whimper while she used tweezers and knife to cut away dead tissue, releasing the putrid stench of rot and pus.

"I thank you," Qaachow said. "Not many of your people would invite us into their homes – in particular, not under these circumstances."

"You're always welcome here," Matthew replied with a stiff little bow. "You should consider spending the night," he added, his offer of hospitality in stark contrast to his strained voice. Alex's eyes drifted over to the Indians waiting outside. Too many of them sported gashes and wounds that indicated recent fighting, and for all they knew there might be a band of enraged Virginia Militia on their tails.

Qaachow smiled in acknowledgement of the offer but shook his head. "We have several days of walking before we reach our home and we have been gone a long time. Our wives will be waiting." Qaachow said something to the man standing beside him, and together they helped their wounded comrade to stand.

"He shouldn't walk," Magnus cut in, jerking his head

in the direction of the bandaged man. "The movement will open the wound." He was still somewhat white around the mouth after watching Alex cut into the infected flesh.

"He can't walk," Alex said. "He's burning with fever."

"He must." Qaachow bowed and stepped into the dusk.

"Oh Lord," Alex said to Matthew once the Indians had dropped out of sight. "I hate feeling so useless." She inspected her darning needle and decided it had to be boiled before she used it again. There were bloodstains on the floorboards and on the light wood of the new wall, and Magnus was already scrubbing the table. Alex poured boiled water into the basin and washed her hands, noting with dispassion that they were shaking – badly. She leaned her forehead against the thick glass of the small window and took a couple of steadying breaths.

"You did well." Matthew beckoned for her to hold out her hands and poured more water over them, rinsing off the soap suds.

"Yes, you definitely looked as if you knew what you were doing." Magnus transferred his cleaning efforts to the workbench.

"I should probably have been an actress. What do you think they've been up to?" Alex grabbed the basin, carried it the few feet to the open door and upended it to the side.

"I don't know, but I suspect we'll find out shortly." Matthew beckoned the children over from where they had been standing in silence throughout the visit and hunched down before them, looking at their three youngest. "Not a word. You mustn't tell anyone your mama helped the Indian." Three heads nodded in acquiescence. "Good." Matthew tweaked Sarah's cheek and got back onto his feet. "The lads, Jonah and Fiona will be back shortly from the fields. I'll tell the lads; Jonah and Fiona don't need to know."

"I don't like it," Matthew said to Ian, standing out of earshot from the rest of his family. He caught Mark's eye and indicated he should join them, biting back a smile at the way Mark straightened up into his new status as a man of the household.

"You must both carry your muskets," he instructed his sons. "And we must make sure your mama has loaded pistols in the house."

"Why?" Mark sounded apprehensive.

"Well, you don't get your flank sliced open like a ripe peach by chance, do you?" Matthew said with a certain edge.

"Mayhap we shouldn't have helped them," Ian said.

"He was hurting and they haven't harmed us. We depend on their goodwill to live in peace." No choice, he thought. Sometimes a man had to walk the tightrope and hope he made it safely to the other side without falling into the abyss.

The pursuers clattered into the yard the next day, six men on winded horses that studied the well-tended buildings with overt interest before turning their attention to Matthew, who was crossing the yard in their direction with Mark and Ian at his heels.

"Indians," the oldest of the men said. "We are on the tail of a band of Indian braves."

"Ah," Matthew said.

"Have you seen them?" One of the men leaned forward across the neck of his horse, brushing at the dirty, black hair that fell over his brow.

"Well, I don't know, do I? What Indians? How many?" Matthew stretched his mouth into a daft smile.

"About ten or so," another man said. "We think at least two are badly wounded." He patted at his sword with grim satisfaction.

"Nay, we haven't seen a band of Indians with several wounded," Matthew said.

"Hmm." The black-haired young man looked at them through eerily light grey eyes.

"What have they done, these Indians?" Matthew asked.

The men shared several looks before coming to some sort of silent accord.

"We had a disagreement," the eldest said, "over some women."

103

"Indian women?" Ian asked.

"Not any more," one of the men muttered. "They're good Christian women now, nothing left of their savage ways. My wife, and his." He used his thumb to indicate one of his fellow riders and shifted in the saddle, looking longingly in the direction of the house.

Matthew bowed to the inevitable. "Will you join us for dinner?"

"Much obliged." The black-haired man swung off his horse with alacrity. He threw the reins at Mark. "Water him, boy." He took a step closer to Mark; sank those strange eyes into the lad. "Are you sure? No Indians come by here recently?"

"No, sir." Mark backed away.

"Really?" The man produced a decorated length of rawhide. "We found this up your lane. It even has blood on it." He turned to face Matthew. "I don't hold with Indian lovers."

"I told you," Matthew said. "We've seen no Indians. That doesn't mean they haven't passed by, does it?"

The younger man looked at him in silence. "No, I suppose you're right," he finally said, smiling at his host. But he didn't believe him – Matthew saw that in his ice-cold eyes.

"I'm not sure what to make of all this." Alex watched the riders disappear in the direction of Forest Spring.

"No." Magnus came to stand beside her. "It was a strange story. I had no idea intermarriage was so common."

"Nor me," Matthew said.

"The question being if it's voluntary or not," Alex mumbled.

"The red-haired one seemed very much in love with his wife and their two children," Magnus said.

"Aye, he did." What a sad tale, Matthew thought. Two Indian women abducted years ago from their families resurfacing as baptised wives of white settlers in Virginia, mothers of several children.

"What was Qaachow attempting to do?" Alex asked. "Buy them back?"

"Aye," Matthew nodded, "and that didn't go down well, did it?" Once the Indians had understood the white men were reluctant to part with their wives, what had begun as pure negotiation had deteriorated into savage fighting, leaving one white settler dead. He gnawed his lip and frowned. "That man, Burley, the one with the strange eyes. I didn't like him."

"No," Alex said, "and it's probably him who abducted the women in question to begin with."

"It is?" Magnus gave her a surprised look.

"Elizabeth told me how a band led by a man named Burley had cornered the wife market – an endless supply of Indian girls offered to whoever is willing to pay." She spat in the general direction of where the men had disappeared. "And it was definitely him I saw back in April, with Sykes. Bastard."

"Why didn't you tell me before?" Matthew said.

"Because they were six, and you're only one, and I didn't want you to do or say something stupid." She shivered. "He scares me, somehow."

"Aye." A man with the eyes of a dead fish was indeed a frightening sight. But gone, thankfully. With a parting pat on Alex's bottom, Matthew went off to finish his chores.

"A word?" Magnus almost overbalanced as he leaned forward over his cane. Matthew straightened up from his inspection of the mare's hooves and nodded. Magnus led the way back out into the September sun, hopping in the direction of the bench under the white oak.

"Only with me?" Matthew sat down beside Magnus.

"I owe you an apology," Magnus said gruffly. "I shouldn't have insinuated that you're forcing your attentions where they're not wanted. It's obvious you don't have to."

"Nay, I generally don't." Matthew leaned back against the broad trunk and stretched his legs out in front of him.

"But you must try and understand. I – we – come

from a time where seven children are seen as excessive, an unnecessary strain on the woman's health. And every time Alex gives birth, there's a risk, right? In the here and now, there's nothing to do if things go wrong."

"Have you shared this with her?"

"Of course not! But I bet she thinks of it," Magnus said.

Matthew knew she did. They even spoke of it at times, and all he could do was promise to be there, as he'd been for Jacob and Daniel and wee Sarah. And this time too he would stay beside her throughout the birth, no matter what the midwife might say.

"She says all your children are planned, all of them wanted. But who in their right mind would want three children in three years?"

"Us, apparently," Matthew replied icily. He relented and exhaled. "They have all been wanted, but not planned. Sometimes God has a finger in the pie as well."

"The only one with a member in the pie is you," Magnus bit back. "And as far as I can tell it hasn't been your finger."

Matthew burst out in surprised laughter, and after some moments Magnus began to laugh as well.

"It isn't easy," Matthew said once they had stopped laughing. He tilted his head in the direction of where Alex was coming out of the house, holding a skipping Sarah by the hand. "I love her, and even if I try to control myself there are times when I can't. There are times when she doesn't want me to…"

"Oh, so this baby is the result of a little accident, is it?"

"The new babe? Ah no, the new babe is planned, but wee Sarah now, or Jacob – Rachel was not yet three months when he was conceived."

"You don't speak much of Rachel," Magnus said gently.

"We don't?" Matthew shrugged. "Aye, we do. With ourselves or the elder lads quite often. Alex says we must, so as to keep her alive in our minds."

"But you don't need to do that. The lost child lives forever in your heart anyway." Magnus sounded sad, and Matthew turned to face him.

"You're disappointed," he said with sudden understanding. "All those years you'd created an image of Alex and what she might be like, and now you find her so different to what you thought she would be."

"She has changed so much."

"Nay, she hasn't. You're looking only at the outside. Inside, Alex is as she always was: quick-witted and opinionated, passionate and reckless..." Matthew stared off into the distance, smiling as he thought of his woman. "She has learnt to hide it better, and that is for the best."

Magnus shook his head. "She has changed. She's an obedient little wife, far from the independent woman she used to be."

"Obedient?" Matthew choked with laughter. "Alex?"

Magnus gave him an irritated look. "Like today. She serves you and all those men dinner, curtseys and leaves the room. That's very obedient in my book."

Matthew just stared at him.

"Or when she spends all evenings sewing and mending, listening to you reading the Bible – that's also a very obedient little wife."

"Today was her choice. Had she wanted to stay she would, no matter what I had told her. As to the evenings, I was under the impression she liked it when I read to her – and it's not always the Bible. I'll ask her, aye?"

"But the thing is you can sit and read while she has to sew. All the time she's working, not once have I seen her idle."

"Nor me."

"No," Magnus said. "You work quite a lot too. But at least you have the evenings off."

Matthew slid his arms around Alex's waist and walked her in the direction of the laundry shed.

"What?" she laughed. "Do I smell?"

"Nay, but mayhap you need a nice hot bath. Time for yourself."

Alex stopped so abruptly both of them almost toppled to the ground.

"Magnus," she sighed.

Matthew urged her on in the direction of the laundry shed and waited until they were inside before replying.

"He says you always work, that you never have time for idleness, and that I at least have evenings free while you must sew and mend. He says how in your old life you'd sometimes spend days on end doing nothing but loiter in the sun." He used buckets to transfer the hot water from the cauldron to the tub.

"Yes, and in between I'd work myself ragged, always in a rush, always with my nose stuck in my computer – so much in fact that Magnus would tell me I had to slow down, that I was working myself into an early grave with these long, long hours. I bet he didn't tell you that." Alex shimmied out of her clothes, folding them neatly on the broad bench that ran the full length of the wall.

"Nay, he didn't mention that." Matthew steadied her as she got into the bath. "Too hot?" he asked when she danced about on the bottom.

"A bit." She remained on her feet until he had poured in a bucket of cold water. She sat down and tilted her head back to look at him.

"I'm fine, okay?" She caressed his cheek with her wet hand. "Yes, sometimes it's a bit much, but it is for you as well, isn't it?" She sank lower into the water and closed her eyes. He didn't reply, deep in thought as he soaped her and washed her hair.

"I'll buy some more contracts." He smiled at the way her eyes flew open. "You need a new maid, and I can use a field hand."

"But you don't—"

Matthew shushed her. "Nay, I don't hold with it, but I won't wear us both to the bone. We can afford it." He did sums in his head. The sizeable amount of money they'd brought across had shrunk alarmingly over the last few years, but there was quite a lot left.

"Yes, I suppose we can." She grinned. "It's sort of fair, isn't it, that dear brother Luke is indirectly paying for all this."

Matthew looked away. A princely sum, Simon had called it once he had concluded the negotiations with Luke. Five hundred pounds as compensation for all the ill turns Luke had done Matthew. Not at all enough, in Matthew's book, and every now and then he would still wake and want nothing so much as to beat his beloved brother's face to pulp. His hands balled into fists.

"And then we have the money for Hillview," Alex said, oblivious to his tense silence. "More than 200 merks when all is said and done." Aye, that remained untouched, a general accrual for the future of their children.

"Does it still hurt?" she asked as she dried herself.

Matthew sank down on the bench and nodded.

"Will it always?" Alex sat down beside him and took his hand.

"It was my place, the one constant in my life. Since I was a bairn, I knew I was born to Hillview and would pass it on to my son. But now I never will. I was incapable of upholding the covenant with my people, with the generations that preceded me and the generations to come. I'm the weak link in the chain, the unhardened metal that gave..." He had to laugh at her expression, wildly rolling eyes and a pretend yawn. She didn't have much patience with him in his maudlin moods, and mayhap that was for the best.

"You did what you had to do, and the chain lives on thanks to your choice. Your sons will grow to manhood in a place where it's up to them to shape themselves a future, unencumbered by the constraints of class or conventions."

"...unencumbered by the constraints of class or convention..." Matthew smiled and used a towel to pat at her wet hair. "A philosopher as well?"

"I've been known to think – women do at times."

"They do? In my experience, they mostly talk."

"Huh," she snorted.

"It doesn't matter," Matthew said as they walked back towards the house. He craned his head back to look at the stars, scattered like randomly thrown specks of glittering glass on a velvet backdrop.

"What doesn't?"

"If I miss it, yes or no," Matthew said. Alex faced him, the whites of her eyes a pale bluish colour in the moonlight. "The bairns don't miss it; to them this is home now. I suppose that means it is."

"*O, my America, my Newfoundland,*" Alex quoted.

"*...My kingdom, safest when with one man mann'd, my mine of precious stones, my empery; how am I blest in thus discovering thee...*" Matthew went on. "John Donne didn't have Maryland in mind, I reckon." He grabbed her arse hard enough to make her squeal.

"Poor her," Alex said. "Imagine walking the world with a name like America."

Chapter 12

"But why did you give it to him?" Alex looked at the velvet pouch on Matthew's desk. A collection of coins – however Magnus had found those – but mostly gold, nine small ingots, three to the ounce according to Magnus, that Matthew had handled with appreciation.

"It's his anyway, right?" Magnus said. "Anything you own is his."

"Well, thanks for reminding me so succinctly."

"It's a belated dowry." Magnus grinned. "But I did actually set some conditions."

"You did?"

"That you buy some ready-made clothes for the whole family and that he please, please bring back some books."

"You might be disappointed," Alex said. "It's not as if there are tons of novels lying about."

"No, but anything else than the Bible, Shakespeare and Don Quijote would be welcome."

"If you'd told me beforehand that the Leslies were coming along, I might have opted for staying at home. As it is, my ears are falling off with her constant talking." Alex smiled pleasantly at Elizabeth, standing on the other side of the clearing where they'd spent the night. "And I'm not quite sure how she does it, but somehow she always makes me feel lacking. Either my dress is not modest enough, or my hair is too uncovered, or I laugh too loud..." A twist and her hair was up, fastened by a couple of hairpins before she covered it with her cap. She pulled up her stockings and gartered them, the bright red ribbons quickly hidden beneath her skirts. Not quickly enough, though, and she turned her head in time to see Elizabeth's mouth set in a straight line at this new evidence of Alex's flightiness.

"And it doesn't exactly help that all you do is talk to Henry Walton." Alex dug a hard elbow into Matthew's side. He uttered a low warning sound and shook his head, stopping with a wince. "Too much to drink?" she said, receiving a beady look in return.

"So what did you talk about all last night?" Alex asked once they were up on the horse, ambling along several yards behind the rest of the party.

"We spoke of his new life here. Of how his building is progressing, and how he will provision himself for the winter, and if the new bairn they're expecting will be yet another lad, and—"

"Okay, okay, I get the picture." Alex looked Henry over and stifled a small laugh. "What does a woman as attractive as Kristin see in this bottle-shouldered man?"

"You're judging by appearances alone." He shifted in the saddle until her bottom nestled snugly between his thighs. "And I know for a fact he is most well-endowed."

"What did you do? Line up and measure them?" She laughed at the resulting image. "It must be a comfort for him to be able to leave Forest Spring and his family in Lars' capable hands – did you notice there was yet another cabin up by now? I suppose it must be meant for when Lars marries that girl of his." Which she hoped would be soon – repeatedly over the last few weeks she'd seen Lars in the woods around their home, no doubt sniffing round for Fiona. She frowned; there was something off about the huge young man, no matter that he'd make Adonis himself weep with envy.

"He doesn't have a betrothed," Matthew said, "or, rather, the betrothed he had is dead."

"Dead?" Alex craned her head back to look at him.

"Aye, very dead: they found her savaged in the woods a year or so ago. A bear, they reckon."

"But why would they say he's still engaged?"

"Mayhap he feels he still is," he suggested.

Well, that would go some way to explain Lars' brooding presence, Alex supposed. "How terrible!"

Matthew grunted. "Aye, a very sad story; sad and well-rehearsed."

"How do you mean?"

"What I said; well-rehearsed, and I doubt Henry was quite as drunk as he appeared to be." He tightened his hold on her waist. "You'll not go to see them on your own."

"Why not? You think it might be dangerous?"

"Grief can be deranging."

"Grief?" Alex made a derogatory sound. "Not much of that around when you gallop around in the woods and bonk your neighbour's maid whenever you can."

"Bonk?"

"You know what I mean." Alex frowned. "He won't like it, will he? That Fiona isn't available to him."

"Probably not. But that's something he must come to terms with. And he's a well-built man, strong and comely. The lasses must be swooning for him."

Not if they had any sense of self-preservation, they wouldn't. Into Alex's brain swam the bruised face of the dead miller's daughter. She had looked as if she'd run into a rabid bear – a human bear. Coincidence, she told herself sternly. Still, the thought lay like a chafing stone in her mind.

"Do you—" she began, but was interrupted by Elizabeth, who'd halted her horse to wait for them.

"You really shouldn't be riding abroad in your present condition," she said to Alex, nudging her horse into a walk beside theirs.

"Oh, I'm alright," Alex said.

Elizabeth snorted. "That was not what I meant. A woman so obviously with child should remain at home."

In Alex's book, that was a huge exaggeration, her hand coming down to rest on the as yet quite discreet swell.

"Really? Why? Do you think I might inspire men to indecent thoughts?" Alex felt Matthew vibrate with laughter behind her.

"Nathan would never allow Celia to leave home while breeding." Elizabeth ignored Alex's question. "He's adamant in that his wife must refrain from too much bustle at present."

"Did she want to come along?" Alex asked.

"She pines for her mother at times." Elizabeth's tone signalled that this was a major weakness.

"To be expected," Matthew said. "She's but sixteen."

Elizabeth's mouth pinched together. "She's a wife now. She should put all her efforts into pleasing her husband and being a dutiful, obedient wife."

"Just like you've always been to Peter," Alex said.

Elizabeth gave her a long look. "Yes, I have always set my husband first and followed where he has led." She kicked her horse into a trot.

"As long as he's walked in the general direction you intended," Alex said to her retreating back.

Matthew laughed out loud. "You think Elizabeth rules the roost?" He laughed some more and looked over to where Elizabeth had now rejoined her husband.

"Don't you?"

"Nay, that I don't. Peter is very much the man in his own house. But he's wise enough to allow his wife some leeway, to let her think that at times it is she, not he, that decides."

"Oh, just like you do then," Alex muttered.

Matthew let his hand slide down to rest on their child and squeezed. "Nay, not as such. You and I take most decisions together."

Two days later, Matthew held in his horse on the outskirts of Providence.

"It's grown, hasn't it?" Alex looked down at the little town spread out before her.

From the docks – about the size of three Olympic pools – four streets, of which three were narrow dirt tracks no more, fanned out up the slope to where the central feature, the meetinghouse, dominated the settlement. To the west a rustic palisade, to the north equally primitive fortifications. Some intrepid souls had built outside the constricting fence, but mostly Providence's inhabitants preferred to live within their walls.

Around and beyond the docks stood warehouses; even

further away were the boarding houses and taverns that served the sailors. The streets were bordered by narrow houses, most of them quite humble, even if here and there somewhat more impressive buildings indicated the worth of their owners. And all of this against the backdrop of the glittering Chesapeake Bay, a wide, smooth expanse of water. A ship was slowly making its way up towards the mouth of the Severn, a dark splotch against all that shimmering blue.

Closer to town came the stink of habitation: privies, piled offal, the disgusting stench of accumulated stale blood and intestines from behind the butcher, the general aroma of far too many unwashed bodies in clothes that had been worn well beyond their laundry date. Alex wrinkled her nose fastidiously, noted a new inn, a bakery, and the colourful sign declaring the presence of a barber surgeon.

"So where is this famous establishment, Mrs Malone's brothel?" she asked.

"Nowhere close to where you will be." Matthew helped her off the horse, dismounted and handed the reins to the stable boy. "You won't go anywhere close to the further docks."

"Not even with you?"

"Not even with me. It's no place for a well-bred woman, and you wouldn't like it – not at all."

"Maybe I should be the judge of that," Alex muttered, but with no real heat. She could imagine just how squalid the area would be. She'd seen her fair share of ports.

"I'm not sure this is how I want to spend a fine autumn morning," Alex said the next day.

Matthew tightened his grip on her elbow and increased his pace, informing her that seeing as it was Sunday they were going to kirk, and that was that. He nodded to acquaintances on his way there, every now and then he stopped and introduced her, and Alex smiled and curtsied, very much the doting, dutiful wife of Mr Matthew Graham. Once at the meetinghouse, she followed him into the whitewashed interior and slid in to sit on a bench.

"Oh God, how much longer?" Alex groaned two hours later. Matthew squeezed her hand and sent her an irritated look. She subsided back against the bench, letting her mind escape from the boring sermon.

The meetinghouse was packed, but whether that was because of devoutness or because of social constraints was up for discussion. To not attend was to risk both fines and public denouncements for ungodliness, and Alex supposed that might be somewhat bad for business in a town dominated by the congregation elders. Her eyes drifted across the women, most of them in muted colours like her own dove grey, and lingered on the impressively silent children, equally soberly dressed. Here and there she saw a dash of blue, of soft russet or pale yellow, but mostly it was grey and brown, and she was swept with a longing for T-shirts in bright colours and with ambiguous messages, jeans that sat tight around your legs and showcased your curves, and Converse sneakers in red or wild purple. She sighed and fidgeted, accidentally bumping into Matthew. She was hot, she was bored, and she went back to her silent scrutiny of the congregation.

Matthew felt Alex stiffen beside him. She sat ramrod straight with her eyes locked on someone sitting several rows down on the other side of the aisle. He followed her gaze and his hold on her hand became a clamp, his fingers twisting themselves so hard round hers that Alex let out a muted little yelp. Jones! Here, in his kirk, for all that he was Anglican as far as Matthew recalled. With him sat his wife, Kate, and a long row of sandy-haired children. Matthew's throat worked with the effort to swallow. Kate... As if he'd called her name, she turned, her eyes sweeping the room and finding his. He saw how they widened, darkening with surprise, and she leaned towards her husband and whispered something in his ear. Jones just nodded, keeping his eyes on the minister.

Kate sneaked yet another look at Matthew, and he smiled at her, receiving a slight curving of the mouth in response. Still with hair somewhere between sun and honey, and dark eyes that had once been his only tenuous link to life. Not only

116

her eyes, but her body as well, wrapping itself around him when he had needed it the most. Kate seemed to see what he was thinking, because her smile widened, a triumphant edge to it as she directed it at Alex. And Alex retook her hand, folding her arms over her chest.

"I thought the purpose of going to church was to concentrate your thoughts on God," Alex said once they were out in the sun. "Not sit and drool over a former lover."

To his irritation, Matthew felt himself flushing. "I wasn't drooling."

"No? I could have fitted an apple into your mouth, so wide did it gape." Alex escaped into the shade of a plane tree, and he followed her, regarding the people as they came out of the meetinghouse. Neighbours and business partners, the men relaxed now that the religious part of the day was over, laughing amongst themselves while their wives made quiet conversation in small groups. Kate was in one of those groups, talking with animation while her eyes scanned the crowd.

"I think she's looking for you. Go ahead, be my guest and go over to her." And if you do you won't be touching me anytime soon, her eyes told him, shards of a dark, daring blue under the brim of her straw hat.

"Alex..."

She turned her back on him and waved at Elizabeth, approaching them through the crowd with Peter and Henry Walton in her wake.

"What a good preacher!" Elizabeth said once she was within what she considered hearing distance, which in practice meant everyone within a furlong heard her. "It's at times like these that I realise how much I miss the spiritual guidance of a minister in my day to day life."

"Yes, it definitely inspired you to pure thoughts, didn't it?" Alex gave Matthew a barbed smile, hooked her arm in under Elizabeth's and strolled off.

Alex threw Matthew a look over her shoulder. Her husband's long mouth had set into a thin, displeased line. Huh, as if he had any reason to be pissed off! It was him and his open gawking at damned Kate that was the issue here, wasn't it? Well, okay, maybe she was overreacting – a bit – but she hated it that he should smile at Kate the way he did, a softness in his eyes and face that made her want to twist his goddamn balls until he squealed.

"Oh look! Celia's parents!" Elizabeth dropped Alex's arm as if stung, grabbed at her husband and dragged him off towards an elderly couple surrounded by three young men.

Alex made a face at being so blatantly dumped and turned with a sigh towards where she'd left Matthew, but he wasn't there anymore and neither was Henry Walton. Instead, Alex found herself eye to eye with Dominic Jones and his wife.

"Great, my favourite people in the world." Alex gave them a false smile. "Why can't you just drop into a hole somewhere?"

Up close, Kate looked somewhat worse for wear, with a dissatisfied set to the mouth and skin that was covered with red, flaking patches, especially over her nose and right cheek. Still, there was no denying Mrs Jones was a handsome woman, her golden colouring expertly set off by the shimmering, tawny velvet she was wearing. Alex twitched at her grey skirts with irritation.

"The sentiment is mutual." Jones twirled the riding crop he was carrying.

"I'm glad we cleared that one up." Alex turned her attention to the Jones' children. The twins were ten she knew, having been present at their birth, and then there were five more, the youngest carried in the arms of a maid. "You've been busy," she said with reluctant admiration. Kate grimaced, and between them flew a look of absolute understanding.

Jones looked at his large family and nodded proudly. "There will be more. My wife is not yet thirty-five."

At this rate his genes would spread alarmingly, Alex reflected, studying Jones' offspring. Not a good thing, in her book.

"I was hoping for a word with your husband," Jones said.

"My husband doesn't want to talk to you."

Jones' small eyes glinted strangely. "It would be unwise of him to attempt me any harm – including defaming my good name."

"Defaming your good name? Why would he want to do that? After all, what have you ever done to him but beat him to an inch of his life and then...oh, yes, then you attempted to pin a murder on him, didn't you?"

"Shh!" Kate said. "People are looking!"

"You give us a wide berth and we'll give you the same." Alex lowered her voice, ignoring Kate. "But if you threaten us or if anything happens to Matthew, I swear I'll tell the whole town about Fairfax's death. Might make it a bit uncomfortable for you – as far as I know, there's no statute of limitation on murder, is there?"

Jones went a sickly white. "I have no idea what you're talking about."

"No, of course you don't. Your conscience is as pure as driven snow." A quick look down the street showed her Matthew making his way back towards the meetinghouse. Alex hurried off to intercept him. She had no intention of exposing Matthew to his former tormentor. Or pretty Mrs Jones, come to think of it.

In the event it didn't help, what with Jones following hot on her heels. Matthew stood like a cornered dog. Very briefly, his eyes flitted over to do a quick inspection of Kate, but then he was back to eyeballing Jones. Of a height, the two men overtopped six feet, but where Matthew was wide in shoulder and chest, Jones was massive all over, although the intimidating effect was offset by the fact so much of his bulk lay concentrated round his midriff, muscles converted to fat.

"Matthew? Let's go." Alex gripped his arm. He didn't seem to hear, eyes glittering a dangerous green. Jones smirked and brought the short riding crop down with a dull thwack against his boot. The sound made Matthew jerk, and Jones smiled, a taunting sneer that made Matthew turn to stone under her hand.

"Matthew!" Alex squeezed as hard as she could. The short whip smacked against the leather again, Jones sinking his eyes into Matthew.

"A beast of burden, Graham," Jones said. "I trust you remember how you bleated to the world that you were nothing but a slave."

"Dominic!" Kate gasped. "That's enough!"

"Bastard!" Matthew spat, and for an eternally long second, Alex was convinced this was when her husband would pull his knife and gut his erstwhile tormentor. So, apparently, was Jones, backing away with some haste.

"Go!" Alex barked, hanging on to Matthew. Kate took hold of her man and dragged him away.

Matthew slowly relaxed. He blinked, shook himself, and without a word led the way to the inn.

Chapter 13

A few days later, Matthew stood by the meetinghouse and watched Dominic Jones lord it over his fellow merchants. Resplendent in a pale silk waistcoat, a matching coat, and with Sykes a few paces behind, all that was missing was a slave carrying a parasol to properly underline just how rich and powerful Jones was.

Matthew's eyes lingered on Sykes. The man was his usual ratty self, armed with both sword and pistol. An idea took shape, and he hastened off to find Peter Leslie.

Sykes looked pale. He licked his lips, eyes darting over to Jones as if he were hoping for some reassurance from his employer. Instead, Jones distanced himself from him, leaving Sykes to face Peter Leslie alone.

"Retribution," Peter said. "I expect compensation for those two girls."

"I've done nothing wrong," Sykes said, "and, besides, I have no money."

"Nay, but your paymaster does." Matthew jerked his head at Jones, sidling away into the crowd. "Why the hurry, Jones?" he called out. "Afraid, are you?"

"Afraid?" Jones came to a stop. "Why should I be afraid?"

"Stealing is a serious offence – and stealing lasses in particular."

"I have no idea what you're talking about." Dominic eyed Sykes as if the man had the plague. Sykes shrank under the weight of the look.

"My wife saw him." Matthew ensured his voice carried over the assembled men. He pointed at Sykes. "She saw him make off with Mr Leslie's property. And..." He paused, swept the small crowd with his eyes. "...Sykes does nothing without Mr Jones' permission, do you, Sykes?" He turned towards the man so abruptly Sykes near on sat down.

"I have no idea what you're on about," Sykes said.

"Very well," Peter said. "In that case, we will take up the matter before the elders tomorrow. I'm sure Mrs Graham will be willing to testify."

"A woman," Jones drawled, "and your neighbour. How are we to know she doesn't lie?"

"For shame, Jones!" Peter might be thin and wiry, but he was tall enough to meet Jones' eyes head on. "Tomorrow," he said to Sykes. "And should you not appear before us, we will hold you guilty and set a price on your head."

"But..." Sykes threw Jones a desperate look.

Jones shook his head and shouldered his way out of the crowd.

"I wouldn't set my hope on him," Matthew said to Sykes. "You're all alone in this." He leaned forward. "He'll see you hang and not lift a finger. So why not tell us the truth? Did you abduct those lasses on his behalf? More money for him, a few coins for you?"

Sykes backed away. "I've done nothing, and your wife is a slanderous witch if she says different." With that parting shot he escaped.

"Well," Peter said, coming to stand beside Matthew, "it seems you've ruffled quite some feathers."

"Alex doesn't lie. If she says she saw Sykes there then she did."

"Ah, yes, but it isn't Sykes you're after, is it?" Peter clapped him on the shoulder. "Go carefully, Matthew."

"I always do. It's something I learnt under Jones' tender care."

Alex listened in silence to Matthew's description of events, sighing inside. This was going to breathe further life into the infected feud with Jones, and not for a second did she believe Sykes would give Jones up.

"He won't show. Come tomorrow, he'll be halfway to Barbados or somewhere."

"Better in Barbados than here."

"Maybe." Alex went back to her packing: salt and sugar, spices and candles, a big chunk of scented soap, ribbons for her girls, knife blades that Matthew would work into wooden handles for their younger sons, but best of all were the bolts of cloth.

"I thought you wanted to buy it ready-made." Matthew fingered the high quality serge and broadcloth. In russet and pewter grey, in a dark blue and a serviceable brown, the various lengths contrasted pleasingly with the pale of the linen lying beside them.

"It made me feel immoral." Besides, she'd found something else she wanted to spend her money on – a present for him, something to make him forget Dominic Jones and his vitriolic comments. Not that she thought it would work, and in particular not now, after hearing how he'd gone after Sykes. Still, she hugged her secret to her, managing not to break out in a wide smile.

"Elizabeth thinks I've lost my mind. She goes on and on about the importance of weaving your own cloth." Alex made a face. Weaving was a skill that eluded her, just as spinning yarn was.

"Nay, she suspects it is me that's gone soft in the head. She's urged me to stop this wastrel behaviour in you; have you produce good homespun for us all."

"I bartered for some of it." Most of it, actually. Her embroidered smocks and shifts had been far more appreciated than she'd hoped for, and so her pouch of coins had remained virtually untouched. Once again, she had to stop herself from grinning, her secret bubbling inside of her, making her want to laugh out loud.

"I have the new serving wench below." Matthew jerked his head in the direction of the door.

Alex got off her knees. "What's her name?" she said as she followed him down the stairs.

"Agnes, and a sweet, soft-spoken lass she is."

Agnes stood very alone in the yard, and Alex took a step back at the sight of her. "How old is she? She looks about fifteen."

123

"Eighteen, she says, and she both writes and reads."

"And her family?"

Matthew looked away. "It's still the same sad story. The lass is from Ayrshire, and her family was fined from hearth and home on account of her father hiding a minister from the soldiers."

"They split them up?"

"Her father died on the crossing, and so the rest of the family must work off his passage as well as their own. Her younger brother has been bonded out for fourteen years."

"Fourteen years? But how old is he?"

"Twelve," Agnes informed her in a high voice. "Wee Angus is but twelve." She fretted with the worn fringes of her shawl and curtsied in greeting to Alex. "I don't know where he is, and he is all I have."

Alex wanted to tell this waif of a girl that they would somehow help her find her brother, but a look from Matthew silenced her. There were no promises they could make, and both of them knew that.

"They said he was a man, and he was sold off the day we were landed. I didn't get to tell him goodbye or to remind him to say his prayers at night. He'll be fine, won't he?" Agnes asked with a pleading note. "He's but a wee lad, and surely they will be kind to him."

"Of course they will." Alex looked at Matthew for help.

"He was crying when they led him off," Agnes said. "Crying for me and Mam."

"Is she here? Your mother?" Alex was willing to take all of their savings and at least reunite this girl with one family member.

"Nay, Mam lies in the kirkyard back home." Agnes' grey eyes softened, and she raised a shaking hand to push an escaped lock of fair hair back under her cap. She was quite pretty in an unobtrusive way, with a fair complexion and a full lower lip. A pity she was underweight and so dirty as to be grey, but none of those drawbacks were of a permanent nature.

Somehow Agnes' sad little tale took a lot of the lustre

out of Alex's gift to Matthew. What had seemed a great idea yesterday seemed ostentatious today, and when a few minutes later a large stallion was led into the yard, Alex watched her husband apprehensively. His eyes flew to the dark bay, a covetous gleam in them as he inspected the deep chest, the white feathered fetlocks and the wide blaze down the horse's face. He took a step towards it and turned to Alex with an expression on his face that made her insides double flip with happiness.

"It's yours," she said. "I thought it was about time you had a horse you want to name something again."

"Mine?" Matthew was already running a practised hand down the dry legs.

"I saw you, the day before yesterday. You were all over him, and when you walked away I decided to buy him for you."

His eyes flashed to hers. "That's why you've been so thrifty in your purchases."

Alex hitched her shoulders. "So what will you call him?" She came over to pat the horse on its withers.

"Moses."

"Moses?" Alex laughed and took a step back. "Well, now that you mention it, he does look like an abandoned baby in a reed basket."

Next morning, they were woken by Peter at dawn. "Come, you must come quick."

"Has he been up all night?" Alex whispered to Matthew as they hurried after Peter in the direction of the docks.

"It would seem so."

"Hmm." The only 24/7 establishment in town was Mrs Malone's. Alex sniffed when they caught up with him, and he smelled of smoke and beer and cheap perfume. Well, maybe Elizabeth didn't mind.

Any further musing on this matter was cut short when they reached their destination: the shoreline of the Severn. There was a small group of men waiting, and Alex recognised three of them as being town elders. Bobbing in the water was a body, and even before they'd turned the corpse over, Alex knew who it was. Sykes streamed water from mouth and nose when they dragged him ashore, and planted in his chest was the handle of a knife.

"Not Barbados." Alex looked down at the lifeless shape.

"No," Matthew said, "but I can't say I feel all that sorry for him, do you?"

"Not really," Alex said.

"An admission of guilt of sorts," Peter put in. "He didn't kill himself, so someone wanted him silenced."

"Aye well, no proof. And if I know Dominic, he was nowhere close to Sykes last night. Someone else did this at his behest." Matthew kicked at the ground.

"Jones was at Mrs Malone's," Peter said. "All night."

Matthew cursed, a long string of colourful expletives involving sheep, livers and the devil's seed. Alex cast a glance at where Sykes was thrown on his back. Having Jones reappear in their lives was like pulling the scab off a healed wound and finding an abscess below, full of putrid flesh and pus. Dear old Sigmund would probably be all for this airing of old hates and remembered wrongs, but Alex wasn't all that sure she agreed with Freud – some things were better left alone.

It was in a somewhat dampened mood that they made their way back to the inn. Halfway there, Matthew ran into an acquaintance, so Alex strolled the last hundred yards or so on her own. She nearly jumped out of her skin when someone grabbed her sleeve, and wheeled to stare into a pair of peppercorn eyes she had never thought to see again.

For a moment she stood there, dumbfounded. Mrs Parson, here! Still those exceptionally white teeth set in a face that was a wrinkled pink, still a plump and inviting chest covered by a pristine white collar over a dark bodice. In fact, she looked not a day older, despite it being almost ten years since Alex had seen her last.

With a shriek of joy, Alex hugged the older woman, dancing them round and round until Mrs Parson recovered sufficiently to dig her heels in, thereby bringing them to an abrupt stop.

"What are you doing here?" Alex couldn't let go of Mrs Parson, had to keep hold of her hand. Shit, she was about to start crying.

"I could ask you the same, and here I was thinking you were back in Scotland."

"But..." Alex looked at her. "I wrote you several letters, telling you the whole story."

"You did? I didn't get them." Her eyes locked down on Alex's belly and she grinned. "Breeding again?"

"No, just some excessive flatulence," Alex said, making Mrs Parson laugh. "So why here?"

Mrs Parson shrugged. "Mr Parson passed away last summer."

Alex waited for more, but apparently Mrs Parson considered that this one-liner clarified everything.

"And?" Alex prompted.

"I couldn't stay in Virginia without him, no? On account of me not being Anglican."

Alex sighed. How could religion cause such rifts?

"Anyhow, it wasn't as if I wanted to stay, not when my sweet man was dead." Mrs Parson threw Alex a brooding look, surprisingly sad for her. "I miss him, and it was hard to stay in a place where I always expected him to walk in through the door." She slipped her arm in under Alex's and rearranged her face into a smile. "And you? Why are you here?"

"We couldn't stay, on account of us not being Anglican."

"Aye?" Mrs Parson came to a standstill. "Nay, you're jesting. Not in Scotland!"

"Well, that is something of an exaggeration, but it's pretty tough to be an outspoken Presbyterian at present. The ministers have been thrown out of their livings; it's forbidden to meet and hold services outside the approved church; and men are jailed and fined and even hanged for aiding and abetting an outlawed man of the kirk."

"And yon Matthew would be one of those aiding and abetting, no?" Mrs Parson nodded sagely.

"Yes, he was." And had they stayed, it would have been their family that was torn apart, the children sold into

127

servitude, she no doubt as well, and her Matthew would have been hanged from the neck until he swung dead.

"Well, it didn't happen, did it?" Mrs Parson pointed out and went on to bombard Alex with questions, ten years of life recapitulated in five minutes.

"Do you have any reason to stay here in Providence?" Alex asked once she'd brought Mrs Parson up to date. She'd even told her about Magnus, receiving nothing but a mild headshake in response – it helped that Mrs Parson already knew the truth about Alex.

"Not really; very full of upright men with inflated views of themselves," Mrs Parson muttered, making Alex burst out in laughter.

"So then you'll come back with us," Alex stated.

"With you? To where?"

"To Graham's Garden, our home."

"Graham's Garden?" Mrs Parson chortled. "And what do you grow there, pray?"

"Oh, you know, silver bells and cockle shells."

Mrs Parson gave her a sharp look. "You're somewhat strange at times, Alex Graham."

"Well, that's nothing new, is it?" Alex grinned and hugged her yet again.

Matthew was as delighted as Alex was, even if he refrained from hugging Mrs Parson, and he definitely didn't break out in a spontaneous dance. But he beamed at her and supported Alex's suggestion that Mrs Parson come home with them, overruling her weak objections by saying she was nearly family – had she not accompanied Alex over the seas all those years ago to buy him free from his unrighteous slavery?

Agnes took one look at the grey-haired woman in her old-fashioned collar and cap and adopted her as a surrogate grandmother, smiling properly for the first time since Alex had met her.

"Is she a relation of yours?" Elizabeth said next day, looking Mrs Parson up and down with an approving expression on her face.

"Not really," Alex smiled, "but we've known each other a very long time."

"Aye," Mrs Parson said from where she sat pillion behind Alex.

"She's a renowned midwife," Alex went on. "She's even been called in to attend the ladies of Jamestown."

"Really?" Elizabeth sounded impressed. "Well, you're a welcome addition to us all, Mrs Parson. I dare say Celia will be most relieved."

"And soon perhaps also Jenny, right?" Alex teased.

Elizabeth gave her a flaming look. "What are you implying?"

"I thought...that maybe she and Jochum..."

"Jochum is German!" Elizabeth's face fell and she looked over at Matthew, at present busy trying out Moses' paces. "It's a suitable match," she said, this time directing herself to Matthew, not Alex, by the simple expedient of kicking her horse into a trot to catch up with him.

"What is?" Matthew sounded confused, drawn back from his contemplation of Moses' smooth gaits.

"Ian and Jenny," Elizabeth clarified.

"Elizabeth," Peter warned from further down the line, "we've already discussed this."

Elizabeth snorted. "It just goes to show, husband, how important it is to raise your children properly. Our daughters have never voiced an objection at your choice of men for them, and our dear Nathan never questioned your selection of a wife for him."

"And look how happy that's made him," Alex murmured.

"Happy?" Elizabeth stared at her. "A marriage is about duty and assets, of obeying the will of your betters to safeguard the future of your family; not about something as frivolous as happiness!"

"I don't agree," Alex said.

"No, my dear, you wouldn't, but then you're so lacking when it comes to instilling obedience in your children that it makes my hands itch at times."

"The day you touch one of my children with your itching

hands is the day you discover what pain is!" In her agitation, Alex almost fell off her horse. Mrs Parson took a firm grip of her waistband and pulled her back into sitting straight.

"Someone should," Elizabeth said. "It seems neither mother nor father have fully understood the responsibilities of parenthood."

Matthew halted his horse, turning Elizabeth's way with a formidable scowl.

"That's enough, Elizabeth," Peter snapped. "You'll ride beside me in silence for the rest of the way." When she hesitated, he rode over and yanked hard at the reins. "Now, wife, or I'll have you walking behind us." Elizabeth's cheeks burnt a deep red, but she meekly allowed her mare to be led off.

"Well, that definitely nailed down the coffin lid on an Ian and Jenny match," Alex said.

Matthew gave her an irritated glance. "It's been buried a long time."

"Really? It sure didn't seem so. And, anyway, what does she mean Jochum is German? Not exactly news to them, is it?"

"He's Catholic," Matthew said.

"So am I. Technically at least."

Matthew smiled and rode Moses as close as he could to Alex's roan. "Technically you were a heathen when I found you. Not even baptised as I recollect it."

Mrs Parson snickered in agreement.

Matthew held in his horse and looked down at Alex. "Ian could do worse than Jenny Leslie."

"Sure he could, but he doesn't love her – he said so."

Matthew sighed. "I've promised I won't force him into marriage – not him or any of our children. But I may still attempt to reason with him."

Alex met his eyes for a long time. "You know as well as I do that if you asked it of him he'd do it, because he loves you too much to want to disappoint you. After all, you're the only parent he has left to him."

Matthew flushed and grudgingly admitted she was right.

"So be careful how you reason with him, okay? A steel hand in a glove of velvet is still a steel hand."

Chapter 14

Ian was not concerned when Alex told him of her latest altercation with Elizabeth and the potential resurrection of his match with Jenny.

"She doesn't want it, and if there's one child in the Leslie household that can wind both parents round her little finger, it's Jenny." He laughed and raised his eyes to Alex. "There are ways of forcing the issue."

"Ian!" Alex shook her head in amusement. "Just like Fiona tried to do with you."

"That was different: she was bedding with more than me."

"Yeah, entrapment; not very nice at all."

Over by the stables Fiona appeared carrying a bucket full of milk, her eyes locked on the ground.

"She's not too happy right now, I think," Alex said.

"Nay," Ian agreed with certain bitterness. "To be wed to the farm hand is less of an achievement than marrying the eldest son." He stretched out his legs and crossed them at the ankles, sitting in a posture that was so like Matthew's that Alex experienced a time warp. Except that she'd never known Matthew this young and innocent – he'd come with his own dark baggage when she met him.

"So, did you enjoy being the man of the house?" she teased, sitting down beside him. She offered him a carrot and bit into one of her own.

"Aye, I did, and it was a right treat to sleep in the big bed."

"What?!!"

He laughed and assured her he hadn't. They sat in companionable silence and ate their carrots.

"I saw her in the forest." Ian tilted his head in the

131

direction of Fiona. "With him: Lars. Should I tell Jonah?"

She thought about that for a moment. "No, it would only make their life more difficult."

Ian's mouth set in a harsh line. "It's wrong; she's a married woman now."

Alex looked away. "Not her first choice, was it?"

She told Matthew some selected bits and pieces of her conversation with Ian.

"I'm not comfortable with having Lars wander about in the woods with a hard-on." And, she added, she was certain it was him she'd caught a glimpse of earlier today as she was returning from a solitary swim in the by now uncomfortably cold river. It made her break out in a rash, to imagine Lars gawking at her as she came up naked from the water.

"What?" Matthew finished his currying and stood back to admire Moses' gleaming hide. He slapped the horse on the rump and came over to where she was sitting on an overturned bucket. "He was spying on you?"

"I'm not totally sure, but yes, I think it was him."

"Hmm." His brows came down in a forbidding dark line over his eyes. "I'll talk to her, and if that doesn't help, I'll talk to him." He pulled her up to stand and kissed her brow. She sniffed at him and wrinkled her nose.

"When was the last time you had a proper bath?"

"Two weeks ago," he said, "before we left for Providence."

"Well then, it's about time, don't you think?" Alex inspected the pale blue of the October afternoon and grinned at him. "A last communal wash for all the Graham men?"

Matthew didn't exactly look thrilled to bits, but nodded all the same.

The boys were no more enthusiastic than their father, but they all recognised the determination in Alex's voice, and so they slouched off, dragging a reluctant Magnus with them.

"Oh, come off it, *Pappa*. You're the man from Sweden. How often have you told me how you used to saw up holes in the ice to go swimming in the winter?"

"Why would he do that?" Mark said.

"I don't know," Alex said. "Ask him. It's all that Viking blood."

"Viking?" Daniel said. "Are you a Viking, Offa?"

Magnus rolled his eyes at Alex and fell into step beside Daniel and Matthew.

"Of course I am. All Swedish men are Vikings – except we don't do much raiding anymore on account of us having become Christians."

Alex followed them down to the river, shouted encouraging remarks to her sons, threatened them all with the lye unless they used the soap properly, and knelt to rub her younger sons dry.

"Jacob, teeth." Alex waved a willow twig in his direction.

"Must I?" he whined, looking at her from below his straight, blond fringe.

"Jacob Graham, cut it out. You've done this morning and night since you were a baby, so why this sudden aversion?"

"But why?" Jacob grumbled. "The Walton lads don't do it, and the Leslie lasses laugh when they see us fiddle around with our wee sticks."

Alex bared her teeth. "See? All my teeth. Next time you're at Leslie's Crossing, check out Mrs Leslie's mouth. It might come as something of a shock. And even Kristin Walton has at least one rotten tooth."

Jacob muttered some more but took the proffered twig.

"I sincerely hope he doesn't ask Elizabeth to show him her teeth," Alex commented to Magnus, who was sitting beside her. "I wonder if it will help, if what I try to teach them about cleanliness will survive down the generations."

"Probably not," Magnus said. "Some of it might, but not all."

"Great. I have these huge babies and teach them to keep themselves clean and healthy, and then what? The genes die out in four or five generations?"

"Not the genes." Magnus laughed. "Just the habits."

"Whatever." She should write them a book, a little tome outlining the benefits of vegetables and hygiene, and hope it would survive a few hundred years, a treasured family heirloom or something. She muffled a laugh.

"What?" Magnus asked.

"Nothing." She tilted her head at him. "Maybe I should use you as an example. Seventy years old and fit like a fiddle, and all due to eating salads and brushing your teeth every day, hey?"

Magnus got to his feet and scowled at her. "Healthy? I've got cancer!" With that he stalked off.

"Bloody hell," Alex muttered.

Later that afternoon, Mrs Parson laughed at Magnus and told him that, to her practised eye, he seemed far from dying, looking remarkably hale for a man of seventy. They were alone in the kitchen, the small space silent for once. Magnus sat down on the bench closest to the window and busied himself with the jackrabbits that had been hanging in the larder for the last week or so.

"It depends what you compare with," he said. "After all, you're comparing with the people of the here and now where the lifespan is somewhere around the late forties." It was a relief to be able to talk to someone about the strange facts surrounding his and Alex's presence in this time.

"Not me, I'm well over three score." Mrs Parson regarded him through bright black eyes. "Why?"

"Why what?" Magnus looked about for the glazed jug.

"Why did you choose to fall through time?" Mrs Parson helped him chop the jackrabbits into small pieces and stuff them into the jug.

"I'm not sure, but I suppose that one driving force was the fact that I thought I was going to die anyway. And I wanted to see Alex again, to verify that she was fine."

"And is she?" Mrs Parson whisked together blood and spices, added juniper berries and a generous amount of Matthew's precious sherry before pouring the pungent mixture over the morsels of meat.

"She seems to be." Magnus waved his hand in the direction of where Alex was chasing an escaped hen, eagerly assisted by Sarah. "But now that I'm here, trapped into staying here until I die, I wish I could go back, because the people who need me are not these people; they're the people I left behind." He fell silent, hoping she would tell him that of course he was needed here.

Instead, Mrs Parson nodded.

"And they're the people I need too – God, how I miss them: Isaac and Eva, John and Diane." Magnus stood up and carried the heavy jug over to the hearth, lowering it carefully into the pot of water that was simmering over the fire.

"That's something else I don't understand, you see," he added in an undertone. "That she doesn't miss them – us. Yes, occasionally I am sure she thinks of Isaac, and I know that through the years she's often thought of me, but all in all she chose to forget us – for him." He nodded to where Matthew had joined the chase, deftly grabbing the hen by its legs. "And I'm so angry with her for that," he ended, hiding his face from Mrs Parson's sharp eyes.

Magnus spent most of the evening feeling just how angry he was. In a silent mating dance, Matthew and Alex gravitated around each other. Eyes met and held, a smile flashing over Alex's features. Matthew's hand lingered on her nape when he leaned forward to add another log to the fire; Alex's fingers brushed at his hair, his shoulders, when she stood to retrieve something from one of the shelves. They conversed with Magnus and Mrs Parson, they laughed and joked and, at one point, Matthew invited Magnus to a game of chess while Alex remained by the fire sewing. But all the time it rippled between them – the unspoken but tangible desire. It was a relief when Matthew stood up, bade them all a good night and escorted Alex from the room.

Matthew was pleased with himself for having thought of lighting a fire in their room earlier in the evening, ensuring the small room was agreeably warm. Alex undid his breeches, tugged his shirt over his head and there he was in only his stockings, his member already hard. Her hands flowed down his back, warm and firm they slid over his flanks, the fingers of her right hand grazing his pubic hair, his cock. It sent tingles through him, prickles of warmth that travelled in concentric circles up his belly, down his thighs.

She knelt, his stockings came off, and he inhaled when she took him in her mouth. His Alex, the only woman who'd ever done this to him, who could set him aflame with but a brush of her fingers. Her mouth was soft and warm, her hands rested on his hips, slid round to cup his buttocks, and he groaned when she tightened her lips round his member. Sweetest Lord, but this was good! Blood rushed downwards, leaving him light-headed and dizzy. He sank his fingers into her hair, threw his head back, and concentrated on remaining on his feet, all of him quivering as her mouth, her tongue, her fingers pleasured him.

"Nay, Alex wait, I…" He raised her to her feet and drew the pins out of her hair to release a cascade of browns and golds and reds.

He worked his fingers through her curls, kissing her earlobe, the corner of her mouth, the point on her neck where he could see her pulse. He kissed his way down her body, undoing garment after garment until all of her stood revealed.

She swayed; he guided her down to the floor. The little rug on the wooden boards was soft and welcoming, and so was she, naked in the reddish light that spilled from the crackling fire. He caressed the smooth, soft skin on the insides of her thighs, stroked her hips, her breasts. She moaned, tugged at him, widening her legs, telling him to please, and still he held back. Slowly, he worked his way over her rounded belly, dropping a line of soft kisses all the way to her pubic mound. He kissed her there, his fingers moving in gentle, slow circles in her moist cleft. He inhaled, savouring her rich female scent in this her most private place. He exhaled, tickling her, and she lifted her bottom off the floor. Her fingers closed around him, flowed up his cock to touch the tip, and he groaned.

"Now," she murmured. "Enough of this foreplay stuff, I want you now, now, now!"

It made him laugh, but he gladly complied and entered her, bracing himself on his arms.

"Yes!" She exhaled. "Oh, yes!"

On the opposite wall their shadows merged, and on the floor below him she shifted her hips to make him come closer, so much closer, a sound of want and need escaping from her mouth. He laughed, kissed her, kissed her again. His Alex, his woman, his heart.

Chapter 15

"I don't like it," Matthew said to Ian, staring down at the hobnailed footprint pressed into the earth below his bedroom window. Someone had been standing here last night, no doubt gawking at them. His cheeks heated with anger and embarrassment – their lovemaking was a private matter, not something to be shared with others. He used the toe of his boot to scuff the mark away and gave Ian a stern look. "Not a word to your mama."

He strode off in the direction of the stables and called for Mark to hurry; he had an errand for him.

"A dog?" Mark said.

"Aye, a dog. Peter Leslie has several half-grown pups from the last litter. Ask him to help you choose one."

"A dog for me?" Mark sounded hopeful.

Matthew smiled at him. "For you, but also for us. We need a new watchdog." He eyed the small bitch they used as a ratter – in no way a deterrent. Besides, she was deaf with age and spent her days asleep, grey muzzle pillowed on her front paws.

"We do?" Mark threw a look at the surrounding woods. "Is it Indians you're worried about?"

"Aye, that too," Matthew lied. Whoever had stood outside their house wasn't an Indian. In fact, Matthew had a pretty good idea who it was, and all of him seethed with anger. He made a mental note to ride over to Forest Spring and have a serious talk with Henry Walton later in the week, once he was done with the barn walls. "Take Jacob with you, and carry your musket loaded, aye?"

Mark nodded and went to find his brother and gun.

"So just like that you decided we needed a dog." Alex set down a bowl of pea soup in front of Matthew. He drew in the strong scents of thyme and salted meat, and picked up his spoon to stir the thick consistency.

"Aye, I did."

"And might this have something to do with the fact that you think Lars is a somewhat too regular and rather intimidating presence on our lands?" She handed him bread warm from the baking oven, poured him a mug of beer, and sat down opposite him.

"Aren't you eating?" he asked.

"I already did – with the rest of the family." She smiled at him. "While you were banging away at your new walls."

"I must finish them. What use is a barn with only three walls?"

"But not all in one day," she said. "So does it?"

"Does what?"

She rolled her eyes. "The dog...does it have something to do with Lars sniffing around Fiona?"

"Aye, it does. You've seen him, Ian ran into him a day or so ago, and I've seen him too. Like a shadow for all his size, flitting away the moment he realises he's been seen." He concentrated on his soup. Something was not entirely right with yon Lars, and he wanted him nowhere close to his womenfolk.

"Wow." Alex laughed, sitting down with her lap full of dog. "I can see how this drooling beast will keep all unwelcome visitors at bay. He'll lick them to death." She shoved the dog away, held her hand out to her son, and heaved herself back onto her feet. "Not a beauty, is he?" she commented, looking down at the sandy-coloured dog.

Mark fondled the soft golden ears. "Nay, he's half mastiff, but he'll be big once he's properly grown."

"He already is big, far too big." She looked at her son. "He sleeps outside or in the kitchen, not in your bed. In fact, he never goes beyond the kitchen, okay?"

"Okay, okay..." Mark glowered at her.

"And his name?" she asked.

Mark tilted his head to one side, studied the dog, and grinned slyly. "Narcissus."

"Narcissus?" Magnus broke out in laughter. "How would you know that name?"

"Why wouldn't he?" Alex said. "What do you think he is: an uneducated farm boy?"

Magnus flushed. That was obviously exactly what he considered Mark to be: a boy that knew everything about the internal workings of a cow but had never studied a foreign language or done advanced mathematics or physics – not at all like his precious Isaac, paragon of virtues that this her firstborn seemed to be.

"I was just surprised." Magnus smiled down at his grandson and the puppy.

"You're so bloody supercilious!" Alex snapped at Magnus once they were alone. "Every time my children open their mouth, I can see you comparing what they're saying – and how they're saying it – with Isaac."

"No, I don't." Magnus sounded defensive.

"They have none of the opportunities he's had."

"But at least they've had a mother!"

"So has he, remember? Diane seems to have filled that role most competently."

"That's not the same! And you chose them – all of them – over him."

"No, I didn't. It wasn't as if I had much say in it, was it? One moment there I am driving my car, the next I'm thrown back in time." But he was right, however awful a mother that made her. Isaac had very quickly faded in her head, replaced by her new, growing family.

"You had one of Mercedes' painted time portals," Magnus said. "You could have travelled back, to us, to him."

Alex looked away. The few times it had seemed she might be dragged back to her time she'd held on for dear life to the here and now.

"Yeah, I thought so. You didn't want to, did you?" Magnus stamped from the room.

Alex watched him stalk off towards the garden, wooden

140

hoe in one hand, a basket in the other, and two little girls skipping after him. She hoped Ruth and Sarah would do a better job of soothing his heartache than she was doing.

It was difficult to hold on to his black, angry mood when surrounded by two chattering girls, who bombarded him with questions and comments while he turned one empty bed after the other. The simmering resentment in him subsided back into a more normal mood, and Magnus laughed and listened as his granddaughters sang and talked.

They played tic-tac-toe in the dirt. After the first few times, Ruth caught on to the fact that it was best to go first, and after that she won every single game. Matthew came by and stood watching, laughing at Ruth's triumphant crowing.

"That girl is scarily intelligent," Magnus told Matthew, nodding his head at Ruth.

"Aye, you would say so," Matthew teased.

Magnus felt yet another burst of anger flare through him. "I wasn't referring to that." He pointed at the lines on the ground. "I was talking about her impressive capacity for numbers. I don't know how she does it, but she does incredibly complex sums in her head."

Matthew grinned. "So do I."

"You do? So what's forty-three times seventeen?"

"Seven hundred and thirty-one," came the prompt reply.

Magnus counted for some time before nodding. "Well done."

Matthew hitched his shoulders. "Da was right fond of ciphering."

"Ruth should go to school, be properly educated."

Matthew turned towards him with a surprised expression. "What for?"

"What for? Because she's talented and should be allowed to develop it."

"Ruth will be a wife and a mother, just as Sarah will."

"A wife!" Magnus said. "What a waste."

"Waste?" Matthew frowned. "Are you saying Alex has led a wasted life?" He looked at his girls and back at Magnus.

"In her own time she would've had a profession, a career, and any gifted child of hers, whether boy or girl, would've had a chance to make something of themselves."

"That was not a reply to my question," Matthew said.

"Yes, it was, if you read between the lines," Magnus answered and slouched off.

What was the matter with him? Magnus took a deep breath of cold October air and counted slowly to thirty before letting it out. He was behaving like an obnoxious teenager – shit, he felt like an obnoxious teenager, his moods disconcertingly erratic. Even worse, he enjoyed needling them, feeling an uncharitable satisfaction at the hurt look in Alex's eyes and an even higher level of black pleasure at the affronted expression on his son-in-law's face.

He exhaled and picked up his pace. What he needed was a long walk to calm down. Alone, he decided when he caught sight of Jacob making towards him. He turned on his heel and walked off.

"Leave him be, lad." Matthew took hold of Jacob. "He needs to be alone."

"If you ask me, he needs to be taught to behave," Alex said from behind him.

"Well, I'm not about to lay my father-in-law across my knee," Matthew replied, making her laugh.

"Maybe we could ask Mrs Parson," she suggested in a low voice. "Who knows, he might even enjoy it."

"So might she." Matthew grinned.

Magnus kept well away from the house for the rest of the day; sat silent through supper before excusing himself, muttering that his head hurt and he needed to sleep. Next morning, he remained in bed until well after breakfast, entering a kitchen empty of anyone but Alex. She nodded a greeting, no more, serving him a bowl of porridge before going back to her sourdough.

"I'm sorry," Magnus said to her back. "I'm not quite sure why I'm behaving the way I am." Well, he was: he was being eaten alive by a corrosive jealousy. And he missed his old life, waking every morning to the dismaying realisation that it was not a dream. He wanted to make love to Eva, to stand in his kitchen and cook surrounded by his family – John and Diane with their twin girls, Isaac and Eva. He sat back on the bench, regarding Alex; always the same clothes, always in the same dull, serviceable colours: grey, brown and green with linen that shifted from white to a yellowish beige. He counted in his head; three skirts at the most was what Alex owned, and nothing in red.

"Do you remember how you always wore red?" he asked her.

"Not always." She twisted to smile at him over her shoulder.

"Red shoes, red jackets, red phone," Magnus teased. He dropped his eyes to the table. "Now all you wear is matronly grey or brown." Well, not quite; the shawl she had on was embroidered with red roses, but otherwise she was all in brown. At least she wasn't wearing one of those ugly caps today, her hair uncovered but pulled back into a neat bun. So boring! "You never wear make-up, you don't do your hair, you have no jewellery except for your wedding ring…"

"For your information, make-up isn't exactly available, and no matter how much I looked I couldn't find a single hairdresser in Providence." She turned to face him, defensively twirling her single ring with its dark blue sapphire.

"You look dull and old. Diane looks at least ten years younger than you. She takes good care of herself, she does."

Alex flinched. Two wide blue eyes met his, and to his shame he could see she was biting her lip, no doubt to stop it from wobbling.

"I'm sorry to be such a disappointment, but as I recall I never asked you to drop by, did I?" And maybe it had been better if you hadn't, her eyes told him.

"Let's just say I hoped I'd find you living a better life,

with a man who took care of you and appreciated you." God, how he regretted diving through that painting!

"He does! He loves me, you bastard!"

"He does? Well, he certainly seems to like making babies with you. But he never gives you any presents, he never—"

In reply, Alex grabbed him by the hand and dragged him to her bedroom. From the large chest she produced a wooden box that in itself was a work of art, the lid a sanded golden brown on which someone had engraved a rose.

"He doesn't?" She threw back the lid before storming out, leaving him sitting on the bed with the box on his lap.

Magnus lifted the small, exquisite wooden figurines one by one, turning them this way and that. Most of them were of Alex, with the odd exception in the form of an animal or a flower. Right at the bottom was a small carving made in pale yellow wood, and when he saw it Magnus knew that this was Rachel, the girl they'd lost. He ran a finger over the soft surfaces, over the details etched out with so much obvious love. He had never felt so ashamed of himself in all his life. He returned the box to the chest and left the room. For a while he stood in the kitchen watching Alex knead bread, but as she refused to meet his eyes or in any other way react to his presence he escaped outside.

"There she goes," Alex said to Mrs Parson, indicating the spot where Fiona had just ducked out of sight. The stupid girl was still seeing Lars, despite Matthew having given her a long talking-to. Apparently, Lars was irresistible, well worth aggravating the master. Alex pulled yet another loaf from the bread oven, knocking experimentally at the crust with her knuckle.

"There goes who?" Agnes lifted her head from the onions she was chopping.

"Nothing," Alex said.

Agnes' brows were so fair as to be almost invisible against her skin, but even so Alex could see the disbelieving curve to them.

"If you mean Fiona, I know where she goes," Agnes said.

"She slips away to meet her one true love."

"Her one true love?" Alex popped a piece of warm bread in her mouth. "Where did you get that from?"

"But he is, and yet the master forced her to marry Jonah on account of her carrying his child..." Agnes broke off, backing away from Alex.

"Whose child?" Alex said.

"The master's," Agnes stuttered.

"Bitch! I'm going to have her off my property the moment she gets back. My husband has never touched Fiona, that I can guarantee you, and should he hear that she's spreading those kinds of lies he's going to be pissed." Alex clenched her fist. "And so am I."

Agnes just nodded and went back to what she was doing, but from the pitying looks she kept throwing at Alex, it was obvious the stupid girl believed Fiona was telling the truth. It made Alex grind her teeth together.

"Where is she?" Alex said an hour or so later, her eyes on the darkening afternoon outside. "It's getting late and she has chores to do or does she expect them to get done by themselves?" This late in November it was far too cold for an amorous meeting to be more than brief, and that worried her. At the moment Fiona wasn't her most favourite person, but she was their responsibility, and now she was missing and night was falling fast. And where the hell was Magnus?

"She'll be back," Mrs Parson said. "There's nowhere else for her, is there?"

"Not unless he's planned a romantic elopement, what with him being her one true love." Alex met Mrs Parson's amused grin with one of her own.

"In my experience your true love elopes with you before you're married elsewhere, no?"

"Probably," Alex said. "Bigamy just isn't the thing, is it?"

Agnes looked from one to the other with round eyes.

"Bigamy?" she squeaked. "That's right ungodly, it is!"

"It was a joke," Alex sighed, eyeing her youngest maid with some exasperation.

"Well, it's not amusing," Agnes retorted with spirit. "Such matters should not be jested about."

"My, my, the mouse that roared," Alex said in an undertone. Beside her Mrs Parson chuckled.

After several hours of walking, Magnus was humming. The anger that had been swamping him for days had been replaced by a sensation of contentment, this helped along by the substantial amount of butternuts he'd found. He was considering just what a treat he'd make himself with all these nuts when a hoarse sound made him stop. There it came again, something in between a howl and a cough. Magnus stood frozen to the spot. A cougar? Didn't big cats sort of cough when they hunted? There was a dull thwacking noise, and this time the hoarse sound became articulate.

"Please," someone slurred. More of those wet, slapping sounds, and now Magnus was moving again.

"Alex? Is that you?" Absolute silence. "Alex?" He picked up pace. "Alex?" He heard the unmistakable sound of something big crashing through the undergrowth, and now he ran, nuts spilling in all directions from the fold in his shirt.

"Holy Matilda!" Magnus skidded to a stop and dropped to his knees beside the half-naked, bleeding woman.

Fiona opened one swollen eye. "Help," she breathed, arms coming up in a weak attempt to cover her nudity.

He found her shawl and covered her with it. *Herre djävlar!* Dear God! Even in the fading light, he could see the poor woman was covered in bruises, in open bleeding wounds, and round her neck blossomed a collar of blacks and blues, as if someone had tried to throttle her.

"I'll go and fetch help."

"No!" Both eyes flew open, one no more than a slit. "He'll come back, he'll kill me!" She crawled, was on her hands and knees. "Please, don't leave me," she croaked in a raspy, barely audible voice.

"I can't carry you."

"I'll walk," Fiona said, panic colouring her reedy voice.

With Magnus' help she was upright, one tentative shuffle after the other in the direction of home.

"Help!" Magnus called out to the surrounding evening. "Come and help!" He caught Fiona as she staggered, knees giving out.

She yelped at his touch, and Magnus had no idea what to do. She was back on her feet, her fingers clawed themselves into his arm, and foot by unbearable foot they moved forward, with Magnus screaming himself hoarse for help.

And there, finally, came Matthew with Jonah and Mark at his heels.

"As she tells it he just lost it," Alex said to Matthew. She sank down on the stool by her dressing table. God, she was tired, and these last few hours helping Mrs Parson with Fiona had sucked the remaining energy out of her. "One moment it was like it used to be, and then suddenly he began punching and kicking, and... Bloody hell, he almost killed her – he would have killed her had Magnus not come along."

"And the bairn?"

"Still there," she said with a sigh. She uncorked one of her stone jars and sniffed at the home-made cream. Goose fat seemed to be the thing, even if it tended to go rancid unless she was careful. She scooped up a generous dollop and worked it into her hands, her forearms, and lifted her shift out of the way to do the same to the distended skin of her stomach.

"Does Jonah know it isn't his?" she asked, frowning down at a new stretch mark.

Matthew batted her hands out of the way and took over the rubbing, letting his hands move in slow, soothing circles up and down her abdomen. She relaxed against him and yawned.

"No one knows. She admits to sleeping with both." He let his hands rest for a moment on her belly. "She'll hold herself to Jonah, and by the time the wean is born mayhap the question of who actually fathered it is no longer important."

"Maybe," she said doubtfully.

Chapter 16

"Is your brother-in-law at home?" Matthew leaned forward over Moses' powerful neck, tipping his hat at Kristin, who had appeared at the door, with Henry at her back.

"Lars?" she asked. "What do you want with Lars?"

"My business with your brother is none of your concern," Matthew said, before turning back to Henry.

"No, I haven't seen Lars all day," Henry said. "I think he's out hunting."

"Ah," Matthew nodded, "and he did that all day yesterday as well?"

"No, yesterday he was here – all day." Two bright red spots appeared on Kristin's cheeks, but her gaze held; unwavering, she met his eyes.

"Really?" Matthew beckoned for Jonah to join him, waiting until Jonah had halted the small mare beside Moses. "My man has a grievance: his wife was assaulted in the woods late afternoon yesterday."

"Assaulted?"

Matthew caught the flash of panic in Henry's pale blue eyes and rode Moses closer. "Aye. From the look of her, one could almost assume she'd been ravaged by a wild beast."

Henry Walton swallowed, and now there was no disguising the expression of fear on his face as he sought his wife's eyes for reassurance.

"Almost," Matthew underlined.

"What does that have to do with Lars?" Kristin's voice trembled slightly. "I already told you – he was here."

"That's not what she says," Matthew replied.

"Then she lies – which we all know she does frequently," Kristin said.

Matthew slid his eyes in the direction of Jonah, sitting

the horse with the grace of a sack of barley, and nodded. "Aye, she's been known to do that. And yet, I find myself inclined to believe her. And then there's the matter of the lassie found dead some months back."

"Lars was nowhere close at the time," Kristin interrupted.

"Really? And you would know exactly what day I am referring to? The lassie was kicked and trampled to death – by someone wearing hobnailed boots. Fiona was kicked as well – by someone with big feet, shod in hobnailed boots."

Kristin's previously so red cheeks had gone a bloodless white, her blue eyes locked in his. "Not Lars, and I'll gladly swear to it."

"Would you now?" Matthew said.

"On the Bible," she said, her chin rising.

"Ah. Well then, I'll not be importuning you any longer." Matthew used his thighs to turn his stallion, levelling a hard stare at Henry Walton. "Tell your brother-in-law he isn't welcome on my land. Who knows, we might mistake him for a bear."

Kristin Walton drew in a long, hissing breath, her hands clasped over her protruding stomach.

"And that's that?" Magnus kicked at the mule to catch up with Matthew. "You just leave it like that? The girl insists it was him!"

"Her word against Mrs Walton's," Jonah said.

Matthew grunted in agreement. "It'll never hold, and, as we speak, Kristin is polishing up her story in such a way that Henry will suddenly recollect that aye, he did in fact see Lars at home yesterday."

"But that's perjury!" Magnus said.

Matthew raised an amused brow. "Oh, aye? And that never happens where you come from?" He looked over to where Mark was bringing up the line. "We must send word to the Leslies," he said to his son. "They must be warned."

"Warned? You think he'll do this again?" Magnus said.

"This was not the first time; we know that." Matthew met his father-in-law's worried eyes and nodded imperceptibly. Alex wouldn't be going anywhere on her own for now.

★

"I'll be alright!" Alex glared from her husband to her father, going on to include her elder sons as well. "I'm not going to spend my days confined to the yard – I'll go nuts!"

"Of course not," Matthew said, unperturbed by her burst of temper. "But you won't step outside the yard without one of us going with you."

"But I like walking alone!" Alex protested.

"You'll do as I say, Alex. I don't want you encountering a maddened beast alone."

"Maddened beast? He's a man, Matthew. Maybe Fiona just managed to drive him totally crazy."

"Mayhap," Matthew said, "but the miller's lass was but a bairn, and the lass back in New Sweden, was she yet another cock tease?"

"But..." Alex hugged herself. "She was killed by a bear."

"Was she?" Matthew shook his head. "I don't think so. Not anymore. So I'll have you promise that you'll do as I say."

"But—"

"No buts, Alex." He held her eyes until she dropped them.

"I promise," she muttered.

Alex set a punishing pace up the wooded slope, walking as fast as she could until her breath began to hitch, her pulse thudded in her ears, and her back broke out in a sweat.

"Holy Matilda," Magnus puffed from behind her, "what are you trying to do? Set a new world record in short-distance walking?"

She looked at him coldly. She didn't feel like talking to him and had been irritated when he'd offered himself as a chaperone on her walk. His comments from the other day rankled, and even if he'd attempted an apology it hadn't been good enough.

"This is my exercise routine. I walk really fast up the long slopes, and then I catch my breath over a stretch before doing it all again. Good cardiovascular training."

"You look trim enough."

"Yeah, but nowhere close to pretty, well-maintained Diane, right?"

Magnus had the grace to look ashamed.

Shit, just the thought of Diane made her jealous, which was ridiculous, given the circumstances. "Anyway, how would you know? You haven't seen me naked, have you?"

"I've seen you in your shift, and with the light behind you that's more or less the same thing."

"*Pappa!*" she exclaimed, making him laugh.

"Seriously," she went on a bit later, handing him the basket while she slid down a slippery patch of ground to land by a late stand of black trumpets. "I work pretty hard at keeping fit."

"I don't see how you can need to," he replied, landing beside her. "It's not as if you spend all that many hours sitting on your bum."

"Mainly it's here." She pinched at her rounded belly. "A permanent squishiness, no matter how many crunches I do."

"That's what you get. All those kids…" He sounded disapproving, making her snort.

"You've met Elizabeth Leslie, right? Fifteen live births, *Pappa*, and four miscarriages. And her sister-in-law has given birth ten times, with two dying young or at birth. So my seven is not much of an achievement."

"But why so many?" Magnus asked.

"Why? First of all because it's difficult to avoid – at least if you like having wild, uninhibited sex." She smiled at his embarrassed expression. "Secondly, because this is a harsh and primitive world. Having many children is a way of ensuring someone will take care of you when you're old and decrepit. And then of course there's the third reason," she said, turning her back on him. "And that's the fact that so many children die while young." Not hers, she thought fiercely, she'd already lost one and had no intention of losing another – not if there was anything she could do about it.

"Come on," she said, retaking her basket. "We'd best get

151

home. I have supper to prepare unless you want yet another of Agnes' specials."

Magnus made a face. "That girl can't cook to save her life, and what's with adding barley to everything?" He looked down at the contents of the basket. "I'll cook; I'll make you a creamy omelette with mushrooms and cheese."

"That sounds nice – or would be if we had the eggs. The hens have stopped laying for the year."

"Bloody hens. In that case, I suppose it's only fair we kill some of them instead and have us a nice casserole." He tucked her hand into the crook of his arm and made for home.

Halfway back, Alex brought them to a stop. "What's he doing here?" she said, pointing at the two men on horses that were riding along the bridle path sixty yards or so ahead of them.

"Do you know them?" Magnus squinted in the direction of the riders.

"The one on the big roan, he's that Burley; you know, one of the men who came chasing after the Indians. The one with the black hair."

Magnus looked again. "Maybe they're on their way home."

"Maybe." It seemed something of a detour if they were making for Virginia.

Magnus narrowed his eyes. "What's that?"

"What?"

"The bundle."

Alex looked closer at the horses. One of the riders had an elongated bundle thrown before him, tied tightly at both ends and squirming wildly.

"Oh my God," Alex said, "that's a person."

One of the riders turned his head, and moments later he had wheeled his horse, raising his musket their way. Definitely Burley; even from here she could see that distinctive lock of black hair.

"Let's go!" Alex tugged at Magnus. She plunged down the hillside behind them, with Magnus at her heels. The last few feet were a sheer drop, and they landed in a heap behind a screen of bushes. "Quiet," she whispered to her father, who nodded, looking pale.

They heard the horses picking their way down the slope, the men exchanging murmured comments.

"Nothing," one of them said.

"Damn!" the other said.

"You know them?"

Someone spat, cleared his throat and spat again. "Not as such, but I think the woman is one Mrs Graham." He hawked again. "I don't like witnesses – unless they're dead."

"Too late for that," the first speaker said. "We must get going; it's growing dark."

But they didn't move, the leather of their saddles creaking as they shifted in the saddles. Alex sank her fingers into Magnus to ensure he kept quiet. There was a muffled yell, followed by several dull thuds – as if someone was beating dirt out of a carpet.

"Hold your tongue," one of the men whispered. "Shut up, you heathen cow, or I'll really hurt you!" And now it was Magnus holding Alex, stopping her from charging to help the unfortunate woman. For a further half-hour they crouched where they were, and it was dark before they dared to move.

"Are you sure?" Matthew said.

Magnus and Alex nodded.

"Bastards," Magnus said. "I bet they've abducted that poor woman from somewhere."

"Obviously," Alex said. "An Indian, I think."

"You do? Why?" Matthew asked.

"He called her a heathen cow." Alex glowered at her father. "If you hadn't stopped me, I'd have tried to save her."

"Thank heavens I did," Magnus replied, and for once father-in-law and son-in-law were in total agreement.

"Two mounted, armed men; what could you have done?" Matthew said.

"You've seen me fight." She heaved herself up on the

balls of her feet, adopting an instinctive crouch.

"That was years ago," Matthew said, "and you're pregnant."

He had a point there, Alex conceded. If she were to be honest, her martial arts skills were seriously rusty, and she decided there and then to do something about it. You never knew when such skills could come in handy.

"What will they do to her?" she said.

"What he's done to all the others, I reckon: sell her. If she's lucky as a wife; if she's unlucky as a whore."

"Bloody hell," Magnus muttered.

"Aye," Matthew agreed. "Quite a nasty little habit of his, and no doubt quite lucrative."

"But why here?" And how did Jones fit in? Was he a silent partner or did he perhaps provide the clients? The thought made Alex sick to her stomach. Poor girl – no, girls.

"Far enough from home – I dare say Mr Burley prefers not to advertise how he makes his ill-gotten gains."

Chapter 17

"She looks awful, doesn't she?" Alex said to Mrs Parson. Two weeks after her ordeal, Fiona's bruises and scratches had healed but her face had acquired a strained look, the full mouth pinched into a discontented spout.

Mrs Parson looked up from her knitting, gave Fiona a fleeting glance and went back to her work. "An unwanted child, and a restless one at that."

Alex let her sewing fall to her knees. "Poor her; all the dreams she ever had of making a new life for herself in a small town wiped away."

"She should have thought of that before she spread her thighs for whoever came her way, no?" Mrs Parson said heartlessly, with Agnes murmuring an agreement from where she was hemming the new sheets.

Alex sat for a while longer watching Fiona. The dark hair was pulled back into a severe braid and when Jonah moved towards her she slumped, nodding at whatever Jonah said before trailing after him. Something about the way her shoulders rounded made Alex suspect Fiona was paying a heavy price for coming pregnant to the marriage bed.

"He's punishing her," Alex told Matthew later, stabbing the needle through the thick cloth of his new breeches. "That's not very nice, is it? He knew she was with child – and potentially with someone else's – when he married her." Matthew pulled off his damp stockings and looked about for a pair of clean, dry ones. "Over there." Alex jerked her head in the direction of the basket with the laundered clothes.

"He isn't punishing her for that," Matthew said. "He's punishing her for making a cuckold out of him, sneaking off for secret trysts with her lover despite being married."

"Oh, and that makes it okay?"

"Aye, it does. No man should be so badly treated by his wife." He adjusted the stockings, retied the garters and stood up, dropping a quick kiss on her cheek. "I would know how it feels."

"But you never hit Margaret," Alex reminded him.

"Nay, that I did not. But I very much wanted to – her and that damned brother of mine."

A week before Christmas, the Leslie brothers rode into their yard, and one look at their faces was enough to know that something bad had happened. Jacob hurried over to take the horses when Thomas and Peter dismounted, with a grim-faced Nathan and one of the indentured hands remaining in the saddle.

"Lizzie," Thomas said. "That bastard has attacked my daughter."

"When?" Matthew clapped his hat on his head, grabbed at his thick woollen cloak, and pulled on his worn boots.

"Yesterday afternoon," Peter said in a weary voice. "We found her late last evening."

"How is she?" Alex had found her cloak and was busy ignoring Matthew's forbidding eyes. If he was going so was she.

"Alive," Thomas whispered, "unfortunately alive." He closed his eyes and emitted a cracked, low howl, the sound making the hairs stand up straight on Alex's arms.

"I'm so sorry," she said. "What can I do to help?"

"I'll go," Mrs Parson said. "Mark here will ride me there."

Mark nodded but looked at his father for confirmation.

"Take your gun, lad," Matthew said. "And you?" he asked Peter. "Are you heading for the Waltons?"

"Oh yes, and this time Mrs Walton will find it difficult to protect her brother."

Matthew hurried over to saddle Moses, with Alex a determined shadow at his heels.

"I don't want you to come," Matthew said.

"Tough, either you let me ride with you or I go on my own."

156

"It won't be pretty."

"What? You think they'll kill him as he stands?"

"Oh no," Matthew said. "Lars Oleson will be taken down to Providence and there be handed over to the constable. But he may arrive very much the worse for wear. He should."

"Kristin is going to be devastated."

Matthew gave her a black look. "She knew – they knew. And still they protected him. He should have hanged the first time."

"But he's her brother!"

"You think Thomas cares? Or his wee lass, not yet sixteen?"

"No," she said, "I suppose she doesn't."

She sat in front of him, aware of the disapproving glances the Leslies kept on throwing in her direction. Alex couldn't explain why she felt she had to be here, but somehow she hoped she'd be able to help Kristin; perhaps offer some comfort as her brother was dragged away to hang.

The boys were out playing in the yard, a wild game of hoops and high voices that was cut short at the appearance of the five horses and their riders. In less than a minute, the boys had melted back into the main cabin, and out of the corner of her eye Alex saw a cloaked shape appear from the back and duck into the surrounding trees. Kristin? She tried to focus on the receding shape. Yes, definitely Kristin, walking into the cover of the trees.

"You must be mistaken." Henry Walton rested one hand on his eldest son. "Has the girl named Lars as her attacker?"

"Not as such," Thomas said. "She's in no fit state to talk."

"Then it might be anyone," Henry said. "An Indian or one of your black men. Everyone knows that black men are markedly lacking in self-control, and your daughter is a pretty girl."

"Was a pretty girl." Thomas' voice broke. "Was, and never will be again."

"I'm sorry," Henry said, "so sorry."

"She was clutching this in her hand when we found her." Peter unfolded his handkerchief. A handful of blond hair lifted in the wind before he closed the cloth around it. "Not an Indian, I think, and definitely not one of my blacks."

"But he was here! I swear, he was here."

"Tread with care, Brother Henry," Thomas said. "Perjury is a crime that carries its own punishment."

Henry's grip on little Per's shoulder tightened. "What will you do to him?"

"Turn him over to the powers of the law and witness as he hangs," Thomas spat.

The boy made a small sound and hid his face against his father's leg.

Alex had kept her eyes on the fringe of trees throughout this little exchange, and now she gripped her husband's thigh hard.

"Matthew! I think Kristin's gone to warn him." Matthew looked down at her and followed her arm to where she was pointing in the direction of Lars' cabin, set a hundred yards or so further into the woods.

"Foolish woman," he muttered, beckoning Nathan over to him. In a low voice he gave his directions, and with a slight nod Nathan and the indentured servant made for the back of the cabin, their horses urged into a swift canter. Matthew nudged Moses forward, with Peter and Thomas following him. Muskets were raised, swords loosened from their scabbards. If Lars didn't come out of his own accord, he wouldn't be moving much any time soon.

"Lars Oleson!" Peter called. "Come out and give yourself over into our hands." There was no reply, and the men walked the horses closer, keeping a wary lookout.

"Lars!" Henry's voice barely carried. "For God's sake, Lars, come out peaceably. Don't let the boys witness something they're too young for." Behind him, the youngest Walton boy began crying, calling repeatedly for his mother.

They were only a stone's throw away when the door to the cabin burst open. A shot rang out. With a squawk, Alex ducked, nearly falling off the horse as a result. Matthew deposited her on the ground and joined her a second or so later.

"There!" Peter motioned to where a large shape was hurtling across the yard, making for the woods on the further side. Thomas barrelled into him, was cast aside as if he were flotsam, but by now Matthew and Peter were closing in on Lars, cutting off his planned escape route. The rye-coloured hair stood like a messy haystack round his head as Lars swerved this way and that, for all the world like a cornered rat attempting to evade a couple of cats. He threw both his pursuers by doing an unexpected turn back towards the cabin and came bounding straight towards Alex, musket in one hand, knife in the other.

"Nay!" Matthew yelled. "Not my Alex!"

It took some time for her to react. At first she just stood there, watching this berserk come rushing at her, but then her survival instincts kicked in, and she turned and fled. A small part of her brain noted with detached surprise that it was impressive how fast she could move when she had to, running flat out with her hands holding her heavy belly to her. A hasty look over her shoulder, and she couldn't breathe with panic. There was no way she'd get away from this madman, and God knows what he'd do to her once he'd caught her. The blade of his knife glittered in the sun, he no longer held the musket, one arm extended as if to grab her. Alex yelped, did a sharp turn to the left, rounded a tree and crashed through a screen of shrubs.

He was close enough that she could hear his every breath, the squeaking sound his boots made when they hit the ground. Fingers brushed over her back. She redoubled her efforts, hands clasped around her unborn baby. Where was everybody? Quick, darting glances, and yes, there was Matthew and here came Nathan, charging towards them with his musket held like a bat over his head.

Something grabbed her cloak. She screamed, wrenched herself free, and the ground below her feet disappeared. She slid down the unexpected incline, landing with an "oof" at the bottom. *Get up, get up,* her overworked brain screeched.

Alex was on her feet, clutching at a piece of rock. There; he came leaping down the slope and Alex snarled, brandishing her weapon.

"Alex? Shush, lass, it's me, it's Matthew."

Alex blinked; once, twice, and yes, it wasn't Lars, it was Matthew. Just like that her legs gave way and she plunked down on the ground, mouth wide open as she gasped and gasped for breath, both in an effort to reoxygenate her blood, but just as much to stop herself from crying.

"Are you hurt?" Matthew was conducting an efficient tactile inspection, his worried frown fading when the child kicked in response to his prodding.

"No, I'm fine." She hugged him. "Lars?"

"Up there, being tied up." He steadied her onto her feet, boosted her out of the little hollow, and took her hand, leading her in the direction of the yard.

"Alright, then?" Thomas raised a bruised face their way. Alex nodded, her eyes stuck on their captive, a struggling tower of a man that kept up a continuous cursing, trying to wrest himself free from the hands and ropes holding him. By the main cabin stood Henry Walton, hands on his eldest son; exiting from Lars' cabin came Kristin, holding yet another musket. She was crying, loud sobs that carried across the yard.

"Kristin! *Hjälp mig!*" Lars twisted to see his sister. "*Hjälp mig, syster,* help me!" His voice was high and breathless, his eyes startling in the paleness of his face. "*Skjut mig,* Kristin, don't let them hang me."

"*Nej!* Don't!" Alex took a couple of steps towards Kristin.

"*Skjuta?*" Kristin's hands tightened on the stock of her musket.

"No, Kristin, don't listen to him," Alex said in Swedish. "Don't, please don't shoot him."

Lars screamed, "*Skjut, syster, skjut!*"

"*Nej!*" Alex yelled at the same moment as Kristin raised the musket and blew a hole through her brother's back.

For about half a minute, the silence was absolute. On the ground Lars jerked spasmodically. Kristin dropped the musket and ran clumsily towards him, and just like that sound came back on, the air full of Kristin's keening, the wails of the Walton children.

"Dear Lord," Peter Leslie said. "What have you done, woman?" He looked down at Lars, now quite still.

"Done? How done? You wanted him dead." A hiccupped sob flew up Kristin's throat.

"We wanted to bring him to justice," Thomas said. "We wanted him publicly condemned for his ill deeds."

Henry had by now joined them and stood a scant yard or so away from his wife, regarding her with an inscrutable look on his face. "Why, Kristin? You foolish woman, why?"

"My brother," she said, "he's my brother."

Thomas spat to the side and took a limping step towards Kristin.

"You'll be coming with us instead, Mrs Walton."

"Me?" Kristin shrank back. "What do you mean? I've never done you any harm!" Her eyes flew to Alex. "Why would you take me?" she pleaded, her hands coming down to span her belly. From nowhere appeared her sons, clutching at her skirts.

"You've murdered," Peter said, "and for that you must be tried."

"No!" Alex tried to disengage herself from Matthew's restraining arms with zero success. "Please don't. What would be the point? After all, he's dead."

Thomas gave Alex a cold look. "She didn't kill him to punish him; she killed him to spare him, and thereby she's robbed me of my revenge on him for what he did to my daughter."

"But how will it help to send her to hang? Look at her, Thomas. She has three young children and another soon to be born. You can't mean to leave them motherless, can you?"

Thomas just shook his head. "My Lizzie will never know the joy of motherhood, so why should I care about her? It's all her fault, isn't it? If she hadn't lied after he'd attacked Fiona then he wouldn't have been free to do what he did yesterday." The men around him murmured in agreement, closing in on the Waltons.

"No," Kristin moaned, hands on her sons.

"Have mercy on her," Henry begged. "I ask you, Thomas, please. How am I to cope without her by my side? How will our sons thrive unless she's here to care for them?"

"You should have thought about that before you chose to protect a madman from justice," Peter said. "As I hear it, he should have hanged well over a year ago."

"He was her brother," Henry cried out. "All the family she has left! And that girl brought it on herself." That comment killed any sympathy he might have hoped for, and the men advanced on them. "No," he groaned, wrapping his arms around his wife. "No!"

"Oh God." Alex twisted in Matthew's arms. "Please stop this, Matthew."

The air was full of the shrill cries of the Walton children, small hands grabbing for their mother, small booted feet kicking at the men who were dragging Kristin towards the horses.

"I can't," he whispered in her hair. "They have the right of it."

"Please," she sobbed, "don't let them take her. What will happen to her family without her? Look at him! He's incapable, entirely dependent on her."

"She killed a man, lass. And, even worse, it is because of her perjury that Lizzie Leslie lies permanently damaged. I don't want to intercede, because all I can think of is what if it had been our Ruth? Or you?"

"But her boys – and the baby!"

"She won't hang until the baby is born," Peter said. "And maybe she won't hang at all."

"Don't lie to me, Peter Leslie," Alex snivelled. "We both know how this will end."

"What will you do?" Alex asked the stunned Henry Walton once the Leslie brothers had ridden off with a screaming Kristin. The air still reverberated with her panicked cries for Per, Erik, Johan.

"Do?" He laughed hollowly. "I have no idea." He was holding his youngest boy in his arms and brushed his lips over the sweaty little head. "I'll never survive here." Henry threw a look of pure desperation at the surrounding forest. "I have no homesteading skills." He set his son down on his feet and collapsed to sit on the door stoop.

"So what are your skills?" Alex asked.

"I'm a glazier, not a profession much in demand here."

"No, not here, but maybe if you go to Boston or to Jamestown?"

"And how am I to get there, Mrs Graham? Beg passage on a ship?" He attempted a slight smile, failing miserably, and instead began to cry, hiding his face in his hands. "Jesus," he wept, "my Kristin! My sweetest wife..."

Alex had no idea what to do. She placed a hand on his shoulder and squeezed.

"I buried him some way into the woods," Matthew said to Henry, setting the shovel against the cabin wall. Henry nodded a thank you and went back to studying his hands. Alex tugged at Matthew's sleeve and pulled him out of earshot.

"We can't leave him here. I don't think he'd even manage feeding them tonight."

Matthew looked over to where Henry was sitting, his three boys hovering around him.

"I suppose they can stay with us until he gets his feet back under him." He exhaled loudly, sending a plume of steam into the cold December air. "I'll go and saddle up the horses and feed the other beasts."

Chapter 18

It had been a strange Christmas, Alex mused as she took a long walk a couple of days before New Year's Eve, wandering in the woods that surrounded her home. The Waltons had moved in and lived like silent wraiths in the midst of the loud Graham family, both husband and sons numbed by the loss of Kristin.

On Christmas Day itself, Matthew, herself and their family had ridden over to the Leslies, leaving a stubborn Henry and his sons behind. He refused to set foot on Leslie land, and in retrospect that had probably been wise, because the Leslie household was still reeling after the attack on Lizzie. And Lizzie herself... Alex's heart twisted into a bundle of pain when she recalled the blank look in the young girl's eyes. According to Mrs Parson, the damage was so severe it was doubtful if she'd ever be able to walk without pain, let alone take a husband to bed.

But foremost in Alex's mind was the tender scene she had stumbled on by accident late on Christmas Day. Despite the cold and the dark, Alex had chosen to slip out to the privy instead of using the chamber pot, and as she was coming back across the Leslie yard she had heard Ian's voice, coming from the direction of the dairy shed. She'd been torn between curiosity and the need to respect his privacy – after all, she didn't want to intrude as he romanced one of the maids – but curiosity had won out, and she'd sneaked closer to where weak candlelight escaped from a crack along the door only to bite back a surprised gasp. There, on the work table, Jenny Leslie had been sitting, her eyes red with crying, and leaning against the table, one hand on her shaking shoulder, was Ian, now talking in a voice so low Alex hadn't been able to overhear a thing. Since they got home, Alex had been dropping heavy-handed hints to Ian, hoping he would tell her why Jenny had been crying, but so far nothing.

She was so deep in her own thoughts she didn't notice Matthew until he appeared before her, blocking her way.

"Hi." She smiled, slipping her mittened hand into his.

"Good walk?"

She nodded. "It's a relief just to get away. That Johan has the most piercing voice I've ever heard. It's like having a whistle screeching you in the ear all day." The little boy kept up a constant, plaintive *Mamma*, tearing not only at Alex's auditory nerves but also at her heart.

"Aye, but they'll be gone by tomorrow."

"They will?"

"He has to be in Providence for the trial," Matthew said. "The summons came today – with an escort. And he has sold the land. He has no plans to return, with or without his wife."

"Without, in all probability." Alex sighed deeply. "Has she had the baby, do you think?"

"I don't know. Henry said it was due in early January, but he's had no word – well, how could he? I bought the land from him – I gave him a good price for it." He had used two of the little ingots Magnus had given him, he told her, and now he had a further five hundred acres of land, enough for a separate living for one of their sons.

"Do you think Ian or Mark would want to live there?" Not that she was superstitious, but Lars had the makings of a scary and persistent ghost.

"Why not? I dragged the body a sizeable distance into the woods and buried him deep."

"Hmm," Alex said.

It was bitterly cold when Henry Walton rode off next morning with his youngest son before him and his two eldest perched atop the pack horse, all four so thickly bundled in shawls that only their noses and eyes were visible. They'd said their goodbyes earlier, and now Henry raised his hand in a salute and clucked his horse into a walk, tugging at the leading rein to start the pack horse. The two escorts fell in behind them, and Matthew stood with his arm around Alex and watched them out of sight before hurrying them both back into the warmth of their home.

"Do you know what he plans to do?" Magnus asked Matthew.

"Nay, not as such, but I reckon he'll leave the colony."

"But first he has to stay and witness his wife's hanging," Magnus said, sounding disgusted.

Matthew raised his brows. "It's the least he can do for her. As she steps onto the scaffold, she'll have him to lock her eyes on."

"Will it help?" Magnus asked scathingly.

"I think it does," Alex replied. "That way she doesn't die alone."

"Whoopee," Magnus muttered.

Alex had noticed for some days that Mark was preoccupied – ever since their Christmas visit at the Leslies, he'd been a distant version of his normal self – and when he once again shook his head at Jacob's invitation to join him for a game of chess, Alex decided it was time for a little heart-to-heart.

"What's the matter?" She sat down beside Mark and gave him a quick hug.

He leaned his head against her. "Naomi says how her father has spoken to her of her future husband, and I don't want her to leave."

"But that's not for years and years. She's only twelve, right?"

He buried his face against her. "You don't understand. I want her to be my wife."

Alex was so astounded she didn't know what to say. Instead, she just held him, wondering if the bubble of laughter that was crawling up her throat would seriously wound his feelings or not. Probably, she decided, and chucked him under the chin to look him in the eyes.

"You're children; neither of you should even be thinking of marriage."

"Naomi's father does. All his lasses have been contracted for marriage before they were fifteen, and now with Lizzie..." Mark cleared his throat and twisted out of her hold. "Well, now that she can no longer uphold the contract, Mr Leslie is planning on offering Naomi instead." He made a small, despairing sound. "And he's already twenty, Mama. He and Lizzie were to wed next autumn."

"So what do you want us to do?"

He flushed a dark red. "Speak to Mr Leslie. I would that Da speaks on my behalf for Naomi."

"But you're too young! You might meet the love of your life five years from now, or in ten years or—"

"Or mayhap I've already met her," he said, looking so much like his father that it made her heart sing inside.

"What does she think?" Alex prevaricated.

In response, Mark opened his fisted hand and showed her a little heart made of braided hair the colour of rich peat. "She gave it to me for Christmas."

"And what did you give her?" Alex stroked his downy cheek.

"I kissed her," he whispered, "on the mouth."

Much too serious, far too soon, Alex thought, but promised she would talk to Matthew about it anyway.

"Naomi, aye?" Matthew laughed. "He has good taste, the lad does. The lass is pretty to look at, taking after her mother more than her father."

"Thank heavens for that," Alex muttered, "and, even better, thank heavens Elizabeth isn't somewhere in her bloodstream. So what will you do?"

"Talk to Thomas, and if he's willing we'll draw up contracts."

"Now?" Alex shook her head. "But they're still so young! What if they change their minds?"

"We cross one bridge at a time." Matthew smiled and tweaked her cheek.

"Absolutely incredible," she said to herself as she made for the kitchen. "He's not quite thirteen, and already formally betrothed." Well, not yet, not until the deeds were signed, but still. She came to a halt in the doorway. Magnus was preparing New Year's dinner, looking harried. His eyes wandered from the baking oven to the pot in which he was

167

reducing cider and broth to a sticky, heavy sauce that had the children wandering in and out of the kitchen with a glazed look of expectation on their faces.

"Need help?" she asked.

"No way." He threw her a quick look. "All I need is peace and quiet, okay?" He made a shooing motion at Sarah and Ruth. "Master chef at work here, people." With a stern look Alex emptied the kitchen of her children, promising she'd help him lay the table later.

It was a pleasant evening, culminating around midnight when Magnus and Alex walked out into the yard and stood staring up at the overcast sky.

"Not a single star," Alex grumbled. "Not fair."

"Oh, come on, Alex, use your imagination." Magnus pointed at a grey cloud. "There, see? The North Star, just at the end of the handle on the Ursa Minor."

"Yes," Alex said, because suddenly she could see a star that wasn't there, remembering all those evenings in her modern life when Magnus and she had stood in their garden seeing stars and constellations that were hidden behind veils of clouds.

"*Gott Nytt År,*" she said to her father, and for the first time in fifteen years she could actually hug him and hear him wish her a Happy New Year in return.

"You haven't wished me a proper Happy New Year," Matthew said once they were in bed. Alex laughed and shifted towards him with the gracefulness of a beached whale.

"Nor have you," she told him, raising her face with pouting lips to his. He kissed her, tasting her deeply. "More," she said when he broke off to breathe.

He chuckled and complied, his mouth covering hers in a progression of kisses that went from soft and teasing to urgent and demanding, leaving them both gasping for breath. He undid her shift, helped her out of it and let his hands travel slowly over her skin.

"You too." Her fingers tugged at his shirt. "All naked before me."

The shirt came off, and her hands touched him across his

scarred back, traced the sword slashes that covered his front and side and slid down to fondle him.

"Hello there," she murmured. "Long time no see, hey?"

"What do you mean by that?" Matthew sounded affronted. "Last time was at most three days ago."

"Precisely," Alex smiled, "ages ago."

"You're insatiable, woman," he sighed, nibbling at her earlobe. "You must take into account my advanced age."

"Advanced age?" Alex chortled. "Oh yes, I forget; soon forty-three and thereby per definition almost dead."

"Dead? I think not." His muscles bunched under her hands, strong arms lifted her this way and that, supple fingers dancing down her side in a way that made her squirm and twist. His mouth; soft and warm, it planted a series of wet love bites along the back of her neck that sent shivers down her spine and made her scalp prickle. She half rose on her knees in invitation, because she wanted him, needed him.

"Not yet," he murmured against her nape. He rolled her over to lie on her back, his exhalations tickling their way down her front as he shifted to lie between her legs.

"I suppose that's why older women tend to like younger men," she said, her hands fluttering around his head. "The stamina thing..." She inhaled noisily when his tongue found her cleft.

"I'll give you for stamina," he growled. "I'll have you taking it back before I'm done with you."

"Really?"

"Aye, really."

"I take it back," she said much later, her fingers playing with his chest hair. "All I ever insinuated about your stamina, I take back." She yawned and nestled closer.

He chuckled. "I'm not done with you yet."

"I'm pregnant," she groaned, "hugely pregnant."

"And juicy with it." It was quiet for some time, the bed creaking as they moved together.

"Oh God, I love you, Matthew Graham," Alex whispered into the predawn grey.

"And I you, my bonny Alex," he whispered back.

Chapter 19

"Why now? Why dump snow on us now, in February?" Alex sat down as close as she could to the kitchen hearth and looked out at where her children were playing in the snow. "They're going to come inside in less than an hour, drenched and cold," she said to Magnus.

He grunted a reply, stirring in the dollop of honey he'd added to his tea – real tea, for a change. His head was aching, an all too familiar throbbing just behind his left eye, and he was trying to pretend he didn't feel anything, that this was just an ordinary headache that would go away with a mug or two of willow bark tea.

"What's the matter?" Alex's voice startled him.

"Just a headache." He sneezed, sneezed again – violently – and pulled out his handkerchief to blow his nose. A cold, he thought with relief, just an ordinary cold.

It wasn't just a cold, it was the grandmother of all colds, Magnus grumbled to Mrs Parson a week later. He swallowed tentatively. The acute discomfort was waning, and at least he was no longer feverish.

He sniffed at the steaming mug she extended to him. "What's this?"

"Ginger and honey." She shook out his blankets, plumped up his pillows and told him to remain in bed at least one more day.

"And the others?" Magnus asked. The house was eerily quiet.

"Sick, most of them." Mrs Parson drew her brows together in a frown and shook her head. "The youngest lad's in a right bad way, and so is Matthew."

"And Alex?"

"Coping. There's not much else to do, aye?"

★

"Here." Alex helped Matthew sit up in bed and handed him a cup of willow bark tea. He looked awful, his normally bright hair dulled into a tangled mess where she saw far more grey than she usually did. His nose was red and chafed after three days of intense nose blowing, and his eyes were irritated slits in his pale, unshaven face. The stubble was also grey, grey with patches of his original dark chestnut.

She set a bowl of hot water on a stool, dipped a cloth in it and washed his face and hands. He shivered when the cool air hit his damp skin, tried to croak a thank you and slid back down into the cover of his quilts. Her hand rested for an instant on his brow. Still hot, as was his cheek, his neck. Hot and yet so cold, constant shivers racking him, no matter that she'd piled their combined bedclothes over him. He hadn't eaten for days, complaining that his throat hurt when he swallowed, and already flesh was melting off him, leaving him gaunt and hollow-cheeked. She gave him one last pat and made as if to stand.

"Stay," he whispered, his hand coming up to encircle her wrist. "Please sit with me for a while." She sat down beside him and held his hand until he was fast asleep.

"It's as if he's burning up from the inside," she said some hours later to Mrs Parson. She was torn in two between her man and her son, but at present it was Matthew's state of health that most worried her. Children were prone to high fevers, but this... She stroked his damp hair and pressed a soft kiss on his forehead.

"Aye," Mrs Parson sighed, wringing out a cloth and patting at Matthew's face, his neck and the uppermost part of his chest.

"What..." No. Alex swallowed back on the rest of the words and crossed her fingers. Of course he wouldn't die; this was just some sort of cold.

Mrs Parson clasped Alex's hand and gave it a little shake. "He's a strong man," she said, picked up the bowl and left.

Strong? At present he looked wasted, and his sleep was anything but restful, him tossing like mad in between

171

shivering like a naked man in an Arctic gale.

For two days straight, Alex sat by Matthew's bedside, restricting her time away from him to her quick visits to Daniel. She washed his face, she spoon-fed him hot broths, she forced him awake every four hours or so to have him swallow down yet another mug of useless willow bark. She helped him with the chamber pot, she changed his shirt, the sheets, and when his teeth wouldn't stop chattering no matter how many quilts she covered him with, she undressed and slipped in to lie beside him, trying as well as she could to hold him close.

By the third day she was so tired she couldn't think straight. Her man continued to sweat and toss, her son was just as ill, a small cocooned bundle that moaned and coughed. She didn't know what to do. At one point she escaped to the privy and sat there for some minutes and wept, huge loud sobs as she prayed and prayed to God to keep them safe, her man and her son both.

"Alex, you need to sleep," Magnus admonished her when she stumbled back inside.

"Not now. I have to…" She hesitated by the door to the boys' room where Daniel was presently sleeping alone. From her bedroom came Matthew's hoarse voice, calling for her, and she stood like the proverbial donkey, not sure who to go to.

"You take care of Matthew, *hjärtat*," Magnus said. "I'll be here for Daniel."

Just before dawn on the fifth day, Alex woke from a heavy if uncomfortable sleep when Matthew stroked her head. She sat up, startled.

"Hi," he croaked, and his eyes were no longer bright with fever.

"Hi," she whispered back, lifting two fingers to his cracked lips.

"Thirsty," he muttered, closing his eyes. "So thirsty…"

Alex rose to her feet and hurried off to fetch him something to drink.

"I'll do that," Mrs Parson said. "You'd best go and see to Daniel." She took the mug from Alex and gave her a gentle shove.

"He's not better?" Alex asked, feeling the relief she'd felt at Matthew's lucid look evaporate, leaving her guts as tightly clenched as they'd been for the last week or so.

"Go see your laddie," was all Mrs Parson said.

The door creaked open, and Alex slipped inside, all huge eyes and a gigantic belly. Magnus threw his daughter a concerned look. She should be resting – and eating – instead she was doing 24/7 nurse duty.

"How is he?" she asked, coming over to join him by the bed.

"Bad," Magnus sighed. "This isn't just a cold; look at the rash." Daniel exhaled, sending a gust of putrid air in the direction of Magnus. "Phew," he said, using both hands to open the boy's mouth. "Strep throat," he concluded after his inspection.

"How would you know?"

"I had it one too many times as a boy." Magnus ran a finger over the exposed, overheated skin of Daniel's chest. "Scarlet fever, I think. After all, it's the same bacteria."

"Scarlet fever?" Alex smoothed Daniel's hair down to lie flat and drew the blankets high around him. "But that's not dangerous, is it?"

"I don't know. How's Matthew?"

Alex gnawed at her lip and got up from her knees, gripping his arm so as not to overbalance. "Better today." She made a face at the loud argument erupting from the girls' room. "Some are much better," she said, looking down at Daniel. "He'll be okay, right? You don't die of something like this, do you?"

Not in our time, you don't, Magnus thought, but in this day and age... But he chose not to say anything, concerned by her apparent exhaustion, and propelled her in the direction of the door.

"Sleep. I'll sit with Daniel."

"Promise?" Her voice wobbled.

"Cross my heart. I won't move until you're back."

"Not good," Mrs Parson said a few hours later, lifting

Daniel's shirt out of the way. The boy was unresponsive, burning with fever, and every time he swallowed he grimaced in his sleep.

"What do we do?" Magnus felt helpless; no medicine, no doctors.

"Garlic for the throat, willow bark tea for the fever, bee balm for his skin, and then it is best we pray."

Magnus shook his head at these futile measures.

"Pray?" Matthew sounded horribly hoarse, but waved away Mrs Parson's concerned exclamations along the lines that he was too ill to be up and about. "Why pray?" He shuffled across the room and sank down on the stool Magnus had vacated. "Measles?" he frowned, squinting down at the bright patches of rash.

"No," Alex said from the doorway. "They've had the measles – all of them." She coughed, muffling the sound against her sleeve, and shook her head at Magnus when he started towards her. She sank down on Daniel's bed, one hand resting on the narrow little back.

"You should be in bed," she said to Matthew. He ignored her, eyes on his fidgeting, burning son.

"How long? How many days has he been this ill?"

"A week?" Magnus said, looking at Mrs Parson for confirmation.

"Something like that," Mrs Parson said. "It'll have to break soon," she added, and Alex uttered a strangled sound that tore at Magnus' heart.

For all that both Magnus and Mrs Parson tried to wheedle Matthew and Alex to bed, neither of them budged, sitting beside their son through the afternoon and evening. Finally, Magnus gave up and, after a mumbled goodnight, went in search of his bed.

"Go to bed, lass," Matthew said. It was midnight or thereabouts, he reckoned.

"I can't. How can I, if he suddenly calls for me?" They were sitting close together on the floor, leaning back against the wall.

"You've been on your feet constantly for the last weeks, minding us." Matthew raised his hand to caress her cheek. So wan, he noted, so totally bleached of colour.

"What if he dies," she groaned, turning to hide her face against his shirt.

"There's not much we can do," Matthew said, pressing her head to him. "All we can do is put our trust in God."

She began to cry. "Please don't let him die, God, please don't! He's going to be a minister when he grows up, and you must like that."

Aye, Matthew prayed silently, please let him live – dear Lord, please accept him as yours and spare my lad.

Somewhere in the wee hours they must have fallen asleep, because Matthew woke with a start when Mrs Parson entered the room, bringing bright daylight in her wake. Alex was reclining against his chest, a damp, heavy warmth that grumbled when he shifted under her. Matthew coughed, tried to pull in some air through his congested nose, and coughed some more. By the bed, Mrs Parson had folded back the sheet and was studying Daniel who, to Matthew's worried eyes, lay very still.

"Is he...?" A wave of ice washed through him.

Mrs Parson threw him an encouraging smile. "The fever is down, and the rash is fading. The laddie will be fine."

Matthew slumped against the wall, closed his eyes and silently thanked the Lord.

Mrs Parson nodded in the direction of Alex. "But you must get her to bed and stay there with her." She put the back of her hand against his cheek and nodded. "You're still feverish."

"So is she," Matthew croaked, trying to lubricate his dry mouth.

Mrs Parson moved her hand and frowned. "Aye, she is. Let us hope the wean stays where it is for now."

"Where he is," Matthew corrected, caressing Alex's belly. "And he will; he's a good lad." The responding kick was impressive.

"Sure he is," Alex mumbled without opening her eyes.

"If you ask me it's a mule in there, not a child." She struggled to her knees. "Daniel?"

"Asleep." Mrs Parson smiled. Alex clasped her hands together and uttered a string of thank yous.

"Bed." Matthew heaved Alex off her knees.

She tottered against him. "Yes," she yawned, "I'm so tired, and..." She gasped, clutching at her belly. "Not yet. Be a good lad and mind your father, okay?"

"All of them have biblical names." Magnus drew the blanket up around his latest grandson's head and handed him back to his mother. "David..."He rolled the name over his tongue. "David Andrew Graham, born on the last day of February in Our Lord's year 1673." Three hundred years before his mother was born, Magnus shuddered inside. He saw the same thought flash through Alex's eyes and smiled slightly. "So why all these Bible names?"

"Ask their father," Alex replied, nuzzling her baby boy. "He names them."

She coughed and grimaced. She was still not fully recovered from her own bout of whatever it was they'd had, and to Magnus' amusement, Matthew was like a protective hawk, flying in her direction if she as much as cleared her throat.

"They're fortunate in each other," Mrs Parson said to Magnus as they watched Matthew crouch by Alex's chair.

"Yes." Magnus batted down the spikes of jealousy he always felt when he watched his daughter with her husband. Instead, he beckoned Daniel over and lifted the boy onto his lap. "How's my Viking today?"

"Tired." Daniel yawned. "And my head hurts something frightful."

So does mine, Magnus thought, God help me, so does mine. He clutched the skinny boy to his chest and buried his nose in the thick, dark hair. It was back: deep in the labyrinth swirls of his brain, the cancer was back. For now it was just flexing itself, sending splinters of pain from behind his left ear towards his frontal lobes, but soon... Magnus swallowed and closed his eyes.

Chapter 20

The shriek froze Matthew to the spot, and after a quick look at Ian, he plunged towards it, musket already at hand. Yet another scream, the unmistakable sound of a woman in fear or pain, and Matthew extended his stride with Ian running beside him.

Now there were other sounds: men laughing, the jangling of a harness. Matthew held up his hand, dropping down to squat behind a thicket. Ian crawled over to join him, and in silence they studied the scene before them.

Indians, several Indians, three men tied up so tightly they could barely shuffle, seven women tied at the wrists. Standing before them, inspecting his catch, was a man Matthew recognised as having been part of the posse that had ridden in pursuit of Qaachow – the man Alex and Magnus had seen late last year: Mr Burley himself.

He dragged at his black hair, said something over his shoulder to one of the other men, received laughter in reply, and approached the woman – no, lass – who had apparently screamed, at least to judge from her bruised face. Like a snake he pounced, hand closing on the long braid to pull her towards him.

Matthew muttered a curse, shifting on his feet. Beside him, Ian groaned when the man pushed the lass to the ground. Burley said something to his companions and undid his breeches.

"Da!" Ian whispered, "He's going to—"

"Aye, I can see that," Matthew whispered back. By now, he'd recognised one of the Indian men, the knotted scar that ran up his side identifying him as the man Alex had sliced open last autumn.

"But we can't let him!" Ian hissed, staring at where

Burley was kneeling between the girl's spread legs. "Da, we have to do something!"

A wail from the lass and one of the other women leapt towards her, tied hands gripping a branch. It was bound to fail, one of Burley's companions wresting the branch from her before cuffing her. The lass screamed; Burley's bared arse bobbed up and down while his companions cheered him on. Matthew swore under his breath, gripping the stock of his musket. Bastard! The lass whimpered and cried; Burley laughed. Ian growled, rising out of his crouch only to be arrested by Matthew's hand.

"Think, lad," Matthew whispered. "They're four, we're only two. To rush out will only get you killed. We need a strategy."

For a few seconds, he sat deep in thought before giving Ian some hasty instructions and sending him off to the opposite side of the clearing. He took a deep breath and stood up; he was laying his life in the hands of his son. Yet another breath and he strode out into the open.

"What are you doing?" he demanded, musket held high.

"Doing?" Burley scrambled to his feet, turning eyes the colour of old ice on Matthew. "Nothing that concerns you, Mr Graham." He adjusted his clothes, smirking down at the weeping lass.

"Concern me? Aye, it does. You're on my land, Mr Burley."

Philip Burley shrugged, keeping those strange eyes on Matthew. The look in them made the fine hairs along Matthew's nape rise in alarm. This was a man without a whit of compassion or warmth.

"Not for long. We'll be well on our way to Virginia before nightfall."

"Without them," Matthew said, indicating the Indians.

"I think not. They go with us. A small compensation for the man who died in last year's raid – and our friend, who died last night."

Matthew just shook his head.

One of the men, still on his horse, laughed and raised

a musket. "And how will you stop us?" Without warning he fired. Matthew threw himself to the side and came back up, his muzzle now aimed at Burley.

"Try something like that again, and I blow his brains out," he warned.

"It must somehow have slipped your notice that we're four and you're only one," Philip Burley sneered. "One shot is all you get, and then..." He mimed a slicing motion over his neck. He yanked the Indian girl to stand and, using her as a shield, advanced towards Matthew. "Go on then," he jeered. "Shoot, Mr Graham. Shoot before I get close enough to disarm you."

One of the men laughed and approached Matthew from the other side. Matthew retreated step by step, luring the two men with him.

"Now!" he called out, and the next moment the mounted man screamed. The handle of a knife protruded from his shoulder, and Matthew congratulated Ian on his aim. Cursing, the man dismounted, yelling at his companion to come and help him. Burley came to a halt, scanning the surrounding woods.

"Not alone, then," he said.

"I'm no fool. Go!" Matthew jerked his musket in a rough south-westerly direction. "Get off my land before we do you bodily harm – and don't return."

"Indian lover!" Burley spat.

"I don't hold with abduction, nor do I wish to have an Indian situation on my hands. We live peaceably with our heathen neighbours and want to continue doing so." He advanced; Burley fell back.

The man on Matthew's right lunged. Matthew whirled and fired. The man collapsed. Burley pounced, as graceful as a giant cat in his movements. God's truth, but the man was strong – and angered! Those ice-cold eyes swam far too close, and Matthew's musket was wrenched from him and thrown to the side. Matthew kicked and heard Burley yelp. He landed a punch, was pushed, shoved back and ducked hastily when Burley's blade swiped by his ear. Matthew backed away. Burley

179

screamed like a banshee and came at him again. Matthew stumbled. Burley screamed again, jumped, and Matthew fell, landing on his back with Burley on top. The knife came down. Matthew grabbed hold of Burley's wrist, thereby arresting the blade a scant inch or so from his exposed throat.

Yet another shot rang out. Burley threw all his weight onto his knife arm, and the blade sank lower. The metal was near on scraping Matthew's skin when the Indian lass kicked Burley in the side – hard enough for the man to grunt, giving Matthew the opportunity to clap Burley over the ear, heave him off, and get back on his feet.

"Da?" Ian materialised beside him. "Are you alright?" He handed Matthew his musket.

"Aye," Matthew replied, watching Burley as he regained his feet.

"You killed him." Burley pointed at the unmoving body a few yards away.

"No loss to mankind," Matthew said.

"He was my friend." Burley grabbed at the Indian lass, backed towards the horses and his two live companions, one clutching at his bleeding shoulder, the other cradling his head. "I avenge my friends, Graham. An eye for an eye, a life for a life." He spat in the direction of Matthew.

"You can try," Matthew said, trying to sound unconcerned. This was not a man he wanted as an enemy, but it was too late to do anything about that.

The man holding his head cursed and tried to get to his feet, but collapsed to sit.

"I couldn't kill him," Ian muttered, "so I just clapped him over the head."

"You did fine, lad." Matthew approached Burley and the lass. "Let her go."

"I think not; she rides with me." Burley cursed when the lass bit him, sinking her teeth into his arm. "Ah!" He hit her over the head with the hand holding his dagger and still she wouldn't let go. "So be it!" he snarled, and just like that slashed his knife across her throat. It was all Matthew could do to hold Ian back.

★

"I must say your life has very few dull moments," Magnus commented to Alex when Matthew ushered a group of Indians out of the surrounding forests. "Since I've been here, we've had Indians, posses, sex stalkers, aggravated bears and now Indians again."

"The bear was pretty scary." Alex grinned.

"Scary? It wasn't you sitting in the privy; it was me!"

Alex laughed. In retrospect it was very funny, with Magnus shooting out of the privy as if his arse was on fire, holding his unlaced breeches with one hand while he kept on hollering there was a bear in the privy.

Magnus gave her an aggrieved look. "It could've eaten me; it was probably starved after months of hibernation."

"No, no," Alex assured him between gusts of laughter. "We wouldn't have let him." And it had been a small black bear, rooting about below the privy holes.

"Huh!" He crossed his arms across his chest and went back to studying their approaching guests.

"Alex?" Matthew motioned for her to come, and she hastened towards him, alerted by the grim look on his face. Curiously, she studied the Indian women, dressed in buckskin skirts and shirts, the hems embroidered with quills and beads. One of them wore a necklace, an impressive work of art that decorated her chest with several multi-coloured strands. She was kneeling by a primitive stretcher, talking in a low, reassuring voice to whoever it was that was lying on it: a girl, a thin little thing who lay wide-eyed but sightless, blood staining the primitive bandage round her throat.

"Oh God," Alex said, and there was Mrs Parson, peering over her shoulder.

"She's dead," Mrs Parson stated. "Fortunately, as there was nothing we could do for her."

"Dead?" The Indian man with the scar approached them. "She dead?"

"I'm afraid so," Alex said. "What happened?"

"As far as I can understand, they were attacked last night," Matthew said.

181

The Indian nodded and haltingly described how five white men had snuck in on them as they made camp for the night.

"One dead," he said, miming a knife in the gut. He pointed with pride at the woman with the necklace.

"His sister," Ian said. "Pretty, isn't she?"

Alex studied the young Indian woman, who was still on her knees in the mud. Pretty? She was beautiful, with dark, gleaming hair, skin a soft bronze and eyes the colour of sloes. Eyes that at present were riveted on the dead girl.

"Yet another sister." Matthew kneeled and closed the staring eyes.

"I wasn't planning on burying a renegade as the first in my graveyard," Matthew said a few hours later. The Indians had already left, taking their dead girl with them.

"If we're going to be correct, you're not. You're burying him just outside." Alex nudged at the shrouded body with her toe. "You shot him?"

"Aye, I had to. If only she hadn't bitten him," he sighed.

"If she hadn't, she'd have been on a horse with him, and God knows what he'd have done to her." Alex helped him hoist the body into the hole and watched as he refilled the grave.

She studied the view, smiling at the sight of their home, their fields and, further away, the glittering waters of the river.

"You chose well; to lie here must be very peaceful."

"Aye, and yet close enough to home to not feel entirely abandoned by the living." He drew her into his arms and they stood looking down at their land.

"You said home." Alex rested back against his chest.

"Aye, I did." He looked around at the small enclosed space. "But I don't plan to lie here for very many years yet."

"Me neither." She snuck her hand into his as they made their way back down. "You think they'll be back?"

"Not likely," he said in a light tone that didn't comfort Alex in the least – not when he'd insisted that his sons keep their loaded muskets at hand.

★

"I should have one too, you know," Magnus said to Alex as they made their way down to the river. The March evening was bright but nippy, and Magnus regretted not having brought his cloak.

"Have what?"

"A gun." Magnus felt distinctly defenceless – and useless – when surrounded by his musket-toting son-in-law and grandsons.

"Can you shoot?" Alex asked, a ghost of a smile on her lips.

"No – but I can learn."

"Right now the guns we have must be carried by those who can use them."

"Use them? Seriously, Alex, Jacob's nine years old, and—"

"Jacob can shoot," Alex cut him off.

Magnus considered protesting further, but decided there was no point. Should he win Alex over, he'd still have to convince Matthew – fat chance. He pursed his mouth and picked up a long, stout stick instead, swinging it a couple of times to get a feel for it.

"Coming?" Alex called. He extended his stride to catch up with Alex and her daughters.

"Agnes says the dead Indian lass will go to hell on account of her being a heathen," Ruth said.

"Agnes has the sense of a fly in a bottle trap," Alex snorted, making Magnus laugh.

"So she won't?" Ruth asked.

"I don't think so," Alex said. "She was a very brave girl, and God loves her just as much as He loves all of us – it isn't her fault that she's an Indian, is it?"

"You think?" Ruth said. "Then why did he let her die?"

"I don't know," Alex sighed. "Sometimes it's difficult to keep up with God."

"Quite an overbearing bastard at times if you ask me," Magnus muttered in an undertone, making Alex elbow him.

One moment things were like they always were, the next

the world was tumbling round him like in a kaleidoscope or the side effects of a bad LSD trip. Magnus came to an abrupt stop, trying to visualise the pain, isolate it and bring it under control. He closed his eyes and gritted his teeth, sinking down to sit on the ground.

"*Pappa*? Magnus?" Alex squatted beside him. "Are you alright?"

"No," he replied through a tight mouth. "No, I don't think I am." He breathed; long, regular breaths that he forced in and out of his nose, concentrating on counting seconds rather than on the burning point inside his head. Finally it receded. His head was no longer banded by pain, and when he opened his eyes he could see Alex's face, only centimetres from his.

"Gone," he said shakily.

"Is this the first time?"

"Of course it isn't. I told you, didn't I? I've had this before, and then the headaches came back last spring. That's why I decided to come here."

"You know that wasn't what I meant," Alex said. "Is this the first time since you got here?"

"No," he grunted, picking at his stockings. "But it's only been a couple of times."

"And that's good, right?" Alex sounded hopeful.

"Yes, I suppose it is." In his head, the pain surged and peaked, but this time Magnus had it under control. He even managed to smile. His hand closed round the pouch that held his small supply of pills and that in itself sufficed to calm him.

Chapter 21

After several weeks of vigilance, life returned to normal. Fields were planted, land was cleared, and what with the workload and the time constraints, the spectre of Burley returning bent on revenge -as he had sworn to do – receded. Besides, the man might be an unsavoury beast of a man, but he didn't strike Matthew as a fool, and an outright attack on the Grahams would be a foolish thing to do, effectively labelling Burley a renegade and an outlaw.

"I thought he already was," Alex said when he told her this. She stifled a yawn. It was well before dawn and she was sitting up in bed nursing their son.

"An outlaw? Whatever for?"

"He kidnaps Indian women and sells them. He even kills them!"

"And you think people will condemn him for doing that?" Indians were heathens that most colonists would gladly either enslave or kill.

"They should."

"Aye, but they won't. And with the escalating tensions in Virginia, I dare say quite a few would applaud Burley for doing what he's doing – the more women he steals away, the fewer new Indians."

Alex made a disgusted sound.

That same morning, she came to find him in the barn. "I'm taking a walk. Want to come?"

"I can't, lass, not now. I have to..." He grunted with the effort of sliding the post into place. "... get this done, aye?"

"Too bad," she said, giving him a blue look. It made him smile, and he moved close enough to kiss her cheek.

"Save that look for later," he murmured. She stood on her toes, took hold of his ears and kissed him on the mouth.

"Later." With a little wave she moved off, promising to bring back something green and edible for dinner.

"More nettles," Daniel groaned, pouting at the dark green soup.

"It's good for you," Alex replied, "and there's pie for afters."

"Can't I just have the afters?" Daniel looked as miserable as possible. "I still feel sick."

"Cut it out," Alex huffed. "That was two months ago."

"Where's Ian?" she asked Matthew, setting his bowl down in front of him.

"I have no idea." Matthew shared a helpless look with his bairns, picked up his spoon and swallowed, pantomiming a horrible throat burn behind Alex's back.

"I saw that," she growled, "and that means you go without dessert, Matthew Graham." The bairns giggled and bent their heads to the soup, filling the kitchen with the sound of their slurping.

"Didn't you hear the bell?" Alex served Ian his soup.

"No," he said, going an interesting pink. As long as it wasn't Agnes, Alex sighed to herself, because however willing and hard-working that girl was, she had at most two brain cells, generally in permanent opposition to each other.

"Hmm." Alex shared a look with Matthew, who shoved his pie plate away with a contented expression on his face.

"Da wasn't supposed to get dessert," Daniel said from the doorway.

"No, you're right, but he apologised so nicely I caved in." She went back to inspecting Ian. "Rolling around on the ground?" She picked a dried leaf from his hair. Daniel snickered, but at Ian's forbidding glare retreated speedily.

"It's a nice day," Ian said. "So I stretched out for a nap. That's why I didn't hear the dinner bell."

"Of course, and that's why you smell so nicely of lavender, right? Maybe you stretched out in my kitchen garden."

Ian gave her a haughty look, muttered something about

being man enough to handle his private concerns, and went back to his soup, refusing dessert in his hurry to leave the kitchen.

"Who?" Alex asked Matthew.

"Jenny Leslie," he replied, grinning at her.

"You think?"

Matthew raised one brow and called for Daniel. "Go on then, tell your mama what you told me before."

Daniel turned to his mother. "I saw Ian, with Jenny."

"Oh?" Alex waited.

"They were talking and holding hands."

"Ah. Just holding hands?"

Daniel wrinkled his brow together. "Aye, I think so."

"Maybe you should have a talk with him," Alex suggested once Daniel had left the kitchen.

Matthew made an indecipherable sound. "Is there more pie?"

"You know there is. Ian just walked out on his slice."

"More pie?" Daniel and Jacob appeared like greased rats from behind the kitchen door.

"Oh, go ahead – splurge." Alex set down the half-empty pan in front of them. "Don't bother with plates," she added a moment later. None of them heard.

"Mama?" Jacob lingered behind in the kitchen, shifting from one foot to the other.

"Yes?" Alex patted David on his back to burp him and laid him to the other breast.

"What's the matter with Offa?"

"How do you mean?" Alex tried to sound relaxed. Jacob came over to her chair and leaned against her, one finger tracing his baby brother's downy head.

"He..." Jacob smiled at David, who gave him a wide, toothless smile in return. "I reckon he's hurting." He gave her a green look. "I saw him in the woods, up beyond the graveyard, and he was crying and calling for Isaac."

"Isaac?"

"Aye," Jacob nodded, "and that's strange because Isaac's dead, isn't he?"

Not quite...if they were to be correct, Isaac wasn't even in the making yet.

"Your Offa was very close to Isaac, and I think he misses him – a lot." Alex ran her fingers through Jacob's thick, fair hair.

"Will he die?" Jacob asked.

"Everyone dies."

He frowned at her. "Will he die soon?"

"Yes, I think he will."

Jacob shifted even closer to her. "Before, I didn't know I missed him, but when he dies now I'll miss him a lot."

"So will I, but I've missed him all the time before as well."

On the other side of the door, Magnus leaned against the wall and didn't know whether to cry or laugh. Maybe this had been the real purpose behind his skydive through time – to meet his grandchildren and leave an imprint of himself on them. If so, it seemed he'd achieved his purpose; his name would be spoken out loud in this household long after he was gone, and even perhaps in his grandchildren's homes. He'd be remembered long before he was born, he smiled wryly – not something that happened to all that many.

He heard Alex kiss her son on his cheek and send him out to play. Magnus remained where he was for some time before going over to the unshuttered window to watch his grandchildren. All five of them were in the yard playing with a makeshift ball, with Jacob testing himself against Mark. Daniel tried to tag after his brothers and leave his tailing sisters behind without any major success because Ruth was fast and lithe and horribly determined in her chase after the ball. Magnus laughed when Sarah picked up the ball, running like a rabbit for the protective shelter of her father. Coming here had been worth it, he told himself, turning away from the window. And he wasn't about to die anytime soon; he had far too many things left to do.

"Like what?" Alex said when he shared this with her.

She poured him a cup of tea and offered him a dry biscuit in lieu of the massacred pie.

"I want to see the sea again. I'd love to attend a religious service—"

"You're kidding," Alex interrupted, "hours and hours of tedious sermon, mainly along the lines of how corrupted we all are by original sin – in particular us women, weak vessels that we are."

"Still, I'd like to go, perhaps even have the opportunity to sit and talk with one of these very convinced ministers."

Alex shook her head. "Not going to happen. You open your mouth and I'll find you burning at the stake or something."

"They don't do that anymore," Magnus scoffed. "That's more fifteenth and sixteenth century."

"Really? And why do you think we had to leave Scotland?" She gave him an irritated look. "What else?"

Magnus sipped at his tea. "I want to see him walk," he said, nodding at David, who was sleeping in his basket.

Matthew found Ian on one of the furthest fields, tilling the recently cleared ground. As he walked towards his son, Matthew noted the lad was nervous, shoulders squaring themselves under his shirt.

"Son." Matthew nodded.

"Da." Ian nodded back, wiping his palms on the coarse cloth of his breeches.

"I hear you've been seeing a lot of Jenny Leslie," Matthew said, dispensing with any form of preamble.

"I have?" Ian tried out his most innocent look, but Matthew wasn't having any, a slight motion of his head making Ian slump.

"We talk," Ian muttered.

"More than talk. I've heard of handholding and kisses." He laughed at Ian's aghast expression. "You have brothers and sisters. They see much more than you think."

"Hmph!" Ian's long mouth set into a straight line.

"So what has changed?" Matthew sat down with his

back against a maple and squinted up at his son.

"Changed?"

"Aye. Not yet a year ago, you insisted you didn't want to wed her, and now you seem to want nothing more than bed her."

Ian went a bright red. "Nay, I don't."

"No?" Matthew laughed. "Now why do I find that hard to believe?"

"I won't bed her without wedding her."

"That gladdens my heart, if naught else because Peter Leslie sets a high price on his daughter's honour."

"It wasn't me!" Ian protested.

"Wasn't you that did what?" Matthew studied him intently.

Ian sat down beside him and let the full story spill from him. "It was at Christmas that I found her crying in the dairy shed," he began, and Matthew remembered that Alex had told him she had seen them there, very late at night. "She was angry and sad, but mostly angry on account of Jochum leading her on when he had nothing to offer her."

"What do you mean?" Matthew found a hairy boiled sweet in his coat pocket, inspected it, and threw it away.

"He's not only Catholic, he's married and was well on the way to committing bigamy until the letter from his wife arrived telling him she was taking the first boat out this year. He didn't think she ever would."

"Does Peter Leslie know this?"

Ian shrugged. "I can't very well tell him, and Jenny hasn't either, keeping Jochum on tenterhooks."

"How did she find out?"

"The letter," Ian explained with an eye roll.

"She reads German?" Matthew pretended to be impressed.

"Nay," Ian said. "He was so shocked he told her – well, he had to, on account of having promised her marriage and weans."

"And why did you say it wasn't you?"

"Because it wasn't. Jenny Leslie is no longer a maid, but it wasn't me."

190

"Ah." Matthew envisioned the total havoc this would cause in the Leslie house. Jenny tied to the bedpost and whipped at a minimum, Jochum out on his ear, probably severely damaged for life. "But she isn't pregnant, I trust."

"Nay, of course not – she isn't a fool."

That made Matthew sit in silence for a while. A young, unwed lass that knew enough to partake of forbidden fruit and not become pregnant was no innocent, not by any stretch of mind.

"And was he her first?"

"Da!"

Matthew shrugged. "You tell me she's bedded a man but has ensured she hasn't conceived. It smells of more experience than I want my future daughter-in-law to have."

"She went to Mrs Parson for help."

This Matthew didn't like at all, for Mrs Parson to be dispensing such advice to the lasses in the area. Somehow he suspected Mrs Parson would give not one whit for his disapproval, and nor would Alex, no doubt haranguing him as to the importance of ensuring no child was born unwanted. With an effort, he pulled himself back to his conversation with his son.

"It wouldn't matter if she were with child," Ian said. "I'd wed her anyway and take the child as mine."

"Oh, you would? That isn't an easy thing to do, and you'd know that better than most."

Ian dropped his eyes to his hands, tearing at a long blade of grass. "I would love it for its own sake, not like Luke, taking me for Mam's sake."

Matthew put an arm around him and gave him a quick squeeze. "And so you love it for its own sake, and then comes a child truly your own. Will you love it still?"

None of them mentioned Luke, or the way his affections for Ian had become permanently eclipsed the moment red-haired Charlie – the spitting image of his sire – was born.

Ian chewed at his lip, deep in thought. Finally he looked at his father with a brilliant smile. "Mama loves me – for my own sake."

"Aye, that she does, so very much does she love you. And she wouldn't like it that you marry for pity. She says you should marry for love."

"It isn't like that," Ian said, looking away into the distance. "I..." In a low, rushed voice he told Matthew how Jenny only had to look at him and he would feel his skin begin to tingle, how her dark voice told him things no one had ever told him before, and how all of her made his insides twist themselves into a ball of fire.

"That's your cock speaking," Matthew interrupted, "not your heart."

"Oh, and it isn't your cock speaking when you go looking for Mama? It isn't your cock that makes you take her up to the hayloft and—"

"Shush, lad," Matthew said, aware of a wave of blood flooding his face. "But you're right: you must listen to your cock as well. As well, mind."

"I want to marry her." Ian's jaw set in a stubborn line. "I ask you to help me."

Matthew looked at him and gave an infinitesimal nod. "I'll do my best." He got back onto his feet and was aware of an urge to find Alex – now. With a quick wave he left Ian to resume his work and strode off across the uneven ground.

Matthew heard her singing in the kitchen garden and moved towards the sound. She was on her knees, her hands buried in the rich soil. She had put her hair up into an untidy bun, locks escaping to wave around her face in the spring breeze, and as he watched, she used the back of her hand to smooth a tendril back behind her ear, leaving a dark smear of dirt across her cheek.

She looked so young, he thought tenderly, not so much in her appearance as in her movements that were still the same restless bursts of energy he remembered from when he first met her. And here she was, nearly fifteen years on, mother seven times over, and at times she still reminded him of that wild, strange lass he'd made love to for the first time on the open moor.

His cock stirred in his breeches, a reaction to the combined effect of the memory of that first time and how she looked today. Something changed in the way she held herself; her back straightened, her head was suddenly at a coy angle, and he knew she'd seen him where he stood among the trees. She sat back, pushed her chest forward, and he smiled that she should still preen for him, want him to like what he saw.

A hand came up to her hair and she shook it free, still without turning in his direction. In her dirt-streaked clothes, loose hair and bare feet, she looked more like an urchin than a wife, and he thought she looked lovely, all of her dipped in gold where the late afternoon sun touched her. He waited until she turned to face him, blew her a kiss and walked off. He laughed at the surprised flash of disappointment in her eyes. That he liked very much.

Chapter 22

Peter Leslie called his daughter into his office, closed the door on his wife, and had Jenny tell him the whole sorry tale – all of it, mind. Matthew would have liked to be anywhere else but there, but Peter insisted he be present, his intelligent eyes wandering from his daughter to Matthew as she told it all. At the end, Peter gave a disappointed shake of his head.

"My daughter," he sighed, "if your mother finds out it will crush her – and with Jochum no less." His non-existent chin jutted as well as it could. "That's what you get; you try to be open-minded and see how you are recompensed. My daughter's honour besmirched, her maidenhead lost forever..."

Jenny paled, squirming on her stool.

"Is your son willing to take her as she comes?"

"Aye," Matthew said, "I have the lad with me if you want to ask him."

"Hmm." Peter studied his red-eyed daughter. "Wash your face, daughter, nip some colour into your cheeks, and tell your mother you're engaged to be married to the eldest Graham son."

Jenny rose and rushed to do his bidding. Peter braced his hands against the desk, stood, and gestured for Matthew to follow him to the kitchen.

"So soon?" Elizabeth looked suspiciously at her husband. "Why the hurry?"

"Jenny is twenty-one come September," Peter said in an offhand way. "It's about time she's wed."

"Has he been on her?" Elizabeth took a menacing step in the direction of Ian.

"Really, Elizabeth," Peter said, "do you think Jenny would allow such without a marriage contract under her belt?"

Elizabeth sneaked yet another suspicious look at Ian, glanced at her daughter, looked for a long time at her, her full mouth thinning into a tight gash while Jenny grew successively paler.

With a visible effort Elizabeth turned to smile at Matthew. "And will you have them with you at Graham's Garden?"

"At first." He'd already drawn up some hasty plans but chose not to divulge any details. He wanted to talk to Alex first.

"How's your grandson?" Matthew asked when they prepared to leave, the contracts duly signed and witnessed.

Elizabeth beamed. "A strong, fine boy. So like his father." She glanced in the direction of the chestnut tree, smiling at the baby basket and the young woman sitting beside it. "And she's a good, doting mother." She looked at Ian and then at Matthew. "I dare say there will be grandchildren soon enough in your household too." She winked and sailed off.

"She winked?" Ian said in an undertone.

"Aye, I believe she did...or mayhap it was just a wee spasm."

"Jointure?" Alex looked from the contract to Matthew, who was jiggling David in his arms.

"Aye, it's a provision for her upkeep should he predecease her."

"Oh." Alex looked at the contract again. "Do I have jointure?"

"Didn't you read our contract before signing it?" he said, setting David down on the floor.

Alex flapped the document at him. "If I'm going to be quite honest, no. I couldn't decipher Simon's handwriting."

"You didn't come with much of a portion, and no portion, no jointure."

She handed back the contract with a frown. "But now there's a portion, remember? The money Magnus gave you."

Matthew took her by both arms and gave her a gentle little shake. "There has always been jointure in our contract. I would never leave my wife unprotected." He kissed her on her nose and smiled down at her, and in the slanting afternoon sun his eyes shimmered a golden green. She rose on her toes to kiss his mouth.

"And dastardly Jochum?" Alex asked once she had disengaged her lips from his.

"Unemployed, I fear."

"That won't please his wife."

"Nor would it have pleased her to find him wedded to another."

"Can you imagine the hullabaloo?" Alex snickered at the thought. "Poor Jochum would probably not have escaped with his balls still attached."

"He might still not. Peter Leslie is quite affronted – and rightly so. To lead an innocent girl on like that!"

Alex had serious doubts as to the innocence of Jenny Leslie – the girl was over twenty, for God's sake. To be quite honest, she wasn't too thrilled about this match, but since neither the bridegroom-to-be nor his father seemed to share her concerns, she chose to keep a low profile in the matter.

"...so what do you think?" Matthew said, recalling her to the here and now.

"Hmm?"

Matthew sighed. "You haven't heard a word I've said, have you?"

"I was thinking."

"Ah. Well, there's always a first."

"Matthew!" She whacked him over the head. He laughed and repeated himself, making Alex stare at him.

"Take them to Providence? But Fiona's big as a house! She can give birth any day."

"Oh, I'm sure the prospect of leaving us will serve as enough of an incentive for her to keep her legs firmly closed round that babe."

Alex chuckled at the resulting image: a red, contorted Fiona twisting her thighs shut. Difficult to do on a horse...

"He needs you." Matthew bent to pick up David, who was grizzling, and waited until she was comfortably seated before handing her the child. "That way Ian and Jenny can live in the wee cabin, and Jenny will be as much help in the household as Fiona is, don't you think?"

"Probably more, although that's not saying much." For the last four months, Fiona had shirked as much as she could, complaining about one thing after the other. And because Alex felt sorry for her, she'd let her be, turning a blind eye as Fiona did less and less. "How leave us?"

"Jonah is a cobbler by trade, and he's thinking of setting himself up in Providence – together with Mr Fuller."

"How? With what money?"

"A loan."

"With what surety?" Alex counted in her head; there was not all that much left of the original 500 pounds, even now that it was augmented with what remained in Magnus' pouch, and she had no inclination to spend any of it on Fiona and Jonah.

"Their contracts; if the loan isn't repaid within three years, I have the right to sell them on for five years. If they pay, I tear the contracts up." He gave her a reproving look. "Jonah is an honest man."

"Jonah is a *poor* honest man with a wife and child to support, but I suppose she can find some employment too."

Fiona was predictably thrilled, and for the last week of her life with the Grahams she bounded about with surprising energy, despite her huge belly. She even offered to help with the laundry but that wasn't a risk Alex was prepared to take, so she set Fiona on other lighter tasks instead.

Mrs Parson examined Fiona, pursed her lips at the thought of this heavily pregnant woman on a horse, but shrugged and said she supposed there was no major risk.

"If our Lord Jesus' mother could ride through the Holy Land on a donkey right up to the night of his birth then Fiona will survive as well."

"The difference being that one was a virgin birth," Alex said, "while the other definitely isn't."

After four days of riding – very slowly on account of Fiona – they entered Providence on a surly April day, clouds gusting across a grey sky.

"Will you be alright?" Alex looked at Fiona and Jonah, standing before a narrow three-storey house. Fiona gawked at everything with the wide-eyed fascination of a country bumpkin in a metropolis. Not that three hundred-odd families was much of a city, but Alex supposed that in comparison with Graham's Garden this must seem a seething melting pot of human flesh. Or not, given the modest attire of the women going about their daily errands.

"Well, take care then," Alex went on, but for the response she got she could have been speaking to a doorpost. Fiona was too busy staring at her new surroundings with a dazed expression on her face, her hand held tight by Jonah.

Magnus was enchanted by Providence, exclaiming with pleasure over the narrow streets and the quaint little houses. He perused the few shops, ignored Matthew's warnings and went down to the docks, coming back white-faced after seeing a slaver unloaded.

"And you know the worst of it?" he said, waving his arms around. "It's that the same men who sit in that meetinghouse on Sunday professing respect for God's creation will turn around on the Monday and treat their fellow human beings like dirt!"

Alex nodded. "Did you see Farrell down there? A small, rotund man?"

Magnus shook his head. "No, I couldn't take my eyes off one Dominic Jones, and at one point I was seriously tempted to kick him into the water. I bet he can't swim, and serve him right."

"Stay away from Jones," Matthew said. "He's a dangerous man."

"I do have eyes in my head," Magnus snorted.

One night, Magnus came back to their room very late, so drunk he could barely walk upright and with a huge, satisfied smile on his face.

"I still could," he slurred. "I could still get it up."

"Oh, aye? That is good." Matthew steadied him over to the pallet bed.

"Mrs Malone." Magnus nodded unsteadily. "What a woman, hey? What a woman..."

"And what if he contracts some unsavoury disease?" Alex asked Matthew once he was back in bed with her.

"He's dying anyway, and I'm sure Mrs Malone is in good health."

"Oh, you are, are you? And how would you know, seeing as it's a year since you last set foot in her establishment."

"Not as such. I took your father there tonight."

"What? You took Magnus to a whorehouse?"

"For the beer," Matthew protested. "I didn't think he'd be interested in anything else."

"Huh." Alex narrowed her eyes at him. "I don't want you going there."

"Alex," he groaned, "I go for the beer and the—"

"I don't care! I don't like it, okay?"

"Fine," he said, holding up his hands. But he didn't promise not to go. Alex turned her back on him, shrugged off his exploring hand and pretended to sleep.

Next morning, Alex woke to an empty bed and a vague recollection of being kissed on the cheek by Matthew before he left for his early meeting with the ministers. Magnus was snoring his head off, and it was with an element of relief Alex escaped outside, with David snug as a bug in his carrying shawl. The day was agreeably warm and, armed with a basket, Alex set off to do some serious shopping.

Alex rifled through the buttons; she wanted something special for the new bodice she was sewing, so she took her time, chit-chatting with the other women surrounding the little stall.

"It's not right, the way he's flaunting her," a woman behind Alex muttered. She turned, following the aggrieved looks to see Jones with a young woman definitely not his wife by his side.

"Who's she?" Alex nodded in greeting at a nice-looking woman she thought might be called Esther Hancock.

"That?" Maybe-Esther made a disgusted sound. "That's our own Babylon Whore, Mrs Graham."

"Oh dear," Alex said with attempted agitation. "And

I thought Mrs Malone's was quite enough to bear."

"This is worse," the woman beside Maybe-Esther said. "That woman has him leaving wife and children, running after her like a rutting beast."

"Poor Mrs Jones," Alex said with sincerity. The other women nodded and went back to watching the spectacle of a middle-aged man fawning on a chit of a girl young enough to be his daughter.

"He's set her up in her own household, pays all her expenses," a third woman said, coming to join them.

"He can afford to," yet another voice interjected, and suddenly Alex was standing in the centre of a group of upset women.

"Witchcraft," one of the women hissed, and a murmur of agreement rose from the others.

"Witchcraft?" Alex laughed. "That's not witchcraft. That's a man being ruled by his member, not his head."

"They all are," an unknown woman put in, and they dissolved into laughter.

"...and then they said she was a witch." She finished recounting the incident to Matthew.

"Mayhap she is." He folded together the long letter from Simon.

"Matthew," she said with exasperation, "of course she isn't."

"How would you know?" He was sitting on the bed, this being the single piece of furniture in the small room – except for Magnus' pallet bed and a rickety stool.

"How? I have eyes in my head. She's a pretty girl who knows how to flutter her lashes."

"Are you saying that all witches are old crones?" He leered at her, hunched his back together, and gave her a cross-eyed look.

"No. I'm saying there are no witches – at all."

Matthew relaxed against the headrest, crossed his bare feet at the ankles and gave her a long look.

"Aye, there are – you know that."

"Mercedes wasn't a witch," Alex said through set teeth. "She was a bit strange, but not a witch."

"Of course she was; mayhap not an evil one, but certainly a witch. Those wee paintings of hers...ungodly, aye, brimming with magic." He shivered, arms coming up in a defensive little hug.

Alex sat down beside him. She couldn't argue with him, because he was right: those small swirling squares of greens and blues were nothing but magic, impossible portals through time. She threw him a sidelong look. If she was uncomfortable discussing Mercedes, Matthew preferred to avoid the subject altogether – which was fine with her.

She shifted closer and rested her head against his shoulder. "I can't help who my mother was."

His fingers picked at her hair, pulling loose long locks that he twisted and uncurled repeatedly.

"Without her you wouldn't exist," he finally replied. "And that would have been a huge loss – to me at least."

Alex nodded and snuggled closer, scrubbing her face against the rough weave of his shirt. In her head, she heard Mercedes laugh, a dark, sultry sound, and there she was, brushes in hand, cigarette hanging out of the corner of her mouth, and on the canvas bloomed yet another weird painting.

"Wherever you are, I hope you're at peace," she whispered.

"Hmm?" Matthew said above her.

"Nothing," Alex answered. Mercedes turned to face her, breaking into a radiant smile, and now she was walking through a sea of golden poppy-dotted wheat, her long dark hair streaming behind her. Alex scoffed. She recognised that scene – she'd seen *Gladiator* about a hundred times.

Mercedes laughed. "I liked that ending," she said, and faded away.

Chapter 23

"I hear you knew her."

Alex jumped at the sound of the voice. "I did, and I'm sorry she's dead."

Kate Jones looked at the single daisy Alex had placed on the plain headstone just outside the graveyard walls.

"She was a murderess."

Alex hefted David close. "She was a mother of four, and the man she killed deserved to die."

Kate made a disinterested gesture. "She died well."

"Do you know if the baby was a girl or a boy?" Alex asked as they walked towards the meetinghouse.

"No, but the husband left on the first boat out – alone."

"Alone?" Alex came to a standstill. "But his boys!"

"They're still here, boarded out with good families." Kate adjusted her straw hat, tipping the brim so that it left her whole face in shadow. In dark green, the bodice piped with red braid and a shawl as gaudy as a peacock's tail, Kate looked quite flashy – and rich. "It was for the best. That man had enough problems taking care of himself – he couldn't have raised those boys on his own."

Alex agreed, but in her head she could see a weeping Kristin raging at having her precious boys raised by others than her and their father, and she thought with some disdain that Henry had taken the easy way out.

Their conversation was interrupted by the sudden appearance of a young man, who narrowly avoided barging into Alex.

"Mrs Graham." The man swept off his hat, a lock of long black hair falling forward over his brow.

With an effort, Alex forced a squeak back down her throat. Him! Here!

He smiled, looking quite charming in a rough sort of way – charming and lethal, given the flinty grey of his eyes. He kept on staring, light eyes inspecting her minutely, and Alex was grateful for Kate's presence beside her.

"Mr Burley, is it not?" she succeeded in saying.

He bowed. "I'm flattered that you remember me, Mrs Graham – and may I say just how becoming that shade of green is on you, Mrs Jones." With a little nod he hurried off in the general direction of the slave pens.

"You know him?" Kate said.

"Not really," Alex replied, clearing her throat. "All I know is his name." And that he was an immoral son of a bitch who thought nothing of enslaving Indian women and raping them. "I'm not sure I want to know him."

"No, that is for the best. Not a nice man, Philip Burley, and unfortunately he has three brothers just like him. A sword for hire, a slave trader of sorts, and a friend of Dominic's."

"Oh." Alex's guts griped in warning.

They continued their interrupted walk. Alex wasn't comfortable walking side by side with Kate, but Kate seemed delighted with this new companion and leeched on, strolling along as Alex did her shopping.

"I can hold him for you if you like," she offered, indicating David, who lay fast asleep in the shawl.

"I'm fine." Alex went back to her list: spices, limes, linseed, poppy heads... She heard Kate hiss and turned in time to see Jones' little piece on the side disappear into an opening between two houses opposite.

"Whore!" Kate said. "Curse him for making a spectacle of us both."

Alex wasn't sure as to what the correct reaction to this was: commiserate or pretend she hadn't heard?

Kate was still staring at the spot where the young woman had ducked out of sight. "It isn't that he takes her to bed; God knows I have no problem with lying alone and unmolested at night. It's that he sets her up, flaunts her in front of all his male companions as if saying look at me, still virile enough to satisfy this young, opulent woman. Fool! She laughs behind his back, disparages his performance but allows him to shower her with gifts."

"A sugar daddy," Alex said. "You know, an older man who buys the affection of a younger woman."

Kate gave an abrupt laugh. "Sugar daddy? Yes, that suits."

"So what will you do?"

"Do? There's nothing I can do, is there? He's a man, and his weaknesses must be forgiven him."

Given her tone, Alex concluded that Dominic Jones would receive a glacial welcome should he find his way back to his marital bed.

Kate went on to change the subject, and over the coming half-hour, Alex found herself beginning to like this woman, who was observant and sharp-tongued and knew more or less everything about everybody. She reduced Alex to helpless fits of laughter when she mimicked Mr Farrell in the pulpit on a Sunday, from the way he would smooth his hand over his head to the way his voice squeaked up into the higher registers every time he said *Our Lord* – which apparently was often.

"He stands there and speak of brotherly love, of how God wishes us to help the weak among us, and come Monday he goes back to ousting people from home and land on account of unpaid rents." She wrinkled her nose. "A man given to hypocrisy is Mr Farrell, and ruthless where his property is concerned."

"Including his slaves?"

"Slaves?" For a moment, Kate looked confused. "Oh, the blacks! I suppose he uses them hard. Tobacco is a harsh crop to raise."

"Yes, and you'd know – first-hand."

Kate eyed her cautiously. "No one here knows of my… err…blemished past and I'd like it to remain that way."

Alex supposed it would be difficult to live down in the hoity-toity society of Providence; three years as an indentured servant on a Virginia plantation, years that ended the day Jones took a fancy to her, bedded her and led her off to marry him when her belly began to expand.

Kate shrugged. She rarely thought about it, she said, having banished the memories of those years to a dark corner of her mind. Hard work, casual abuse, and one day she ended up the property of Mr Fairfax, set to work in the tobacco fields.

"I wasn't quite as fresh and pretty as when I first landed," Kate explained wryly. And then Matthew Graham had arrived on the plantation, and long before he'd noticed her, she'd noticed him, how hard he struggled to retain some element of dignity in this new world of his. A beautiful man, she said with a little smile, even damaged and half-starved. Kate sighed, her eyes acquiring a wet sheen.

"He was mine long before he was yours," Alex said with an edge, recalling just how much she should dislike this woman with her thick, golden hair, her dark eyes and a soft mouth that had far too intimate a knowledge of her Matthew.

"Mine?" Kate shook her head. "He was never mine. He never promised me anything, because all he ever talked about was how you would come; soon you'd come and save him." She fell silent and looked off in the direction of the sea. "And you did, didn't you? I stood in the door to the kitchen and saw him stumble towards you, and you picked up your skirts and flew in his direction. It was perhaps the most beautiful thing I've ever seen..." She wiped at her eyes and gave Alex a watery smile. "It was hope running across that dusty yard; hope and love and faith."

This was getting far too emotional. With a rueful gesture at David, Alex explained she had to be getting back to the inn to feed him. Kate nodded and fell into step, offering to carry Alex's overloaded basket. They had to stop, crowded back against a wall, when a slow train of people and horses headed by a team of oxen hitched to a flatbed cart made its way towards the port area.

"Who are they?" Alex stared at the huddled women on the oxcart.

"Refugees," Kate said. "They've been coming for some weeks now from Virginia."

"Refugees?"

"Yes, there's unrest there. A treaty line with the Powhatan has been violated, and the settlers are being pushed by force back across the border. So they come back here from where they once started out, and they have nothing but the clothes on their backs. Some return widows – some don't return at all. There's angry talk among the men, about how it's time the Indians be taught a lesson."

"But if it's their land…"

To Alex's surprise, Kate nodded in agreement. "All of it is theirs; all of it we want to take from them."

"All of it we will take from them," Alex said in an undertone, studying the blank faces of the white women in front of her.

"It was nice talking to you," Kate said as they bade each other farewell. "It's rare to find someone with whom to share your thoughts."

"Likewise. Not that I want to like you, but it seems I do."

Kate laughed. "I can assure you that sentiment is mutual, Alex Graham." She pecked Alex on her cheek and swivelled on her toes, walking off in the direction of the harbour.

Matthew sat back. "It's not our concern."

"No, not for now," Mr Farrell said, "but it might be."

"Why would it? We're not breaking any treaties with our Indians, are we?" Matthew said.

"Commercial interests," Dominic Jones drawled, sitting down to join the group of men. He nodded in greeting to all of them but Matthew. "But maybe you wouldn't understand the concept, Mr Graham, seeing as you don't have any, do you?"

"Aye, I do, but I keep my business transactions above board, Mr Jones. That might be a novel concept for you."

Jones flushed, going an unhealthy pink. "What is it you're insinuating, Mr Graham?"

"You know, Mr Jones, don't you? And however impolite I might seem in saying so, this is a meeting to which you're not invited, so I'd appreciate if you left us to it."

"Really!" Jones glared at them. "I'm a prominent member of this town, am I not?"

"Mayhap," Matthew said, "but we're discussing kirk matters, and you're not an elder."

"I will be," Dominic Jones said.

"I think not," Minister Walker put in. "Not while you're living with that concubine of yours."

"Morals, Jones," Matthew sighed. "Now that is an entirely incomprehensible notion, is it not?"

"You shouldn't goad him like that," Minister Walker chided once a flustered Jones had left them. "It doesn't do to have someone like Mr Jones as your enemy."

"Too late for that, I'm afraid; well over ten years too late."

"What did you mean, about his commercial interests?" Mr Farrell asked.

"Ah, no, Mr Farrell, it would be indiscreet of me to tell."

Once, very many years ago, Matthew had been taken by surprise in a dark alley. It had cost him several years of his life, months of servitude and chains, so now he went canny, an ear out for anything unusual whenever he walked alone through the night. Which was why Dominic Jones' fist crashed into a solid wall instead of Matthew's head, and by the time Jones had stopped cursing and recovered somewhat from the pain of near on crushing his knuckles, he was under violent and relentless attack, Matthew's fists flying through the air to connect with Dominic's head, shoulders, gut.

Jones had brawling skills of his own, and after a few minutes he was giving as good as he got, large, meaty hands connecting painfully with Matthew's body. Matthew hissed when a fist drove into his side, smashed an elbow into Jones' face, and leapt to the side to avoid the responding kick. They were both panting, Matthew mostly with rage while Jones sounded like a drowning man, air rattling up and down his windpipe. All it would take was a knife in that huge stomach and Jones would die in agony, here in the moonlit alley. Matthew pulled his dirk; Jones backed away fumbling for his own weapon. Matthew prepared to pounce.

"Now!" Jones yelled.

Matthew had no time to react. A kick to the back of his

legs made him fall to his knees. Another kick to the small of his back sent him sprawling in the mud, his knife slipping out of his hold. Yet another kick, but Matthew succeeded in grabbing the booted foot, pulled, and sent this new assailant tumbling. Jones; where was Jones? He groped for his dirk. A hand closed on his hair.

"I warned you," Jones wheezed. "I told you not to slander me!" His hold tightened, forcing Matthew's head back.

Where was his blade? There! His fingers closed round the familiar handle. Something sharp nicked his neck. Matthew went for Jones' face with his knife. With a howl, Jones released him, clapping a hand to his eye. Matthew got to his feet. The other man charged; Matthew sidestepped and kneed him in the gut. The man grunted, staggered for a few paces before regaining his balance. He turned, knife in hand. Matthew pulled his sword.

Jones collared his accomplice and dragged him away. Moonlight struck Jones full in the face, revealing a gaping cut that bisected his eyebrow, and a rapidly swelling nose. Blood trickled over his face, dripping onto his collar. Matthew's back was roaring in protest after the savage kick to his lumbar regions but he managed to remain upright until both men had disappeared, after which he slid down to sit against the wall, legs extended before him.

"Matthew?" Alex's voice startled him out of an uncomfortable doze. "Matthew, is that you?"

"Here," he croaked, and there came his wife, lantern aloft and a pistol in her free hand.

She gasped when the light struck his face. "Bloody hell! What happened?" She was on her knees beside him.

"Help me up." He groaned out loud as he slowly straightened up. "I..." he began but she shushed him.

"Inside, then we'll talk."

He recounted the events as she washed his face and helped him out of his clothes.

"Jones?" She dabbed at the shallow cut on his neck.

"Aye, and that misbegotten son of a whore I chased off my land some weeks back – Philip Burley." He winced when she placed a hand on his back, twisting to study the discolouration that flowed up his left side. "How did you know?"

"Mmm?" She was busy with his face, washing his bruised cheek. "Oh, the maid told me she'd seen Jones and another man staggering out of the alley, and when you didn't show..." She hitched an expressive shoulder. "They succeeded in giving you quite a bashing."

"You haven't seen Jones." Matthew glowered at nothing in particular. Damnation! Why did Jones have to resurface here, with Burley as his henchman?

"Why?" Alex asked.

"Umm," Matthew said.

"Why?" Alex insisted.

"We had words," Matthew muttered.

"Oh, you did, did you? I thought we'd agreed you'd stay well away from him."

"It wasn't me; it was him coming to taunt me before the kirk elders." He sank back against the pillows, turning his head in the direction of Magnus' empty pallet. "Magnus?"

"Magnus? He's out partying, taking a fond farewell of Mrs Malone." Alex made a dismissive sound and went back to inspecting Matthew.

"Are you sure you're alright?" She kissed his broken mouth gently.

"Now I am." He snuffed out the headboard candle with his fingers and pulled her close. "Sleep, aye?"

By the time Magnus was capable of uttering more than single-syllable words next morning, they had already left Providence far behind.

"I've found Jacob an apprenticeship," Matthew said. He looked terrible, half his face one huge bruise.

Alex nudged her mount closer. "You have?"

"A lawyer, Mr Hancock."

"The lawyer," Alex corrected. "He's the only one in town." Maybe-Esther's husband was a grave man with far too much hair sticking out from his ears, but on the whole a nice, soft-spoken person with eyes a most unusual and quite attractive light brown colour, like brandy, or whisky.

"Educated at the Inns, no less," Matthew went on with some awe.

"You're supposed to be an obdurate Scot," Alex reminded him with a smile. "Not at all given to being impressed by anything English."

Matthew made an amused sound.

"So why is he here, then?" Not the most obvious of career moves, in her book.

"Mr Hancock is of staunch Puritan leanings, so staunch that his wife is the niece of one of the men who signed the death warrant of Charles that was."

"A regicide." Alex nodded.

"Regicide? Aye, but what manner of a king goes back on his sworn word?"

"One that has his back against the wall?" Alex smothered a smile at the irritated look Matthew threw her. "And Jacob?"

"He's willing to take the lad on as clerk and ensure he gets some hours of schooling each day. I assured him Jacob has a strong clear hand and a good head on his shoulders."

"When?" It came out more breathless than she'd intended, and Matthew gave her a concerned look.

"The lad is nigh on ten; it's time he's set to learn a trade."

"But not yet, not for some years more." Her Jacob; how would he cope without her? Who'd make sure he had clean shirts and darned stockings, that he ate properly and... Her eyes filled with tears that she blinked way. "We need him at Graham's Garden. You said so, didn't you?" And even more now with Jonah gone, no matter that Peter had promised Matthew the loan of one of his hands over the harvest.

"He's owed the opportunity to make his own way, and he's by far the brightest of our lads. He deserves more than to be a farm hand on his brother's farm, don't you think?"

"Yes, but not for some more years."

Matthew smiled down at her. "We've accorded the summer of next year. Do you think you'll be able to let him go then or will you want to keep him tied to your apron strings for longer?"

"Do I have a choice?"

"Nay."

She prodded her horse into a trot and for the coming hour rode some distance ahead of him. She didn't want him to see she was crying.

Jacob didn't say much when Matthew explained what arrangements had been made for him. If anything, his eyes lightened with excitement, an expression replaced by a concerned frown when he understood he'd be living so far away he'd only see them a couple of times a year.

"Will you come to see me?" he asked Matthew later that evening. For once, it was Matthew who was putting his sons to bed, and now he sat on the bed's edge and took Jacob's hand in his own. Daniel was already asleep, his dark hair lying in feathers across the white pillowcase.

"Of course we will, you wee daftie, and you'll be home for harvest and Hogmanay as well."

Jacob shifted closer and rubbed his face against Matthew's shirt. They all did that, his bairns, rubbing their faces affectionately against his chest or his back – just like their mother did.

Matthew lifted the lad to sit on his lap. "You'll do fine, lad. And you've always said how you want to see the world."

"Providence isn't the world," Jacob said. "Mama says it's at most a country town, a place rife with bigots and narrow-minded fools."

Matthew rolled his eyes. "Your mama is at times too outspoken, and some things she says you mustn't repeat."

Jacob laughed softly. "Mrs Leslie didn't like it when Sarah told her Mama said she was an uneducated, meddling woman that kept her dairy shed cleaner than she kept herself."

"Nay," Matthew sighed. "I can imagine she wouldn't like that."

Jacob leaned back against him, eyes blinking. "The world..." he breathed. Matthew laid him back down and pulled up the quilt. Jacob yawned and promptly fell asleep.

Chapter 24

"Ian!" Jenny hissed.

"It's alright," he whispered back. "It's not as if it's wrong, what with us getting married within a week." The hay rustled when he renewed his attack, stretching out to his full length beside her and kissing her. She kissed him back.

When his fingers worked their way under her bodice, she sat up to help him get at the laces and laid back while he explored her breasts; through the thin cloth of her shift at first, his open hands brushing across her nipples until they stood like pebbles against the linen, but soon his hands were on her warm skin and she seemed to like it, her face acquiring a pink hue while her breathing quickened. He slid his hand down her flank, noting that she broke out in goose bumps, a shiver rippling through her.

"Take it all off," he said in a strangled voice and sat back to undress.

"Here?" Jenny looked about the hayloft.

"No one will come."

"I..." Jenny sat up half-dressed. "I've never seen a naked man in daylight before." Ian felt somewhat flustered, but drew the shirt over his head, leaving himself nude to her eyes. He was painfully aware of his cock, rising from its fuzzy nest of hair. She extended a hesitant finger to touch his member and at her touch he experienced a jolt, a spark of live energy that flew up his spine. Her hand on his stomach, and it was as if a red-hot iron pressed into his skin, a delicious but singeing warmth shadowing her hand as it moved from his navel and downwards. His hand came down to stop hers, his breathing loud gulps.

He stood up, helped her up, and her skirts were a puddle around her feet, her shift floated down on top, and still they remained a scant foot or so apart. The hair of her crotch was much darker than on her head. And her breasts…small and topped with pink nipples that he just had to brush his fingers across. She was his; all of this creature standing in front of him was his, and whatever he saw he could touch.

He knelt, guiding her down to lie in the hay. Her thighs spread at his touch, and he slipped his fingers into her private place and looked at her, amazed. So warm…he wiggled his fingers, and her pupils widened and unfocused, her hips shifting towards him. So warm and so wet, her curls damp with her moisture.

His cock was screeching with pent-up need, screaming that it had to, God it had to, and somehow he was inside of her, in so deep he could feel how his balls crushed themselves against her. In his head, it all went red and purple and red again, and then he came, holding on to her as a shipwrecked sailor to a rock.

Ian propped himself up on his elbow and looked down at her, and she gave him a slow smile from behind half-closed eyes. His wife…soon, anyway. His to bed, his to care for. He drew a hand over her soft stomach and wondered how long it would be before she carried his child.

"You must be getting back home," he said.

She nodded but showed no inclination to move from where she was. Instead, she widened her legs in an inviting gesture, stretching herself to show off her neat small breasts. Ian didn't need more encouragement; he rolled back on top of her.

"The foul deed is done," Alex said to Matthew, leaning forward on her wooden spade. He was helping her manure the new beds of her expanding garden, and at her comment lifted his face to where Ian and Jenny were walking through the closest meadow in the general direction of the grazing horses.

"You think?" He came over to stand beside her.

"Definitely; look at how she's walking."

He tilted his head to one side, and in his head flashed

a memory of Alex walking before him up a small hill on a Scottish moor, her gait wide-legged and unsteady after an afternoon spent on her back with him on top. He slipped an arm round her waist and squeezed.

"You don't walk like that anymore," he said with some reproach.

"You don't make love to me like a rutting stag all through an afternoon anymore either, do you?"

"A rutting stag?" He nuzzled her hair. "Would you want me to?"

"This is when I should slap you over the head and tell you you're out fishing for compliments, Mr Graham. But being a dutiful and most loving wife, I'll do this instead." She stood on tiptoe to kiss him before whispering a hot "yes" in his ear.

"Mama?" Ruth's voice rang with uncertainty.

"Yes?" Alex stepped out of Matthew's embrace with a wry shrug. "What is it, honey?"

"It's Offa. I think he's hurting." Ruth pointed up the slope towards the little graveyard.

Magnus was lying on the ground, curled shrimp-like with his hands held hard around his head. The skin around his mouth was numb with the effort of stopping himself from uttering a sound, and he'd squished his eyes shut to keep out the fucking painful light that was setting his damn brain on fire. It was a relief to feel Alex's hands on him, to hear Matthew assure him they were here, both of them, and did he want Matthew to help him inside?

He closed his fingers round his son-in-law's wrist and held on as the fire in his head burnt and raged, huge soaring flames of pain that abruptly flickered and died, leaving his brain sore but functioning.

An hour or so later, the pain had abated.

"This is ridiculous," Magnus groused, looking at Mrs Parson for support. "I don't need to stay in bed; it's just a headache."

"You'll stay in bed for the rest of the day," Alex replied,

214

"and Mrs Parson here has promised to bring you something to drink and to keep you company."

"I hope by drink she meant whisky," Magnus said to Mrs Parson once Alex had left them alone.

"Later, perhaps, but for now it's a good cup of wintergreen and St John's wort tea. It will relieve that remaining headache—"

"I don't have a headache!"

"Oh aye? And is that why you squint at the light from yon window?"

He drank the tea under protest, complaining that it was too hot, too bitter, totally useless, and anyway he didn't need it. Mrs Parson just went on with her knitting. He fell silent and closed his eyes. This had been the worst one yet, and soon there'd be more.

He rolled over on his side and studied Mrs Parson's flying hands. "You're quite good at that."

"Well aye, seeing as I've been doing it for close to sixty years." She inspected the long knitted tube. "Stockings for you. The ones you came with are nothing but holes, and the wool is so poor they can't be darned."

Magnus eyed the dark grey stocking growing from her hands. "I'll probably never get to wear them."

"Aye, you will."

He felt a flash of irritation with her, sitting there and telling him that he'd be around for yet another winter. But instead of saying something rude, he shut his eyes. Click, click, click, click...her needles beat out a steady drumming, and he fell asleep comforted by the sound and her presence.

"Are you better today?" Mark asked next morning, appearing by Magnus' side as he made for the vegetable beds.

"Yes, it was only a headache."

Mark scratched Narcissus on the broad, flat head. "A headache? It looked far worse when Da brought you in yesterday."

Magnus looked at the lanky thirteen-year-old and sighed. "I'm going to die."

Mark's brows pulled into a little frown, hazel eyes

regarding Magnus. "Everyone dies. Naomi's wee brother passed away just after they got here, Rachel died when she was but four, our neighbours back in Scotland died of starvation and exposure… You're lucky in that you'll die of old age, not violent, untimely death."

"I'm not sure that's much of a comfort." Magnus was taken aback by Mark's laconic answer.

"Are you afraid?"

"Of dying? No, I don't think so. Maybe of how I'll die…" His hand closed around his secreted stash of pills. He shook himself free of all these dark thoughts and turned to face his grandson with a smile. "So, what are weddings like over here? Wild parties or sedate affairs?"

"Wild parties," Mark grinned, "and Da is adding casks of beer and whisky just to make sure."

"Do you dance?" Magnus waggled his hips in a stiff demonstration. Mark nodded that they did, but perhaps not quite like that.

"Mama says how you do it differently in Sweden." To Magnus' amusement, Mark began to hum something that sounded very much like a late seventies disco hit while dancing quite competently on the spot.

"Well done!" Magnus said. "But you have to work on the butt shakes."

"Butt shakes?" Mark twisted to study his backside.

Magnus closed his eyes, pretended himself back in a hot, steamy Seville night a year or so before Alex was born, and danced. And there was Mercedes, alluring as ever with her long hair flying as she twirled and laughed, and she was spinning round him, faster and faster, and he could no longer remain upright because the whole world was tilting violently from one side to the other. He sank down on the ground, his chest heaving with a combination of exertion and plain simple fear.

"I'm too old for this," he muttered.

"Just as well. Mrs Leslie wouldn't have been impressed."

"Of course she would," Magnus joked. "She'd be all over me."

Mark looked at him strangely. "Who would want that?"

Alex detoured by the kitchen garden to ensure Magnus was okay, and got a black look in return for her effort as he told her to stop mollycoddling. She scowled back at him and flounced off to check on her chickens and the impressive sixteen piglets.

"All that nice ham," she cooed at the small, black-spotted animals. "Won't that be nice come Christmas?" After giving the sow a long rub behind her ears and commending her on her exemplary motherhood – not one piglet bitten to death – she stepped out into the June sunshine in time to see Ian walk off towards the river and hurried after him.

"Are you nervous?" Alex swept her skirts round her legs and sat down beside Ian. He nodded, his eyes locked on a hawk in the sky.

"I'm not sure. I like her but I'm not certain that I'm in love with her – but I would very much want to be."

"And why are you marrying her if you're not in love with her?" More to the point, why had he made love to her yesterday if he wasn't sure? She stared up at the bird, thinking that there was something very self-sufficient about Jenny. She still had her doubts about this match.

"She came to me when she needed help, and I liked that." He liked a lot more about her, he mumbled: the way her hair whorled over her left temple, how her tongue would peek out of the corner of her mouth when she concentrated, the way her hand felt in his...

Alex laughed and gave him a shove. "It seems you're well on your way there."

He made a non-committal sound and threw himself back to lie in the grass.

"It's not like with you and Da." He turned his head to look at Alex, a hesitant expression on his face. "But you grow into it, don't you?"

"Absolutely," Alex said – well, what could she say? "It's just a matter of nurturing it."

"Aye." Ian closed his eyes.

"How utterly archaic," Alex said to Mrs Parson when they trailed the bride and her female well-wishers from the candlelit barn to the wedding chamber prepared by Elizabeth. Mrs Parson beamed and took a firmer grip of Alex's arm in an attempt to walk as straight as possible.

Alex stood back, pitying her new daughter-in-law as she was undressed, perfumed and led to lie waiting in the bed, her long hair artfully arranged around her. Thank heavens they'd already gotten the sex part out of the way, Alex reflected, watching with some amusement when the bridegroom was led through the door, his shirt already half out of his breeches thanks to the many helping hands that surrounded him.

Alex escaped outside, leaning back against the warm wooden wall. Above her hung a fat full moon, a greenish white against the dark night sky, and a weak breeze caressed the leaves of the closest plane trees into a whispering rustle. She was tired. Spring had been one long hectic stretch of work except for the few days in Providence, and she would far prefer sleeping with Matthew in her own bed tonight than cramming down to sleep with Ruth and Sarah. She sighed and decided no one would miss her if she chose to retire. Besides, David needed to be fed.

"If you want, we can ride back home tonight." Matthew's dark voice startled her.

"What are you? A mind-reader?" Alex yawned widely.

"At times." He came to stand beside her. He smelled of wood smoke, of beer and barbecued pork, but under it all was his own fragrance, warm and salt and startlingly fresh, like that of ice-cold water in a mossy spring.

She sniffed and broke out in a pleased smile. "You still smell like you did when we first met."

"So do you," he concluded once he'd done his own sniffing. "Of tart green apples and fresh split wood and warm milk."

"Warm milk?" Alex unstuck her breasts from her shift – she had to find David soon – and shook her head. "I didn't smell of warm milk when we met."

"Aye, you did; you always smelled like a mother – the mother of my bairns." For some strange reason, that comment made Alex ridiculously happy.

They stood side by side in the night for some time. From the barn spilled light and noise, loud laughter interspersed with the sound of fiddles and stamping feet.

"What is it, lass?" he said, taking her hand.

"I don't know. I'm just tired, I think, and then all of this… Our oldest boy married, our next son already contracted for marriage, and Jacob on the threshold of leaving us. I guess it makes me feel old, to see them begin to grow away from us."

"But you have a wean and two wee daughters and a lad just seven. And you have me, and I'll never grow away from you."

"No," she ran her hand down his smooth, well-shaven cheek, "you won't, will you?

"And then it's Magnus," she went on. "I'm not sure I'm going to be good at nursing him as he gets worse. He goes all snappy and I bite his head off when I should be understanding and supporting."

"He doesn't want you to be mild and meek; he wants you to be as you are, to treat him as you always have."

"You think?"

From the barn came a wild round of applause, and Alex recognised Sarah's high voice, heard her say something and then begin to sing.

"Sarah? Isn't she in bed?" Matthew cocked his head and turned to look at Alex with an expression somewhere between wild amusement and desperation. "What is she singing?"

"Oh my God," Alex groaned, "please don't let this be true." She wheeled and rushed in the direction of the carrying voice.

"You could have stopped her," Alex said to Magnus once he'd stopped laughing.

"I could," he said, and began to laugh again. "Her face, Alex, you should've seen her face!"

"Who? Sarah's?" Alex asked with irritation.

"No, no. She looked the same angel she always does, no matter what dark thoughts might be lurking in her little devious brain, but Elizabeth… For a moment there, I thought she was going to die of an apoplectic attack."

"It's a trifle uncommon," Matthew interjected, looking flustered. "A lass of four singing songs about virgins and fucking…" He shook his head at Alex. "How could you teach her something like that?"

"Me? I didn't teach her that!" After all, she'd only sung it to Ian and Mark – well, perhaps to Jacob as well.

Chapter 25

Agnes inspected the curd, looking quite pleased.

"See how it has begun to crumble, mistress? This will make good cheese."

Alex nipped off a piece. "Doesn't taste much."

"Not yet, but it will. My mam was a good cheese maker, and I learnt the making from her as a wee lass." Agnes patted the two tightly packed wooden moulds and wrapped them in cloth. Alex went back to her churning, bringing the wooden plunger up and down, up and down, in a steady rhythmic movement.

"I can do that." Jenny appeared in the doorway and smiled carefully at Alex.

"Be my guest." Alex let go off the long wooden stave. Her hands were reddened and a long, narrow blister had formed along the heel of her left hand. "Well, two's company, three's a crowd." She smiled at the two girls before leaving the dairy shed with a relieved sigh.

Jenny and she weren't comfortable round one another; the daughter of the house relegated to being a newbie in a world ruled as firmly – but totally differently – by Alex at Graham's Garden as Leslie's Crossing was by Elizabeth.

At times, Alex would catch Jenny staring at her with something like awe in her face; at other times the expression was one of incredulity – like the other day, when Jenny realised that late supper was a meal consisting entirely of vegetables and nothing else. She had eyed the boiled new beets, carrots, potatoes and onions with open disappointment, and had watched with amazement when the Graham children ate platefuls, slathering them with butter and salt.

Thankfully, Jenny and Agnes seemed to get on well,

even if Jenny found it strange to see Agnes included so naturally as a member of the household, eating all her meals with the family and generally treated as a relative rather than the servant she was.

"It would be a bit more difficult at your home," Alex had said when Jenny commented on this. "You're so many, and you have what? Four serving girls?"

"Five," Jenny said with some pride. "And six field hands and five slaves."

"Hmm," Alex replied, non-committal.

"They're blacks," Jenny pointed out.

"Hmm," Alex had repeated, conveying with precision just what a disgusting practice she thought slavery to be.

Alex was feeling cranky. She was tired after several nights of disrupted sleep thanks to David, her back hurt, her hands ached – a consequence of far too many hours in her garden – and, on top of it all, she had a huge pile of unwashed linen to take care of. Not today, she decided, no, today she'd take it easy for once; maybe throw herself on a bed and browse through a book or two, or why not watch something on the telly. She grinned at her own joke and made for the kitchen.

"No, no," Magnus was saying when she stepped over the threshold, "don't put it anywhere near your mouth. It burns like hell." He looked up and smiled at his daughter. "True, right?" He held up a small, circular pepper, the size of a small plum.

"A chilli," she said. "Well done, *Pappa*, you got it to grow!"

"Of course I did, I'm the botanist," Magnus retorted, somewhat puffed with pride. For months he'd been pampering his pepper plant, driving Alex nuts by moving it so that it always stood in the window with the best light, and now the scraggly little plant had five undeveloped fruits, all of them still green, plus the three red ones that now lay in Magnus' palm. "They're not fully ripe, but at least I stopped little Miss Stickyfingers here from popping them in her mouth."

"I'm not a Miss Stickyfingers," Sarah protested.

"Yes, you are," her grandfather said. "I'd told you not to touch it."

Sarah turned cornflower blue eyes to her mother. "They fell off."

"Sure they did," Magnus snorted.

"Go and wash your hands," Alex told her daughter before producing a cutting board and a knife, feeling quite reenergised. "Chicken, I think, and we'll use chillies and garlic, and then we'll have..." She frowned, trying to recall exactly what they had in their bare storing sheds.

"Rice," Magnus said. "You still have some left."

Alex nodded and concentrated on her chopping.

"Hot." She raised wet eyes to her father. "Very, very hot!"

"I told you," he said, uncorking the stone bottle that contained their precious olive oil. "You should be wearing gloves or something. These peppers are among the hottest in the world."

"Too late, and besides, I think it would be difficult to do this with mittens." But he was right; her skin was tingling, and her lips stung from where she'd inadvertently wiped at them with her hand. She transferred the chopped chillies to the mortar, added garlic, salt and a dollop of oil, and picked up her pestle, pounding it all into a fragrant, extremely spicy oil.

They were concentrated on their cooking when the dogs began to bark.

"What now?" Alex jerked so that the chilli oil ran over her hands.

"Alex! Hold still!" Magnus snapped.

"Sorry, sorry," she muttered, squinting out of the window. "Bloody hell!" Without bothering to wash her hands, she strode outside. "What do you want?" she asked, planting herself before the rangy roan.

"Mrs Graham, as always a pleasure," Philip Burley replied, doffing his hat in a courteous gesture.

"Not mutual, and no, don't bother getting off your horse."

Philip ignored her, dropping to land beside his mount. "Is Graham not here?"

"As you can see," Alex replied, made uncomfortable by the way he was staring at her, the children, the buildings – everything. She threw a look at Burley's companion, a middle-aged man that remained on his horse, returned her eyes to Philip, who was now far too close. Alex backed away. "I don't want you here, so please leave."

"I have a letter to deliver," Philip Burley said, "to Mr Graham."

"Then deliver it and be gone." Alex held out her hand. Her cuticles were burning with the chilli, and she had to stop herself from putting her fingers in her mouth to cool them. Philip snickered; took yet another step towards her. This time she stood her ground, staring firmly into eyes that liquefied her guts.

"No dinner?" He handed her a small paper square that she tucked away.

"Nope. I don't feed rapists – or assaulters."

Philip laughed, straightened up and let his eyes travel the household. "Quite a few pretty wenches." He nodded in the direction of Jenny and Agnes. "Maybe we should take them with us," he commented to his companion, who grunted, eyes never leaving Agnes.

"Get out," Alex spat. "Leave or—"

"Or what, Mrs Graham? Your husband and sons aren't here, are they, so what can you do to stop us?" His face was inches from hers, his hand closed on her left arm in a way that had her skin shrinking away. "We could take you along as well."

"You wish!" She clapped her oily, burning hand to his face and smeared his eyes, his nose, his mouth.

At first Burley just stood there, a sneer on his face. And then his eyes began to tear up; he dropped his hold on Alex's arm and staggered back, knuckling at his eyes.

"Aagh! What have you done to me?"

"Chilli pepper. Now go, before I kick you in the balls."

"Burley? Are you alright?" The companion rode his

horse closer, his hand closing on the butt of his pistol.

"He will be," Alex said, "but his eyes will burn like hell for a couple of hours – serve him right!"

"You will pay for this!" Burley scrubbed his sleeve over his face. "I can't see! And my nose, it's on fire!"

"What have you done? Have you hexed him?" the unknown man said, watching Burley stagger towards his horse.

"Don't be ridiculous. I'm a good cook, that's all. Now, get off my land."

As if to reinforce the threat, Magnus appeared at the kitchen door, one of Matthew's cavalry pistols pointing at Burley, who was still cursing as he fumbled with his stirrup leathers.

"What took you so long?" Alex demanded once the two horses had dropped out of sight. She had to sit down, her knees morphing into quivering jelly.

"I couldn't load it. Ruth here had to help me." Magnus gave Alex an admiring look. "You were quite impressive."

"Huh, somehow I don't think that puts me at the top of Philip Burley's Most Favourite People list, do you?"

Matthew listened in silence as Alex retold the events of the day, brows successively forming one dark line of impressive anger.

"The gall of him!" she finished. "To ride in here cool as a cucumber, and more or less threaten to abduct Agnes and Jenny. Who does he think he is?" She gnawed at her lip. "He scares me, and what if he'd decided to take them with him? What could I have done?"

"You stopped him this time," Matthew said.

"Pure luck," she muttered.

"Lass," Matthew said, drawing her close enough that she could rest her head against his chest. "He wouldn't do something like that. He was just trying to intimidate you."

"He did." She rubbed her cheek against the soft weave of his shirt. He put his arms around her, and they stood like that for some time. "What did the letter say?"

"Summons. I have to ride down to Providence for a meeting regarding a militia company."

"Militia?" In Alex's head swam images of men in combat boots and semi-automatics that chose to create enclaves where their word was law. "Why?"

"The Indians; the situation is set to explode, and so—"

"But not here, right?"

"We live under treaty with the Susquehannock." Matthew kissed her brow. "It will be no great matter. Now, where's my supper?"

The following morning, Matthew woke to find himself regarded by two light hazel eyes, copies of his own. On the other side of David, Alex slept on her back, snoring loudly. Her shift was damp with milk, their son was damp all over and, from the way he attacked Matthew's proffered knuckle, very hungry. Matthew hefted him up and padded over to change him.

"He's very well endowed," he commented with a grin once he had Alex sitting up in bed nursing the wean.

"Maybe that's why he eats like a horse." She yawned, blinking at him from sleep-encrusted eyes. "Look what he's done to me," she complained, indicating her swollen breasts.

"Very nice," Matthew replied, eyeing her bosom. He brushed at her free nipple and it stiffened immediately, a wet spot appearing on her shift. With a little chuckle he settled himself beside her, placing his hand on her thigh. Inch by inch, he moved his hand upwards, fingers caressing her warm, soft skin, while he amused himself by telling her what he was planning to do with her once the wean was fed, starting with a thorough inspection of her bosom.

"Matthew!" Alex nodded at their son.

"Dead to the world." Matthew lifted David out of her arms. "And even if he weren't, he doesn't understand, does he?" He placed the wean in his cradle and returned to the bed. "So beautiful," he said, tugging at her hair, her lacings. The shift was discarded, her hair lay unbound, a mass of curls that decorated their pillows. "So pink, so round, so strong," he went on, inspecting in turn her breasts, her arse, her thighs. She reclined against the pillows, fluttered her lashes at him and coyly crossed her legs. "That doesn't work," he laughed, clambering over her to kiss her on the mouth. "We both know you're quite the wanton."

"No, I'm not," she protested, was kissed, and kissed, and kissed. "Well," she murmured, licking her lips, "maybe I am – a little."

"A lot," he whispered in her ear. "And I can prove it to you."

"Really? I don't think so."

"No?"

He began by kissing her ankles. Her knees, her thighs, her pubic mound, her navel, her breasts...

"You're going the wrong way." She laughed when he nuzzled her throat. He kissed her silent. Her tongue darted out to meet his; he bit down ever so gently on her lower lip. His fingers threaded their way through her bush, slid in to touch her moist centre.

"Ah," she groaned, her hips shifting from side to side. "Oh," she added, and her thighs widened, her hands reached for him, but he took hold of her wrists, shaking his head.

"Lie still," he murmured.

"Matthew," she groaned, raising her hips off the bed.

"Lie still, wife." He stilled his fingers.

"Tease," she whispered.

"And I haven't even begun yet," he said, smiling wickedly.

"You sleep," he told her a while later. David was fast asleep in his cradle. Matthew was still in only his shirt, and Alex was a jumble of rosy limbs and wild hair. She made a happy sound and burrowed into their pillows. He covered her with a sheet before leaving the room.

"Except for the few times when I've been ill, maybe four or five times all in all," Alex replied to Magnus' question later. She was still in her shift, despite it being almost noon, and

David was back in her arms to eat. "There's too much to do, and with the children and Matthew to feed, the hens and the pigs to tend, the garden to take care of, well, time just flies..."

"So, in fifteen years five lie-ins." Magnus shook his head. "What a life of drudgery."

"At times." Alex inspected the heel of her stocking; yet another hole to darn. "But now I have a daughter-in-law to help, and Jenny's a competent young woman." As if on cue Jenny appeared at the kitchen door.

"You'd best get dressed, Mother Alex. My parents and my uncle have just ridden in."

"Shit," Alex muttered and handed David to Magnus. "If she sees me like this, Elizabeth will think me even more of a slothful wife than she already does."

They were still outside when Alex joined them, the men speaking in low, hushed voices, with Elizabeth making the odd comment.

"What?" Alex went to stand by her husband.

"Indians, my dear." Peter shook his head so that his fair locks stood in a parody of a lion's mane around him.

"Oh, that," Alex sighed, "all that militia nonsense."

"Nonsense? How nonsense? They're attacking defenceless settlers in the northern part of Virginia as we speak." Peter looked quite upset, with Elizabeth nodding vigorously beside him.

"Not our business, is it?" Alex shrugged. "And the question is why the Indians are attacking."

"Aye," Matthew put in, "one could argue they are but retaliating."

"The Powhatan and the Nanticoke have transgressed against us, and then there was that group of Susquehannock who attempted to abduct those two wives last year." Peter frowned.

"It depends how you see it," Alex said. "Those women might have been married when they were carried off from their Indian village, so maybe last year was an attempt to free them."

Elizabeth snorted. "You can't think that a woman happily

228

married to a Christian man would ever consider returning to a life in longhouses and skins."

"Maybe they were happily married before," Alex said, "and being forcibly converted to Christianity is probably not much of a spiritual experience. More like being raped."

Elizabeth's mouth shrank into a prune, but she didn't reply.

"Whatever the case, we have to defend ourselves," Thomas put in, "and it's better for all if the militia is capably manned. Men like me and Matthew, with experience of warfare, will be able to temper the more hot-headed amongst us."

"Matthew?" Alex shook her head. "He can't go! We... I need him here!" She gripped her husband's hand and swallowed. Him gone? How was she to manage without him?

"One man from each household," Thomas said. "You could send Ian instead," he added, directing himself to Matthew.

"I think not. I will go, but I don't like it, nor do I intend to be gone over the harvest. My fields are ripening as we speak, and I'll start taking in my crops within the fortnight." Matthew gave Alex's hand a little squeeze.

"Of course not," Thomas said. "That's why the meeting is called for next week. We'll be home in time, and then the militia will ride out late autumn – if necessary."

"If necessary," Matthew repeated.

"I don't want you to go," Alex said once the Leslies had left.

"I have no choice, lass."

"But why? We're not the ones having issues with the Indians! Let them who've provoked them sort it. I..." She broke off. Words failed her, and she concentrated on finding her voice again, swallowing a couple of times to rid her throat of its sudden congestion. She hated the idea of being left behind here, all alone with their children. Even worse, how was she to stand it with him gone, not knowing if he'd come back safe and sound? And what if that Burley... No;

she shoved the unfinished thought out of her head.

"It will be fine." He cupped her chin and lifted her face to meet his eyes. "I am no rash, untried youth, Alex. I will take no risks. A few weeks, no more. Surely you can survive without me that long?"

"Barely," she muttered, making him smile. "But I don't want to. I want you here, with me."

"And this is where I want to be: with you." He kissed her on the brow. "Besides, it's not yet, is it? And, who knows, by autumn it may all have died down."

Chapter 26

"I'm taking a walk," Alex said to Magnus. "Now that the baby tyrant is fast asleep for the first time in days, I'm going to take my overworked tits and escape into some solitude, okay?"

"Okay, and should he wake from hunger pangs, I dare say he'll survive until you're back." Magnus smiled down at his grandson, who lay like a frog on his blanket in the shade.

"Will you stay with him?"

"No," Magnus said. "Given my advanced senility, I will amble off and leave him to be eaten by a raccoon or something."

"Raccoons don't eat humans," Alex snorted.

"Something as fat and juicy as this? I wouldn't gamble on it." He laughed at her. "Go on. Look, I'm here and so is our faithful hound, dear Narcissus." The dog raised one silken ear at the sound of his name before subsiding back to sleep, his big head on the bottom corner of the baby blanket.

She felt free; no hollering baby, no constant weight in her arms. She braced her aching back against her hands and, after a quick peek to ensure Jenny wasn't anywhere in sight, lowered herself to the ground to do a set of push-ups. Then she got to her feet and ran into the cover of the trees before any of her other children should discover she had slipped her fetters and was available to them.

It was a normal, humid July day. After half an hour of brisk walk, her chemise clung to her back, and the down on her upper lip was beaded with sweat. God, how she longed for Scotland on days like these! For the crisp dawns of the northern summer, the dry heat of the days, and the long, soft summer evenings. Things she would never again experience, she thought, kicking her way through the high grass of the

231

meadow. Never again would she stand on a Scottish moor and see the flaming pinks of the autumn heather; never would she break off a branch of blooming gorse to set in a stone jar on her kitchen table.

Homesickness draped itself like a wet blanket over her, and she longed violently for Matthew, for his hand round hers. She missed him – had missed him since the moment he rode off two days ago.

"You're being ridiculous," she chided herself. "Get a grip, Alex Lind, before you turn into a needy old cow." It made her laugh, and in a somewhat better mood, she cut in towards the abandoned Indian village. She went there quite often, sitting for some moments in solitude while she thought about Rachel. Just thinking her name made her lost daughter spring alive in her head, untidy braids bouncing round her sturdy little body. And then the horse's hoof came down and crushed the skull to pulp. Oh God; Alex wiped her hand over her eyes.

Alex didn't see him until she had sat down on her normal perch, a fallen log just to the east of the clearing. He was sitting in absolute stillness a bit further on, his eyes locked on what Alex supposed had been the main house of the settlement but that now reminded her of an elongated tomb. She shivered at the thought; after all, to some extent it was.

"I'm sorry." She stood up. "I didn't mean to intrude…"

Qaachow tilted his head to show he'd heard her but otherwise remained where he was.

"You come to think of your daughter," he said, gesturing at the 'RACHEL' she had carved on a nearby tree. "Those thoughts do not intrude on mine."

Alex sat back down again. Not that there was any possibility of her thinking about Rachel now, with this slim, half-naked Indian some yards away, but it would be rude to walk away and disturb his meditation again. He was gaunter than last time she'd seen him, more careworn. He shifted on his perch and the breechcloth rustled, releasing a fragrance of crushed pine needles.

"I sit here at times and remember the life that was.

Before…" His low voice cut through the silence.

"Before we came," she filled in, following the dancing beams of afternoon sunlight that fell in from the west to pattern the ground with eerily lifelike shades of that long gone existence.

"Yes, before John Smith brought the white man over." He looked away through the screen of trees towards the river, barely visible from here. "He came to our village once."

"He did? What was he like?"

"I'm not that old." He smiled. "I never met him in person, but my grandfather did. We should never have let you land," he added in a darker voice. "We should have listened to our wary brethren of the north and pushed you back into the sea."

Alex quietly agreed. Soon nothing would be left of the Indian way of life.

"We still could, we still might."

"Too late," Alex said. "We'll never let this go. Not now."

Qaachow gave her a look of grim amusement. "We could steal in like shadows in the night, and none of you would notice until you lay dying in your blood."

Alex huddled together with physical pain at the thought. "But you won't, will you? You won't kill my babies."

"No, my people will not. We owe you lives."

"Your people? Are there any other Indians we need to worry about?"

Qaachow hitched his shoulders. "This is our land. They will not touch you. But, elsewhere, white women and children will be slain, and their men will be killed slowly and in agony. The coming years will be bad, Mrs Graham, very bad."

Alex nodded and bent to pick up a pine cone from where it lay on the shimmering green of the moss.

"I know. That's why Matthew's been called down to Providence."

Qaachow looked away, saying something in his own language that sounded very sad. For some time he sat sunk in

233

thoughts, eyes lost in the dappled shadow of the surrounding woods.

"I've never thanked you or your husband for what you did for my people, in particular for my wife." Qaachow stood up in one fluid movement. He was an attractive man, Alex reflected, his hairless torso outlined with muscles without becoming too excessive. Long, beautiful hands, and a mouth that, when relaxed, was soft and tender – kissable. Their eyes met. For a couple of heartbeats he held her eyes, the shadow of a smile playing round his mouth.

Alex cleared her throat. "Your wife?"

"Thistledown-in-the-wind; it was her sister that died."

"She's very pretty," Alex said, thinking of the young Indian woman with the thick braids – young enough to be his daughter, but apparently his wife. He seemed to see what she was thinking and smiled crookedly.

"I loved my first wife very much, and it took many moons before I wanted to look at another woman." He stared off into the distance. "Morning Dream – always first in my heart."

"Morning Dream, what a beautiful name."

"As was she." With a courteous nod in her direction, Qaachow blended into the surrounding trees.

"She'll never know," Thomas said, setting yet another mug of frothing ale before Matthew. He smiled at two of the working lasses and elbowed Matthew hard. "See? They're giving you the eye. Pretty girls, both of them."

Matthew had to agree that they were bonny – and frighteningly young. "Nay, I'll sit here and drink my beer and wait for you."

Thomas exhaled. "After riding the same mare for so many years, why not try out a hot new filly? Are you worried you won't be able to perform?"

Matthew ignored the slur and concentrated on his beer. "You go."

He was sitting there, as lost in his own thoughts as it was possible to be in a tavern populated by men with the expectant look of male baboons every time one of the whores smiled at them, when he became aware of someone looking at him. Matthew kept his eyes on the table, peeking through lowered lashes until he saw him, sitting straight across.

Dominic Jones wasn't sitting alone: beside him sat that little strumpet of his, a right bonny woman with hair the colour of a fox pelt in autumn. Just like Luke's hair... As always the thought of his brother made a surge of bile rise through him, even if there were times when the anger was accompanied by a tinge of regret that his brother should be so completely lost to him. Matthew scraped at a blob of wax, refusing to raise his eyes to where Jones sat staring at him.

"Graham." Dominic Jones didn't wait for permission. He just sat down at Matthew's table, ignoring Matthew's instinctive recoil.

"Jones, what business brings you to my table? You prefer skulking in the dark."

To Matthew's surprise Dominic scrubbed his hands over his face and groaned. "I have enemies enough in my life; chief amongst them my sweet wife."

"Aye," Matthew nodded in the direction of the lass who was laughing with a comely lad. "She would be a trifle upset, what with yon lass." And she had the right of it, to be so openly spurned, and she a dutiful and fertile wife and handsome to boot.

"Upset?" Jones spat on the floor. "I fear to return home lest she castrate me." Matthew smiled faintly. Not a major loss, he reflected, sipping at yet another mug of beer that had miraculously appeared before him.

"I wish to make you a deal," Jones said. "Retribution, if you will."

"Retribution?" Matthew echoed. "For what? For your unprovoked ambush last time we met? Or for kicking my dignity out of me all those years ago? For treating me like an animal despite me being a man as good as you are? Or for attempting to have me hanged for a murder you committed?"

"Shh!" Jones glared at him. "For all, I suppose," he said in a surly voice.

Matthew shook his head and pushed back from the table. "You can't give me back what you took, no matter that you pile rubies and pearls on the table before me."

Jones looked at him from under lowered brows, one of which was neatly bisected by a glossy pink scar – a permanent remembrance from their last meeting. The small, light eyes regarded him with a mixture of caution and dislike.

"We're to serve in the same militia company," Jones said, "and I don't want to be constantly looking over my shoulder to ensure you're not aiming your musket at my back."

Matthew eyed the man in front of him and decided then and there to have a long talk with Thomas about the need to have someone always covering his back. In the darker recesses of his mind woke the thought that it would be so very easy; for a man as good a shot as he was, it would be no great matter to permanently rid the world of Dominic Jones.

"Can we then at least agree that while serving together we'll do each other no harm?" Jones asked.

Matthew grinned wolfishly. "If anything befalls me, dear Dominic, you might find it all a wee bit too hot under your feet."

"There's nothing you can prove!"

"Nay, not as such; but a providential date on the will that gave you Fairfax's whole estate and an extensive description of events might make it difficult for you. Gossip sticks like tar, and once it sticks it burns itself into your skin and never, ever washes off." He was enjoying this. Jones squirmed like a fat worm on a hook before getting to his feet.

"I make an uncomfortable enemy."

"So do I," Matthew replied, baring his teeth. He frowned down at the table for some heartbeats before looking at Jones. "But if you give me your word you won't harm me, I'll give you my word I won't harm you – not as long as we serve together."

"My word," Jones nodded, "it's given." He spat in his hand and held it out to Matthew, who after some consideration spat in his own hand and took it. The revulsion that ran through him at Jones' touch made him want to void his guts, and he retook his hand to wipe it against his breeches. Besides, he didn't believe him.

Matthew stared down at his mug, drained it and slammed it down on the table, beckoning to one of the wenches for a refill. Where the hell was Thomas? He nursed yet another mug of beer and another, and suddenly there was a lass sitting beside him, and she was laughing at everything he said. When her hand brushed at his crotch, his cock sprung into beer-sodden life, vociferously demanding to be let out to run a chase or two. Matthew blinked at the girl; she was very bonny, with dark eyes and hair the colour of honey – like Kate.

"Kate," he slurred and the girl nodded.

"Kate," she said.

"Sweet, sweet, Kate," Matthew enunciated, making a huge effort. His cock was being expertly fondled and he heard himself groan. What was he doing? With a huge effort, he slapped her hand away and scooted away, but she came after him and there was her hand again, and it was almost like Alex... Alex! Matthew sobered up so fast he nearly fell off the bench.

"Nay, lass." His tongue was thick in his mouth. She ignored him, no doubt assuming it was but a matter of minutes before he followed her upstairs, and then it would be quick and neat, with her much richer and he rather poorer. Sweetest Lord, but he wanted to! He sat back against the wall, his legs spread as her hand found its way into his breeches. His head was spinning with too much beer, his pulse thundered in his head, and his balls ached with lust.

"Matthew?" Thomas leaned across the table, beaming. "Do you want me to wait for you?" He jerked his head in the direction of the stairs.

"Nay." Matthew batted away the long-fingered hand and got to his feet, trying to order his clothes. His cock protested; it needed to, it screeched, and this lassie definitely knew her business. "For the love of God, Thomas, take me away. I don't want to do this, however much my cock wishes to."

★

Next morning Matthew woke to a throbbing head and an acute sense of self-disgust. Had Thomas not appeared when he did, he would've gone with the pretty little whore and...

"But you didn't." Thomas sounded irritated. "And even if you had, how would it have harmed? Alex would never have known."

"Aye, she would. She would have had it out of me in less than an hour, and then my married life would have morphed into a bed of thorns." Matthew threw a look out of the window and rolled out of his side of the bed. "Kirk?"

"Oh, of course," Thomas agreed and stretched.

It was therefore in a penitent state of mind that Matthew heard Richard Campbell for the first time. Sitting ashamed and hung-over in a pew, he listened as this small man with an unattractively high voice laid out the text around the fall of Sodom and Gomorrah – in Scots. Afterwards, he felt flayed, but somehow much relieved, and he approached the minister for a private discussion that ended with Richard Campbell promising to come home with him. Matthew was elated; a minister in his home – it was going to be like old times, long nights spent in religious debates with Sandy Peden or Minister Crombie.

He was substantially happier when he made his way back to the inn. Judging by his behaviour last night, it was evident he needed to shore up his moral backbone, and now he had found someone to help him with it.

Chapter 27

It was dislike at first sight. Alex looked the small, pompous man up and down before dropping him a swift curtsey and disappearing inside the house, carrying the bundles Matthew had offloaded into her arms.

"Why has he brought wee Richard Campbell with him?" Mrs Parson muttered, shaking her head.

"You know him?" Alex was wondering the exact same thing.

"Not as such. Fiery preacher, I must say, a man that can inspire a crowd to do great things in the name of the Lord."

Magnus glanced at their guest. "Difficult to believe; he looks about as inspiring as a turnip – a very dirty one at that."

"*Pappa!*" Alex laughed. "Shush, the children will hear you." But he was right; Mr Campbell looked as if he and water had a very distant relationship – like once a year at most – and he smelled accordingly.

"David can't talk yet." Magnus hefted his grandson higher into his arms. "And the others are standing in an adoring circle round their father, in case you haven't noticed."

Over the coming days, Richard Campbell was horrified by what he saw in the Graham household: lads well over the age of six still under their mother's tutelage, a wife who spoke her mind, not only to her ageing father and sons, but also to her husband. Even worse, Matthew Graham minded what she said, upholding her authority when necessary. Not that there was much need of that, the sons leaping to do their mother's will with alacrity.

He studied Alex as discreetly as he could, trying to calculate how old she could be. Seven children, and the eldest was nigh on nineteen, so she must be some years shy of forty.

She didn't look it, her carriage erect, her skin a soft, glowing pink except on her uncovered hands and forearms. Eyes of a startling blue, dark hair that was mostly covered, even if now and then a long curl would escape to bob enticingly below the cap – all in all, Alex Graham was an attractive woman, with a high bosom and what even Richard Campbell could recognise as a promising swell to the hips. He noted how Matthew's eyes followed his wife around and sighed; a man enslaved to his bodily needs and a wife who knew how to keep him enthralled. No, this needed to change.

"And what are you studying in the Bible?" Richard asked Daniel, receiving a blank stare in return.

"The Bible? We read from it at times, but mostly it is ciphering and writing, and Mama teaches us about geography and history. I know all the capital cities of the world."

"Capital cities?" Richard shook his head. "But can you name the books of the New Testament?"

Daniel admitted that no, he couldn't – not all of them.

"Can you cite me the ten commandments?" Richard asked, and Daniel assured him that aye, those he knew. "Well, all is not lost then," Richard muttered.

After some days of interrogation, Richard cornered Matthew in the stable and told him he was failing in his responsibilities as a father.

"I am?" Matthew said warily. Richard Campbell as a constant presence was somewhat less enchanting than he had been as a motivating speaker, and he was already having regrets about having brought him home – particularly as Alex left neither Matthew nor Richard in any doubts as to her opinion on the matter, silently supported by both Magnus and Mrs Parson. It irked Matthew to have all three ranged against him, and it gave him a certain amount of satisfaction to insist that Richard stay a bit longer, making a clear point as to who decided what in his family.

"Your lads are sadly lacking in Biblical knowledge," Richard said. "You've left their schooling in the hands of a woman with no understanding of the Holy Book."

"I read to them myself; every Sunday I read a text and discuss it with them."

"And yet they can't name the books of either the Old or the New Testament, they can't name the twelve tribes of Israel, have but a rudimentary knowledge of the Epistles, and have not fully studied Revelations. You've been remiss, Matthew Graham, and your sons will suffer for it."

Matthew's ears were tingling with shame.

"Fortunately, I'm willing to stay for some weeks, and I'll take over their schooling for the length of my stay. If you want, I'll be glad to undertake to do something about your wife's ignorance as well, but that requires she be of a willing disposition."

"My wife isn't ignorant, and I'll not have you talk of her like that. But I'll gladly take up your offer to school my lads."

"I don't want that man teaching my children anything!" Alex said when Matthew informed her of his arrangements with Campbell. "Every time he opens his mouth, in creeps an insinuation that women are somehow deficient to men."

"He will only be here for some weeks, and it won't come amiss to have the lads taught the Bible, will it?"

"The lads? So Ruth and Sarah don't need to be taught? On account of them being too young or too inconsequential?"

"Too young," Matthew lied. He looked at his father-in-law for support. "You agree, Magnus? That it can't do any harm?"

"Hmm," Magnus said, looking anything but encouraging.

"I've asked him to stay August out," Matthew informed them rather coolly. "He'll be tutoring the lads a couple of hours each afternoon, after they've finished with their work for the day."

"Well, thank you for discussing it with me beforehand," Alex said.

"I don't have to," Matthew retorted, stung into anger. "It is I that decide what's best for my children, not you."

"Well done," Magnus murmured to Matthew, clapping him on the shoulder. The room was still reverberating with the crash of the slammed door.

★

It went nasty very quickly after that, a previous silent hostility degenerating into open war with Mark, Jacob and Daniel the contested territory. If Richard decided it was time for Bible class, Alex contrived to be on hand, adding elucidating comments whenever she thought they were needed.

"The Queen of Sheba was a fair-skinned beauty of great renown," said Richard.

"The Queen of Sheba was a beautiful dark woman," Alex scoffed. "She was queen of Ethiopia which is in northern Africa."

Richard scowled at her interruption, his substantial lower jaw jutting out in a way that made him resemble a frog attempting to catch a fly. He cleared his throat and opened his Bible at Psalms. "Today, we will talk about King David, a man of utmost piety and righteousness."

"King David was also a womanizer who didn't think twice about arranging Uriah's death to get his hands on Uriah's wife," Alex reminded her boys. She swallowed back on a cackle of satisfied laughter at the look on Richard's face. Instead, she pretended an interest in her sewing.

When Richard came to find Matthew, he was so upset he near on stuttered. A woman to take it upon herself to correct him, a minister! Matthew sighed inwardly as the wee minister listed one example after the other of how Alex had undermined his authority, and promised to talk to his wife. He found her in the parlour, singing under her breath as she worked. At the sight of him she fell silent, sitting up straight.

"Richard says you are purposely disrupting his teaching."

"On purpose? I happen to be in the room. Surely I should correct him when he gets it wrong."

"He doesn't want you to be present."

"Oh really? So now I'm not allowed to sit in my own front room?" The blue eyes narrowed dangerously, and Matthew found himself with a pile of mending in his lap. "In that case, dear husband, it's best you take over the mending. Or do you want me to repair to the laundry shed to do it?"

"Alex," Matthew sighed, shamed by the look on her face.

"Don't you Alex me!" she spat and stormed off.

After that, Alex avoided the front room, remaining either in the kitchen or retiring early to their bedroom. And the mending lay untouched, with Richard commenting on how sad it was to find a woman idle.

On purpose, Matthew tore a gash in his shirt and came to Alex with the ragged sleeve.

"Will you mend it for me?" he asked, hoping she would see this as the olive branch he meant it to be.

"Ask your pet minister – he has sole access to my parlour these days."

"Only for class."

"Oh, good. In that case please ask him to take his leisure elsewhere. I have no intention of having him disrupt my evenings of calm and quiet with his grating voice and inane braying."

"I can't do that," Matthew said. "He's my guest and must of course be welcome in my home."

She gave him a long look and handed him the shirt. "Mend it yourself. Or have one of the girls do it." She sat down with her back to him to feed their son.

"But Mama says—" Jacob began, only to be interrupted by Richard.

"Your mother has no idea what she's talking about; she's a woman."

"Mama says women are as intelligent as men," Mark put in.

"Foolishness!" Richard Campbell said. "Man is set to rule over woman on account of his intellect and spiritual strength. Women are more prone to be taken over by the devil, seeing as they're weaker souls."

"That's nonsense," Magnus said from where he was sitting by the window. "That's like saying women are more given to evil, and yet, if you look about the world, men seem to be overrepresented when it comes to crimes."

Richard sniffed. This tall Swedish man disconcerted

him, and even more when he turned eyes as blue as his daughter's in his direction.

"We were discussing the exodus from Egypt," he reminded his class of three. "And here we have the truth." He held up his Bible.

Magnus made a derisive sound. "I bet there's no mention of Hatshepsut in there."

"Hatshe who?" Jacob asked.

"A female Pharaoh," Magnus said. "A fantastic ruler, as I hear it."

"Hmph!" Richard straightened up. "One swallow does not a summer make. And, mark my words, had she been a man, she'd have been an even better ruler."

"How would you know?" Magnus said.

"Common sense," Richard said. "A quality men share but women rarely enjoy."

With a snort Magnus left the room.

Richard sat back and unbuttoned his coat, quite pleased with himself. "Now," he said to the Graham lads, "let's get back to the Scriptures."

An uneasy truce settled over the household. Richard seemed content enough with the lads' progress, and from what Matthew could make out the lads were not suffering unduly from their imposed hours with the minister, even if Mark muttered something about not liking it: how Mr Campbell addressed his mother.

Matthew sighed inwardly. Alex remained aloof and distant, minimising her communication with Richard. All in all a good thing, Matthew supposed, but he didn't like it that she treated him the same way, shoulders and mouth set in a constant expression of reproach. At times, he wanted to take her by the arms and shake her, telling her that he was doing this for their lads, for their immortal souls.

"A pretty lass," Richard said, pointing at Ruth, who was out in the yard playing with her brothers in the summer twilight.

"Aye." Matthew threw a look at his wife, sitting as far

away from him as she could. "Like her mother." He'd hoped for a smile, but was disappointed, Alex keeping her eyes on the bread she was slicing.

"Umm," Richard said. "A bit wayward; should a lass really be allowed to run that wild? She's old enough to spin and knit. As I recall, my own sisters went about with their spindles from their fifth year or so."

"She helps enough as it is," Alex said. "She's not yet six."

"She must be taught to be a good helpmeet," Richard continued, ignoring Alex. "She should be knitting stockings for her brothers, learning to serve them first."

Matthew looked at his lass, not quite sure he agreed with the minister.

"Not in my home; in my home we treat our children as equals. We do, don't we?" Alex challenged, glaring at Matthew.

"Of course we do," he said.

"Except, of course, that our boys have to put up with him." Alex made a contemptuous gesture in the direction of Richard.

"Alex!" Matthew said.

"Luckily, there will be time afterwards to correct all the nonsense he's trying to fill their heads with. After all, I don't suppose you plan on having him here forever, do you?"

Matthew compressed his mouth, giving her a warning look.

"Well, do you?" she demanded. "Because if you do, please let me know so that I can start making arrangements to go elsewhere – with my children." She banged the door on her way out.

"A cross," Richard sighed, "a cross to bear."

In reply Matthew flung himself out of the kitchen, hot on Alex's heels.

"How dare you?" He towered over her, near on stuttering with rage.

"How dare I? How dare you! With what right do you force that idiot of a man on us all?"

"He's a minister." Matthew swallowed in an effort to

keep his voice controlled. "He's here to teach our sons the things we can't teach them."

"Which adds up to the impressive sum of zero, *nada*. And on top of that, you expect me to feed him, I'm forbidden access to parts of my home, and my boys..." She gave him a bright look, eyes wet with unshed tears. "I want him to leave; now."

"We have accorded until the end of August. That's four more weeks."

Alex studied him in silence. "I see, your pride must come first, right?" Her tone cut him, even more because she was right.

"August, Alex. That's what we decided."

"That's what you decided." She turned to walk off; he blocked her.

"You're making this more difficult than it has to be." He brushed at a lock of escaped hair.

She reared back from his touch. "I am? I don't think so, Mr Graham. I didn't bring him here, did I? And now, if you'll excuse me..." She dropped him an ironic curtsey. "...I'm going for a swim."

"Do you want me to come with you?" he asked, trying out a smile.

"No way," she said. "Whatever for?"

Over the coming week, Alex more or less stopped speaking to Matthew – she was so pissed off with him she preferred not to. And he, typical man that he was, pretended things were just like normal, even if he was smart enough not to try cuddling her. He probably realised he risked being kneed in the balls if he did, given her present mood. So they went to bed together – in silence – they rose in the morning – in silence. Well, except for the more basic communication along the lines that were there any clean stockings, or was Sarah's scraped knee healing as it should. And all day long that enervating, brain-dead excuse of a man hovered around her children and her man, a self-satisfied simper on his lips. Worst of all were the mealtimes, dinner conversation shrinking to

Richard Campbell's long, haranguing monologues.

"But that's how it is," Richard stated. "No matter how hard she tries, a woman remains a simple, immoral creature, ruled by her lusty nature, not by sense."

Okay, that was it, she'd had it; not one more night listening to his misogynist crap.

"What?" Alex said.

"Oh, yes, Mrs Graham, that's how things are ordered. Even a male child has more intellectual capacity than a grown woman, which is why, of course, it is so important that boys be schooled by men, not by their deficient—"

"Take that back!" Alex glared at Richard across the table. "Don't sit in my kitchen and tell my sons that their mother is a simple creature on account of her sex!"

Richard gave her a bland smile. "It's the truth. Eve was made a helpmeet to Adam, a weaker vessel that relies entirely on her husband for guidance and protection. Women lack the cerebral power of men."

"Bollocks," Alex said. "And I must say that for a man that professes such great insight into the mysteries of life you're woefully ignorant."

"Ignorant?" Richard cleared his throat. "And you'd know better? I think not, Mrs Graham. Loud you may be, opinionated too, but your understanding of intellectual matters is at best limited, at worst non-existent."

"Oh, shut up! I know more than you do about everything – anything – but the Bible. And even there I'd argue that while you know huge chunks of the Bible by rote, you've totally missed out on the underlying message." She stopped to fill her lungs with air, throwing an angry look in the direction of her silent men. Why the fuck didn't Matthew or Magnus agree with her? How could Matthew allow this toad of a man to say these things? Richard opened his mouth but Alex raised her voice. "But of course you have; you lack context because you have no understanding of history or geography, and you scoff at any ideas that don't fall exactly within your limited understanding – extremely limited, if you ask me."

"Alex," Matthew interrupted, "that's enough. You'll not insult the minister further."

"Insult him?" To her irritation, her voice wobbled. "And what about when he insulted me just now? Why don't you berate him for calling me a foolish, opinionated woman?" She slammed the pitcher of beer down so hard the earthenware cracked, leaking beer down the sides to puddle on the table. "So seeing as you won't defend me, I'll do it myself, okay? In my opinion, Richard Campbell, you're nothing but an uneducated charlatan with your head so far up your own conceited arse all of you smells of the shit you spout."

There; that shut him up. In fact, it shut all of them up. Matthew was looking at her as if he dearly wanted her to go up in smoke; Magnus was biting down on his lip, eyes glittering with laughter; and Richard, well, he'd forgotten how to close his mouth. Alex decided it might be wise to take a little time out and went to check on the soup.

For a couple of seconds, the silence was absolute. There were none of the normal sounds a dozen people would make while seated at a table. Instead, it seemed to Matthew that his household had turned into pillars of salt. And then Sarah sneezed, Jacob shifted on his rump, and life returned. Breathing was resumed, feet scuffed at the floor. Spoons were raised, bread was torn off in chunks, as his family continued with their meal. But Richard remained immobile, arms folded over his chest while he stared demandingly at Matthew.

"Apologise," Matthew said. Goddamn the woman! Aye, Richard had been out of line, but how could she do this to him, humiliate him in front of a minister, showing him to be a man that had no control over his own wife?

Alex ignored him, busy stirring the pot. The kitchen filled with the rich scent of chicken soup, complete with sage and garlic.

"Alex," Matthew injected his voice with ice, "you'll apologise to Richard. Now."

"Matthew..." Magnus said in a warning tone.

Alex turned to face the table. "No, I won't. He's a despicable narrow-minded little worm, and if anyone should apologise to anyone it should be he to me."

"He's a guest in our home, and you've insulted him." Matthew was all too aware of their silent audience, his sons, his lasses, all looking at him with huge eyes.

"Not my guest, remember?" Alex shrugged, ladling up the soup.

"You must curb that wilful tongue, brother," Richard said. "A wife to speak to her husband like that...sometimes the only thing that helps is the belt."

Alex wheeled and swung at him with the ladle. "Get out! Get out of my kitchen!"

"Alex!" Matthew roared, leaping to his feet. He grabbed her, ignoring her angry struggles as he carried her to their room and set her down inside.

"You must apologise."

"Go fuck yourself," she spat, face red with anger.

He walked out of the room and slammed the door behind him. He heard her shoot the bolt into place.

An hour later, Alex unbolted the door, stalked out to the kitchen, heaved a bawling David from Ian's arms, and without a further word returned to her bedroom. She had a writhing snake pit inside of her. Never had they argued like this, and had she had Richard bloody Campbell in front of her, she would have been tempted to kick his teeth in. Her stomach growled with hunger and anger, but with an effort she emptied her head of anything but the image of her baby boy, his wide eyes smiling up at her as he fed.

She sat for a long time with him in her arms, hearing how the house went to rest as the summer sky shifted to the dark of an August night outside her window. Finally, she placed David in his cradle and tiptoed out into the kitchen for something to eat, only to find Matthew waiting for her with Richard beside him.

"Apologise to the minister," Matthew said. In that moment she hated him. How could he betray her like this?

"No." She blinked back tears she had no intention of spilling — at least not in front of them. "Not unless he apologises to me."

Richard coughed. "You must go first. You've insulted a man of God."

"A man of God?" Alex laughed hoarsely. "What a joke... an insufferable bigot, that's what you are."

"Alex," Matthew sighed.

"What would you have me do?" Alex swung back to Matthew. "Prostrate myself and abjectly beg for forgiveness?"

"You'll apologise for the name-calling and for swinging at him with the ladle."

"Or what? I don't get to eat in my own kitchen?" She was getting angry again, regretting she hadn't whacked Matthew over the head with the ladle instead.

"Apologise, Alex." His voice was cold.

She took a big breath, turned towards Richard and curtsied deeply.

"My apologies," she said with no attempt at sincerity. "Happy now?" she asked her husband.

"Aye." He tried to catch her eyes, but she wasn't having it.

"Well, that's good. At least one of us is." She turned on her heel and made for her bedroom, closing the door in his face.

Chapter 28

On the surface, things were back to normal next day, with Alex her usual capable self around the children. She set Jenny and Agnes to do the laundry, busied herself with her preserves, and had Ruth sit on the kitchen table and go through all the multiplication tables. She joked with her boys, sang to David while she nursed him, and served the household both dinner and supper. But some things were different: she chose not to eat with them, and she avoided any kind of contact with Matthew. Richard she treated as if he didn't exist, staring straight through him with a vague smile on her face.

"You're making too much of it," Mrs Parson said, serving Alex a huge slice of honey cake.

"You think?" Alex shook her head. "He humiliated me, in my own home."

"Ignore him, aye? He'll soon be gone."

"I'm not talking about Richard Campbell; I'm talking about Matthew." She traced a complicated pattern on the table top, a large loopy M. A warm, wrinkled hand came down on hers, giving it a little shake.

"Talk to him, lass."

"I can't." She was tongue-tied with anger, a huge lump of hurt lying across her vocal chords whenever she saw him.

The boys didn't know what to do. Intensely loyal to their mother, they became belligerent and downright rude to Richard, slyly commenting on things he so obviously had no idea about. After a particularly embarrassing situation in which Daniel made it clear he didn't believe one word of what Richard had to say about the heathen Indians, Richard decided there was nothing to it but to administer a beating. Daniel shrieked like a gutted pig when Richard forced him

251

down over the table, and suddenly Mr Campbell was flying across the room to land hard against the wall.

"If you touch any of my boys again, I will flay you," Alex told him, eyes boring into him. "You have their father's permission to teach them, but I, their mother, forbid you to touch them."

Once again, Matthew came to berate her, demanding what she was thinking, to so discourteously throw his guest against the wall. Alex stared straight through him, giving no sign of hearing one single word.

"I'm talking to you!" Matthew snapped.

Eloquently, she raised first one then the other shoulder. For a moment her eyes met his, and Matthew's stomach shrivelled at the absolute hurt in that blue gaze. He opened his mouth to say something, anything, to make things better, but he never got the chance. Without a word, Alex left the room.

Matthew had no idea what to do. His wife evaded him, fleeing at his approach. So he concentrated on the remaining harvest work instead, escaping out to the fields early in the morning, returning weary to the bone in the evenings. Not once did she touch him or suggest he should take a bath or in any way indicate she cared one whit for his comfort apart from setting food on the table in front of him. She never spoke to him, her eyes blank the few times he managed to catch them with his own. He hated the silence that grew between them, but he was waiting for her to do something, because he didn't know how to break through the walls of impenetrable ice she was putting up around herself.

Every attempted conversation was stonewalled. When he reached for her brush to help her with her hair, she stood and left the room, returning only when she assumed he was asleep. Once he reached out to touch her, hoping that by loving her he'd somehow repair this breach, but she lay as stiff and unmoving as a corpse beneath his hand, her face turned to the wall until he gave up and rolled to face the other way. But the night he lay coughing because of all the dust in his lungs, she stood up and went out in the kitchen to return with a mug of raspberry cordial which she handed to him without meeting his eyes or saying a word.

All through this time, Richard walked beside him, an ongoing whispered sermon as to the importance of casting away everything that was not to God's liking, and surely a wife as wilful as Mrs Graham had to be taught to obey. What had he ever seen in this man to make him quarrel so devastatingly with Alex over him? Matthew wanted to take the minister by the scruff of his neck and shake him into silence, because somehow it was his fault that his wife no longer spoke to him, sprang away at his touch and never looked at him.

After a week of this torture, Matthew had had enough. "You must leave," he said to Richard.

"Leave?" The wee man straightened up to his full height and filled his lungs with air to protest.

"You heard." Matthew crossed his arms over his chest.

"But...your lads, your sons! They have need of me, of the schooling I can give them."

"We'll manage." From what he'd overheard yesterday, Alex was correct: Richard Campbell might be well schooled in the Bible, but on any other subject he was most ignorant.

Matthew twisted inside. What had he done, bringing this man back to his family? And all because of a tender conscience on account of that soft, fondling hand and his all too willing cock.

"I can't go on living in discord with my wife," he said, irritated for feeling he owed the man an explanation. "And you're the cause of a rift I must attempt to heal."

"I am?" Richard stuttered. "You mean she is! A wilful, temperamental woman that is lacking in discipline and respect for her betters."

Matthew eyed him with a sudden flaring dislike. "Alex is my dearly beloved wife, and you'd best remember that." He nodded in the direction of Ian, who came over to them leading a saddled horse. "My son will take you to the Leslies or see you some way down the road to Providence if you prefer."

"Now?"

"Now." Matthew nodded, wanting him off his property as soon as possible.

"Matthew has sent Richard away," Magnus told Alex, lifting a gurgling David out of his basket to set him in his lap. Alex shrugged and continued with her work, her hands flying as she reaped redcurrants.

"That's good, right?" Magnus wiped his finger clean before offering it to David to chew on. "Shit! You're right, he is teething."

"Tell me about it," Alex said with her back to him.

"So will you start talking to Matthew again?" The present atmosphere in the household had the consistency of cheese curd, thick enough to slice with a knife.

"Do you think I should?" She sounded disinterested.

"It would help. It's not much fun being around you at present."

"Right now it's not much fun being me," she said, "but if he thinks sending Richard away is all he has to do to have me mellow on him he has another think coming. Had he done it that same night it might have been enough, but now it's just too little, too late. Maybe you should tell him that."

"Me?" Magnus shook his head. "Oh no, Alex, you're old enough to sort out your own marital issues. I won't be your go-between." He placed a hand on her arm. "You're being childish."

"I can't help it," she whispered, and he could hear how close she was to crying. "I'm so mad at him, and..." She closed her mouth and ducked her head. Magnus sat waiting, but apparently Alex had nothing more to say.

As the days progressed without any change in her attitude towards him, Matthew came to understand that he was being punished, that Alex was making him pay for the humiliation he'd put her through. One part of him recognised that she had the right of it, while the other raged at her for doing this to them, and so they drifted further and further away from each other until the day Matthew came into the stable to find her sitting staring into space, the cat purring in her lap.

"What are you doing?" he asked, noting with a twinge to his heart how tired she looked. And today was her birthday, and he wanted to... He sighed, not sure now was a good time to give her the little carving he'd made her.

"Avoiding you." She tumbled the cat to the floor when she got to her feet. "Although that didn't work very well, did it?" She moved over to the door but he blocked her way, and just like that he kissed her. He had thought she might perhaps slap him, or not kiss him back, and he was pleasantly surprised to discover she was warm and pliant in his arms, pressing herself as urgently against him as he to her – at least initially.

"No." Alex twisted out of his hold, scrubbing the back of her hand across her mouth in a gesture that cut him to the quick.

"No?" Matthew gripped her arm. He was panting with arousal and didn't understand. Only moments ago she'd been like a bitch in heat in his embrace.

"You heard me, I don't want you to touch me – or kiss me. It disgusts me."

He looked at her for a long time before releasing her, sending her staggering backwards. He swivelled on his toes and walked off, all of him vibrating with hurt.

Alex straightened her bodice, eyes on his retreating back for as long as she could see him. Maybe she should... No, no way. He was the one who owed her an apology, not the other way round.

She didn't see him all morning and, when he wasn't back for dinner, Alex began to get nervous.

"Oh God, what am I doing?" she said to Mrs Parson. "How can I risk my marriage because of an overheated verbal exchange with that turd of a minister?"

"Aye, I told you so, no? This has gone on for far too long. It's time to swallow that pride of yours, Alex Graham."

"My pride? What about his pride? This is his fault and—"

Mrs Parson held up a hand. "He's a man. He is entitled to his pride." Her face softened into a little smile. "They need it so much more than we do."

Alex wasn't sure she agreed with her, but their conversation was interrupted by Mark and Jacob coming in from the fields with a tired Daniel trailing them. None of them had seen Matthew.

"He said he'd come up after us." Mark poured himself some barley water. "He never did."

Ian returned from where he'd been working, and he hadn't seen his father either. Nor had Magnus, even though he did think he'd seen Matthew earlier, somewhere in the general direction of the river.

"Stupid man," she said in an attempt to be mad at him as she jogged towards the woods. "Run off and sulk." She tightened her shawl and plunged in among the trees, heading in the direction of the river. "And what if you've broken your leg or something," she went on with her little rant, her heart catching at the thought of Matthew physically hurt in the woods. She increased her pace, convinced that he had stumbled over a stone to break his neck, or been bitten by a rattlesnake to die in agony, and all because of her and her need to wound him back for listening to bloody Campbell over her.

Her breathing was coming in loud, uneven gasps by the time she reached the water. He wasn't there, and Alex gyrated for a while before setting off again, this time deeper into the forest. If he wasn't here, there was only one place he could go, she told herself, and now she was running in her haste.

Her shoulders sank together with relief when she saw him. He was sitting with his back to her, just on the edge of the abandoned Indian village. If he heard her, he gave no sign of it, remaining very still with his head bowed. In the late August sun, his dark hair showed glints of chestnut, and Alex was overwhelmed by a wave of tenderness for this man that meant everything and more to her. She took the last few steps towards him and put a hand on his head, trailing her fingers through his hair.

He made a strangled sound at her touch. "I was wrong. I shouldn't have done as I did."

"No, you shouldn't." Alex stepped over the fallen log and kneeled down to see his face.

He shoved his hair out of the way and locked eyes with her. "Will you forgive me for not defending you as I should have done?"

She cleared her throat repeatedly to say something and finally gave up, nodding instead.

His stance relaxed and he raised his hand to rest the back of his fingers against her cheek. "Do you recollect once, very many years ago, when you told me I was all you had?"

Of course she did; a dark night in Scotland when she'd pleaded with him to put her and her children first – before his religious convictions.

"It's the same for me. You're all I have, Alex. All I want and all I need, and when you choose to close me out as you've been doing these last few weeks, you leave me standing very alone in a cold and unwelcoming world." He rested his forehead against hers. "I don't like it out there on my own."

"Nor do I." She cupped his head in her hands and kissed him, allowing him to pull her close.

It was needy and urgent, uncomfortably damp and very fast, with Alex tumbled on her back and Matthew already deep inside of her. He was rough, and so was she, sinking nails into the flesh of his lower back. He bit her, he kissed her, he slipped in a hand below her and lifted her closer and then he came, while still inside of her. Alex stiffened and opened her eyes to his, so close and so green. There was a silent challenge in them, a reminder that she was his wife and she shouldn't forget that – ever again.

"Happy birthday," Matthew said with a crooked smile as they made their way back home. He stretched out a hand to clasp her elbow when she nearly overbalanced on one of the mossy stones.

"Thanks." Between her legs she could feel his stickiness, and all she really wanted to do was to ask him to love her

257

again, but her breasts were beginning to ache and she knew David needed her, so she lengthened her stride and took his hand.

That night, he loved her again, and next morning, and next night… And every time he came inside of her, always with that bright green sheen in his eyes, and Alex was torn between the fear of conceiving again and the burning hunger he woke in her. Oh, what the hell, she thought and succumbed to his touch and his will, leaving it all up to fate. Because it was so wonderful, and he was so gentle, and his mouth made her gasp and beg him to please…and he did, impaling her with slow, forceful movements that made her wriggle and twist with desire.

"I think I'm pregnant," she told him some weeks later in passing.

"Good." He kissed her on the cheek before going back to his work.

"Good?" Alex shook her head. "I'm not sure it's good."

"But I am, and it's good for our wee laddie, to have a brother or sister close in age."

"Extremely close," Alex muttered.

Matthew let his hand rest for an instant on her belly. "A lass." He smiled. "It will be a lass."

Alex didn't reply. For the first time the thought of yet another child filled her with far more apprehension than joy.

Chapter 29

"Another one?" Magnus sounded disgusted. "But David's just seven months old!"

"And you think I don't know?"

"So what does he think you are? A cow?"

"What a bloody insulting thing to say!" Alex exploded. "As I said, it isn't always easy to avoid."

But, of course, in this specific case there'd been no question of attempting to avoid it. Matthew had set out to make her pregnant and she had silently acquiesced without really knowing why. That was a lie. She knew exactly why: because the loving had been spectacular, a reconfirmation that it was she and Matthew against the world – and because he'd demanded her submission.

"And, as I said, use your brain a bit more. And if he doesn't know how, let him come to me and I'll explain the basic principles behind pulling out in time."

"Magnus!" Alex began to laugh, overwhelmed by a far too graphic image of Magnus demonstrating how to do it and when.

Mrs Parson expressed her congratulations, saying that Alex would no doubt have it easy this time as well.

"As will she," she added, nodding in the direction of Jenny.

"She's pregnant too?"

"Och aye, anyone with half a brain can see it, no?"

"Thanks very much," Alex huffed, even more irritated when Matthew shrugged at this news, telling her he'd suspected Jenny was breeding for some weeks now. He laughed at her and led her off to sit on the bench under the white oak.

This was by far Matthew's favourite place, and he settled

back against the gnarly stem of the tree, pride bubbling through him as he regarded his home. Neat and well ordered, his homestead was still nowhere close to what he wanted it to be, but these last few years had seen a lot of progress, and next year he'd clear some of the woods separating the house from the river proper. He wanted meadows and cows, some more fields of wheat and... He sighed; so much work left to do.

"What?" Alex reclined against him, resting her head on his shoulder.

"Nowt." He extended his legs and crossed them at the ankles. The expansion plans would have to wait until spring. A warm hand slipped in under his shirt to rest above his heart, teasing fingers tugging at his chest hair.

"Love you," she murmured.

"And I you." He draped his arm round her shoulders in a hard but brief one-armed hug.

"We haven't even spoken about your visit to Providence," she said some minutes later. "And the bundles you brought back still lie unpacked in a corner of our room."

Matthew looked at her in surprise. "You didn't unpack?"

"Let's just say I didn't feel like it."

"But the letters!" Matthew sprang up from the bench. "I forgot, aye?"

There were a lot of other things in the bundles: ribbons for the girls, a bone rattle for David, and a book that Matthew handed over with a flourish to Magnus.

"I thought it might be of interest," he said with a grin.

"*Gustavus Adolphus, the scourge from the North.*" Magnus turned the book over and over. "There's no author."

"Aye, there is," Matthew said. "It is just that he chooses not to give his name."

"From the initial paragraph, I can glean he isn't a Swede," Magnus said some minutes later.

"You only needed to look at the cover to understand that," Alex said. "The king looks as if he's eating a baby."

"He is," Matthew said after studying the engraving. "You do that a lot in Sweden?"

"Do you do what in Sweden?" Jacob asked, coming over

to where his Offa was sitting with a new book in his hands.

"Eat babies," Alex replied in a distracted voice, holding several letters.

"You do?" Jacob sounded aghast.

"Of course not, not unless the winter is uncommonly long and cold." Magnus grinned and led his grandson off to study his new treasure together with him.

"Why is there a letter for me?" Alex said.

"Because someone wrote you one?" Matthew teased. "An ardent admirer, perhaps?"

"An unknown admirer," Alex muttered. "I don't recognise the handwriting." Neither did Matthew, so he suggested she turn it over to study the seal.

Matthew frowned at the bold L and G that decorated the blob of wax. "It's from Luke."

"From Luke? Why would he..." She broke the seal and unfolded the crackling, thick paper. A wrinkle formed between her brows as she read the letter, and well before she was done, Matthew knew the news was bad. He could see it in how her shoulders curved, in how she gnawed her lip. She held it out to him, wordless. Matthew took the letter from her, had to read it twice to take it in. Margaret dead! Not yet forty and now gone, leaving four bairns and a devastated husband.

Matthew was stunned; all that life, all that astounding beauty, snuffed out by fickle fate. It wasn't fair, not on her or on Luke – no matter how big a bastard his brother was – and definitely not on the bairns, left motherless before they got the chance to know her.

"Why did he write to me?" Alex said. "Why not to Ian? Or you?"

"To me? Nay, he would never write to me. Mayhap he thought it best to tell you so that you could tell Ian, soften the blow, like." Matthew threw himself backwards onto the bed and raised his hand to trace her spine through her clothes. What would he do if she died and left him alone to cope with life? The thought filled him with a dull numbness that settled across his chest, snaked into the pit of his stomach, and made his throat itch. "I'll write him."

Alex turned to look at him. "You will? You've not exchanged a civil word with him since the day you found them in bed."

"That was eighteen years ago. It would seem time to let it all go."

Alex made a vague, distracted sound, her eyes on the door. "We have to tell Ian."

"Aye," he sighed.

"Shall I…"

"Nay, lass, this is something I must do. But I'd not mind you being there."

It was a terrible thing to do. Matthew cleared his throat, took a deep breath and… Yet another deep breath, and as gently as he could, Matthew told Ian his mother was dead. Not a word did the lad utter, he just sat there, and when Matthew was done, he extended his hand for the letter, making it very clear he considered it his full right to read it.

He just held it at first, and Matthew was certain he was playing one of those foolish games where you hope that as long as you haven't read or seen something for yourself it isn't true. Finally, Ian dropped his eyes to the brownish ink and, when he was done, folded the letter together.

"I…" Ian stood up. He looked at Matthew for a long time before leaving the room.

"Oh dear," Alex said. "Maybe I should go after him."

"Not yet, leave him be for now. I'll go and find him later." Matthew got to his feet and straightened up. "And you and I have work to do."

"Always." Alex grabbed a basket. "Agnes! Come on then, girl. We have a whole vegetable garden to get into the root cellar."

"Mama?" Daniel dug his toe into the turned earth and leaned forward on his hoe.

"Mmm?" Alex looked up fleetingly before going back to filling her basket with potatoes and beets.

"Will I be like him, Mr Campbell, when I grow up?"

Alex was so surprised she dropped the potatoes she was holding. "Richard Campbell? Why would you think that?"

Daniel twisted a bit. "He's a minister."

"Most ministers are nice people, and I'm sure you'll turn out one of them." She picked up the dropped potatoes and brushed them off before putting them in with the others. "Do you think a lot about it? Being a minister and all that?"

"Sometimes. But it's years before I have to go to school."

"Of course." Alex smiled. "After all, you're only seven."

He came over to where she was kneeling, and she wrapped her arms around him and held him until he began to squirm.

"Da says how he and I will begin reading the Bible together," Daniel told her, helping Alex to hold the heavy door to the root cellar. Due to the inventiveness and sheer persistency of the raccoons, the storage cellar resembled a fortified bunker, with walls that were constantly checked for recently dug holes and a door that weighed half a ton and which bolted shut on all four sides.

"Oh, you will?" Alex stuck her head out and held up her arms to receive yet another full basket.

"That's good." Agnes smiled down at Daniel. "It's important that you know the Holy Writ. My da used to read the Bible all the time with wee Angus, and he was so proud on account of Angus being such a dedicated student. He knew all the books of the Bible when he was your age."

"And that's good to know why?" Alex asked.

Agnes frowned. "You should know."

"Why? If you want to know, you just open the Bible and read the index, right?"

"Index?" A new word for Agnes, Alex could tell. "All good Christian people know their Bible well enough to name the books," Agnes said instead. Alex laughed as she ducked into the cellar.

"And all good Christian people know it is the sun that rotates around the world," Agnes said to Daniel just as Alex popped back up for another load.

Daniel shook his head. "It has been proven that it isn't

so, by scientists such as Co... Coperniclas and Gallyley."

"Nicholas Copernicus and Galileo Galilei," Alex corrected. "How do you know that?"

"Offa told me and when I asked Da he said that aye, it was so." And of course whatever his father said had to be true, Alex smiled.

"Once I find the time, aye I will," Matthew said when Alex asked him about these Bible lessons. "He was right in that at least, Richard Campbell, that I've let my sons grow up somewhat unschooled in the Holy Writ."

"And daughters," Alex corrected with some sharpness.

"And daughters." He was sitting with his hands held apart holding a skein of wool while she rolled it into a ball of yarn. "Daniel must come well prepared to school. I won't have him ridiculed on account of him not knowing his texts." He stretched and smiled lazily at her. "It might do you some good as well. We could spend time studying the Song of Solomon."

"Now?" She dropped the balls of yarn into her basket and stood up. "*Thou art fair my love, behold thou art fair...*" she quoted. "Although I actually prefer another line...*let my beloved come into his garden and eat his pleasant fruits.*"

Matthew chuckled and hooked a finger into her waistband, drawing her close enough for him to wind his arm around her waist. "I am here. So where is my fruit?"

Sometimes it was very slow, an unhurried exploration of bodies so familiar they were but an extension of each other. Her hand – or was it his? – on his member, his fingers, her fingers, exploring her moistness. Skin on skin, the delicious sensation of his – her? – weight on top, the slope of a hip, the ridge of a collarbone. Murmuring voices, a sudden laugh, more hands, lips that were wet and soft, exhalations that tickled exposed necks, breasts and thighs. Toes that caressed their way up shins, hands that smoothed down unruly hair, stopped to trace a brow, the curve of a lip.

A kiss...a long, long kiss, and in her chest her heart picked up speed. A hand on her thigh, insistent, strong, and her breath became ragged. A low, dark voice that told her just how much he loved her; more kisses, fingers that knotted themselves into hair. Her head forced back, laying her throat bare to his lips, his nipping teeth. His body rising above hers, her hand on his arms, on his shoulders, gliding down his back to his waist, his buttocks. Her man, her Matthew. Her legs twisting into his – or was it the other way around? – hips, definitely her hips, that rose of their own accord from the bed, and there! Oh yes, there.

"Matthew?"

"Aye?" He spooned himself around her, drawing in her warm, moist smell.

"What if..." Alex broke off and twisted round to face him, propping herself up on an elbow. Matthew sighed inwardly. Why was it that so often she had a need to talk just when he was on the verge of sleeping?

"What if..." he prompted, stifling a yawn.

"Well, what if Daniel doesn't want to be a minister?"

"Sometimes you don't give them a choice. Since he was a wee bairn, we've told him that he'll be a man of God once he grows up. And we won't encourage him to question that now, aye?"

"But—"

"No buts. Daniel Elijah is meant for the kirk. You know that. Through God's grace was he saved when he was ill, and to God we've promised him in return."

She mulled this over for some time. "Okay, no buts. However, we're going to spend a lot of time finding him a cheerful and competent wife, okay?"

Matthew lay in astounded silence and then he burst out laughing.

"What?"

"Nowt," he said, still laughing.

"What's so funny? You don't agree?"

"Aye, of course I do." He rolled her over on her side, slipped his hand in to cup her breast, and smiled. Find him a wife indeed... Mayhap Magnus was right; Alex had changed, much more than she fully noticed herself. To the point where she was even contemplating an arranged marriage for their seven-year-old son. He grunted contentedly and shifted closer to her.

Chapter 30

"I don't like it." Alex hid her face against Matthew's chest. The summons had come late – so late Alex had begun hoping that maybe the militia wouldn't be called out at all – and now he was off to participate in some ridiculous punitive operation. She didn't like it one whit; months away from her, months at close quarters with Dominic Jones.

"Nor do I, lass, but it can't be helped, can it?" He disengaged himself from her hands, kissed her on the mouth, close-lipped and warm. "But I'll be back."

"Promise?"

"Like a dove to his dovecote," he smiled. Assuming he didn't die out there in the wilds, she thought with a little gulp.

"He'll be fine," Mrs Parson said, coming to join Alex in the yard.

"Of course he will." Alex raised her hand in one last wave. "It's just..."

"I know, you hate it when he's gone from you."

"Ridiculous, right?"

"Very," Mrs Parson said, "but I suppose you can't help it, can you? Weak and clinging, that's you, Alex Graham."

"No, I'm not!" Alex retorted before she saw that Mrs Parson was smiling, her black eyes sparkling with amusement.

The old woman gave Alex a maternal pat on the cheek. "It's not so strange, is it, lass. You've almost lost him a couple of times, and that makes you overprotective of him."

"He wouldn't like to hear you say that. In Matthew's view of the world, he protects, not me."

"Aye well, that's men for you, no?" Mrs Parson shrugged, hastening off in the direction of the closest storage shed.

Alex sighed and wandered off up the lane in the futile hope of catching one last glimpse of Matthew. Once she'd gotten to the top, she decided she might just as well take a walk, keeping an eye out for anything edible.

She meandered her way along the overgrown bridle path that led to Forest Spring, her eyes on the ground, her mind with Matthew and Moses, now well on their way to Leslie's Crossing and beyond. At least he had a friend with him, she thought, finding some comfort in that. Thomas might be dull and somewhat staid, but he was a competent fighter and a loyal friend. She found a briar rose full of hips and, for the next half-hour, she stripped the thorny bush of the small red fruit.

"Do you recall the first time we picked hips together, you and I?"

Alex jumped at the sound of Ian's voice.

"Don't do that!" she scolded. "You scared me half to death. Besides, you're not picking now, and you weren't picking all that much that time either."

"Aye, I was."

They fell silent, working side by side to fill her apron.

"He'll be fine," Ian said, echoing Mrs Parson's earlier comment.

"I hope so. I don't like it, Ian; him and Dominic in the same militia..."

"He's twice the man Jones is."

"Absolutely, but it doesn't do to underestimate Dominic Jones." Alex chewed at her lip. "Men that do end up dead."

Ian went off to continue with his hunting, and Alex was back to walking alone, humming something under her breath. The wet late October day was quiet, birds a muted background noise no more. She strayed off the path to inspect a stand of mushrooms, but as she didn't recognise them she chose to leave them standing. She was still squatting when the unexpected sound of male voices made her freeze.

She recognised the horse first, gulped and tried to make herself as invisible as possible. Difficult to do when one was wearing a flowered shawl and a white cap, and with a low whoop Philip Burley brought his horse to a halt.

"Well, well, if it isn't Mrs Graham." His mouth stretched itself into a cold smile. "And what may you have in your apron? More of those peppers you so kindly anointed my eyes with last time we met?"

"No." Alex succeeded in sounding much more relaxed than she felt. "These are hips."

"Hips, you say?" Philip let his eyes travel up and down Alex.

"She has good ones," one of his companions piped up, eliciting a snicker from the other two.

Alex looked from one to the other. "Oh my God, it's actually true. You do have three brothers."

"Why is that so surprising?"

Alex just shook her head. Dark-haired and light-eyed the lot of them, the youngest not much more than a boy, the other two closer to Philip in age, somewhere in their late twenties. "I was commiserating with your mother. Imagine giving birth to four like you."

"Seven actually, but the three eldest were girls," Philip said.

"Lucky her," Alex muttered.

"Very," one of the other brothers said. "Four sons to keep her well protected – unlike you, Mrs Graham." He looked over to Philip. "Is she the wife of the man who stole the Indians from you?"

"Stole? Matthew stopped your creep of a brother from abducting them!" Alex shifted a couple of yards further away from the path, eyeing her surroundings.

"Yes, she is." Philip rode his horse into the underbrush, and Alex retreated behind a stand of maple saplings. "Think you can run?"

"Run? Why should I? Matthew will be here any minute."

"Really?" Philip drawled.

"Really," Alex said, taking yet another step away from him. "What are you doing here? Aren't you supposed to be in Virginia?"

"Our business is none of your concern," Philip said.

"Business? Here?" Alex swept her arm at the surrounding wilderness. "What do you do? Sell nuts to the squirrels?"

Philip laughed. "There are always buyers for our goods – and services." He turned to his brothers. "What do you reckon she's worth?"

"Worth? Me? Why you—" Alex broke off at his look and backed into the closest bramble.

"She's quite old," the youngest of them said.

"Yes," one of the others agreed. His eyes stuck to Alex's chest, did a cursory inspection of the rest of her and returned to her chest. He had eyes as light as Philip, eyes that made her knees wobble.

"Just because she's old it doesn't mean we can't sell her," the third brother said. "Some sort of compensation for the lost Indians."

"Just because you walk on two legs and can talk, it doesn't follow you have a brain, does it?" Alex retorted.

"Feisty," Philip said. "I like that in a woman. Makes it more fun to..." He made a rude gesture and his brothers grinned, eyeing Alex hungrily.

"I just told you. My husband will be here shortly."

"Now why don't I believe you, Mrs Graham?" Philip Burley leaned forward over the neck of his horse.

"Because you're stupid?" Alex said.

"Stupid? I think not, Mrs Graham." He rode closer. Alex groped for her knife and raised it high. Philip looked at her with a glimmer of admiration in his eyes. He smiled, a slow, dangerous smile further enhanced by the lock of coal-black hair that fell forward over his face. For eternal seconds, she was nailed to the spot by his eyes. The palms of her hands, the insides of her thighs broke out in a cold sweat.

Finally, he wheeled his horse. "I'll be back," he threw over his shoulder. "If nothing else to offer my condolences to the recently bereaved widow."

She couldn't help it, she gasped, making him laugh.

"We don't have time to waste. We have a militia to join – coincidentally the same company your husband belongs to."

270

"But…" the youngest whined. "I thought we'd—"

"Not today, Will," Philip cut him off. He smiled at Alex and touched the brim of his hat. "We know where to find her when we want her." With that he was off, his three brothers in his wake.

Alex sank down to sit where she stood.

"Mama?" Ian crouched before her. "What's the matter?" Alex just couldn't stop crying, throwing her arms around her eldest son while she tried to explain why she was sitting here in the dusk, a mile or so from home.

"Shush, Mama, he'll be fine. And he has Thomas with him."

"They're four," she sobbed. "Five, if you count Jones."

"Mama!" Ian gave her a little shake. "Look at me."

Alex sat back, snivelled, and wiped her nose on her sleeve.

"You'll have to trust him to take care of himself."

She nodded. "He'll be fine," she said in a voice hoarse with crying. "Of course he'll be." She twisted at her wedding ring, round and round it went. "But what if he isn't? What then?"

Chapter 31

Matthew had forgotten how tedious life was when spent entirely in the company of men – in particular men young enough to be his sons and with one single thought in their brains: to prove themselves men by slaying an Indian or two. After five weeks, he worried he might lay into one of these young hotheads, but he held his tongue and avoided them as much as possible, riding with the other officers instead.

He adjusted his bright sash, pressed his hat down harder on his head, and urged Moses into a trot to catch up with Thomas, who was riding a few horse lengths ahead, involved in a heated debate with the men beside him. The conversation died away the moment he joined them, and from the strained look on Thomas' face, Matthew understood it had been him they'd been discussing. Again. It made him seethe inside, and instinctively he turned, looking for that goddamn Dominic Jones, preferably to tear that lying tongue out by its roots.

Everywhere Matthew went among his contemporaries, he was now met with glances that spoke of distrust and caution – after all, Matthew Graham had at an earlier point in his life been sent over as an indentured criminal.

"It doesn't help, does it?" Matthew said. "I can repeat that I was unlawfully abducted until I'm blue in the face, but he got there first, and anything I say will be taken as a weak attempt to defend my reputation."

Thomas made a non-committal sound. "Dominic Jones is not the best liked of men and, once the novelty of it has worn itself out, men will forget. After all, quite a few of the elders in Providence were shipped over against their will."

"Aye, but he's painting me a common criminal, not a prisoner of conscience." Matthew tightened his gloved fist around his reins and glared at Jones' back. "All to discredit me and any story I might have to tell – be I dead or alive."

Thomas nodded; he was one of the few Matthew had told the whole sorry tale that had ended with an innocent man hanging for the murder Jones committed down in Jamestown.

Matthew was sorely tempted to plunge his dirk in the broad back some horses ahead of him – sink it in and twist it until Dominic Jones shrieked in pain. He eyed Jones' band of companions and spat in the dust. The four Burley brothers – Philip, Stephen, Walter and Will – shadowed Dominic like half-tame wolves, their light eyes nailing into any man that came too close. Unkempt, with an air of savagery to them that had most of the men avoiding them, the brothers kept to themselves, always sitting to the side with Jones.

Every now and again, Matthew caught Philip Burley studying him, eyes travelling up and down Matthew in a way that made all of him crawl. Matthew spat again; unsavoury, the lot of them! The youngest was recently bearded, but with the same avaricious look in his eyes as his older brothers and a constant dim-witted smile on his face. There was something unnerving about them; even more when Matthew realised the Burley brothers had a tendency to follow him around. Four against one... Matthew swallowed.

There was a yell from behind them, there were several calls for help and pandemonium reigned, the small group of militia overrun by a party of Indian braves. Before Matthew and Thomas had managed to bring the men to order, the attack was over, with two men lying thrown to the ground and their horses and muskets gone.

"To show us what they can do, should they want to," Minister Walker said.

"Aye, and to show us what they chose not to do. They're still alive," Matthew pointed out, earning himself an approving nod from the minister.

"Yes, Brother Matthew, very much so." Their nominal commanding officer called a halt and had the two wounded men helped to their feet and inspected for damages.

"Not much more than bruised pride," Thomas said in an aside to Matthew.

"Why are we doing this?" one of the Burley brothers said several hours later. "Why don't we ride into the closest Indian village and pay them back in blood?"

"For shame," Minister Walker said. "We're not here to spill the blood of innocents."

"One dead Indian is as good as another dead Indian," Philip Burley voiced, receiving murmured approval from the other young men. "They're driving off our people from their land, and in some cases they've even killed colonists."

"And raped the women," another man said, "and you know what they do to the children: they carry them off into slavery."

"Three colonists," Minister Walker retorted, "and it could be argued the Indians were provoked. And as to the stories of rape and pillage, so far they have proved unfounded." He stepped closer to the fire, and Matthew was yet again impressed by how such a small man could exert such confidence and leadership, simply in the way he modulated his rich, carrying voice. In his dark coat, his old-fashioned white collar that he insisted on wearing no matter weather or occasion, he looked every inch the man of God he was, a man who wouldn't countenance the slaughter of innocents however heathen they might be.

"We ride to find the perpetrators and bring them to justice," Minister Walker said, "and that's what we'll do."

There was a lot of grumbling among the men who were all of them beginning to tire of this impossible cat and mouse game. November had been for the most part bearable, but since the advent of December the nights had become colder, and every day men would turn to gaze at the skies, sniffing for the first sign of snow.

Dominic objected this was a waste of time. "I can't spend the whole winter chasing elusive Indians. I have a business to run, and every day away is costing me a small fortune. So why don't we capture a few, string them up and leave them to rot as a deterrent?"

"Or enslave them," Philip Burley said. "That might even make us some money."

"We will not lower ourselves to killing innocent men," Minister Walker said, "nor will we take them into slavery."

"Easy for you," Dominic Jones muttered. "You get paid – by us, no less – no matter where you are. But the rest of us suffer financially. Besides, they're all savages. Despicable heathens, the lot of them."

"Mr Jones! For shame!"

"Well, they are. There is only one use for them, and that is as slaves."

"Hear, hear," someone called out.

Dominic expanded his chest further. "A week; I'll not give this nonsense more than one more week. I have other matters to attend to."

"Let me remind you that you've signed up to serve for as long as necessary," Matthew said. "All of us have."

"Ah, the redoubtable Mr Graham has spoken," Jones smirked. "The difference being that while I have business interests to protect, you have but a small farm lost in the wilds."

"Most of us do," Matthew said.

"And I say it is time we end this business so that we can all return home – in a week, not a month."

Some of the men muttered their agreement; all of them no doubt harbouring a niggling feeling of unease that while they were here, halfway into Virginia, the Indians might in fact be back home, harming their families. Matthew sighed; he'd spent endless, sleepless nights worrying about Alex and his bairns.

"We will do what we set out to do," Minister Walker said. "And we will do it no matter how long it takes." He sank his eyes into Dominic Jones. "That goes for all of us, Mr Jones."

Dominic gave the minister a cold look and shouldered through the assembled men.

Some days later, they made camp in a grassy hollow, and after an agreeable evening spent with Thomas and the two Chisholm brothers, Matthew was lying in his pile of

275

blankets, attempting to ignore the fact that his bladder was on the verge of bursting.

Finally, he bowed to the inevitable and stood, moving in the direction of the lines of horses. The sentry by the fire nodded, and Matthew ducked below the lines and walked some feet away to piss. Too much salted pork, too much beer and too little else... He longed for one of Alex's winter stews, with thick chunks of carrot and cabbage and meat, all of it liberally spiced with thyme and garlic. He almost smacked his lips together, but was shaken out of his daydream by the sound of twigs snapping. He crouched and remained unseen when Dominic Jones passed by only a couple of feet from him, moving stealthily in the direction of the camp. As always, he was tagged by the feral Burley brothers. Matthew frowned. Where had they been and why did they smell of smoke?

Late next morning, the militia company came upon a small homestead. The men gaped in horror at the scene in front of them, and several of the younger men vomited, while the elder sat in a silent ring upon their horses and surveyed the carnage.

"Ah, Jesus sweet," Thomas groaned, "what have they done?"

"See?" Walter Burley's voice shook with indignation. "Are these not innocents, Minister Walker? Have they not been slaughtered like lambs despite doing no harm?"

There was a loud sound of assent from the shocked men. What had been a small, thriving farm was a smouldering ruin, the chimney stack the single remaining structure that exceeded three feet. By what had been the door was the charred corpse of a man, and halfway to the stable a bairn lay curled up on her side, dead. Her fair hair lifted in the cold December wind, long tendrils snaking round her head. The stable was burnt to the ground, and from the heavy stench in the air, it was obvious its inhabitants had gone up in smoke with it.

"This is wrong," Matthew murmured to Thomas. "This isn't the work of Indians."

"Matthew! How can you defend those accursed heathens when confronted by this?"

"They didn't do it. They would've taken the beasts. And look at the bairn, Thomas. A wee fair lass... They wouldn't kill such a one. They'd carry her off and sell her."

Thomas gave him a thoughtful look and went back to studying the desolation before him. "So what do you think happened?"

"Tinder to the powder." Matthew pursed his mouth. Was this why Jones had smelled of smoke?

"Don't be ridiculous. White men do this? For your own sake, I suggest you don't repeat these follies elsewhere." Thomas nudged his gelding in the direction of the minister, leaving Matthew sitting quite alone on Moses.

Thomas avoided Matthew for the coming days, restricting himself to the odd polite word, no more. Matthew felt somewhat abandoned, but concentrated on the few tasks he had. He heeded Thomas' advice and kept his suspicions to himself. He was no fool and had no wish to end up with his throat slashed. Besides, it seemed to him that Jones and the Burley brothers hovered that much closer to him, five pairs of eyes following him everywhere he went. So he made a point of spending most of his time with the Chisholms, and at night he lay back to back with a silent Thomas, his dirk held in his hand.

"Why the knife?" Thomas asked one morning, thereby normalising their friendship.

"I don't like the way he's watching me." Matthew nodded in the direction of Jones.

"He'd be a fool to try anything," Thomas said.

"Oh, he won't, he'll set his wolves on me."

Thomas eyed the Burley brothers and looked back at Matthew. "We sleep in turns."

Late in the afternoon a week later, their scouts returned in a state of agitation and told them they had come upon an Indian camp some miles off.

"And they didn't see you?" Minister Walker asked.

"No," one of them said. "We counted to twenty braves – and they're driving several heads of cattle."

"Thieves!" someone hissed.

"Murderers," someone else added, and the whole company was on their feet, demanding that they go and wipe these heathens off the face of the earth.

"We arrest them and take them back with us." Minister Walker sank his eyes into the by now mounted men. "No killing!"

It was a bloodbath. Too late, the Indians noticed their presence, and then the militia was upon them, fuelled by weeks of anger and fear and by those haunting images of the destroyed homestead.

Minister Walker's cries that they must take them alive went unheard, and no matter that Thomas and Matthew shouted themselves hoarse, the men ignored them, bashing heads with unloaded muskets, slashing at unprotected bodies with their drawn swords.

A sword flashed to Matthew's right. Philip Burley bore down on him, and Matthew parried the blow. Stephen appeared on his other side, herding him deeper into the heaving mass of men. Two swords, one to his right, one to his left, and Matthew was fighting for his life, parrying, thrusting and ducking. The tip of Stephen's sword nicked Matthew's thigh; Philip's blade near on severed his arm. In the distance, Matthew could hear Thomas screaming his name. He stood in his stirrups, Moses skittered to the left, and Matthew brought his sword down. It glanced off Stephen's raised blade and struck Stephen full in the face.

Stephen shrieked, hands on his bleeding face. Philip screamed a curse. His horse barged into Moses, his blade swished through the air, narrowly missing Matthew's head. Moses snorted and reared. Matthew parried yet another thrust from Philip and set his heels to Moses in an attempt to evade Philip's determined attack. The horse took a leap, crashed into the bay mare belonging to Jones. Moses neighed and reared again. Matthew was nearly unseated, and only his instinctive grab for the pommel kept him astride.

A hand closed around his boot. Matthew tried to kick loose, but to no avail. A determined yank, and Matthew was pulled off his horse. More Burleys! Goddamn, there was Walter, and the young, grinning face before him was Will, brandishing an evil-looking knife. Matthew scrabbled away. Will giggled and came after, and for all that they were surrounded by men, men that screamed and cursed and fought, all Matthew could see was Will, now poised to pounce like a human cat. Matthew rose to his knees. Will lunged, and Matthew's arm moved of its own accord, the sword severing Will Burley's windpipe. Merciful Lord! Warm blood cascaded over his hand, and here came Walter, screaming his brother's name. Matthew crawled backwards, looking for his horse.

Someone screeched him in the ear, there was a stinging pain high up on his arm, and Matthew turned, coming up in a crouch with his sword held high. Only yards from his face was the muzzle of a pistol, and on the other side of it grinned Dominic Jones. For an instant, Matthew thought this was his last moment, and then Thomas barged into Dominic from behind. Matthew launched himself to the side, the gun went off, and the ball whizzed by Matthew's head to bury itself in the back of a dying brave.

"Of course not!" Dominic protested. "You're misconstruing what you saw, Mr Leslie. It may have appeared that the gun was levelled at Graham, but in truth it was pointed at the Indian behind."

"Who was already mortally wounded, lying face down." Thomas was shaking all over, his eyes blazing with dislike as they stared at Jones. Matthew dragged a hand over his face. The damned Burleys had melted away like mist into the forest and God knew where they might be by now, having left behind the body of their brother. "You set those brothers on Matthew," Thomas continued, "and had I not seen that Walter Burley pull Matthew off his horse, he would've been dead by now!"

"That is a very serious accusation," Minister Walker broke in. "We all saw the brothers set upon Brother Matthew, but from there to implicate Mr Jones... Vermin, those brothers, unstable all four of them, and even as a minister I can't say I much regret the death of one of them."

A consenting murmur rose from the older men.

"They've been living in Jones' pocket since the day they joined up," Thomas said, "and I saw how the gun was levelled point-blank at Matthew."

"At the Indian behind him," Dominic insisted.

"Well, maybe that's what Dominic is most comfortable with," an unknown man piped up. "He prefers to shoot them when they're already dead." Nervous laughter flew through the small knot of men surrounding them.

"Or drunk," someone else added, and the laughter spread, making Jones' face shift into a deep red at these slurs on his courage.

By morning, most of the company had left, a spontaneous disbanding that had Minister Walker sighing loudly before concluding it was maybe for the best. Matthew was tightening Moses' girth when out of the corner of his eye he saw Dominic Jones approaching. He continued with what he was doing, ears strained in the direction of Jones to ensure he wasn't caught by surprise. Matthew adjusted the stirrup leathers, fussed with the harness and turned to face Jones, who was leaning back against a tree some yards away.

"What?" Matthew demanded.

Dominic just shook his head. "Thinking of how things could have been."

"Unhappy, are you?"

"Not particularly." Dominic straightened up from his reclining posture. He gave Matthew a malicious look. "Sooner or later they'll get you, Graham. Those Burleys have an axe of their own to grind with you now."

Matthew's guts heaved. He took a steadying breath, took two.

Dominic snickered. "Tenacious, the lot of them. And vindictive – very vindictive." He backed away when Matthew advanced. "Now, now, this isn't my fault. You're the one who slit Will's throat and nearly killed Stephen."

"And why is that? Because you set them upon me!"

"Proof, Graham," Jones sneered. With that he turned and left.

Chapter 32

"He's doing poorly today," Mrs Parson commented to Alex, who glanced in the direction of Magnus' room and sighed. She could almost see the headaches rolling in over him, and at times they were painful but bearable, while sometimes they seemed to spike into cruel shards that left him blind and incapable of moving.

"There's not much we can do, is there?" Alex looked out of the window at the dull grey skies and made a face. Eight weeks Matthew had been gone, and she was increasingly restless, spending far too many hours looking up the lane to where she hoped to see Moses materialise. Every night, she woke to a racing heart and a sweaty shift after yet another nightmare featuring Philip Burley, and at times she was convinced it would be Philip, not Matthew, who came riding down their lane. And God help them if that were to happen...

"Nay, nothing but help him with the pain," Mrs Parson said, recalling Alex to the present. Mrs Parson wrinkled her nose at the sweet, cloying smell of yet another pipe of cannabis that drifted through the half-closed door. "That helps."

"Stoned out of his head," Alex muttered. "Of course it helps." She smiled at Jenny, who appeared from outside, balancing a bucket of milk.

"The last, I think." Jenny set the pail down. "It was a struggle to get this much out of her."

Mark stuck his head into the kitchen and announced there were horses coming, and for a moment Alex thought it might be Matthew, before realising that of course it wasn't, as in that case Mark wouldn't have looked so unimpressed.

"Who?" she asked.

Jenny mumbled something under her breath. Elizabeth's

recurring visits were somewhat of a strain on all of them, her daughter included.

"It's because she's worried about you," Alex said. "Now that you're with child, she wants to check up on you."

"She's bored, is what it is," Mrs Parson said. "Yon Mary is no fun to bully on account of her being a meek and insipid person, wee Celia is besotted with her son and breeding again, and apart from her husband she doesn't have many to converse with."

"She doesn't converse," Jenny said. "She hectors."

Alex hid a small smile. Elizabeth came because she missed her daughter, and even more because she resented the way Jenny was integrating herself with the Grahams.

"There you are." Alex poured them all some herbal tea and added a generous dollop of honey to her mug.

"You look well," Elizabeth said, although her eyes remained on her pregnant daughter.

"Thank you." Alex ran a hand over her belly; five months to go and already a pronounced bulge. "I wouldn't mind if this was the last one." She caught the amused glance that flew between Mrs Parson and Elizabeth and frowned. If she had any say in things, this would be the last one.

"I've myself birthed fifteen, and four of them after my fortieth birthday." Elizabeth looked over to where Jacob was helping Ruth and Sarah with their numbers. "It's them that are your crown of glory," she said, her eyes softening when they rested on Jenny. "It is in procreation that woman fulfils her destiny and does penance for the fall from grace."

Mrs Parson nodded in agreement. "A man blessed with a fertile wife must ensure she gives him as many bairns as she can, for they in turn will also be fruitful."

"How Darwin," Alex muttered under her breath. "But what about the women who can't?" she said out loud. "Those who are barren or who for some other reason just can't?"

"They must pray," Elizabeth replied. "Somehow they've displeased the good Lord and must abjectly beg for his mercy and forgiveness."

"Oh." Alex sipped at her tea.

"I have news," Elizabeth said, in an abrupt change of subject. "Our militia rode down a group of those heathen savages, south-west of here, and now peace has been restored." She gave a satisfied little cackle. "I suppose the sight of real soldiers made them think twice about disturbing the order of things."

"The order of things?" Alex couldn't help it; she just had to bait this woman.

"White man, Alex. You know that, surely? White man is set to rule his coloured cousins on account of his greater wisdom and spiritual development."

"Lucky them; here we come, steal their land, break the treaties we have negotiated with them, and when they protest and try to push us back, we ride out in force to kill them. Seems very fair and just to me – God-given proof of the white man's spiritual supremacy."

"You have no understanding of what you're saying," Elizabeth said. "This land has been granted us by God that we may build a society founded on God's word here in the wilderness, where no man was before."

Alex opened her mouth to launch herself into a heated reply but what could have become an infected discussion was cut short by loud, agitated barking interspersed by what Alex recognized as Mark's voice, raised in alarm. She flew out of her chair, and at her shoulder went Elizabeth, both of them making for the door.

"Sweet Jesus in his meadows," Elizabeth exclaimed.

"A bear?" Alex swallowed and rushed towards her son, the perpetually loaded musket in her hands.

"Can you shoot?" Elizabeth panted from beside her.

"Not really." Alex could barely talk, her eyes glued on the large yellow dog and what looked like a gigantic brown shape snarling at it. Behind the dog stood Mark, with the rounds of sausage he'd been sent to collect from the smoking shed cradled in his arms.

"I can." Elizabeth took over the musket.

By now the bear had seen them, turning small, ill-tempered eyes in their direction and rising to stand on its hind legs. Narcissus growled. With lowered head, bared teeth and the hackles along his yellow back standing straight up, he looked menacing, and apparently the bear thought so too, swaying from side to side. The dog lunged and the bear roared, its front paws swiping.

The musket exploded, and there was blood and skin everywhere. For a shocked instant, Alex was convinced Elizabeth had missed her target, blasting Narcissus or Mark into non-being, but then the bear dropped back onto all fours and lumbered off in the direction of the forest, blood flowing down its flank. Halfway there it crumpled, slowing over several paces before it hit the ground with an excited Narcissus leaping around it. Alex stumbled towards her son, who fell into her arms with a muffled whimper.

"Why didn't you throw him the sausages?" she said. "Why not yank down a ham and throw it at him as well?"

"I couldn't," he said into her shawl. "I couldn't move so scared was I."

A wild-haired Ian came galloping from the woods where he'd been logging, musket in one hand and axe in the other, and skidded to a halt.

"Are you alright?" His eyes flew over them.

"More or less," Alex said, and they were – well, except for poor Narcissus, who was standing with one leg held clumsily off the ground.

"Good shot," Ian said to Elizabeth before raising his own musket and blowing a hole in the bear's head.

"Good shot?" she snorted, but smiled all the same. "With less than fifty feet between me and the beast, it's not that impressive, is it?" She came over to where Ian was standing beside the dead animal and prodded at it with her toe. "Young – and very thin, considering the time of the year." Which was probably why it was skulking round the farm to begin with, she theorized.

"Aye." Ian lifted one of the oversized paws. "Old injury."

"I want to see." Mark squirmed in Alex's arms. "Let me go."

Alex reluctantly did, following him to where Elizabeth was peering at the badly healed cut across the pads.

Ian straightened up and frowned in the direction of the stable. The animals sounded half-crazed with fear, and from the pig's end came a series of loud thumps.

"I'd best go see to the beasts," he said to Alex, who was staring at the brown heap that had until recently been a bear. "Mark, you come with me, and then we'll see to your dog."

Mark nodded and hurried after Ian. Alex was tempted to rush after him, but knew Mark would prefer if she didn't. Instead, she retrieved the sausages from the frozen ground and made her way back to the house with Elizabeth in tow.

"So much snow," Alex said a couple of days later. She shoved open the door and placed a booted foot on the thick white carpet. It crunched beneath her weight. "He'll be cold," she added in a worried tone.

"Perhaps, but snow insulates." Magnus gave his daughter a reassuring hug before calling his grandchildren together, promising them they were going to do some serious playing in the snow.

"Did you get much snow, back in Sweden?" Daniel wallowed after Magnus up the hillside. His woollen cap was pulled down tight over his ears, and he had to hold his arms out from his body on account of the two shawls he had cross-tied over chest and back. Magnus smiled down at mini-Michelin and looked at the others, just as bundled.

"Masses and masses," Magnus exaggerated, hoisting Sarah to sit on the primitive sled he'd knocked together in Matthew's wood shed. "So we did this a lot." He shoved at her and stood back to grin when she flew down the inclination, squealing with exhilaration.

"Do you miss it?" Jacob asked.

"Miss what?" Magnus' head was beginning to throb. The sunlight threw reflections off the pristine snow that hurt his eyes. He squished them shut to block out the spinning circles of black that were crawling across his field of vision.

"Offa?" Jacob stuck his hand into Magnus' and squeezed.

"I'm okay." Magnus took a series of short, quick breaths. He opened his eyes wide. "See? Right as rain." He even managed to smile. "Yes, I do miss it," he said, in an effort to think about anything, anything at all but the clanging in his head. "Just like your father misses Scotland."

"Very much," Jacob nodded, "but not all the time – not anymore."

"Do you?"

Jacob looked at him and smiled, his hazel eyes a brilliant emerald green in the sunlight. "Nay, not really. But one day I think I'll go back, to see it. Da never will." It sounded so much as a prophecy that Magnus felt the hairs stand up along his spine and shoulders.

"You don't know that. Look at me: seventy years old and here I pop up in Maryland. Not something I expected to happen." No, because he'd assumed he'd be ending up in Hillview. "Go on," he motioned Jacob towards the others. "Take your turn, son." He remained where he was, gritting his teeth as he battled the pain in his head. His fingers were already digging for a pill, a momentary relief. Still enough, he comforted himself. Even if I take one now, there's still enough to end it all before it becomes unbearable.

An hour or so later, a very happy but very wet troop of children entered the house. Alex alternated between scolding and laughing as she undressed them and rubbed them warm before serving them all something hot to drink.

"Will you ever go back, do you think?" Magnus asked Alex once they were alone in the kitchen. The whole space was garlanded with drying clothes, the smell of damp wool overlaying the rich scent from the pot of hip soup that stood on the table. Alex dipped her ladle, brought up a serving of dark red hot soup and poured them both a refill.

"No," she said. "How can we?"

"But you'd want to?"

She shrugged and looked away. "If wishes were horses... Anyway, what is there for us to go back to? Hillview is gone, and Matthew is still a convinced Covenanter, a man who won't back down from his Presbyterian beliefs and kowtow to the Church of England. Besides, we could never afford to." She surveyed the whitewashed walls of her kitchen, ran a hand over the table top, and smiled. "So this is home for us now; until we die."

"Until we die," Magnus echoed. Which in his case was going to be bloody soon. He gave Alex a little smile. "A good home," he said, and was gratified by how pleased she looked.

"You think?"

"I do." He closed his eyes and yawned. Beside him, she fidgeted, and he opened one eye to see her twisting her wedding ring round and round her finger.

"He'll be back," he said, one hand coming down on hers.

She nodded, one single tear sliding down her cheek. "I pray, all the time I pray that he'll come back to me this time as well."

Magnus didn't say anything. He just squeezed her hand.

He came riding down the lane just after daybreak, and the first person he saw was his wife balancing over the frozen ground, emptied chamber pot held aloft. The early morning sun threw shards of glittering light off the snow at her feet and touched her dark hair to glint in deep bronzes and reds. He opened his mouth to call her name but she was already darting towards him, and he smiled at how her hair came undone from its messy braid, how her face was lit from within at the sight of him.

He was off the horse and she threw herself at him, arms winding themselves tight around his neck as he swung her round in a slow arc before setting her down again.

She raised her hand to his face to trace a shallow cut on his newly scraped skin. "You've shaved," she said.

"I had to. It was mostly grey; made me look frightfully old." He hugged her again, smiling at how her womb had hardened into a perceptible roundness.

"And the babe?" He placed a tender hand on the small of her back to hold her closer.

"He's doing quite well, I assume," she replied, and in her eyes he could see she already loved the unborn wean.

"She is," he corrected, and kissed her brow.

"He – yet another boy that looks just like his father." She ran light fingers over the skin under his eyes. "You're tired."

Aye, he was tired and dirty, and in his head were images he didn't want to have of defenceless Indians being put to death by enraged colonists, of Jones staring at him along the length of a pistol, certain death gleaming in his eyes. He closed his eyes at the memory. He'd tell her later, but not now.

"Bath?" she suggested.

"Bath," he agreed and lifted her onto her toes to kiss her.

The laundry shed was cold, their exhalations blooming like miniature clouds in the frigid air. Soon she had the fire going, and Matthew swung the cauldron to hang over the flames. He sat down on the bench, exhaustion creeping through his limbs. Three days of hard riding, cold nights and bad food were taking their toll. When Alex came to sit beside him, snuggling up close enough that her hair tickled his nose, he sneezed, slipping an arm round her waist to hold her close. The fire crackled, the bench creaked, and he could have sat like this for ever, relishing her proximity.

"Okay?" she asked after a long while, tilting her head back to regard him.

He nodded, struggling with his boots.

"God, I've missed you," she said.

He threw her a look, thinking she was right bonny in only her shift and her cloak.

"Here I am." He reclined against the wall. "Have your way with me, woman."

She laughed, placing a hand on his crotch. His cock swelled under her touch, and he spread his legs for her, closing his eyes as her deft, strong fingers caressed him through the heavy cloth of his breeches. She had a good hand, his wife, and his member stretched and preened, warmth pooling in his loins.

The water came to the boil, and Alex rose and retook

her hand, leaving him bereft. She filled the wooden tub and steam enveloped them, the scents of crushed lavender and rosemary making him sniff in appreciation.

"Come here." Alex beckoned, and he complied, shedding clothes in his wake. Hot water sent painful tingles through his cold extremities, his skin going from white to bright red in a matter of seconds. His wife knelt by the tub, dipped the washcloth and began washing him. Hands, shoulders, stomach...he sat forward to give her better access to his back. Her arms came round his neck, her mouth leaving a series of soft imprints down the side of his face. The washcloth travelled over his chest. She repeated the movement, but this time she rubbed the wet cloth over his left nipple. It hardened into a miniature pebble.

"Close your eyes," she murmured. He did, and the cloth traced the scars decorating his front, stopping for a while to inspect his bruised ribs.

"What's this?"

"I fell off my horse." Albeit with a little help... He grimaced, shoving the unwelcome images of the Burley brothers away from him.

"You fell?" She sounded incredulous.

"Not now; we can talk about that later. Go back to your work, lass."

"My work?" She kissed his shoulder. "Aye, aye, sir." Slowly, she dragged the cloth down his front to his privates. The cloth stroked his crotch, his balls. He opened his eyes.

"Close them." She stilled her hand. He closed his eyes. Her tongue flicked against his lips, but when he opened his mouth in expectation of more she laughed. The washcloth on his member, wrapped around him as she moved her hand up and down, and Matthew groaned, lifting his buttocks off the bottom. That tongue again, now on his chest, her mouth closing round his right nipple. Teeth nibbled him, her grip on his cock tightened, and he opened his eyes again.

"Kiss me, wife."

Alex brushed her lips against his.

"I said kiss me," he growled.

"What, like this?" She took hold of his ears, holding him still as her lips moved against his. He raised a hand to her head and kissed her back, his tongue invading her mouth. She spluttered and tried to rear back. Matthew took a firm grip of her waist and pulled her into the tub.

Alex gasped. He kissed her again. Her wet shift clung to her skin, outlining her breasts, her swelling belly. His woman. He suckled her nipple through the sheer linen, and her mouth fell open, hands fluttering around his head. Blood rushed through his body, his pulse pounding loudly in his temple. His cock thudded, his balls near on ached. So many weeks without her, so many nights longing for her warmth. He gripped her round arse and lifted her on top. With a little sigh, she took him inside. He lay still, she moved – up and down, up, up, down. Alex leaned over him, her eyes burning into his.

"Welcome home," she said. "Welcome home to me!"

Chapter 33

"For God's sake, Alex, you're what? Seven months pregnant? Let me do this, okay?" Magnus snatched the spade from her.

"For God's sake, Magnus, you're what? Seventy-two and with brain cancer? I can do this myself," she bit back, attempting to take the spade off him. She scraped one clog off against the other to dislodge the damp earth that had gotten stuck underneath and inspected her little kingdom. Magnus began to laugh, but insisted that she wasn't doing any more digging.

"You know Matthew would agree with me, so no digging. You have sons to help you if you consider me too decrepit."

"Decrepit? With the amount of food you put away, how can anyone consider you anything but hale and hearty?" Mrs Parson made an amused sound and bent down to inspect the lavender bushes.

"Look who's talking. It's not as if you live off salad leaves and water, is it?" Magnus extended his hand to help Mrs Parson straighten back up. "I'll take the girls with me and go nettle hunting. I'm sick of cabbage and wrinkled carrots."

"That makes two of us." Alex waved him off.

"How can he eat so much and dwindle as quickly as he does?" Alex asked Mrs Parson once Magnus was out of earshot. The last few weeks had tinged Magnus' skin a permanent grey due to fatigue and illness.

"It eats him from within, and I think he's in constant pain."

"How much longer do you think?"

Mrs Parson muttered that she had no notion but thought it doubtful he would live over the summer.

Alex looked in the direction of their little graveyard, and a whisper of cold crawled up her spine.

★

Increasingly, Magnus began escaping into the woods, ostensibly to collect nettles, or check on his maple trees. He'd spent the winter carving a number of wooden spouts and now had several trees from which he was collecting sap. In reality, he wanted to be alone, and during the long walks he took mental stock of his life, from those early years of protected childhood in the far north to these last few years in a day and age he shouldn't be in. Sometimes he spoke to Matthew about God, amazed and reassured by Matthew's bone-deep conviction that God did indeed exist.

"Do you truly believe that you'll go on living after you're dead?" Magnus said.

Matthew looked down at his long legs and inspected his hands. "Not in this form, and I'll find it a great loss not to have carnal knowledge of my wife in the hereafter, but aye, I do believe that somehow we will still be here." He looked up at the spring sky and pointed at a spot high up above. "Somewhere up there, so that I can peek at my bairns from time to time."

"...so that's where I'll be, I hope," Magnus said to Jacob some days later, pointing at the sky.

"Like Rachel." Jacob nodded. "You'll like Rachel, I think. I don't truly recall her, but I know she was a high-spirited lass. Like Mama, Da says, and then he laughs."

"I'm sure I will." From above came the honking of a V-shaped flight formation and they craned their heads back to look at the geese.

"Every year they fly all the way back north," Magnus said. "It always impresses me that they do that. It's like swifts: they come back year after year to the same breeding place, and when the parent birds die, the young still keep on coming back."

"How do they know where to go?" Jacob asked.

"I don't think anyone really knows, but it might have something to do with magnetism."

Jacob gave him a confused look.

Magnus smiled. "Like a compass. The needle points to

the true magnetic north. The birds seem to have an inner compass, and as long as they have that they can always find their way back home."

"So how do sailors find their way?" Jacob said, lugging the bucket full of sap he had insisted on carrying – fortunately, as Magnus had to stop frequently to catch his breath, a numbing exhaustion creeping up his body to centre somewhere in his brain, where a small voice was pleading with him to lie down and die – get this over with.

"I told you," Magnus snapped, irritated by Jacob's youth and apparent health, by the fact that he had all his life in front of him while his, damn it, was turning into its final, very short stretch. "Compasses, remember? And quadrants."

Jacob ignored his tone and helped Magnus sit on a log, waiting while Magnus drew in huge gusts of crisp spring air.

"Do you need such to find your way to heaven?"

"No, I don't think so," Magnus said with a weak smile. "I think that sorts itself." Or not, he added darkly to himself.

Matthew waited until Jenny was safely inside her cabin before returning to the big house. Not that he got much more than a grunted 'thank you' for his efforts. The lass was right ill-tempered at present, cranky and sore with the bairn that seemed in no hurry to leave the comfort of her womb. It made him smile; Ian was somewhat intimidated by his great-bellied wife, and so it fell upon him to help the lass as well as he could. He strolled across the yard, stopping by the oak. The spring evening was scented and warm, and he stood for some moments enjoying the silent peace.

"It makes you feel very patriarchal, doesn't it?" Alex said once he was back inside.

"Hmm?"

"Jenny. You hover around her, always there to help."

"The lass is having a hard time. No harm in making things easier for her."

"I can't recall ever being that pampered."

"That's because you don't like to be pampered," he said, receiving a black look in return.

"Yes, I do. It's just that I don't remember what it feels like."

He caught the edge of reproof in her voice and opened his mouth to list examples of how he'd pampered her, but shut it when he realised he couldn't cite one occasion in the near past. Somehow he suspected letting her sleep late those nights when David had been feeding round the clock wouldn't count.

At times, he took her far too much for granted, he admonished himself, expecting her to see to his needs but not always giving her quite the same attention back. Here she was, heavy with their eighth child, and he spent more time informing himself about Jenny's present state of health than hers. So the next day, Matthew took a day off from the spring planting, leaving Ian in charge, and went to find his wife where he knew she'd be, tending the tender shoots in her garden.

"Will you come and walk with me?" All of him warmed at the pleased look of surprise in her face, at how her cheeks coloured a pretty pink. He offered her his arm, leading her off towards the river. It was a warm early April day, and he adapted his stride and pace to hers, strolling through stands of maples and oaks in the general direction of the beckoning blue of the water. Here and there could be seen a dash of bright yellow flowers, especially on the sunny southern slopes, and the huge stands of lupines Alex had been culling for flowers the last few years were already in full leaf.

"I miss the windflowers," she said. "Do you remember the drifts of white blossoms under the trees back home?"

"Aye, of course I do." And no matter that soon the woodslands here would be covered in flowers, it would never be the same as seeing the early anemones transform the bare ground below the trees into carpets of white and bright green as they did back home.

He spread a blanket for them and helped her to sit, using himself as her back prop.

"He'll die soon," she said.

"Aye, he's busy making his farewells."

Alex didn't reply, grunting when his strong fingers massaged her neck and her scalp. She bent forward and piled her hair out of the way, baring her vulnerable and oh so white nape to him. He rested the back of his finger against it, running his digit up and down the downy skin.

"The first time you lay in my arms, crying for your wee lost son, Isaac, it was all I could do not to touch your exposed skin here. I'd never seen such an uncovered neck before, never seen a lass in short hair."

"You must have thought me awfully forward; first I throw up all over you, then I cry in your arms..."

"... and then you turned to me when you heard me hurting and held me."

"Yes, I did, didn't I?" She threw him a look over her shoulder. "It was meant, wasn't it? There was no choice."

"Aye, I think it was, and I thank God nigh on daily for you."

"Yeah, in between thinking I'm something of a handful, right?"

"The thought has crossed my mind." He laughed, placing his hands on her belly. She covered his hands with hers.

"If I die—"

"Nay, Alex, don't even say it."

"I have to," she said and turned round to face him, sitting with her hands on her crossed legs. "If I die..." she started again, and this time he closed his eyes but sat quiet. "Promise me that you won't marry someone who isn't good to our children."

"Oh Jesus, lass, do you think I'd ever wish to wed again if you were gone?" It made his insides turn to gravel to consider a life without her, his woman, by his side.

She took his hands. "You're a man – a relatively young man with a healthy libido. You can't go through life in permanent celibacy."

"And if it were you? If I died, would you wed again on account of you being incapable of sleeping alone?"

"If you died, I'd never marry again. I'd prefer living with

my memories of you and me." The thought obviously filled her with desolation, her spine curving into a dejected 'c'.

"As would I," Matthew said gently. "So don't insult me by telling me I must wed on account of my cock. You won't die," he added, placing both arms round her to hold her to him. "I won't allow it."

"Well, that's good to know." She laughed against his linen shirt. "I had no idea I was married to God himself."

Chapter 34

"Will that be all?" Mrs Redit placed the bundle of rolled hemp leaves on top of Matthew's other purchases.

"Aye." He nodded his farewell and exited her shop, only to run straight into Kate Jones.

"Why if it isn't Matthew Graham," she said, helping him retrieve the hemp leaves from the ground.

"Kate." He dipped his head in a little bow. She smiled, fair lashes lowered to shade her eyes.

"So many years since last we spoke," she said.

"Aye, at least ten."

"No wife?" She fell into step with him.

"Wife? Oh, nay, Alex remained at home. She's expecting – any day now." Which was why he was riding home on the morrow after only two days here... He had promised Alex he'd be back in time, had even considered cancelling the trip down to Providence, but that was never a realistic option. They had no salt, he needed a new coulter and share as well as a large axe head, and Alex required spices and sugar – and the hemp, for Magnus.

"Again?" Kate's brows rose.

"Aye."

Matthew threw her a look. She was all in pale green today, skirts of shimmering velvet enhanced by a bodice he'd never have allowed Alex to wear, what with how it lifted and exposed Kate's bosom. The linen of the shift beneath did cover most of her chest, but the fabric was rather transparent – too transparent.

"Finished gawking?" Kate said, and Matthew felt his face heat.

"You look well."

Kate laughed, a low, sultry sound. "Why thank you,

297

Mr Graham. So do you." She leaned close enough that her exhalation tickled his cheek. "Almost as good-looking as you were last time we spent time alone."

"Kate!"

"Well, it's true; the years have been far kinder to you than to my beloved husband." Kate's mouth twisted into a sour grimace. "Fat and big, that's what he is now."

"That's what he was then as well. Is he still…"

"Being openly unfaithful?" Kate lifted her skirts and sidestepped a puddle. "Yes, he is. She, apparently, understands him as I do not." She snorted. "Understand him? What is there to understand? He wants to be petted and pampered; he wants her to gaze at him with adoring eyes – preferably while his member is in her mouth."

Matthew choked.

"What? Do I shock you?"

"Aye."

Kate shrugged. "'Tis the truth. My dear beloved husband doesn't want a woman with whom to share his thoughts; all he wants is a strumpet that does as he bids her. Good riddance, I say."

"It must be a mite lonely."

"At times." Kate looked away. Then she turned to face him. "Do you ever…" She broke off and cleared her throat a couple of times. "Do you ever think about those nights with me?"

Matthew shuffled his feet, not knowing quite what to say. Aye, of course there were times when he did – like right now, with her standing a scant foot away. But mostly he didn't, and when he did what he felt was shame, for having used Kate and betrayed his wife. Kate's eyes were hanging off him, two bright red spots on her cheeks.

"Now and then," he said. "But it should never have happened."

"But it did – and I think of it often."

"Ah." Matthew pretended an interest in his purchases.

Kate burst out laughing. "I've discomfited you – twice."

"Thrice, actually," Matthew muttered. Kate chuckled, placed a hand on his arm and pecked him on the cheek.

"I'm glad we met," she said before dancing off on light feet. Just as she reached the corner of Main Street, she turned, sending him a mischievous look. "And it's true; I do think of those long-gone nights – very often." She winked, waved, and was gone.

Apart from his run-in with Kate, this had been an uneventful visit to Providence, Matthew reflected as he set out that evening. After an afternoon spent discussing kirk matters with Minister Walker – and it had gladdened Matthew to hear that Richard Campbell had chosen to leave Providence, called to serve elsewhere – he was somewhat late for his appointment with Thomas and Peter at Mrs Malone's.

So far, he had avoided running into Dominic Jones, but the first thing he heard when he opened the door to the tavern was Jones' voice, loudly calling for beer. Matthew vacillated, uncertain whether to stay or leave. Over by the counter, Jones said something that made Mrs Malone laugh, and there was Mr Farrell, tipsy to the point of requiring the support of a nearby table not to fall over.

As Matthew heard it, Mr Farrell had matrimonial issues that had him spending most of his evenings here, with the madam and her jolly whores, rather than at home. Not that such behaviour would endear him to Mrs Farrell, but mayhap she preferred it that way – at least for now. Minister Walker had confided certain concerns as to how to resolve the infected quarrel regarding Mr Farrell's decision to sell Mrs Farrell's childhood home without informing his wife beforehand.

"Matthew!" Peter stood up and waved. Jones swivelled on his toes and scowled. That sufficed for Matthew to make up his mind, greeting Mrs Malone with a bow before going over to join the Leslie brothers.

The meal was, as always, excellent. Matthew licked the grease from his fingers and sat back, shaking his head at the last of the pig trotters.

"You take it," he said to Thomas, who eagerly complied.

Peter wiped his mouth and sighed happily. "Good food,

good beer, pretty wenches; what more can a man ask for?"

"Not much." Matthew smiled at the lass who set down a new pitcher of beer before them.

"What did Minister Walker have to say?" Thomas asked. Matthew sighed. It was all about the Indians, about white man being threatened, about homesteads being razed to the ground.

"Ah," Thomas said, and Matthew could see in his eyes that his friend was gripped by an urge to hasten back home.

"Not here, but in Virginia..." Matthew shook his head. It had surprised him to hear that the Virginia governor had so far shown little interest in organising a decisive action against the natives. As he recalled it, Sir William was a man of much courage, but mayhap the man was too old and too set in his ways to countenance military action.

"It will spill over on us soon," Peter said. "Mark my words, if the Virginians don't sort their Indian issues, we will have outright war here as well."

"It's the Susquehannock," Thomas said. "It's them that are the instigators."

"It's us," Matthew said curtly. "We broke the treaties, aye? Not them. Not that it helps." He drank deeply, wondering if Qaachow was involved in the ongoing hostilities in Virginia. He hoped not, because if he was... He drank some more, swallowing down on the fear that his home would end up a charred ruin, his family dead or destroyed.

"What else did you discuss?" Thomas asked, and Matthew was grateful for the opportunity to change the subject, spending the following minutes telling the Leslie brothers about the minister's plan for a school.

He was halfway through when Thomas stood up. "Him! Here!"

"Who?" Matthew turned towards the door and near on choked. Sitting beside Jones was that accursed miscreant Philip Burley, looking as if butter wouldn't melt in his mouth. Thomas was already moving towards them, his hand on the handle of his knife. Matthew followed, fingering his dirk.

Philip Burley rose to his feet at their approach. "Mr

Graham, Mr Leslie." He sketched them a bow, his hand gripping the butt of his pistol. Burley must have come into money recently, Matthew concluded as he took in the velvet coat, the tailored breeches and the polished boots.

"What are you doing here?" Thomas demanded. "How dare you even show your face here."

"Mr Burley is here with me," Jones said. "We are discussing business."

"Business? With him?" Thomas spat to the side. "And what services does he offer? Assassinations on request?"

"Among others," Philip drawled, looking at Matthew. "But at present it is the slave business we're discussing. Most lucrative, as you can see." He leaned forward, bracing himself on the table. "Not that my recent commercial successes have made me forget my other pressing matters."

"Such as being dragged to trial for your attempt to murder me?" Matthew shot back.

"I'd like to see you try." Burley squared his shoulders.

"We'll do more than try," Matthew said.

"I think not." Jones snapped his fingers. Four men stepped forward, armed to the teeth. "Mr Burley is my guest, and I'll not have my guest arrested."

"Your guest? Strange company you keep these days, Jones. A respectable man to consort with a villainous cut-throat... Ah, but I forget; it was you that hired Burley and his disreputable brothers," Matthew said.

Jones stood. "I did? I think not and—"

"My brother is dead! Killed by you!" Philip interrupted, pointing at Matthew.

"One less to worry about, and once we've put you in chains, that leaves only two." Thomas made as if to grab Philip but was shoved back. Steel grated on steel, a blade swished through the air.

"Enough!" Mrs Malone appeared at the table. "You know better than to have your men come in armed, Mr Jones. I'll not stand for it, so take your quarrels outside, gentlemen. Now."

"Gentlemen?" Thomas laughed. "Not these two, Mrs

Malone. Dominic Jones and Philip Burley are scum, and you would do well to bar them from your establishment."

"You impinge my honour," Jones growled.

"You have no honour," Thomas said. "A man who tries to shoot one of his own is a rogue."

"I did not!"

"Aye, you did. We both know it," Matthew said.

"And I'll insist on it 'til my dying day." Thomas shook his fist at Jones.

"Which might come sooner than you think if you repeat such slanderous nonsense." Jones scowled.

"A threat?" Matthew shook his head. "Now, now, Mr Jones, we can't have that, can we?"

"Outside, all of you!" Mrs Malone yelled, but no one moved.

"I did not attempt to shoot you, Graham. That is a misconstruction. I have repeated over and over again that it was the Indian I was aiming at. To hear Mr Leslie insist I had my gun levelled at you…well, I find it most hurtful." Jones placed a hand somewhere in the region of his heart. "And I will not tolerate such calumnies. I have a reputation to uphold."

"Aye, that you do; a reputation as a cold-hearted, greedy bastard who stops at nothing to line his purse with an extra shilling or two."

Jones laughed. "That's called being a trader, Mr Graham. Profit is always profit, however small the amount. And if you excuse me, I shall now comply with Mrs Malone's wishes and leave – as should all of us."

"Not him." Thomas pointed at Burley.

"Oh, him as well. Or else I will be obliged to have my men kill you, which would, of course, be most unfortunate and cause Mrs Malone substantial distress."

"I'll kill him first!" Thomas pulled his knife. Peter grabbed hold of his arm, shaking his head.

"Most wise." Jones nodded. "And one shouldn't make threats one can't deliver on, Mr Leslie. Philip Burley would make mincemeat of you – in a matter of seconds."

Thomas blustered, Peter hung on to his arm, and Matthew could do nothing but seethe as Jones and his party made for the exit.

At the door, Philip Burley turned. "Just so you know, Graham, I don't make empty threats. And one day…" He dragged his finger over his throat, laughed and hurried outside.

"You were there!" Matthew glared at Mr Farrell. "You heard the man, you saw that damned Burley."

Mr Farrell squinted at the sun and muttered that, even if he had been there, he had no recollection of the events as such.

"He threatened me," Matthew said, "and that Jones—"

"That Jones what?" Dominic said, joining them. He nodded at the two ministers and murmured a greeting to Mr Farrell.

"You're harbouring a man who tried to kill me," Matthew said, "at your behest, no doubt."

"At my behest? And you have proof of this?" Jones looked Matthew up and down. "You must stop this, Mr Graham, all these accusations levelled against myself. Figments of an overheated imagination, gentlemen," he added, directing himself to the ministers. "Yes, Graham and I have a past, but from there to want him dead? Really!"

"You do, and we both know why."

Jones waved Matthew silent and pursed his mouth. "As to Burley, I dare say you're right. The man is a scoundrel, and I have therefore decided not to do business with him, however lucrative. And I had him forcibly removed from town this morning." His eyes met Matthew's, a triumphant gleam in them.

"Forcibly? You had him aboard one of your sloops," Thomas put in.

"Most forcibly. Burley had matters he wanted to attend to – here." Jones grinned. "It may be I saved your life, Graham."

"Saved it? It was you…" Matthew closed his mouth,

irritated by the mild look of disapproval on the ministers' faces. "You were there, Minister Walker."

"I was. And while I saw the Burley brothers attack you, I did not see Mr Jones doing so." Minister Walker patted Matthew on his shoulder. "I understand you find this most distressing, Brother Matthew. But leave Mr Jones out of it – unless, of course, you have proof." With an apologetic shrug he was off, with the other minister and Mr Farrell in his wake.

Thomas said something about having to visit the farrier before they set off and left Matthew alone with Jones.

"I should tell them," Matthew said. "And maybe I will; the whole sorry tale starting with Fairfax's murder."

"You do that and I'll put you through hell." Jones' previously so affable mien was replaced by an intimidating scowl. "As I said, you have sons, Graham. One word from you and who knows what will happen to them?"

"You wouldn't dare!"

"I wouldn't? I don't make idle threats either. Best you keep it in mind." Jones stretched to his full height. "As I said, stay out of my life and I'll stay out of yours – well, what remains of it, now that Philip Burley has his eyes set on you." Jones smirked and sauntered off.

"It's all conjecture," Matthew said some hours later. "I can never make a case against him. All I have is a murder and a last-minute will that named Jones as the benefactor of estates previously left to a relative." He was still shaken by Jones' parting comment, his mind invaded with images of his sons dead, he himself dead, his wife... Matthew took off his hat and scrubbed at his hair in an effort to dislodge these disconcerting visions.

"Have you at least written it all down?" Thomas said, from where he was riding just in front of Matthew.

"I have. I've left it with William Hancock – together with my will."

"Good." Thomas nodded.

"Good? If it comes to that, I'll be dead." But it wouldn't

come to that, he comforted himself. Burley was far away, and he was capable of defending himself, a better swordsman by far than most.

"Nothing will happen." Peter held in his horse to wait for them. "As long as you don't say anything, Jones won't do anything."

"It's not Jones I'm worried about," Matthew said. "It's Burley."

"A long ride from where he lives to where you live," Peter said. "With time, he will forget, Matthew."

"You think?" Philip Burley struck Matthew as a man capable of holding a grudge for a lifetime.

"Or die. Men as disreputable as he is tend to live brief lives." Peter clapped his heels to his mount, making the horse break into a trot. "We'd best pick up pace," he called over his shoulder. "If you're not home in time for the birthing, you'll be a dead man anyway."

Matthew laughed and urged Moses into a canter. His wife waited for him; a wean was soon to be born. Life would go on, he told himself. Nobody would kill him; nobody would tear his family apart. He wouldn't allow it, and for now he was strong enough to keep them all safe. For now.

Chapter 35

"I don't think I want to do this ever again," Alex said, and Matthew wasn't sure if it was her that was incapable of unclasping his hand, or him that just couldn't let go. Her hair was plastered to her sweaty brow, her legs were still shaking with the effort of giving birth, and on her stomach lay the latest addition to their family. Her left arm encircled the wean – a lad. She licked her lips and took a shaky breath.

"I don't think I want you to either," Matthew said just as unsteadily.

It had been a long, hard struggle, this their eighth child, and Matthew was washed by a wave of tenderness at the sight of her reclining against the pillows, still in her soiled shift, the entire room smelling of blood and sweat and fear.

His son mewled and moved his limbs in a crawling motion, the small head lifting and butting hard in its search for food. Matthew disentangled his hand from Alex's and lifted the wean to lie at her breast, watching with the same wonder he always felt as this new life latched onto the offered nipple and began the arduous work of feeding. Alex moaned, a hand coming down to press at her lower belly. She made a face at her as yet uncovered legs and the mess between them.

Mrs Parson patted her on her thigh. "I'll fetch some warm water and then we'll get you into a clean shift and clean sheets."

"Sounds wonderful." Alex smiled, her eyes blinking. She shifted the wean to her other breast and leaned into Matthew, her head heavy on his shoulder. For a moment, he thought she might have fallen asleep like that, the babe at her breast, and he draped his arm closer around her and the wean both.

"You were wrong." Her voice drifted up with a note of satisfaction. "And I was right. A boy."

"Aye, you were." Matthew laughed into her ▮, then he began to weep, and she crawled as close as she ▮ and cried as well.

"So what's his name?" Alex asked some time later. There was some colour in her cheeks, the room had been aired and cleaned, and she was sitting up in her best chemise, ready to receive the rest of the family. Matthew stroked her hair and kissed her brow.

"Samuel." Matthew lifted his son to lie in his arms. "Samuel Isaac Graham."

"Samuel? Such a big name for such a wee lad."

He smiled at Alex's choice of words – she didn't even notice. "He'll grow."

"Oh, he will, and let me tell you he was pretty big to begin with." She grimaced, unlaced her chemise and placed their bonny lad at her breast.

"Samuel Isaac," Magnus held the baby in his arms and studied him for a long time. Two new grandchildren in fifteen months and both so alike at the moment of their birth they could be twins. A tuft of dark hair, eyes that were an indefinite shade of muddy blue, and a long mouth, curved into an involuntary smile.

"They could bear a stamped legend," Magnus joked. "You know, *Made by Matthew Graham.*"

"It's a good mould, and if they turn out anything like their father once they've grown up—"

"Spare me the panegyrics. I already know you consider Matthew Graham to be God's gift to womankind."

"No," Alex yawned, "but he's definitely God's gift to me."

"That's what you've been waiting for," Mrs Parson said to Magnus some weeks later, nodding her head in the direction of the baby basket where Samuel slept under the cover of a thin linen cloth.

"Yes, I thought that I should at least get a peek at him before I died."

...ied him with her head tilted to one side. ...nus of a huge magpie, with those bright ...by a white linen cap and white linen collar. ... mumbled, "I look more dead than alive." ... made a dismissive sound. "You look very ... even. But that isn't dead, is it?" ...; soon." These days, the headache was a constant, and increasingly the pain was such that he wanted to yank his left eye out to allow whatever it was that was growing in him expansion room.

"Aye, probably." Mrs Parson folded together her knitting and came over to place a hand on his head. "Another pipe?"

He gave her a grateful look. Alex had this strange notion about rationing his weed, insisting overconsumption would make him an addict. Rather hilarious, given that he would be dead long before his addiction became a problem. Magnus sighed. Right now, all he wanted was for this to be over.

"What day is it today?" Magnus asked Alex a few days later. He craned his head back to look out at the pale blue summer sky but closed his eyes with the effort.

"Midsummer's Eve."

How apt, Magnus thought, to die on the longest day of the year. He lay in silence, listening to the sounds around him. Sounds of life, of continuity: Samuel's soft snuffling from where he slept in his basket only feet from his ear, David's piercing screams from outside, and Agnes' low soothing voice, shushing him. In the distance he could hear a horse – probably Moses – and there were birds, and hens cackling, and the ubiquitous sound of young, vibrant beings, his grandchildren, tumbling around in the summer afternoon.

He smiled at Jenny's tuneless singing, recognised the tread of Matthew's feet on the kitchen floor – there was that damned plank that always creaked – and from beside him came the clicking sound of Mrs Parson's knitting. He listened some more and heard that one sound was missing. Alex was holding her breath, and that meant she was trying very hard not to cry. He moved one hand in her direction and immediately her fingers closed over his.

"It's not too bad," Magnus lied. It was fucking terrible! Whenever he opened his eyes, it was like having a red-hot needle poked through his tender cornea, so he preferred to keep them closed. Behind his eyelids swirled blacks and blues and the occasional dash of bright vermillion and orange and sometimes – thank heavens – a soothing green, and then it all began again and he was in so much pain that sometimes he could feel each individual strand of hair as a hurting, aching extremity. He sighed; he should have taken his planned overdose months ago, but he'd been too much of a coward, and since then he'd used up all his pills, buying himself short reprieves from the pain.

He heard Matthew enter the room, hesitating for a few seconds before pulling up a stool to sit beside Alex. It almost made Magnus laugh; like a *lit de parade*, the adults of his family converging to watch him die. He twisted his face towards the twilight that hovered outside the small window.

"I always knew," he said.

"Knew what?" Alex asked.

"That I'd die at dusk." He turned his face to the wall. Soon he'd be dead, and never again would he see the trees or the clouds, never would he walk over fields, brush his legs through knee-high grasses. Not that it mattered. Nothing mattered except for the pain that inhabited his head, the humongous effort it was to keep on breathing. There was a numbness in his chest, a squeezing sensation as if his heart was cramping. Air. He needed air, and he sucked and sucked, but nothing seemed to reach his lungs. No click, click, click from his right-hand side; instead, Mrs Parson's hand closed over his, her breath warm on his cheek as she leaned over him.

"Go with God, Magnus Lind," she said, and he heard it in her voice that he was dying, that any moment now he'd be dead, and he didn't want to be.

In Magnus' head, things happened that were frightening and awe-inspiring – like being high on something far more potent than marijuana, his brain dissolving into extraordinary

309

fireworks. Everything was spinning; he saw bands of shifting colours and he shot forward through time and there was Isaac – in Stockholm, Magnus noted with pleased surprise. He was dragged backwards in time, he whizzed past Alex, and there was his Mercedes. He squinted because he'd never seen her so old, but there she was, her dark hair a beautiful silvered grey covered by a lace mantilla, and he realised she was back in her time, living out her life, and all of him shrivelled in panic. I don't want to die if she's not there waiting for me! Idiot, his brain jeered, no one's waiting for you – you don't believe in the afterlife, do you? No, Magnus Lind, this is the final curtain call, and soon… No! He shrieked in protest at God, at the bursts of light that were falling like confetti in his head.

Hands on his arm, someone kissed his cheek, dragging him back to a glimmer of real life. With an effort, he opened his eyes.

"Alex? *Lilla hjärtat?*"

"*Pappa.*" She clasped his groping hand and held Magnus as he began the final fall from life. It no longer hurt. It was all a soothing cold that was like rustling silk over his poor, aching brain. It grew dark. The spinning slowed to a gentle twirling and he could no longer hear, but he could still feel Alex's hand in his.

It grew even darker and it was very cold but it didn't matter because now there was a growing point of light and in it he saw Mercedes. She was young, her hair fell free down her back, and she held out her hand to him and smiled.

"Mercedes?" he whispered.

"*Estoy aquí,*" she murmured. "I'm always here, *amor mío.*"

"He's gone," Mrs Parson said.

Alex extricated her hand and placed it on Magnus' cheek. So cold, so no longer him… She turned to Matthew and held out her arms. Wordlessly, he gathered her to him, and she sat in his lap and was rocked like a child while she cried. But in her head she saw Magnus and Mercedes wander off hand in hand into a deep, restful blue, and very faintly she heard her father laugh, a sound of pure, unadulterated joy.

Chapter 36

The coffin was lowered into the waiting hole, and on shaky legs Alex took the few steps required to deposit her posy on the dark wood.

"Alright?" Matthew's hand rested for an instant on her arm. She nodded and retreated to stand to the side while the men began filling in the grave, shovelful after shovelful of dark, moist soil landing with a thud on the wooden lid.

"Devastated," Jenny told Elizabeth in an undertone. "She took to her bed for the following day."

Alex frowned, but pretended not to hear, keeping her eyes straight ahead.

"Really?" Elizabeth whispered — well, tried to. "She looks strangely ravaged for an expected death. It's a miracle her father held on this long, what with him being nothing but skin and bones."

"Ian says it's on account of her only ever having had a father," Jenny said.

"Ah," Elizabeth said. "Yes, she is a singularly lonely person, isn't she? No siblings, now no parents…"

Alex turned their way, tired of pretending she couldn't hear a word.

"How's Celia?" she asked Elizabeth, smiling down at Jenny's baby, Malcolm, fast asleep in his mother's arms.

Elizabeth's lips pursed for an instant. "She has me a trifle concerned. She has swollen most significantly of late in both hands and feet, complains about headaches and a constant mauling backache."

"Swollen? Like with dropsy?" Mrs Parson popped her head in between them.

"Yes." Elizabeth gave Mrs Parson a worried look.

"She's due shortly, no?" Mrs Parson asked.

"In a fortnight, we reckon."

"Any bleeding?"

Elizabeth made a scandalised sound. "I won't discuss my daughter-in-law's private matters at a funeral. It isn't seemly!" She swivelled her head this way and that to ensure no one was listening and then dropped her voice. "Yes, but not much."

"Hmm," Mrs Parson said, looking very concerned.

"She's dead?" Jenny stared at Mrs Parson. "Celia? But..." Jenny sat down with a thud. "How?"

Mrs Parson's shoulders were bowed, and for the first time Alex noticed that Mrs Parson was in fact quite old – even very old by the standards of the here and now: sixty-four or thereabouts.

"Sit down," Alex said. "I'll bring you something to drink, and then you can tell us."

Mrs Parson just nodded, yet another indication of how affected she was by the whole thing. Alex returned with a mug of sweetened tea and a slice of rich currant cake.

"Thank you." Mrs Parson placed her hand over Alex's.

"The baby?" Alex asked as a starting point.

"A lassie," Mrs Parson said, stirring her tea. "Healthy enough, although not as bonny as her brother was when he exited the womb. The afterbirth came undone during the birth, and there was nothing I could do to stop the bleeding. She bled to death." The mug shook when she raised it to her mouth. "Not a sound did she make. She just looked at me..." Mrs Parson's voice broke. "She just looked at me."

"I'm so sorry for your loss," Alex said to Elizabeth at the second funeral in less than a month.

Elizabeth looked at her from dull eyes. "Thank you, she was a good daughter-in-law, was Celia, and we'll have problems finding someone to fill her shoes."

Alex looked over to where Nathan stood white-faced beside his father with his little son in arms. "It must be difficult for him."

"Yes, they were fond of each other." Elizabeth sounded a bit strange, her eyes stuck on one of her maids. The girl, a delicate blonde with a baby in a shawl, squirmed under her mistress' look.

Once Celia was safely in the ground, Peter Leslie invited the men to his study. Alex wanted to go home, but Matthew gave her a helpless look and followed his host, leaving Alex to trail Elizabeth and the other Leslie women to the kitchen.

The table groaned under the combined weight of the platters holding everything from cheese to pickled tongue, and after a few mugs of beer, Elizabeth was back in good old form, haranguing everyone within earshot about the deficient morals of her papist maids.

"Little slut!" she spat, jerking her head in the direction of the girl with the baby. "No sooner did she get here but she ended up pregnant."

"All on her own?" Alex said.

"Of course not," Elizabeth snorted. "No divine intervention, just a scheming wanton taking advantage of my poor Nathan."

"Poor Nathan?" Alex set down her mug. "What if it's the other way around?"

Elizabeth's face took on an unhealthy hue, so when Mary grabbed at Alex's sleeve and suggested they step outside, she complied.

Matthew spent an hour or so enclosed with the Leslie men and a good whisky, after which he went to find his wife. Alex was sitting in the shade with Mary and, from the set of her mouth, he could see she was right upset. Once he followed her eyes across the yard to where the serving wenches were sitting, he knew why.

"Fond of each other!" Alex said as he helped her up on Moses. "He was so fond of his wife he impregnated one of the indentured girls. And now that unfortunate woman – who, by the way, has had her contract extended – is nursing not only her child by Nathan, but Celia's little girl. Probably apt poetic justice in Elizabeth's book."

"You're being unfair," Matthew chided. "She's the only nursing mother there."

"Huh," Alex sniffed and took off her cap, complaining she was hot.

"Will he marry her, do you think?" she asked a bit later, leaning back against him. Samuel squirmed inside her shawl, a small red fist appearing to wave at the world.

"She isn't good enough, and if I'm not mistaken she's also Irish." But she was a comely lass, wee Ailish, with those elfin features and eyes like crushed violets.

"Irish? And what does that have to do with anything?"

"She's not of the right faith, she being a papist and all."

"Sometimes..." She threw both arms up in the air in an exasperated gesture which almost led to them falling off the horse. "Oh, what the hell!" she finished. "It's a petty, small-minded world at times."

"Aye, but now and then people surprise you."

"They do?"

Matthew chuckled and held her tight. "You wait and see, lass. I fear Elizabeth and Peter Leslie have somewhat of a surprise coming."

"You do?"

"Och, aye, I do." He slowed Moses to a walk and buried his nose in her uncovered hair. "I love you," he murmured.

"You're only saying that because you're hoping for some action, Mr Graham. More or less now."

"I am? And how would you know?"

"Let's just say that I have a long-standing relationship with that part of you that's presently nudging at my arse."

He laughed, pressed himself a wee bit closer and turned off the bridle path. Once he'd halted Moses, he dismounted, somewhat gingerly because of his erection.

"Will you join me?" he asked, bowing.

"As if you need to ask." She smiled down at him.

"You look like a fairy, or a wood sprite," he said drowsily, lying back with his head pillowed on his arms. The sun filtered through the canopies of the tall trees that surrounded them, casting dancing shafts of golden light to gleam on moss and stones, on his discarded boots and on her, his woman. She was rosy from their recent lovemaking, sitting in only her shift, her hair hanging undone round her shoulders, their son at her breast.

"You look pretty other-worldly yourself." She smiled, drawing a finger down his naked torso. He shivered at her touch, the skin prickling in anticipation. Samuel burped, expelled something that sounded like a contented mewling and fell asleep, his head pillowed on his mother's shoulder. She placed their son on his chest, and he cupped his son's head, his wee bum.

"Did you think it would be like this?" she asked, lying back down beside him on the makeshift bed consisting mainly of her skirts and shawl.

"Like what?" He let his head fall over to meet her eyes.

"Did you think it would get so much better as we got older?" Her cheeks coloured a deep pink. "Or maybe you don't think it has gotten better," she said, making him smile.

"It has, on account of us knowing better how to please each other." He shifted Samuel to lie beside him before rolling over towards his wife. With a light finger he traced her brows, the delicate pointed tip of her ear. "I didn't think it could get better, and in some ways it hasn't – after all, I no longer rouse as easily after the first time as I used to." He brushed her nose with his own, kissed each of her eyes in turn.

"You don't?"

His thighs parted under her touch. "Nay, not as fast, but fast enough." He kissed the corner of her mouth and laid her down on her back, drawing out long strands of hair to decorate her pale skin. "We didn't get very far with the Song of Solomon, did we?" he said, sliding his hands up her thighs. Skin as soft as velvet, smooth and warm under his palms. His thumbs brushed over her privates. She sighed, lifting her hips towards his touch.

"No, we never get very far beyond the first lines. But I do believe we have the sentiment down pat."

"Aye," he breathed against her ear. "That we do."

★

"I'll be riding down to Providence at the end of next week," Matthew said once they were back on the horse. "I have to be there on the first of August." A long, slow afternoon spent in a clearing in the forest had left him heavy with sated desire, somnolent near on, and it would appear his wife was in the same state, seeing as it took her some time to reply.

"To Providence?"

"I must be there for the meeting of the militia." Matthew grimaced. "What with the repeated attacks on outlying settlements during the summer, it's all set to explode. Thomas and I will be riding down together. With Jacob."

"Jacob?" Her voice squeaked.

"As we decided – the lad's to go into apprenticeship, setting him up on his way to becoming a man."

"You decided." She closed her arms round the wean and said nothing more.

Matthew sensed the tension radiating from her but chose not to say anything. She had to learn to let them go.

The night before they were scheduled to leave, Alex came and found Matthew in the stables.

"I can't," she said, her voice heavy with tears. "Please don't make me let him go."

"It's a good opportunity for him. And you've had a year to prepare yourself."

"I can't send away my ten-year-old boy, not now, with the countryside in upheaval and you soon off to ride with the militia and…" She took a big breath and knotted her hands in her apron. "I just can't."

Matthew went back to his currying, thinking as he worked. Behind him, he could hear her breathing, the restless shifting from foot to foot as she waited for him to reply.

"One more year," he said, turning to face her.

"Thank you," she whispered, "thank you so very much." She almost curtsied but stopped herself at the last moment. He smiled slightly. Some weeks shy of forty-two, his wife

316

had seemingly learnt that ultimately most things were his decision, not hers.

"You may kiss me if you wish to show your gratitude in an appropriate, wifely manner," he teased.

Alex's head flew up and a bolt of bright blue hit him squarely in the eyes. "I don't."

"Oh aye? But I do." He grabbed at her and pulled her close, ignoring her half-hearted attempts at wresting herself free.

"I'll take him down to Providence with me anyway," Matthew said to Alex as they made their way to the house. "It might be good for him to meet Hancock in person already now." He frowned at the thought of the upcoming discussions with the lawyer, but decided Hancock would understand the motherly concerns – in particular given the escalating tension between natives and whites. "That way he can see where he will live and acquaint himself with the town – and meet the Hancock lasses."

"Lasses? They have children?"

"Six lasses, the three eldest wed already, but the three youngest remain at home." The youngest was of an age with Jacob, he told her, and as he recalled a cheerful, polite lass. "It won't come amiss with a friend."

"No, a friend is always good."

He smiled. The Hancock lassie would be a good match for his Jacob, but he saw no reason to broach this subject yet.

Alex had to bite back a smile at her son's over-excited face. Jacob was bouncing up and down on the mule, so eager was he to ride off alone with his da.

"I'll bring you back something nice," he told his sisters. "Mayhap some of those sweets you liked so much last year?"

Sarah nodded eagerly.

"A book," Ruth said gravely. "Could you find me a book, do you think?"

Jacob promised he would try, his hand clutching the few coins Alex had given him.

"What do you want, Mama?" he asked when she came over to pat him on the leg.

"Me?" She raised her eyes to his. "I want you to come back, Jacob. That's the best gift I can wish for."

She laughed at how pleased he looked, patted him on the cheek and went over to where Matthew was already astride Moses.

To her husband, Alex had other words to say. She stood holding on to his stirrup and waited until he bent his head to hers. "Stay away from him, Matthew. This time don't go anywhere close to Dominic Jones. Promise me you won't."

"I'll give the man as wide a berth as I can."

"Good." Her eyes moved to the loaded pistol at his belt and she nodded approvingly. One doesn't enter the viper's nest unarmed.

Chapter 37

Jacob had never ridden so far before, and by the time they made their way into Providence, three days after setting out, all he could think of was the sore, chafing skin along the crease of his buttocks and down the insides of his thighs. For three days he'd listened to Mr Leslie and Da while they discussed the latest incidents of burning and pillaging, and he could hear in Da's voice that he wasn't happy about leaving his own home unprotected to go and protect elsewhere.

"It's them that provoke the Indians that should handle it themselves," Da said at one point. "I've had no problems with them; none at all."

Thomas Leslie agreed, saying that the colonists were in flagrant breach of the treaty lines, and he could understand that the Nanticote and Powhatan settlements were irritated by this encroachment.

"In Virginia in particular," Mr Leslie said, "it's not that long ago since Berkeley fought them to submission and signed treaties with them that are now being trampled underfoot."

"Long enough." Da smiled. "About the time you and I were fighting for the Commonwealth."

Jacob listened avidly. Rarely did Da talk about the four years he had served in the Horse, and then mainly to bewail the futility of war or to tell them harshly that war was not about glory and honour; it was about blood and pain and being hungry and cold and wishing desperately to be back home with your mam. Needless to say, none of his sons believed him, and in secret they played out long battle sequences between Roundheads and Royalists, with Ruth and Sarah being roped in to add to the numbers.

"When we were both young men." Mr Leslie twitched

at the ancient buff leather jacket that strained over his middle despite the extra panels in it.

"Did you both serve in the Horse?" Jacob asked.

"Aye, but not in the same regiment." Da twisted in his saddle towards Mr Leslie. "Did you ever meet him? The Protector?"

"Not as such, no. I saw him at the battle of Naseby, and once I saw him in London. And you?"

Da hitched his shoulders. "Nay, but then why would a man such as Oliver Cromwell notice an eager farmer's lad with his head and heart full of convictions but nothing much else?"

Mr Leslie smiled. "It was people like that who changed it all — at least for a while. It was all those that burnt with these new ideas of self-governance and equality that achieved a time when England was not ruled by a king but by free men."

"A very short period, all in all," Da said.

"A precedent." Thomas Leslie nodded. "And one day that precedent will be followed by others."

"Do you think he's right, Da?" Jacob asked later. It was a relief to be walking, not riding, and he hurried as best as he could to keep up with Da through the narrow streets of Providence.

"Who?" Da shortened his stride.

"Mr Leslie. Is he right when he says you all set a...a precedent with the Commonwealth?"

"Shh!" Da looked about before returning his attention to Jacob. "These are things you don't discuss openly and never with people you don't know and trust."

"Sorry," Jacob mumbled, allowing his thick hair to come down like a curtain before his face.

"Aye," Da said some moments later, "I think he is. And it will all start here."

"Here?" Jacob surveyed the small, nondescript town around him.

Da smiled and straightened up to his full height. "Aye,

here. I won't see it, you won't see it, but mayhap your children, or at least your grandchildren. This is the cradle, and it's already being set in motion." He laughed and ruffled Jacob's hair. "That's what happens. Most people you see here have come on account of convictions, lad. They have come determined to build a new life for themselves, free of persecution and ancient constraints... There is no turning back the flood, and this particular tide will build until it one day washes away all vestiges of the old." He peeked down at Jacob. "You didn't follow, did you?"

Jacob shook his head ruefully. "No, I don't understand. Not yet."

One look at Betty Hancock and Jacob understood why Mark so often would choose to spend time with Naomi instead of with him. The lass standing in front of him reminded him of a squirrel: bright brown eyes, bright brown hair that was so curly it stood like a fuzz around her head despite the tight braids, freckled skin that hued in browns and dusky pinks, and a wide, welcoming smile that broadened as she appraised him. Betty dropped Da a polite curtsey and went back to staring at Jacob.

"Come," Betty said. "If you come with me to the kitchen, Mother will give you something to eat." She sniffed. "She's making pie. Do you like pie?"

Jacob assured her that he did and followed her out of the front room.

"I hear you have yet a son," William Hancock said to Matthew, motioning for him to sit. Matthew nodded and accepted the proffered mug of beer. "You're fortunate in your wife." There was a slight tinge of envy in Hancock's tone. "What is it? Six sons?"

"And one grandson."

"Ah, yes..." Hancock smiled into his beer. "I have three grandsons." He looked towards the kitchen from where came the sound of girlish voices raised in a heated discussion. "Women," he sighed. "I live surrounded by women. Like an isle in a sea of sirens."

"And rarely do you complain about it," Mrs Hancock said from the door, a loaded tray in her hands.

"I wouldn't dare to," William said, smiling at his wife. Pregnant, Matthew noted, and no doubt praying that this time it would be a lad, a son that lived beyond his first year, unlike all those wee laddies William had told him about last time they met.

"Esther is most devout," William remarked once they were alone again. "She rises well before dawn to read her daily lessons and meditate upon the Holy Writ."

"Ah," Matthew said with mild approval, wondering if this specific characteristic would endear Esther to Alex or not.

"And she's strict with the children when it comes to God and the Bible, but I'm assuming that is as you want it."

"Aye." Matthew studied the small room, noting it was clean and uncluttered. The food set before him was tasty, and Mrs Hancock looked neat, her grey skirts and bodice offset by a starched white collar, her hair decorously covered by a cap. Yes, this would be a good home for his son, and if it also led to him developing a fondness for the wee lass that was not so bad, was it?

"Do you think you'll settle in with them?" Matthew asked Jacob once they were back on the street. Jacob nodded, telling him that Mrs Hancock reminded him in some aspects of Mama; and Betty: she was like he imagined Rachel would have been had she still been alive.

Matthew laughed. The lad was right: wee Betty had that air of bubbling energy that had accompanied Rachel from the moment she was delivered into his arms to the day she flew to his defence and met her death.

"Do you miss her?" Jacob asked.

"Aye I do, very much." The child of his heart, the lass whom he had loved so intensely from the first time he saw her.

"Would you..." Jacob broke off, eyes stuck on the cobbles.

"I would," Matthew said, "of course I would. Every one of you, I would miss as much had you been taken from me."

★

It seemed to Jacob that every soul in town knew his father, their progress halted repeatedly as Da stopped to greet yet another acquaintance. Minister Walker hailed them on the dusty street, beamed down at Jacob, and launched himself into a long discussion with Da, leaving Jacob to stand bored by their side.

He scuffed at the ground, studying the people that moved around them. Most of them were adults, men in hats and coats, with a sprinkling of women and children. He smiled politely at the pretty lady coming their way and was surprised when she stopped and smiled back. Another person who knew his da and, from the way Da shone up, someone he liked, initiating a long conversation that had Jacob stamping his feet.

She was very pretty, the lady, a wafting fragrance of lilies of the valley clinging to her deep blue skirts. He took in her bodice, thinking that there was quite a lot of white skin visible, and studied what little he could see of her light hair under her hat. She put a hand on Da's arm and Jacob didn't like that at all, just as he didn't like it that Da laughed a bit too loudly at something she said.

"Who was that?" he asked, once the lady had bid them both farewell.

"Mmm?" Da smiled in the direction of the lady's back. "Oh. A friend," he said, leading the way towards the little inn.

"Da?" Jacob tugged at his sleeve. "Will you take me there?" He pointed towards the harbour where two ships lay at anchor. Even from here, he could make out the smell that emanated from one of them, and when he looked up he saw that Da's brows had pulled together into a dark line.

"Not today, lad, perhaps some other day, when yon accursed ship is gone."

Jacob pouted. He wanted to see the ships up close, not the harbour as such, but he tagged after his father as he went on his way. He was on the verge of asking Da about why the ship was accursed, but a quick peek at Da's face made him think better of it.

★

Jacob had never been to a service before. He sat at attention for the first half-hour, his eyes flying from congregation to minister and back to congregation, barely listening to the service as such. The next half-hour he amused himself by swinging his legs back and forth and counting the number of times the minister stopped to repeat what he had just said. After one and a half hour, he was so bored he began to fidget, only to have Da's hand come down like a clamp on his leg. After that he sat very still, eyes straight ahead and ears shut. Poor Daniel; this was what he was going to do when he grew up – talk people to sleep on a Sunday.

After the service Da told Jacob to wait for him under the plane trees and settled down to a long debate with several of the men. There was an obvious agitation in the way they held themselves, and repeatedly they nodded in agreement with each other, listening attentively when Thomas Leslie or Da held forth. It made Jacob proud to see his da like this, surrounded by men who seemed to defer to his judgement, most of them forced to crane their heads back due to Da being that much taller than them. But it was boring to sit and wait, and it was hot despite being in the shade, so without really knowing how, Jacob wandered off in the direction of the glittering water.

He hesitated when he got closer to the port area, surprised to see so many women and men about on this day of rest. And the women! He gawked at them in admiration; he had never seen something as pretty as these painted girls before.

Finally, he reached the wharves, and up close the ships were huge, creaking in the wind. Just opposite to where he was standing were what looked like huge holding pens. For an instant, he supposed it might be for cattle and pigs and such, but then he saw people moving behind the fence and gaped. So many, and so black! The stench that wafted across the water from the enclosure made him back away, falling flat on his back when his foot caught on a pile of coiled ropes.

"What have we here?"

Jacob looked up to find himself surrounded by four

men, their heads backlit by the sun. They reeked of beer and grime, three of them swaying unsteadily on their feet, while the shortest was leaning over Jacob, his hair standing like a messy haystack around his ratty face, made even more disconcerting by his drooping eyelid.

"Sirs." Jacob scrambled to his feet. He didn't like the look of them, of how they eyed him as if he were a juicy bone of meat and they starving dogs.

"They pay well for boys as comely as that," the short man said to the others.

Jacob could barely breathe. How pay? He clenched his fist around his little knife.

"Too old. They like them younger than that," one of the other men said.

"We could always cut him – that'd keep him downy cheeked for ever," the fattest of the men suggested.

Cut him? You cut horses and pigs and even bull calves, but Jacob had never heard about cutting lads.

"Cut?" the man with the drooping eyelid snorted. "You know they don't hold with that, infidel though they may be."

"Still…" the fat man said.

"He'll sell for a high price anyway," the fourth man voiced. "They like 'em fair, don't they?"

Jacob looked from one to the other, trying to see if they were jesting, but their expressions indicated they weren't. Out of the corner of his eye he saw another man, a huge man in a curling hairpiece and a magnificent coat who was standing close enough that Jacob could see the scar that bisected the closest eyebrow.

One of the men, the fat one, made a grab for him, and Jacob backed away, slamming into the wooden wall behind him. The big, well-dressed man fiddled with his wig, clasped his hands behind his back and stared out at sea, but not before Jacob saw small eyes darting in his direction, eyes that were averted while a small smile played on his heavy face.

"Sir," Jacob croaked, but his voice didn't carry all that far – at least the large man seemed not to have heard. The short man laughed, fingering his drooping eyelid.

"Come here then, laddie," he crooned. "Come here and we won't hurt you."

"We might," his fat companion said, "but it's quick." He made a slashing motion with his hand and moved to block Jacob when he tried to sidle off. His comrades laughed.

"Come, come, little piggy," the one with the drooping eyelid said. "You'll squeal for sure if you don't come along nicely."

They had him trapped. The four men approached him from all sides, and Jacob had nowhere to go. His knees wobbled, wet warmth trickled down his legs, and Jacob was ashamed for being so unmanly, and at the same time incensed that these horrible men should talk about him as if he were an animal. He took a big breath, pulled his knife and ran, lowering his head like a small ram. He butted one man full in the stomach, stabbed another in the thigh hard enough to make him yelp, and there was the gap that Jacob needed, flying like a hare towards the edge of the wharf. Behind him, he could hear them cursing when they came after him. The water was dank and dark, making Jacob hesitate.

"Nowhere to run, laddie," the short man said.

Jacob took a deep breath and dove in. He swam a long way under water before coming up for air. On land, the four men were already moving away, and Jacob made his way back slowly, looking for somewhere to clamber up.

"Here, young Master Graham."

A rope landed in the water, and Jacob was pulled out to stand dripping on the wooden planks. Two men stood before him, one the very large, well-dressed man he'd seen before, the other an older man he recognised as Mr Farrell.

"How fortunate, Jones, that you were here," Mr Farrell said. "Those sailors carry their sport a bit too far at times. Antagonise a young boy!"

Fortunate? Jacob shoved his hair off his face, was about to tell Mr Farrell what had happened, but there was a light in the big man's eyes that made him decide to hold his tongue, trying out a weak smile instead.

"Thank you, kind sirs." Jacob bowed.

For a long time the large man – Mr Jones – stared at him, and it was all Jacob could do not to squirm.

"I'll talk to the captain of the *Henriette Marie*," Mr Farrell said. "It would do those ruffians good to spend a day or two tied to the mast."

"Indeed." Jones returned to staring at Jacob. "Your father will be most displeased. I'm sure he has warned you to stay away from here."

Jacob nodded mutely. Da wouldn't be displeased; he would be angry – very angry.

Jones swivelled on his feet and beckoned for Jacob to come with him. Jacob wasn't sure he wanted to, but Mr Farrell shooed him along, telling him Mr Jones would be kind enough to see him back to the inn. As a precaution, Jacob maintained a distance of some yards.

"Thank you." Matthew opened his arms to receive his son. "It was most kindly done." It stuck in his craw, those words did. It was an effort just to force them up his throat. To be beholden to Jones!

"Make sure he keeps away from the harbour," Jones said. "Next time there might be no one there to save him from being carried off. Slavery is colour blind, and from what I hear white children carry a high price on the slave markets in Arabia. And he's comely, your son."

"And disobedient."

After a few more pleasantries, Matthew bid Jones farewell and turned to the task of disciplining his son. By the time he was done, Jacob was no longer crying; he was hiccupping, hands covering his bright red arse. Matthew tightened his belt back into place, helped Jacob out of his wet shirt and handed him a dry one.

"You'll never disobey me again," Matthew said.

"I promise," Jacob said in a small voice.

Matthew picked up a towel and poured some water from the ewer into the shallow basin.

"Come here." He dipped the towel and washed his son's tearstained face, unclenched the small fists and washed them too before using his comb to bring some order into the damp, fair thatch. He hugged Jacob and kissed him on his brow.

"I could have lost you. God's truth, lad, do you realise how close you were to being carried away from us?"

Jacob nodded, looking at him from below his lashes. "He was there all the time."

"Who?" Matthew frowned down at him.

"The man who brought me back: Mr Jones. He was standing to the side, watching. I don't think he would've helped me if Mr Farrell hadn't shown up."

For a moment, Matthew was sure he would faint, blood rushing to collect in his gut. He squashed Jacob to him. Sweetest Lord! His son!

"God curse you, Dominic Jones, and may I be granted the opportunity to send you to hell myself."

Chapter 38

"Truly?" William Hancock shook his head. "I must say I find it hard to believe."

"Well, as yet I don't know, do I?" Matthew said. "But I aim to find out."

"Hmm." Hancock sucked in his lower lip. "There have been a few cases of disappeared children over the last few years." He threw a look at Jacob, sitting with his youngest daughters on the bench in the backyard. "But to think... No, I can't get my head around it; white men to do something so despicable. He might have misunderstood them."

"Only one way to find out." Thomas got to his feet.

"Aye," Matthew agreed, standing up as well. "She hasn't sailed yet, has she?"

"No," Thomas said. "Last I heard, the *Henriette Marie* will sail on the morrow – she's waiting for the tide."

"No time to waste," Matthew said.

"I'm coming with you." William shrugged into his coat.

"I think not," Matthew said. "We may use methods you'll not approve of."

William raised his brows. "I am no innocent. I have served my years in the armies of the Commonwealth. I dare say I'll manage."

Despite it being Sunday, the waterfront was busy in the early evening, whores conducting a brisk business with an endless line of sailors.

"We just grab a few and ask them," Thomas suggested.

"You think the common crew will know? I doubt it. No, we need a bosun, perhaps even a first mate." William studied the men around them more knowledgeably than Matthew had expected. "I do business here," William said with a crooked smile. "Almost every day I am down here on one matter or the other." He led the way to one of the taverns, talked for a few minutes with the landlord and returned with a painted girl in tow.

"Felicity," he introduced, and Matthew and Thomas inclined their heads, making the bonny little whore giggle. "Felicity here knows the first mate of the *Henriette Marie*, and she's somewhat aggrieved with him, are you not, my dear?"

"Dawson scarpered without paying last night," she said, "and I don't hold with that, do I?"

"No," Matthew agreed, "I imagine you don't."

The girl gave him a wide smile, displaying several blackened teeth.

"I've promised Felicity a finder's fee," William said. "Enough to compensate her for some hours of lost business."

"And how were you planning on doing this?" Matthew asked.

"Well, I was thinking that we'd settle ourselves here and wait." William pointed to a nearby table.

"He always comes here," Felicity put in, ruffling at her long black curls in a way that made Thomas' eyes hang off her hand. "Him and that sleazy Wilkes, his bosun." She smiled at Thomas and dropped her hand to trace her neckline. Most of her bosom was visible: two pert breasts that near on hung in plain sight. Pretty she definitely was, but Matthew shuddered at the thought of ever being desperate enough to bed a lass so...hmm...well used.

An hour or so later, a ruddy man entered the tavern with a small rat-faced man in his wake. After a word or so with the landlord, he scanned the crowd and brightened at the sight of Felicity.

"There you are, my pet!" He ploughed through the crowded room towards her.

"I'm not talking to you." Felicity sniffed, slipping her arm in under Matthew's. "That's Dawson," she whispered.

Dawson stopped, looking confused. "Why ever not? If I'm interrupting, I can wait. I dare say none of these gentlemen will last very long under your expert hands." He winked, receiving a pout in reply.

"I won't be going anywhere with you, Dawson. Not until you pay me what you owe me for last night."

"Of course I will, and look, I bought you something, didn't I?" Dawson produced a set of ivory combs from his pocket and held them aloft.

"Oh!" Felicity was up on her feet and dancing towards him.

"Move," Matthew hissed. "She'll warn him."

Thomas was on his feet, William was halfway across the room, and Matthew closed in on the little whore, now hanging like a limpet round the first mate's neck.

Felicity squealed. "Run, Dawson, they want you for something!"

Matthew threw himself forward to block Dawson's escape, but Dawson was quick, he was strong and agile, and to top it all he had Wilkes, the small man who'd entered with him and who now produced a cudgel. The cudgel whistled through the air, Matthew ducked, got hold of Dawson's breeches and yanked him to a stop. An elbow connected painfully with his face, but Matthew held on, using his weight to topple them to the floor. The bosun brought down the cudgel, raised his arm to do it again, but was stopped by Thomas.

Matthew was back on his feet and forced Dawson to follow suit by the simple expedient of pulling at his hair while William kept a shrieking Felicity from coming to the sailor's aid. When Dawson produced a knife, Matthew had had enough, kneeing the man hard in the groin before disarming him. The first mate staggered, and Matthew dragged him towards the door, helped by the landlord who loudly told his patrons that he had no tolerance – *none, y'hear?* – for violence in his tavern.

The bosun was struggling in Thomas' hold, and at one point he tore himself free, backing away with a sneer. With a little sigh, William clapped him over the head with a bottle, and so it was that a short while later they were standing outside with their two captives.

"We just want to ask you some questions," William said. "What harm is there in that?"

"Depends on the questions," Dawson retorted.

"I suggest you come with us," Matthew said, "peaceably, like."

"Peaceably?" Dawson struggled. "This is abduction, is what it is."

"Aye, and you'd know all about that, wouldn't you?" Matthew shoved at him.

The first mate paled. "I have no notion what you mean."

"We'll see." Matthew gripped Dawson by the arm and towed the protesting man with him.

William led them towards one of the warehouses, and a few minutes later they were inside a cramped little room that smelled of mildew and yeast.

"This is trespassing," Thomas muttered.

"Oh, Jones won't mind – he'll never find out, will he?" William gestured at the unswept floors and the rickety furniture. "He doesn't use this premise much; it's prone to flooding."

"Ah," Thomas said.

Wilkes took the opportunity to tear himself free and rushed for the door. Thomas yelled, William latched on to the bosun's shirt, and Dawson butted Matthew in the stomach. The enclosed space was a whirlwind of limbs, of stoutly shod feet and shouting men.

"The door!" Matthew called, and Thomas launched himself towards it, slamming it shut.

Wilkes shrieked. "My hand!" He tugged his hand free from the door.

"Enough!" Matthew grabbed hold of Dawson and threw the man against the wall.

"Uuhh," said Dawson, sliding down to the floor.

Wilkes was sobbing, cradling his bleeding hand. Matthew secured his prisoners to the two chairs in the room and stood back to look at them.

"Right, we can do this two ways: either you tell us everything we want to know immediately, or you don't. And if you don't, well then..." Matthew shrugged.

"This is unlawful," Dawson said.

"Aye, it is. But so is abducting wee lads."

"Lads?" Dawson swallowed. "What are you talking about?"

"No, no, Dawson, that won't do at all," William put in. "This is where it behoves you to tell the truth."

"What truth?" Dawson tried, but his eyes were wide with fear, and beside him Wilkes had shrunk into a silent ball, eyes locked on the floor.

"Four men, including him, tried to steal away my son today," Matthew said, jerking his thumb at Wilkes.

"Me?" Wilkes squeaked.

"Aye, you. You have a distinctive appearance – all that hair and that drooping eyelid."

"Really, Wilkes! How many times have I told you not to frighten young lads?" Dawson attempted a smile. "It's just a jest. Wilkes enjoys riling the lads a bit. No harm done."

"I don't believe you," Matthew said. "So, the truth."

Both men shook their heads.

"Fine," Matthew said, cracking his knuckles.

"Merciful Christ!" William sat down on the small table, groped for his handkerchief and wiped his face. Matthew rested back against the wall and closed his eyes. His hands hurt, the two men slumped in their ropes, blood patterned their shirts, their breeches, and still he had to fist his hands around the desire to hit them some more; a just punishment for the atrocities they had finally admitted to – unfortunately without naming Jones.

"So many lads." Thomas sank down beside William, eyeing the semi-conscious men. "We should kill them."

"Aye, but they were only doing what they were told to do," Matthew said.

"You think?" Thomas spat in Dawson's direction. "Me, I think he enjoyed it."

"Oh, most definitely, and as to the other one..." William studied his hands for a while and looked at Matthew. "This is not enough to lay anything at Dominic Jones' door, at most you can accuse him of watching and not interceding, but based on Jacob's word alone it won't carry much weight." He smoothed at his coat, regarding his bloodstained cuff with disgust. "But that ship, well, we must make sure no more boys disappear."

"Aye," Matthew agreed, "that we must."

"And those two?" Thomas jerked his head at their prisoners.

"They must not rejoin the crew of the *Henriette Marie*," William said. "We don't want them warned, do we? No, I'll see to them, I'll have them aboard a different ship come morning – destined for Jamaica or such."

Matthew raised an eyebrow. William had quite the ruthless streak in him. Not that he minded; he'd gladly have sold these ruffians as galley slaves to the Turks had he had the opportunity.

"Now what?" Thomas asked as they made their way back to the inn.

"I don't know." Matthew kicked at a stone, sending it to bounce off a nearby wall. "Damn him! He was going to let them take my Jacob. Not one fat finger would he have lifted to save my son."

"Yes," Thomas sighed.

"But this time I'll bring him down," Matthew vowed. "Even if I must wait a year or two before I have the whole puzzle neatly laid and solved."

"You don't know—" Thomas began.

"Aye, I do! It's his ship. He inherited it when Fairfax died." He spat to the side, his mouth filling with bitter bile as he recalled his miserable months aboard the *Henriette Marie*, chained like a beast in the hold.

"It is?" Thomas came to a halt. "But if it is, well then—"

"Not enough, Thomas. He can maintain he had no idea, that this was the captain's own little sideline."

"And you don't think it is?"

"I think the captain of one of Dominic's ships risks his life if he does something without Jones' approval – and I dare say they know it. So, for now, we do nothing."

"Nothing." Thomas nodded.

"And we don't tell anyone Dominic Jones owns that accursed ship either."

"No, of course not," Thomas said.

It was all Matthew could do not to pull his sword and run Jones through when he ran into him halfway across the little town square next day. As it was, he clasped his hands behind his back and advanced on Jones.

"Graham." Dominic Jones backed away.

"Jones." Matthew took yet another step towards the retreating man. Oh, how he wanted the satisfaction of seeing this man cringe before him, mayhap even kneel and weep, begging for his life. He wet his lips, swallowing back on the hot accusations that were thronging his throat, tickling his tongue.

"What?" Jones straightened up, set his shoulders and lowered his head, reminding Matthew of a cornered bull.

"Well, you see, my lad is convinced that you were standing to the side all the time those ruffians were threatening him." There was so much more he wanted to say but this was not the time – not yet.

"That's preposterous!" Dominic glowered at Matthew and tugged his waistcoat into place over his expanding middle. "Of all the ungrateful—"

"Really, Brother Matthew! It was him that helped me pull Jacob out of the water." Mr Farrell looked from one to the other and sighed. "I have no notion what lies behind this enmity, but isn't it time you moved on?"

"I am willing," Dominic Jones said. "I have said so before."

"To be quite correct, what you said was that we should promise each other not to harm each other while serving in the militia," Matthew said, "and then what did you do? Set those Burleys on me!"

"I did no such thing – as I said last time we met." Dominic rolled his eyes. "How many times must I repeat myself? They had their own reasons to wish you dead. You hindered them in their business pursuits—"

"Business pursuits? They were abducting Indian women! Was I to stand by and watch while innocents were carried off into slavery?"

"Oh, dear." Dominic smiled maliciously. "Quite the sore point, isn't it? But then you would know everything about being enslaved, would you not?"

"And I was innocent too," Matthew spat.

Dominic laughed. "They all say that, Graham, and yet very few are."

"I was, you knew I was, because I was part of your little business concern. How much money did you make by abducting innocent men back home and selling them like slave labour here?"

"How dare you!" Dominic spluttered.

"I am but telling the truth. You know that, and I know that."

"Enough!" Minister Walker shouldered his way through the small group of men that had gathered around them. "This is unseemly, two adult men quarrelling like fishmongers' wives!" He clapped his hands together, glared at the collected audience until they dispersed, with only Mr Farrell remaining. "Put it behind you," the minister suggested, making Mr Farrell nod and mutter that was just what he'd said a few minutes ago.

"I can't, and I doubt he can either." With a curt bow to the minister, Matthew left.

"Well, that didn't paint you in the best of colours, did it?" Alex said several days later, having listened to Matthew's terse recap. They were in the laundry shed, just the two of them. The small space was suffused with the scents of crushed mints; a single lantern cast a weak, yellowish glow over the tub, leaving the rest of the room in darkness.

"I don't care. What was I to do? Lie and say let bygones be bygones, when all I want to do is rip his entrails out?"

"That bad, huh?" Alex sank lower into the tub.

"Aye." He went back to washing himself. "Our Jacob," he said, scrubbing at his heel with the pumice stone. "If the laddie hadn't saved himself, he'd have been gone, and we'd never know what had happened to him."

Alex gulped down on the fear that invaded her at the thought. "You still don't know if Jones is in on it."

"Aye, he is; it's his ship. And do you know what has befallen those lads?"

"No, and nor do you, Matthew."

"Aye, I do. With some persuasion, the first mate and his bosun became quite voluble. They trade them with the Arab slave traders for black men. The lads end up as unwilling catamites, most of them dead from excessive abuse by the time they turn fifteen."

"No way, that can't be true!" Alex suppressed an urge to storm stark naked into her sons' bedroom and clutch Jacob to her.

"But it is. The *Henriette Marie* does best in staying away from Providence in the future. William Hancock has done a good job of letting people know about its most profitable – and despicable – sideline, so by now there is a long line of aggrieved fathers who will demand justice to be served on that accursed ship."

Alex sent him a slanting look. "I suppose for now you've held back on the information that Jones owns the ship?"

"For now, and as yet he doesn't know that I know... I would keep it like that, aye?"

Chapter 39

"Be careful," Alex said to Matthew. "Come back to me safe and sound." And never take your eyes off Dominic Jones – but she didn't need to say that out loud.

He kissed her and held her close one more time before turning to say his farewells to the rest of his family.

"We'll be back in a month," he said as he sat up on Moses. "By then, I expect you to have finished the new cabin." He smiled down at his eldest son. "You take care of them, lad." Ian nodded and placed a protective arm around Alex.

All of them stood silent and watched him ride off with two of the Chisholms. The October day carried a promise of cold nights and rain, and Alex huddled together under her cloak. She hoped he'd make sure to dress warmly and change clothes when he could and... She sighed and ruffled Ruth's hair. "Come on, let's get back inside. If you want we can make cinnamon rolls."

The kitchen smelled of warm rolls and brewing tea when Elizabeth Leslie stormed into the yard on her grey mare, her appointed companion galloping in several minutes later with a harried look on his dark face.

"Now what?" Alex said, not at all liking the thunderous expression on Elizabeth's face.

"Oh, dear." Jenny went a bright red.

"What?" Alex asked, but any further investigation into her daughter-in-law's guilty face was cut short by Elizabeth's entry into the kitchen.

"This is all your fault!" Elizabeth was spitting with rage, her small eyes narrowed at Alex. "You put him up to this."

"Put who up to what?"

"Don't give me that! Look at how you run your household! Your serving maid sits at the table with the rest of you; your children are encouraged to raise their voices and express opinions in the company of their elders..." Elizabeth stopped to draw breath, eyeing Alex with open dislike.

"Get out! Unless you can explain what it is you're upset about without insulting me, I suggest you leave – now." Alex turned her back on Elizabeth, served her children tea and rolls, and sat down to nurse Samuel.

"It's Nathan." Elizabeth spoke in a controlled tone. "He's run off to marry that little slut."

"The mother of his child, you mean," Alex said acidly, "and the foster mother of his other child."

"See? This is how I know it is you that have influenced him! The girl should have kept her legs closed!"

Alex was on the verge of telling her that she didn't think that was an option for a bond servant and that it was common knowledge Peter Leslie sampled his way through a number of the girls in his service, but decided that would be like adding petrol to a fire totally out of control.

"I have at most exchanged ten words in a row with your son," she said instead, "and the last time I spoke to him at all was at Celia's funeral."

Elizabeth collapsed to sit by the table and grabbed a bun.

"By all means, please help yourself." Alex adjusted Samuel in the crook of her arm.

Jenny deposited Malcolm in his grandmother's arms and poured her mother a cup of tea.

"Tell us," Jenny urged her.

Tell us? Alex threw her a look. She'd wager little Miss Jenny knew all about this.

Elizabeth smoothed back Malcolm's impressive crest of dark hair and exhaled. "He left us a letter, telling us he and Ailish are off to be wed." She groaned. "Our eldest son, married to a papist!"

Mrs Parson made a sympathetic noise from where she was sitting by the hearth. "Did he take the wee lad with him?" she asked.

"Who? Henry? No, Henry he left behind, but the two girls he took with him."

"Ah well," Mrs Parson said, "then he's planning on coming back, no?"

Elizabeth relaxed, giving Mrs Parson a wobbly smile. "We must hope so." She helped herself to yet another bun. How could he do this to her, his mother, she moaned to the room at large; where had she gone wrong in the raising of that apple of her eye, her eldest son? She'd indulged him, she chided herself, and she hadn't been vigilant enough, bringing girls lacking in spiritual rectitude to live amongst them. Nathan was but a man, and what could she expect of him when that girl had flouted herself, thrown herself at him.

"Maybe it was him that threw himself at her," Alex said. "As I recall, Ailish is very pretty, isn't she?" A definite one up on poor Celia, at any rate.

"He would never do that. No, it was the girl, gold-digger that she is."

"Your daughter-in-law," Alex reminded her, which made Elizabeth go puce. Alex handed Samuel to Agnes and walked over to the door.

"Where are you going?" Elizabeth asked.

"Going? I'm not going anywhere. I'm just going to invite your man in from the cold."

Elizabeth stared at her as if she'd taken complete leave of her senses. The man outside was a slave, a black man.

"That won't be necessary," Elizabeth said. "I'm leaving."

"You don't really like my mother, do you?" Jenny asked once Elizabeth was gone.

"She's too quick to judge," Alex said, "and for all that she professes to be so religious, she seems to miss out on the most important message in the Bible."

"And that is?" Jenny said.

"Do unto others as you would have others do unto you. If everyone lived according to that, it would be a very nice world, wouldn't it?" Alex rather liked the admiring look in Jenny's eyes.

For all that Matthew had told her about running into Philip Burley back in April, Alex had succeeded in convincing herself the Burley brothers were gone from their life, melting back into the obscurity from which they had sprung to never bother them again. Until now, that is, when the three remaining brothers came riding through the forest in the late afternoon. Weak sun gilded the damp hides of the horses, exhalations stood like steam from both beasts and humans – very many humans.

Alex squeezed Daniel's arm, crouching down behind an ineffectual screen of shrubs. "Go," she whispered into Daniel's ear. "Run home and find your brothers."

Her son nodded, eyes huge in his pale face.

Alex grabbed at him. "Go quietly," she admonished and let him go. She returned her eyes to the elongated clearing, shifted on her feet, and dug her hand into the slit of her skirt, relaxing somewhat when it closed around the familiar hilt of her knife. Fantastic: one knife against three armed Burley brothers – this was going to be a walk in the park.

Further down the slope, the Burley brothers were herding three dozen or so Indian women and girls, all of them gagged and tied. Bringing up the rear came two unknown men, one of whom looked like an Indian to Alex, despite wearing breeches and a soiled coat, his long hair topped by a slouching hat. Alex's eyes flew over the captives, wondering if they might be of Qaachow's tribe. She didn't recognise any of the women, and she hunched lower in a combination of relief and fear.

From behind her came the sound of snapping twigs, and Alex swivelled, catching a glimpse of Daniel ducking out of sight. Philip Burley had also heard the sound, and here he came, cantering up the incline. In a matter of minutes he'd see her boy, and Alex had no doubts he'd ride him down and carry him off should he consider it necessary. She swallowed and barged out from her hiding place, causing Philip to exclaim and hold in his horse so brutally the animal sank back on its haunches.

"Well done," she said when Philip remained in the saddle.

"Mrs Graham," he said through gritted teeth. "Now why doesn't it surprise me that it's you?"

"Maybe because you're on our land. To be quite exact, you're trespassing."

"We are?" He looked down at her, eyes an almost white when a shaft of sunlight hit them square on. "And what do you intend to do about it?"

"Nothing. There's not much I can do, is there?"

"Wise of you," he said, nodding so that the signatory lock of black hair fell forward over his brow. He looked over to where his brothers seemed to be joining them and shook his head. "Stay with them," he called. "They'll run like deer if you give them the opportunity to."

"So many. What did you do? Stamp out a whole tribe?"

"More or less." A small smile played over Philip's mouth.

"And the others?"

"What others?"

"They're not all women, are they? There must have been men and boys and small children, even babies..." Her voice wound down at the expression on his face. "Oh my God! You killed them!"

"No, no, Mrs Graham, of course we didn't – well, except for the men. We just left them behind." He sounded as if he considered this to be to his credit.

"But..." Alex stared at him, shocked to the core. "The babies, how will they live? The little children?"

"What do we care? They have no value to us."

"They're human beings!"

"They're Indians, dispensable and heathen to boot."

"Heathen?" Her voice squeaked with rage. "And what are you? Devils risen from hell?" She shook her fists at him. "You'll die for this, one day you'll pay, and I for one will dance on your grave."

"That depends on if you're still alive," Philip snarled, struggling to control his horse, which was spooked by Alex and her angry arm flapping. "After all, why not take you with us as well? Sell you off as a slave somewhere."

"You wouldn't dare! Matthew would—"

Philip laughed. "Not here, is he? And by the time he finds out, you won't be in a position to care – and he'll not want you back." His eyes glinted as he dropped off the horse.

Alex's instinct was to turn and run, but she suspected that was just what he wanted, because there was no doubt he was faster than her. He took a step towards her. Another, and she backed away, thinking that if he came close enough she'd kick him in the head. These last few years, she'd worked regularly on her sadly forgotten karate skills, and even if she was far from the black belt competences she once had, she had regained some of her agility and body control. She crouched, hand gripping the knife she kept hidden in the folds of her skirt.

Philip gave her a little bow. "You don't scare easily, Mrs Graham, do you?"

She didn't trust her voice to reply, so instead she shook her head, planning on where to sink her knife. She'd only get one shot at this, she thought, licking her lips.

There was a commotion down in the clearing, and for an instant Philip's attention wavered. That was all she needed. She launched herself at him, kicked his legs from under him and bolted, darting like a hare between the shrubs. She ran until she could taste blood in her mouth; she ran until she barged straight into Ian, sending them both to the ground.

"Quick, quick, get up," she panted, struggling back to her feet. "They're coming, Ian, run!"

"Who?" Ian said. "There's no one there."

"There isn't?" Alex peeked over her shoulder before sort of melting into the ground, listening with detachment to her own heavy breathing. "Oh, Jesus," she whispered, and hid her face against her knees.

"Gone," Ian said when he and Mark returned home. "And from the looks of it, in quite a haste." He flung himself down in one of the armchairs and extended his legs towards the hearth.

Alex turned from where she was sitting by the little desk, ledgers lying open before her. "Well, they don't want Matthew on their tail, do they?" She gave herself a hug, rubbed her hands up and down her arms. "Those poor people, and the children, the little babies." Her guts shrivelled with compassion. "Do you think—?"

"No," Ian said, "I don't. We'll never find the village they came from. How can we?"

"Where will they take them?"

"To Virginia, I imagine. There's always a market for slaves there."

"It's wrong! We should—"

"Do what?"

"I don't know, but to just watch and do nothing... It sticks in my craw." With a sigh, she returned to her accounts, brows pulled together as she tried to get the shillings and pence to square.

"We have to find more labour for next year," Ian said, probably to distract her. "We can't manage one more year with only the three of us." He nodded over to where an exhausted Mark was half asleep on the floor, Narcissus' huge head pillowed on his lap.

"I know." Alex frowned down at the meagre pouch, hefting it to hear the reassuring clonk of the six small ingots left. "Have you thought about Forest Spring? You know, moving there?"

"Aye. Jenny thinks cows – a lot of cows. She's good at dairy work, and the beasts can be left to pasture among the trees during the summer."

Alex grunted in agreement. "You do the cows, I'll do the pigs." This year as well she'd been very successful with her piggies, and Ian and Matthew had ridden down to the Michaelmas market with two overloaded mules carrying hams and sausages, smoked ribs and jellied trotters that had brought in a sizeable amount of money, most of it immediately spent on cloth and sugar and salt, her precious tea and two new muskets with rifled barrels.

"I'll write to Minister Walker," she said.

"The minister?" Ian looked totally lost.

"About the Indians. Maybe he can do something to help them."

"Maybe." Ian rose and came over to give her a hug.

"Most colonists don't care, and in particular now they won't much mind if an Indian village or two are eradicated."

"I know, but that doesn't make it any better, does it?"

Ian kissed her on the brow. "My mama," he said, and she could hear the pride in his voice.

"Do you think he's alright?" Alex asked Mrs Parson a couple of weeks later, indicating with her head the full-blown storm outside the windows. "Will he have somewhere to sleep that is moderately warm and damp free?" Well over six weeks he had been gone, and she worried about everything: if his clean shirts had run out, if she should have sent along more woollen stockings, if he was eating properly, if, if, if. And foremost was the eternal question: if he was still safe and whole or if he'd been wounded and oh, dear God, killed, in an unnecessary skirmish defending those who had been too greedy from the legitimate reprisals of the aggrieved natives. She refused to think about Dominic Jones. Matthew would make sure he kept himself safe from him.

"I told you many years ago, didn't I?" Mrs Parson replied without lifting her eyes from the rakish striped stockings she was knitting. "You sense him, no?"

Alex closed her eyes and raised a clenched hand to her chest, taking long breaths. And there, deep inside of her, she felt his beat, the slow steady pulse that told her he was still alive and well.

She gave Mrs Parson a teary smile. "Still there." She fell to her knees before the old woman and buried her head in her lap. "What would I do without you?" she murmured, closing her eyes when Mrs Parson's hands came down to wind themselves in and out of her locks, to brush back and soothe.

"Cope, I imagine," Mrs Parson said, but there was a wobble to her voice that made Alex smile.

"Mother," she said into the dark skirts beneath her cheek.

"Daughter," Mrs Parson murmured. "A most beloved daughter, aye?" It was calming to sit like this, but the moment was interrupted when the door flew open.

"Mama?" Jacob fell into the kitchen, shadowed by Daniel.

"Yes?" Alex frowned at the expression on their faces. "What's the matter?"

"In the stables..." Jacob began.

"... and we thought she might be dead," Daniel said, "but she opened her eyes."

"...but the baby, Mama, the wean looks awful," Jacob went on.

"Dead, almost," Daniel nodded.

Alex was already on her way out, throwing a shawl over her shoulders against the biting north wind.

"It'll snow before evening," she muttered as she hurried after her boys.

"Aye," Jacob agreed, "look at yon clouds, near black."

"Why is it that snow comes out of black clouds?" Sarah asked, having joined the party. "Snow is white. Shouldn't the clouds be white?"

"I have no idea." Alex smiled. "Why don't you write that question down and we can ask your da when he comes home."

"Will he be back for my birthday, do you think?" Jacob slipped a hand into hers.

"I hope so," Alex said, "both for yours and Ruth's."

Alex took in the awry nativity scene: hay, farm animals, but instead of a rosy Virgin, a woman that looked half-dead.

"Thistledown-in-the-wind." Alex fell to her knees beside the woman. The once so radiant Indian woman was the colour of dirty linen, a dull grey that highlighted her wasted face and contrasted eerily with the thick black hair that hung in a matted mess around her head.

"What has happened to you?" Alex asked, without receiving a reply. The eyes remained closed, shallow breaths steaming into the air.

"The wean, Mama," Sarah whispered, her little arm shaking when she pointed at the cradle board lying some distance away.

Alex crawled over to it. "Oh, Jesus." If the mother seemed to be hovering between life and death, the little baby looked even worse. Snot-encrusted eyelashes glued the eyelids together, the mouth hung open and a soft wheezing accompanied every breath.

"Here." Alex thrust the cradle board into Daniel's hands. "Run inside and give it to Mrs Parson." Daniel flew, with his sister at his heels, and Alex turned to Jacob.

"Can we lift her between the two of us, do you think?"

Jacob inserted his hands under the woman's legs. "Aye, she doesn't weigh much."

"No," Alex said, "and that's the problem, isn't it?"

Chapter 40

"Starvation," Mrs Parson said, stating the obvious. "The wean is near to expiring."

"Not anymore." Alex looked down at the coal-black head at her breast.

"It must suckle, lass. You can't swallow for it."

"It will live, but what about the mother?"

In response, Mrs Parson pinched the skin of the young woman's arm and let go. The skin remained creased for quite some time before smoothing itself out.

"Undernourished, no liquids..." Mrs Parson sighed. "Honey, I think, and a rich broth."

Agnes came over with linen and hot water. Together, she and Mrs Parson undressed their surprise guest, washed her, and got her into a clean shift before placing her on a pallet bed as close to the hearth as possible.

"Do you think she'd mind if I comb her hair?" Agnes asked.

Alex looked up from the baby. "I think she'd appreciate the kindness," she said and went back to prodding the baby to eat. Every time it tried to fall asleep, she pinched it gently, using her finger to tease the mouth open. Suddenly, it clamped down and suckled hard, choking on the resulting gush of milk. Again and again it sucked, the milk began to flow, and the baby swallowed and swallowed.

"Not too much at one time," Mrs Parson warned. Too late, and Alex made a disgusted face when her bodice was covered with baby puke. The child in her arms wailed piteously, but at least it was moving and making noise.

"You'll do," Alex shushed it. "Now, let's try and do this again, okay?"

Some time later she wrapped the clean infant in a shawl

and placed him beside his mother. A thin arm came out to hold the baby close, and Alex patted Thistledown on her cheek before getting off her knees.

Two weeks later, Alex moped her way down the lane towards the house. No sign of Matthew today either, and she had no idea where he was, or, more importantly, how he was. She tugged at her best bodice, feeling foolish for having dressed up yet again on the off chance that this was the day he'd come galloping home.

She entered the front room where Sarah and Ruth were playing something in a corner, generously including David as well. By the fire lay a quilt-covered shape, soft snores escaping from the open mouth. After days of competent care, Thistledown had regained a more normal skin colour, even if she was still too weak to do much more than sleep and eat.

Her son had recovered much faster, and was now fast asleep on his belly beside his mother. Alex eased her aching breasts. Feeding two children was becoming something of a strain, and her poor tits were constantly overproducing, leaving her tender and damp. Samuel grunted when she settled him in her lap, and for half an hour it was all peacefully quiet, pale December sun leaking in through the small glass panes to pattern the scrubbed floor with squares of light.

"Mama?" Daniel shook her awake. "Jacob says you must come, and come quick." He held out his arms. "I can take care of Samuel."

"You do that." Alex stood up with a flutter of apprehension in her stomach. By the fire, Thistledown was awake, sitting up with her son cradled to her chest.

"See?" Jacob was standing by the kitchen door, musket in hand, indicating the group of riders coming down the lane.

"Mother! And Father..." Jenny frowned. "Why have they brought the Chisholms with them?"

"I have no idea, but I suppose we're about to find out."

Alex grabbed her cloak and went outside to face their visitors.

"Good day, Mistress Graham," the elder Chisholm said, bowing in her direction.

"Andrew, how nice to see you." It pleased her that he flushed. She remained where she was, arms crossed over her chest, and waited for them to state their errand.

"We've come for the Indian," the younger Chisholm explained.

"The Indian?" Alex raised her brows. "What Indian would that be?"

"Oh, don't you try!" Elizabeth snapped. "We know you're harbouring one of those heathens, and we have come to take her away."

"Really," Alex said, "and why would you do that? Do you intend to offer her the hospitality of your own home?"

"She's a heathen!" Elizabeth said. "It's her menfolk that are killing white men and their families all over the colonies, and by offering her succour, you're betraying your own!"

"She is Susquehannock," Alex replied. "As far as I know, we're not in conflict with them."

"Our brethren in Virginia are," Peter broke in. "And as my wife rightly points out your Indian is an enemy to us all."

"Besides," Andrew said, "God knows what plagues she brings with her, weak and starved as she is."

"And how would you know that?" Alex asked. "Unless of course you've seen her and chased her off, despite her being near dead."

Andrew's skin mottled under his grey stubble as he muttered something about not knowing what was ailing her, and he couldn't risk bringing disease into his home.

"Ah." Alex was quite pleased by how that one syllable had Andrew looking as if he'd prefer to disappear into a hole.

"Why this palaver?" Elizabeth said, sliding off her horse. "We've come for the Indian, so you'd best move out of the way."

"Make me." Alex planted herself before her door. Elizabeth looked somewhat taken aback – for like a microsecond. Then her eyebrows rose, two rather hairless crescents that all but disappeared into her hair.

"She's one of them," she said. "She has to go – she's a danger to us all!"

"Yeah," Alex said. "I can just see her, axe-murdering us in our sleep. She can barely stand, for God's sake! And the Susquehannock have never harmed us."

Andrew grunted, throwing Alex a long look.

"Okay, so they've stolen a horse here and there, but all in all—"

"They're thieving heathen," Peter interrupted. "And now they've risen in rebellion against their rightful masters."

"Their rightful masters? Would that be the king and his governor, who has signed the treaty and then allowed violation of the drawn up borders?" Alex said. "Or are we talking about the rogues who ride in under cover of the night and steal away Indian women to sell them as wives?"

"Those women are better off," Elizabeth said. "They exchange a life in the wilds for a life with a Christian, civilised man."

To his credit, Andrew Chisholm protested, saying that he did not agree with any woman being abducted from her family – no matter if she were Indian.

"Enough of this," Elizabeth said. "Surely you won't let a woman hinder you? Go and fetch her!"

"Try." Alex crossed her arms over her chest. It was obvious neither Peter nor Andrew were all too keen, both of them remaining where they were.

"The first one that takes a step towards Mama is dead," a cold voice said.

Ian used his thighs to ride his horse down, his musket levelled at Peter Leslie, who swallowed noisily. Behind him came Mark, eyes as icy, hands as firm on his musket. Wow, her own Light Cavalry. Alex's chest expanded with pride at the sight of her sons.

"Son," Peter raised his hands in conciliation, "this has taken on ridiculous proportions. Can you not make your mother see sense? The Indian woman must be driven off."

"To die," Ian said.

"To be taken care of by her own." Peter backed away from the catlike quality of Ian's eyes.

"She stays until she wishes to leave," Ian said. "She's our guest and as such it is our obligation to protect her. And we will."

Half an hour later, the yard was cleared of their visitors. Jenny was devastated. In between crying and wringing her hands, she apologised for her mother, saying over and over again that this was most unlike her, and mayhap she was not all herself what with Nathan and Ailish and...

Alex waved her quiet. She would happily have brained Elizabeth had she been given the opportunity, but it was the men she was seriously angry with. "Intimidation," she said, "that's what it was."

"Well, that didn't work very well, did it?" Mrs Parson commented from her place by the fire. "In fact, it would seem to me that it was you that intimidated them, no?"

"Me and Ian." Alex nodded. "And Mark," she added, seeing his face cloud.

"They're frightened," Ian said, "and all Indians are now potentially dangerous."

"It's the other way around, I'm afraid," Alex sighed.

After a night spent tossing from side to side, Alex gave up just before dawn. She pulled on stockings and a thick flannel petticoat, slipped on her knitted bed jacket and her skirts before making her way through the sleeping house towards the kitchen. Her boots...she hunted around for them as silently as she could, finding them propped against the hearth where Agnes had placed them to dry. At the door hung her cloak and in less than five minutes after waking she was outside, walking up the lane.

A brisk walk would do her good, she decided, if nothing else to work off the edgy restlessness that plagued her. She stepped off the bridle path to walk through the woods, brittle ice crunching underfoot as she stepped through shallow puddles. Here and there, the odd bird called, things rustled through the shrubs, and the bare trees were decorated with a delicate latticework of frost.

She was almost back home when she heard the sound of hooves, and just in case she ducked behind a stand of trees. But when she saw who it was, she stepped out into the open so abruptly Moses shied, causing Matthew to curse.

"Alex?" He looked down at her. "What are you doing here?"

"Waiting for a lift?"

He laughed and helped her up to sit behind him. "Why are you here?"

Alex wrapped her arms round his waist and gave him a long squeeze before replying. He was back, and she just had to rest her face against his back and scrub it up and down a couple of times, hearing him hum in response.

"Why?" he repeated.

"I'm not sure. I woke very early and felt like a walk – I missed you."

"And I you, lass." He reached backwards to pat her on her thigh.

"Did things go alright?" she asked.

"Alright? I don't think so. It's war on all Indians now, and it's us that are in breach, not them."

"So why are you home then?" Alex asked with a sinking sensation in her gut.

"To keep you safe. Thomas and I and some other homesteaders were relieved of our duties to protect our families instead." He exhaled. "Difficult times ahead, lass."

Anything else Matthew wanted to tell her had to wait, because when they turned into Graham's Garden they found Elizabeth and Peter Leslie at the top of the lane, the former looking decidedly the worse for wear.

"Matthew!" Peter said. "Does this mean it's all over?"

"Rather the reverse, but I hope it won't be as bad here as it will be elsewhere." Matthew looked them up and down. "Is there any particular reason why you are visiting this early?"

Peter doffed his hat and directed himself to Alex. "My apologies, Alex, for what we put you through yesterday. It was unacceptable, and I can only put it down to a combination of anxiety at the general state of affairs and our difficult private situation, what with Nathan and Ailish."

"Apologies?" Matthew looked from Peter to Alex. "What have you—?"

"Later." Alex patted his leg. No way was she going to have Matthew's homecoming marred by a full-out quarrel with Peter, no matter that what she really wanted to do was punch Peter in that glib mouth of his. He'd had a whole night to mull over the implications of being on strained terms with his neighbour and had obviously concluded this was not to his benefit – something he ought to have considered before setting out yesterday, the jerk. What she did, however, was to give Peter an insincere smile and inquire if they wished to eat breakfast with them.

Chapter 41

It was only for Jenny's sake that Matthew didn't throw them out. Ian had given him a quick recapitulation of events while in the privy, and Matthew stood in the doorway and scowled at the Leslies, wishing them gone. Besides, he had other matters to attend to now that he was finally home; foremost among them his wife. He wasn't sure if it was his glares or the silent presence of the Indian woman that did it, but finally the Leslies caught on and left – none too soon in his opinion.

"What were you thinking of, inviting them to breakfast?" Matthew fell full length across their bed.

"I hoped they'd say no, what with the dangerous heathen still being here," Alex said.

Matthew drew his brows together. Dangerous? The woman was still in a bad way. He yawned and stretched luxuriously before rolling over on his side to look at his wife. "Your generosity towards Thistledown will serve us well."

"That's not why I did it."

"Nay, of course not, but all the same." The situation had escalated beyond the point of no return, and he had no doubt in his mind that the coming years would be full of fear and strife. Fools – on both sides – hotheads eager to prove themselves men by slaying a man or two, and the incident some time back when the local militia had killed fourteen Susquehannock in their sleep had not much helped. He shivered and turned to cast a look out of the window. How was he to keep his family and home safe? Tomorrow; he would address that issue tomorrow.

"My back," he said. "Can you perhaps give me a wee massage?"

Alex helped him out of his breeches and stockings and wrinkled her nose. "Long time since you saw a bath tub, Mr Graham."

"Aye," he agreed sleepily, "a very long time." She patted his bare rump and promised she'd be back with hot water and some towels.

He was almost asleep when she returned, submitting to her ministrations with pleased "mmms". Only once he was reasonably clean did she pour some oil into her hands and begin to work her way up his back.

"I nearly killed Jones," Matthew said out of nowhere. "It was that close that I shot him, and no one would ever have known."

"So, why didn't you?" Alex concentrated on his right shoulder, making him hiss in protest when she sank her elbow into a particularly sore point.

"Too easy," he said through gritted teeth. He protested when she used the same elbow technique on his buttocks, but she ignored him, telling him not to be such a baby.

He rolled over on his back once she was done. "He near on shat himself. There he was, taking a wee turn round the camp, and suddenly I pop up before him, pistol in hand." His fingers had itched with the need to squeeze the trigger, blow a hole through Jones. "It was almost enough to see him so frightened – almost, mind."

He yawned, overwhelmed by weariness now that he was home safe in his bed, and turned towards her, pillowing his head on her lap. One part of him wanted to bed her, while the other, cock included, suggested it would be best to sleep. He yawned again and nestled closer, all of him relaxing when her hand came down to rest upon his head.

Three days later, Qaachow appeared in their yard at dusk, a wild-eyed, desperate Qaachow, far from the controlled man Matthew recalled from their previous meetings.

"My wife!" He gasped. "The village...raided, all dead, so many dead, but my wife, my son—"

"They're here," Matthew said. "They're both fine, aye?"

Qaachow looked about to weep. When Alex came through the door with the Indian wean in her arms, he rushed towards her, coming to a halt when Thistledown followed Alex outside. Two pairs of dark eyes that met, two sets of legs that moved of their own accord, two bodies that for a few seconds fused into one – until an aggravated squeal from the wean had Thistledown turn with a worried frown in the direction of her son.

"Thank you." Qaachow held his son as if he never intended to let him go.

"You're welcome," Alex said. "I'll fetch you some food; you look as if you could do with it."

Qaachow bowed in reply, and Matthew was left standing alone with him, two men with weans in their arms.

"Foster brothers." Qaachow nodded in the direction of Samuel. "Our son and your son."

Foster brothers? Matthew looked down at his sleeping son, not sure he liked the sound of that.

"I will come for him," Qaachow said. "When your son is ready to be a man, I will come for him and take him with me that he may do the rites of manhood with my own son."

Matthew had no idea what to say. It behoved him to keep this man as his friend – in particular given the present situation – and it was obvious Qaachow felt he was presenting Matthew with a gift, a most precious one at that. Strange images of painful initiations popped through his head and made him tighten his hold on Samuel. Before him, Qaachow stood waiting, an avid look on his face, and to his own surprise Matthew nodded. At Qaachow's insistence, they clasped hands – a formal handshake that felt as binding as a blood vow.

Alex returned with food and drink, she laughed and talked, and all the while Matthew stood silent to the side, his son a heavy weight he couldn't bring himself to let go. He saw her throw him a look, a concerned frown on her brow, and no sooner had the Indians departed than she came towards him. What he wanted to do was to turn and run; what he did was lead her to their bedchamber and tell her.

"You did what?" Alex stared at him, sinking down to sit on the bed.

"You heard," Matthew replied, adopting a casual tone. "It will serve Samuel well to have friends among the Indians. So I gave him my word that he can have my son for some time." And, in exchange, Qaachow had promised Matthew that the home of his – Qaachow's – foster son would not be harmed by his brethren.

"And for how long will he be gone?" Alex asked with a quaver.

"Some months? A year?" Matthew shrugged. "But not yet; not until he's twelve." He twisted at the thought: his son, alone in the woods with Indians.

"No," Alex said. "I won't let him. How could you promise him that?"

Matthew fell to his knees beside her. "What was I to do, lass? We need Qaachow's goodwill. Besides, it probably won't happen. By the time wee Samuel is old enough, Qaachow will have forgotten."

"You think?" She gave him a doubtful look.

"I do," he said, praying that in this he be proved right.

"Oh well then, that's okay," Alex mumbled, clutching her son to her chest.

"Qaachow is taking his tribe further north of here. He may never return. But he has left us well protected."

"He has? How?"

"Word of mouth. There's not an Indian living within a hundred miles from here that hasn't heard that you took in his dying wife and saved both her and his son."

"Oh." She brushed her nose back and forth over Samuel's head. "I still don't like this foster brother business."

"Neither do I." Matthew ran a finger down his son's cheek and gave Alex a reassuring smile. "It won't come to anything."

"Of course it won't. He tries to take my boy and I'll rip his balls off."

He laughed. "I'm sure it won't come to that."

Alex hadn't said much for the last half-hour, eyes turned inward as she nursed Samuel and put him to bed. She undressed down to her shift, washed and moved over to sit before the looking glass, removing her cap from her hair.

"Let me." He covered her hand with his. She sat still while he unpinned her hair to fall down her back. He brushed for a long time, her hair crackled with static electricity, and still he brushed, slow long strokes that brought her hair alive into dark browns and deep reds and here and there the odd glint of lighter hair, a polished bronze. The dash of grey by her temple had expanded, and there was a sprinkling of grey all along her hairline. He set his chin on her shoulder and smiled at their mirrored image.

"A wee bit more worn, the both of us," he said.

She nodded and dipped her hand into one of her jars, rubbing sweet-smelling grease all over her hands and arms. She applied oil to her face and neck, and in passing rubbed some into his face as well.

"Do you mind?" she asked once she was done, raising her hand to his face.

"Mind? That we grow older together, you and I?" He laughed softly and bit her ear. "It seems far better than the alternative. Besides," he added, cupping her breasts, "we're not old yet, are we?" He undid the lacings of her shift and eased it off her, studying her in the candlelight.

Eight children hadn't passed unnoticed, and she was rounder of hips, but he found that attractive. Her arse was still firm and high, and her breasts, despite being so much in use, retained their overall shape, even if they were heavier. Strong, shapely legs, skin that shimmered in the soft light of the candle, eyes that regarded him from under half-lowered lashes… A smile tugged at the corner of her mouth, her tongue darted out to lick at her lips – such delectable lips. He looked down at his cock, poking at the cloth of his shirt. No, he wasn't old, not at all; and his wife was warm and welcoming, her body so familiar and yet at times so unknown, with so much left to explore.

With her houseguest gone, Alex found the time for an overdue visit to the graveyard. Pale blue skies sparkled above, a couple of sparrows squabbled in the closest mock-orange, and under one of the pines she found a little stand of ferns, only lightly dusted with snow. She broke off a frond and placed it on Magnus' grave, thinking that as a botanist he couldn't complain about this his last resting place; so many trees around him, and she could hear the awe in his voice as he craned his head back to exclaim at the height of the closest chestnut.

"Do you miss him?" Ian's voice cut through Alex's reverie, making her start. She brushed Magnus' headstone free from snow and let her fingers trace his name.

"Yes." She held her skirts up high as she made her way back across the snowy graveyard. "Mostly, I think it's realising that I never really knew him, and now I never will. And you? Do you miss your mother?"

"Aye, at times…" Ian helped her over an icy patch, and threw with his head in the direction of the river. "Walk?" Alex nodded and fell in beside him.

"It's strange, isn't it?" she said, reverting to her previous thoughts. "How ultimately you don't know them; not your parents, not your children…"

"You know me," Ian protested. "You know all my siblings."

"I do?" Alex shook her head. "I know you as children, but will I ever truly know the adult? I don't think so. You really only ever know yourself, and many people don't even achieve that."

"And Da? Don't you know him in and out?" Ian teased.

"It's more the other way around: he tends to brag he reads me like an open book."

"And does he?"

Alex grinned. "Sure, when I let him. Seriously, some of us are lucky enough to meet that soul mate, that one in a million man or woman that slots seamlessly into you, knows all your quirks and secrets." She looked over in the direction of the closest shed, raising her arm in a wave to Matthew, who waved back from where he was sitting on the roof. "That's how it is with me and Matthew."

"Do you know immediately?" he asked, and Alex heard

the controlled yearning in his voice. She threw him a quick look and chewed her cheek. Ian talked much more with her than he did with his wife.

"Not always," she lied. "Sometimes it takes years. And as I said, it's very rare.

"Have you read it yet?" she asked a bit later. Ian had, to his surprise, had a letter from Luke.

"Aye, very short, but a good letter all the same – he even sent his regards to Da."

"Wow." She sighed. "Such a waste, isn't it?"

"What is?"

"Matthew and Luke; brothers should love each other."

"Too late for that, too many sharp words, too many ill deeds."

"Yeah."

Matthew had sent off a stilted note of condolence to Luke, and received an equally stilted reply, and then there was nothing more to say. There was no vocabulary between the brothers to express anything other than hatred, no words to help them find their way back to each other should they want to. Which in Alex's opinion was doubtful to begin with, however much Matthew insisted he was willing to try.

"Malcolm senior really screwed up," she said.

"He did?"

"Well, he started all this, didn't he? The day he threw Luke out on his ear after finding him with Margaret."

"Luke shouldn't have bedded her."

"Probably not; they were too young. But he loved her. That's something that none of us can ever take away from him." She scooped up a wad of snow and shaped it into a snowball, sending it to land with a dull thud against a tree. "She wasn't good enough, far too poor to be the wife Malcolm wanted for his younger son."

"But he allowed Da to wed her."

"He didn't need a rich wife; he was the heir, remember? So in that case her gorgeous looks were considered quite enough."

Ian came to a halt. "You're jealous!" He ducked to avoid

the snowball she sent flying in his direction. "How can you be?" he asked, bending down to arm himself.

"Because," she replied, and hit him squarely in the head with her next projectile. She darted away from him and grinned when his snowball missed her by a foot or so. "She was very beautiful, and we were alike enough for everyone to see she was prettier than me."

Ian fell backwards into the snow, laughing.

"What are you doing?" she asked with irritation.

"A snow angel," he said between gusts of laughter, waving his arms up and down.

"Did you ever love Margaret like you love Mama?" Ian asked Matthew as they hefted yet another heavy log onto the wood pile. Matthew grunted, busy avoiding getting his fingers squashed.

"No." Matthew pulled off his glove to study his skinned knuckle. "Never." He looked defiantly at Ian, receiving an amused stare in return.

"Alex and I…" Matthew stared off in the direction of his home. Winter dusk was falling, and he smiled when he saw Alex come out to help Ruth and Sarah light their snow lanterns. From the way she was jumping from side to side in the snow, he could tell she hadn't bothered with pulling on her boots, wee daftie that she was at times. "…we just are," he finished. "Mind you," he said, bending down to grip the next log, "she isn't always easy – very opinionated and all."

"Was Mam easy?"

"Margaret? I didn't know her well enough, lad. There were parts of her she always kept secret from me." He grimaced; starting with her passion for his brother. "We didn't talk, she and I, at least not much." He straightened up and rubbed a hand up and down the side of his back. "It's the talking that does it, to talk, and to keep on talking, all through your life. Not that the bedding isn't important," he said, grinning at Ian's expression, "but one thing doesn't exclude the other."

Chapter 42

Late one Monday in March, Robert Chisholm and his youngest brother Martin came riding down the lane to Graham's Garden. Matthew saw them coming, and with a reluctant little sigh he straightened up from where he'd been standing by the door to his finished barn, enjoying the warmth of the spring evening.

"Indians," Robert said. "We were raided by Indians this morning."

"Ah, was it bad?" Matthew asked.

"A few cows." Robert's bushy brows came down into a ferocious scowl. "And two of the wenches."

"I'm sorry to hear it," Matthew commiserated.

"Yes, well." Robert scuffed at the ground. "Father is not convinced."

"Not convinced? Of what?" Alex popped up beside them.

"It's a mite unusual for an Indian to ride with saddle and bridle," Martin said.

"So we think..." Robert retook the story. "Well, we wondered if this might be the work of those renegades, the Burleys."

"Ah." Matthew nodded.

"Father thought it best to let you know," Robert said. "In view of what happened a few years back."

"Not that they're anywhere close; we've been scouring the woods for them." Martin frowned. "Strange, I would swear at least two of them were real Indians – long black hair, dark of face."

"I suppose there are renegade Indians as well," Alex said.

A couple of minutes later, Matthew had a clear picture of the events. Six men, at least two of whom they thought were white, had ridden in just before dawn. The two unfortunate lasses had been milking the cows, and it was Robert's opinion that taking them had been a spur of the moment thing, while the real target had been the beasts. The men had threatened to kill the wenches if the Chisholms rode after them, and something about how it was said had made Andrew Chisholm hold his sons back until noon.

"That sounds like a Burley to me," Alex muttered.

"That sounds like a rogue — any rogue — covering his retreat." But Matthew took a private decision to not go about alone or unarmed, at least not for the coming few weeks.

Five days later, Matthew grabbed his musket and his axe and told Alex he'd be spending most of the day up on the new clearings with Ian. It was a longish stretch through the woods, and they walked in silence, neither of them having any pressing matters to discuss.

"Hot," Ian commented a few hours later. He'd discarded his shirt, working in only his breeches.

"Aye." Matthew wiped his brow with his shirt tail, straightening up to stretch his back. Something flashed by, a blur, no more, right at the edge of his peripheral vision. Matthew stooped, closed his hand on his axe and listened. No birds.

Ian stopped mid-stroke. "There's someone in the woods," he said, taking a couple of paces towards Matthew.

"I know." Matthew looked about for his musket, propped out of sight in a nearby shrub. The skin along his back was rising, his nape prickled, and with a certain detachment he noted how all of his body bunched. "Go, run, lad."

Ian shook his head. "Nay, I stay. Besides—"

Whatever else he had planned on saying was drowned in a war cry. Out of the forest came four men, black braids down their backs, leather leggings and bare torsos. Except that one of them had short hair and eyes too light to be an Indian. Walter Burley. Last time Matthew had seen him was when the accursed whelp had pulled him off his horse.

"For Will," Walter shrieked and raised his musket.

A good shot. Matthew hurled himself to the ground, imagined he could feel the ball graze his skin. Up; on your feet, man, and where was Ian? Where was his axe? He groped for it, fingers grazed on the smooth worn wood of the handle, and then Walter barged into him, bringing him down to the ground.

Matthew heard his son cry out. There were shots, more cries, and all the while Walter Burley was on him. Something slashed down his arm. A nick no more, and now he'd gotten his dirk free, hearing Burley gasp when he cut him. Too shallow, in the wrong place, and, dear Lord, but this man was strong, light eyes far too close, close enough that Matthew could see the streaks of darker pigment that bordered the pupil.

"Da!" Ian screamed, and Matthew's blood ran cold at the thought of his son dying. He grabbed hold of Burley's ear and twisted. The man roared, his hold on Matthew slipped, and with a grunt Matthew regained his feet. Ian was standing a way off, two men circling him while the third was lying at his feet.

The musket. Matthew threw himself towards it. Something grabbed at his legs, his feet, and Matthew kicked. Walter groaned, but held on. Ian screamed again. Out of fear? Rage? Matthew had no idea; all he knew was that he had to go to the aid of his son, because the lad was untried in battle, and the two vultures circling him most certainly were not. They were but playing with the lad.

There, he was free again, and now there were only feet between him and his musket, and then he'd... Aaaah! He couldn't breathe, couldn't scream. He clapped his hand to his thigh, fell to his knees. He raised his eyes, and there was Walter, and in his hands was Matthew's axe, and why was the head red with blood? Up went the axe. Matthew followed its arc, incapable of moving, of even attempting to save himself. I die; Alex, my Alex.

The clearing erupted with men. Walter faltered; Matthew dragged himself out of range. In his dazed state, all Matthew registered were Indians, many Indians. Burley stumbled backwards, dropped the axe and clutched at his shoulder. A loud, keening sound, and Burley turned and ran. Ian? His son? Blood, so much blood. Ian; arms round his shoulders, helping him to lie down. The sky, so blue, a beautiful, beautiful blue, and was that Rachel coming dancing towards him? Pain jolted through his system. Hands on his leg, sweetest merciful Lord but that hurt! A face swimming very close to his. Dark eyes, hair braided back. Qaachow. Ian said something, Matthew couldn't hear him. Alex, I want Alex.

They brought him in on a rudimentary stretcher, and for an excruciating moment Alex was convinced he was dead, and then her skirts were in her hands and she was running, a wild, breathless spurt with her heart clawing its way up her throat.

He tried to smile at her, drawing his lips wide in what looked more like a grimace. "It's alright," he breathed. "I'm still here."

"What happened?" Alex was running beside them as they rushed towards the house.

"Attacked," Ian panted, "up in the woods..." He was the colour of old porridge, an ugly greyish beige.

"And you?"

"Da," was all Ian said in a cracked voice. "Help Da."

Qaachow carried Matthew inside, staggering under the weight. He laid him down on the table and nodded for Alex to begin. She forced herself to look at his leg. Jesus! His breeches were sodden with blood, from somewhere at groin level all the way down to his knee. Ian had wound his shirt tight around the upper thigh, and the grey linen was liberally stained with dark red splotches.

"What—?"

"Not now," Qachow said. "That we can talk about later."

Yes, of course. First things first, except she couldn't quite remember what would be the first thing to do. So much blood... She swallowed and, with a decisive movement, tore the cloth off his skin, ignoring his inhalation, the way his eyes went round with pain. Blood welled in alarming quantities.

"Shit, shit, shit," she said. "*Djävla skit*," she added for emphasis and looked down at his face. "You could have died," she squeaked, her fingers shaking as she tied a primitive tourniquet into place.

"But I haven't, not yet," he croaked. "Although, if all you're going to do is stand and gawk at me, it seems I still might."

She laughed; cried. Still alive, still capable of talking.

"I'll do this." Like a saving angel, Mrs Parson appeared at her side. Alex backed away, rushed to boil water, find bandages, fetch the catgut, bring the quart bottle of brandy, sear the needle – in short, supply Mrs Parson with everything she needed to save her husband's leg. Over Mrs Parson's shoulder she peeked at the long, deep gash, and her stomach cramped, sweat breaking out along her back.

Mercifully, he wasn't all there when Mrs Parson began her work. Hot water, so much water. The stench of a heated blade against his flesh, and Alex had to bite her knuckles not to cry.

"I have to," Mrs Parson said. "I must stop the bleeding." Please do. The wound kept on welling blood, a sluggish trickle that dried up successively as Mrs Parson worked her way up the gash. Matthew was out cold, slumped like a dead jellyfish on the table, and Alex had to put a hand on his chest to reassure herself that his heart was still beating.

An unbearable hour later, Matthew's cleaned and sewn leg was bandaged and he was transferred over to his bed. He had regained consciousness halfway through Mrs Parson sewing the gash together, and had since then refused to let go of Alex's hand. That was perfectly fine with her, because at present all she wanted to do was crawl into bed with him and somehow fuse herself with him. But she had guests to see to, Ian to check on, and so she kissed him and tried to disengage her hand.

He tightened his hold. "Stay," he whispered, "stay with me."

She sat down beside him and shifted so that he could pillow his head on her lap, stroking him over his head and down his shoulder, long rhythmical movements that soothed them both. Only once he was asleep did she leave the room.

"Ian?" she asked, collapsing to sit on a bench. She managed to give Qaachow a smile, but when Mrs Parson set a plate in front of her, she shook her head.

"No great matter, a flesh wound no more." Mrs Parson poured out a generous quantity of whisky and set the pewter cup in front of Alex. "Drink."

"I…" Alex made a face; she rarely drank.

"I said, drink."

So she did, and to her surprise it was just what she needed, a bubble of comforting heat that unclenched her gut.

"What happened?" she asked Qaachow, pillowing her head on her arms.

"Indians," he said with a crooked smile. "One was a white man; the other three were Iroquois."

"White?" Alex quavered.

"Your man called him Burley. I wounded him." Qaachow mimed a knife throw.

"And where is he now?"

"He went into the river, as did one of the others. The other two are dead."

"Oh," Alex said.

"He would be a fool to come back," Qaachow said, "and I dare say he knows it."

"That's a relief." It wasn't, not really.

"He probably thinks your man is dead – he looked as if he were dying – so why risk returning?"

That made some sort of awful sense, and Alex's shoulders fell to a more comfortable level.

In a low voice Qaachow went on to tell her that they'd found one of the abducted girls, gagged and tied beside the ruffians' horses.

"She'll live," he said, "but as to the other…" One shoulder came up in a shrug.

It was dusk by the time Matthew woke.

"Hi," Alex said, and the rope frame squeaked when she sat down on the bed. He shifted to give her room, the movement arrested by the way his leg screeched in protest. A peek under the bedclothes, and he stared at his thigh, bandaged from groin to knee. He swallowed. Had the axe hit him a few inches higher up, he'd be dead by now, blood spurting out of him like a fountain.

"Does it hurt?" Alex asked.

"Aye." He closed his eyes. "Ian?"

"Okay. I think he's more shocked by the fact that he killed one of them than by the wound to his arm."

"He killed?" Matthew struggled to sit. "That's a terrible thing to do; gives you right troublesome dreams."

"He's with Jenny. I'm sure she'll take care of him."

Matthew smiled lopsidedly. As he recalled it, all he'd wanted to do was drink – and swive. A spurt of heat rose through his groin, his cock twitched into life. He slid his hand down to cup himself, a warm heaviness that reconfirmed that he was here, with her, not exsanguinated in the woods. He looked at her. His cock thudded.

"Come here," he said, lifting the bedclothes out of the way.

"But, you're..."

He took hold of her nape, pulled her close and kissed her. Her hair, her beautiful hair, now undone and floating like a veil around her. Her breasts; his hand closed on one and it was soft and warm. All of her in his arms, and he gasped when her leg knocked against his.

"Sorry, sorry," she muttered, but he didn't care, not really. Pain was good. Dead men felt no pain; dead men didn't have their cock straining upwards, inwards, while their wives straddled them. He held her hips as she settled herself on him. His hands slid down to grip her buttocks. Warm skin under his touch. Alive, like him...

"Slower," he said, "move slower." So she did, a sinuous movement that sheathed him inside of her, all the way from his balls to the tip of his cock. Up and down, slowly, slowly, and Matthew's buttocks bunched, his legs tensed, and with a loud exhalation he came.

★

369

Six days and he was up on his feet; a further week and he insisted he had to get back to work.

"You know what? I don't care, okay? If you want to go gallivanting around on your unhealed leg, fine, go ahead. But don't expect me to come rushing after you like some bloody Florence Nightingale and put the pieces back together afterwards!"

"Florence Nightingale? Is she someone I should know?"

"No," Alex said, "seeing as she's not even in the making yet."

"Ah." Matthew nodded. "Nice name. Sounds like a peaceful, soothing woman, all cool hands and a low sweet voice."

"Bastard," she muttered.

"Bitch," he whispered back, amused by her indignant start at his use of this future pejorative. He grabbed at her hand and pulled her close.

"I can't sit idle with the spring planting going on." He flexed his leg experimentally, biting back when the skin strained. "Ian and Mark are worked to the bone, and had we not had two such good workers in Jacob and Daniel..." He looked over with pride at the two lads, both of them half asleep over their supper. "I'm on the mend, and you'll have to trust me to know my own limits."

"Now why is that absolutely no comfort whatsoever?" Alex said, with an unwilling smile curling the corner of her mouth. He kissed her and hobbled off.

Not that he would ever admit it, but by the time the bell rang for supper next day, Matthew's leg was numb with tension. It took considerable effort to walk across the yard without gritting his teeth at every step, but he managed well enough, he reckoned, sinking down to sit in his chair with relief.

"Massage?" Alex murmured while serving him beer. "You look as if you need it."

"I do?" He shrugged. "Not really, but mayhap it helps in the healing."

Alex grinned. "Sometimes you're as transparent as a fishbowl, Mr Graham."

No sooner had he finished eating but she led him off to their bedroom. Matthew stretched out on the bed; she kneeled beside him.

"I actually think the sow understands me," Alex said, rubbing her oiled hands together. "So I'm somewhat circumspect in what I say around her, because it might hurt her feelings to know I only see her babies as hams on trotters."

Matthew laughed, grunting when her hands became a wee bit too hard.

"It's scary at times, how she stands on her hind legs and crosses her front legs. It makes her look horribly human." She frowned at the pink bubbly scar tissue and prodded at his thigh muscle.

"Do you mind?" He made an effort to sound relaxed.

"Mind?" Alex raised her eyes to his face. "Do I mind you have a scar the size of a normal kitchen knife decorating your thigh?" She bent her head and kissed his exposed skin. "I'm glad you're still here, so, no, I don't mind." She rested her cheek against his leg and moved so that her ear lay closer to his groin. Her hair tickled him. "My favourite sound in the world, the sound of your pulse."

He stroked her dark, soft hair. Alex made a contented sound, no more. Matthew continued playing with her hair, ran his fingers down her cheek in a soft caress. Her breathing deepened, and he lifted his head to squint down at her. He smiled. She was fast asleep.

Chapter 43

Mrs Parson uttered a colourful curse, rubbed at her buttocks and hobbled over to the fire.

"Yon animal has a spine like a razor." She cast a baleful look at the rangy gelding she was sharing with Jacob. Alex agreed, but wasn't about to switch places from where she rode perched behind Matthew.

Alex stretched. The June night was balmy, a soft darkness that had her thinking of moonlit beaches and midnight swims. No such luck – at least not here. Instead, she busied herself with the food, produced a stone flask of beer and sat down.

"I plan on selling him when we get to Providence," Matthew said, tearing off a chunk of bread to go with the thick slice of cheese. "He's not much use on a farm anyway."

"Oh aye?" Mrs Parson lowered herself to sit. "Am I to walk back then?"

"You can ride on the mule," Matthew said, "and the new bondsman will have to walk."

"That's a long walk." Alex reclined back on her arms.

"Aye, and yet we did it. Five bairns and you breeding, and we set out with nothing but two mules and a horse, and they were fully loaded." Matthew smiled over to where Jacob was sitting. "Do you remember, lad? You were only four and yet you walked most of the way."

"As I recall, it rained," Jacob said.

"Rained?" Alex laughed. "It poured! The skies opened and drenched us to the bone, and there was no dry wood, and what food we had we had to eat cold, and it was absolutely horrible."

"You didn't say it at the time," Matthew said.

"What would have been the point?" She leaned forward

and touched his cheek. "You were desolate," she said in a voice meant for his ears only. "The boys didn't know what to think, Ruth was bawling her head off with the damp and all the flies... How would it have helped if I started whining? It wasn't as if there was anything you could do about it, was there?"

She'd never seen him as helpless as he had been those months after leaving Hillview. It was as if some mainstay in him had been sliced in half, and he had stared out at this new world where the one single constant in his life – his home – was permanently lost to him with fear leaping in his eyes. Never had he been so vulnerable, never had he depended so completely on her... Her eyes met his, and she could see her own thoughts mirrored in his face.

"That was a difficult time," he said.

She took his hand. They'd been lucky. Thomas Leslie had come to Providence to meet them, and so they'd had someone to guide them through a landscape that was frightening in its majestic wilderness. And as to Matthew, it had all changed the moment he had set foot on the land that was now his, a rectangular oblong bisected by the river, bordering the Leslie land to the south-east and the Chisholm land to the east.

"It helped once you saw Graham's Garden," she said.

"Aye, strength flowed back in me." From the soles of his feet it had risen, he told her: an assurance that here, on this virgin land, he would carve out a new home for his family.

"And you have," she said, resting her head against his shoulder.

"We have," he corrected her.

By the time they reached Providence, Mrs Parson was complaining about piles and other nasty afflictions caused by the thin nag she'd been forced to ride, and no sooner did she touch ground but she took off, making for the Apothecary.

"I wonder how one cures piles," Alex murmured. As far as she knew one cut them off, and no way did she intend to help with any such surgical effort.

"Prunes, a lot of prunes." Matthew helped her unload,

led the horses over to the inn's stable, and told her over his shoulder to make haste as he wanted to be at the Hancocks' within the hour.

"You arrive most auspiciously," William Hancock said in greeting, ushering Matthew into his home. "There have been developments." He bowed in the direction of Alex, ruffled Jacob's hair and suggested they all repair to the kitchen where his wife was baking.

"Betty!" William raised his voice, and swift feet came rushing across the landing upstairs and down the stairs. "Help Jacob carry his belongings to his room, and then you might wish to show him round."

Betty curtsied to Matthew and Alex, grabbed Jacob by the hand and rushed off as quickly as she had appeared, her bare feet drumming on the floorboards. Alex had the impression of a sparkling exuberance, of glittering red brown eyes and hair that stood in a burnished halo. She smiled when she heard the girl begin to talk, a bubbling stream of words that wound themselves around Jacob's long replies.

"Auspicious how?" Alex asked once the children were out of earshot.

William gave her a blank look, before directing himself to Matthew. "I suggest we speak of this in my study," he said, extending a hand in the general direction of his office. Matthew winked at Alex and followed his host.

"Some cider?" Esther placed a hand on Alex's arm and guided her in the direction of the table. "I'm almost done, and then we'll settle ourselves in the parlour."

It was a small but neat home, the ground floor given over to William's office, a kitchen and the small parlour that obviously was Esther's territory. Two wooden armchairs, one with a soft shawl thrown over it, several baskets filled with ubiquitous mending and, in one corner, a baby basket.

"Six months." Esther smiled at her son. Alex made adequate congratulatory sounds.

"I pray," Esther said. "Every day I kneel and pray to our Lord that this time we be allowed to keep him a bit longer than his brothers."

"He looks very healthy," Alex said, studying the rosy baby. And relatively clean, as was the whole home, the floors scrubbed, the table top in the kitchen looking as if it was regularly attacked with lye and brush, the few cooking utensils as clean as she kept her own. "What's his name?"

"William," Esther replied with a weak smile. "After his father – like all his brothers."

A few hours later, they bid William and Esther farewell and left. It was like chopping off a hand. Okay, so that was an exaggeration, but Alex had to bite down on her lip not to cry when they left Jacob behind.

"He's too young," she moaned to Matthew as they walked through the late evening in the general direction of their inn. "What if he hates it there?"

"He'll be fine. The wee lass is quite taken with him, and he with her."

"Huh, and that's all part of your elegantly laid plans, right?"

"He's not yet twelve, so we shall see." He lifted her hand to rest in the crook of his arm and smiled down at her. "You'll see him tomorrow – and for a few days more."

Once at the inn, Alex went in search of water, balancing the heavy pitcher up the rickety stairs to their little room, uncomfortably hot in the summer heat. She filled the basin to the brim, stripped down to her shift and spent a few lovely minutes cooling herself with the cold water. As a final touch, she dipped her face, did it again, and decided not to bother with the towel. It was refreshing to feel the water on her skin. She braided her hair and came over to join him by the small window.

"So what was so auspicious?" Alex shook her head at his proffered pewter flask. Matthew swigged a couple of times, corked the flask and turned to look at the dark alley below.

"The captain of the *Henriette Marie* was arrested in Jamestown. A Providence elder was there when the ship sailed in with its latest load of slaves, and at his insistence the captain was seized and sent here to answer on the count of several disappearances. He didn't survive long. A rabble of citizens broke in to where he was being held and battered him to death."

"Oh dear," Alex said, "what a loss to humanity."

"And how fortunate for a certain Mr Jones, because had the captain decided to talk, well then..." He faced her and smiled in a way that made her suppress an urge to recoil. "However, there's a witness to their perfidy. A man you know."

"That I know? How would I know—?"

"Think, Alex. A seafaring man we both know." Well, that was an extremely short list, topped by the captain who'd carried her thrice over the Atlantic. The first time when she set off in search of Matthew, back in 1661; the second time when he transported them back home to Scotland in 1663; and the third time when he carried the Graham family from Scotland to here, in 1668.

"Captain Miles?"

Matthew shook his head. "Nay, Alex. A cook, a man who served for some time on the *Henriette Marie* but chose to abscond without pay at what he saw."

"Iggy? But he was on the *Regina Anne* when we came over."

"And he's back there now," Matthew said. "They're here, Captain Miles and Iggy. We will see them on the morrow."

Yet another scorcher of a day, still not a swimming pool or a bikini in sight. Alex hurried towards the port area, her hand held in Matthew's, Mrs Parson at their heels.

"I haven't seen the captain in nigh on a decade," Mrs Parson had said over breakfast. "Best I take this opportunity; neither of us are getting any younger."

"Ah, so you're going after him?" Alex had teased.

"Go after him? How go after him?" Mrs Parson had looked quite affronted.

William was waiting for them by the waterfront. Matthew pointed at the ship, anchored a fair bit off the harbour proper.

"Just seeing her makes me queasy," Alex said.

"Aye, well, a sailor you're not." Matthew chuckled,

handing her down into the longboat that was to take them out to the *Regina Anne*.

"Seasick?" William said.

"Very," Alex sighed.

"Me too, I voided my guts for most of the journey over." William gripped the side of the boat. "The sea is best when seen from land."

"Yeah, it makes a nice backdrop." Alex dipped her hand and kept her eyes on the receding shoreline.

Not much later, she was safely aboard, and at the sight of Captain Miles she grinned and hugged him, ignoring Matthew's black look at this excessive familiarity. She stood back to allow Captain Miles to greet Mrs Parson and was rather amused, in a tender sort of way, by how flustered both of them were. It was obvious the captain still thought Mrs Parson to be utterly delectable, eyes drawn like by magnets to that most ample bosom, as always modestly covered. The captain cleared his throat, greeted Matthew and William, and led them off to his cabin, calling for Iggy to join them.

Iggy gave Alex a cautious smile, no more. She smiled back, thinking he looked much the same as last time she'd seen him, nearly seven years ago. Tall, with red hair that was tied back from his face, and light green eyes, he bore a passing resemblance to Luke – except that where Luke was broad over chest and shoulders, Iggy was narrow like a girl, bony shoulder blades visible like folded wings under his worn shirt.

"It wasn't a voluntary employment." Iggy wiped his hands on his apron before shaking Matthew's hand. "It was a matter of being in the wrong place." He threw a look at Captain Miles, who nodded for him to go on. "Their cook was taken ill and they needed to replace him. I saw how they threw him overboard."

"Overboard?" Alex said.

"Smallpox," Captain Miles explained, "and they didn't want to be quarantined."

"Oh." Alex nodded. "Was he dead when they threw him in?"

377

Iggy shook his head. "Not then, no, but right soon after. He didn't know how to swim." He fidgeted on his feet. They had cornered him just off the old customs house in Jamestown, given him the choice of dying or coming with them, and so he had found himself aboard the *Henriette Marie*.

"I didn't much like the company, and I didn't like it at all when I found the lads." With a minimum of detail, Iggy explained how seven small boys had been kept under lock and key in one of the cabins, and how he had come upon them by chance, hearing one of them cry for his mother. He shuddered. "Poor lads, all alone in the world, not understanding what had happened or where they were going.

"I didn't dare to do anything, but once we anchored off Cadiz I jumped ship." Iggy gave them a weak smile. "I can swim." Since then, the memory of those abducted boys had hung over him, and after finding his way back to Captain Miles, they had together decided it was best to advise the authorities.

"And how does all this tie in with Jones?" Alex said.

"He was on board the ship in Jamestown – difficult to miss him, what with him being the size of a carthorse." Iggy licked his lips. "I think I saw him enter the lads' cabin, but I couldn't swear to it."

"It's his ship," Captain Miles said. "From what I've gathered, they've been at it for years."

"Still..." Alex said. Circumstantial evidence, no more, and knowing Jones he'd wiggle out of this little trap as elegantly as always.

William nodded. "We need more than this."

"Oh aye, we do." Matthew smiled wolfishly. "And I know exactly where to find it."

Chapter 44

"Wait, wait, wait." Alex was panting in her efforts to keep up with Matthew. "You want *me* to talk to her?"

"You were right friendly with her last time you met her."

"As I hear it, so were you. At least that's what Jacob said."

Matthew ignored her, lengthening his stride.

"I gave her a good day, no more," he said after a while. "You spent a whole morning in her company."

"That was two years ago!"

Matthew made a guttural sound, indicating this was irrelevant.

"So what am I supposed to say? 'Hi, Kate, listen we want to nail your husband's sorry arse once and for all, and we need your help'."

"Aye, why not? She's a mother. Do you not suppose it might strike her as perfidious to steal away wee lads?"

"As you say, she's a mother, and the father of her children is Dominic Jones."

Matthew didn't reply, his eyes fixed on the distant white house.

"Wow." Alex turned this way and that, taking in the Jones' residence. The whitewashed two-storey house was adorned with dark green woodwork and shutters; the inner yard was cobbled, with a neat path of stone flags leading from the gate to the main entrance. All the windows had glass in them, the chimneys were bricked creations that rose like elegant fingers towards the sky, and, from what she could make out, the roof was of slate. To one side was a sizeable stable, also with a second storey, and on the other side stood a row of small, identical buildings which Alex assumed to be storage sheds and the like.

Inside, the floors were of dark, heavy wood, the walls plastered and the furniture impressive, to say the least. In pride of place was a gilded mirror. There were decorated chests with intarsia work that drew the eye, several elegantly carved high-backed chairs complete with embroidered cushions, and an assortment of tables, most of them decorated with beautiful silver candlesticks.

"He's done well for himself," she said.

"Aye, built on the backs of his fellow men."

"Not entirely," Kate said, coming in from the direction of the cook house. She nodded in greeting, dark eyes lingering a moment too long on Matthew, and to Alex's huge irritation he smiled at her, a softening of his long mouth that she resented seeing directed at anyone else but her. Alex stepped closer to her man and slid in her hand to rest possessively in the crook of Matthew's arm.

After Alex had half-heartedly attempted to explain the reason for their visit, Matthew took over and filled Kate in. She didn't seem surprised; rather the reverse.

"You knew?" Alex asked.

"Of course not, but I found it coincidental, that so often did boys go missing while the *Henriette Marie* lay at anchor."

"Oh." Alex didn't even attempt to disguise how incredible she found this.

"Greedy fool," Kate said after a long and strained silence. "I wouldn't mind being a widow." She directed herself to Matthew with a cold glint in her eyes. "It wouldn't impact my life, what with him being always with her, never with me."

"Kate!" Alex said, shocked by her callousness. "We're talking about your husband, the father of your children."

Matthew gave Alex an exasperated look. "We're talking of a man that abducts wee lads and sells them as slaves, a man who once tried to have me hanged for murder."

"Yeah – with her collusion." Alex gestured in Kate's direction.

Kate's cheeks turned a dark red. "I needed him then, heavily pregnant as I was. And Fairfax was a miserable worm of a man – he deserved to die."

Too right about that, Alex thought. Her brain clouded with unwelcome memories of a long gone afternoon, that fat, horrible man, and the things he did to her and had her do to him to give her Matthew back.

"But still," she said, "you were willing to let Matthew take the blame – you'd have let him hang to save Jones' neck."

"But it never came to that, did it?" Kate moved over to the writing desk, long fingers sorting through the neat piles. "Here." Kate handed Matthew a number of documents. "His correspondence with the captain of the *Henriette Marie*. I dare say you'll find what you need in there." With a curt nod to Alex and a far too warm smile at Matthew, she exited the room.

"Beware of a woman scorned," Alex said to Matthew as they walked back towards town, now at a more sedate pace. "Pretty cold-hearted. Seven kids that will potentially soon be fatherless..."

"From what I hear, they don't see much of him as it is. It's always with the other lass he spends his time, and she has just given him a son."

"She has?"

"Hancock had a visit some days back. A certain Mr Jones wanted to set up provisions for this new child of his. A most substantial provision..."

"And Kate knows." Alex nodded, things tumbling neatly into place.

"Aye, I suppose she would, on account of Mrs Hancock being her friend."

It was one of the best moments in his life. Matthew entered the inn and stood for a while to the side, savouring the sweet taste of revenge. Mean spirited, not at all in line with Kirk teachings, and yet it was with a spring to his step that he led the three elders in the direction of where Dominic was dining.

Jones looked up from his meal, knife poised halfway to his mouth. Conversations died away, and the whores scuttled over to stand like a flock of chickens round their mother hen, Mrs Malone. Jones pulled the napkin free from his collar, dabbed at his mouth and stood.

"What? More unsubstantiated accusations about me attempting you harm, Graham?" Jones lifted his lip into a sneer. "As if I would even bother! You're nothing but a homesteader while I am a man of wealth and influence – friend to the governor, no less." His small eyes darted round the group of men.

"No unsubstantiated accusations this time, Jones." Matthew couldn't keep the triumph out of his voice. "This time there is plenty of proof – and witnesses."

"Witnesses?" Jones laughed. "Then they lie. I haven't raised a finger against you"

"Against me? No, no, Jones, you have it wrong. We're here on account of the missing boys." Matthew took a step closer to Jones. "It was a foolish thing to do, to abduct children in your hometown. And it must have been God that ensured Jacob was saved that day last summer, by the propitious appearance of Mr Farrell. After all, we both know that had he not been there, you yourself would have carried my son aboard your accursed ship."

"I have no idea what you're talking about." Dominic Jones straightened up to his considerable height.

"You would say so," William Hancock snorted.

"It is best you come with us," Minister Walker said, and there was nothing for Jones to do but to obey.

"No!" Jones wet his lips and looked from face to face. "No, of course not! It's all conjecture." The collected men facing him stared at him in stony silence.

"My son! My Sydney!" one man moaned, stumbling to his feet. "Where is my son, goddamn you?"

"I don't know; it isn't my doing." Jones' eyes flitted over the room, rested for an instant on Matthew, moved on.

"It was your ship," another man said. "You were even on board when some of the lads were carried off."

"That doesn't mean I knew everything that went on," Jones protested.

William Hancock flipped through his papers. "And yet it would seem from this correspondence that you were aware of this lucrative sideline."

"Correspondence?" Jones' voice was breathless. "What correspondence?"

In reply, Hancock waved several sheets at him. Jones sank down on the chair behind him and hid his face in his hands. Matthew suppressed an urge to whoop. Jones was as dead as the chickens that hung plucked in the poultry shop. For the rest of the proceedings Jones sat as still as a statue, his eyes locked on the floor between his feet. Twice he repeated that he wasn't guilty, but his voice was flat and lifeless, and when he stood to hear the foregone verdict, a tremor wobbled through his huge frame. When Minister Walker pronounced sentence, Dominic Jones blinked, a large, meaty hand coming up to caress his fat neck.

Matthew stood to one side, his hat crammed down on his head to leave his face in shadow. The square was full of people, and unlike him, most of the men were accompanied by their wives. To his surprise, Kate Jones was there as well, coming to stand not very far from him. She seemed ill at ease, her hands fiddling repeatedly with her dark shawl and the brim of her equally dark hat.

From the other side of the square came repeated shrieks, and when Matthew looked that way he caught a flash of red hair. He winced when he realised Dominic's mistress had been forced to attend, her hair uncovered to signal her adulterous behaviour, her arms held by two of Providence's worthies. He felt a twinge of pity for the lass and her wean, but closed off that section of his brain. He was here to gloat. Except that he couldn't, disturbed by the whole sorry spectacle, the eggs that whistled through the air, the howls of rage that met Dominic Jones as he stepped onto the wooden platform. Grudgingly, he admitted that he acquitted himself well, Jones did; all through the extended proceedings the man kept the fear he must be feeling well under control. Not once did he look in the direction of his wife; to the last his eyes locked themselves on the weeping, terrified young woman and the wean she held in her arms.

"For a man Walter swears is dead and buried, you seem in the best of health," a voice whispered in his ear, and Matthew wheeled to find Philip Burley staring at him from below a broad-brimmed hat. At his back was Stephen, his face bisected diagonally by a vivid red scar that had healed badly, giving the impression his nose was about to fall off at any moment. Only two, Matthew comforted himself, and his hand dropped to his dirk.

"Mr Graham." Philip bowed. "And so we meet again."

"I can't say I'm glad," Matthew said. His thigh itched.

"No, I assume not." Philip moved an inch or so closer.

"You killed him!" Stephen looked as if he was about to launch himself at Matthew but was held back by his brother.

"Not here, you fool!" Philip snapped, gesturing at the crowd.

"He was condemned and executed in due course," Matthew replied.

"Who? Him?" Philip jerked his head in the general direction of the body that swung from the gallows. "What do we care about him? You killed Will, you bastard."

"Self-defence, Burley." Matthew stood his ground, pitching his voice to ensure it carried. Out of the corner of his eye, he saw Minister Walker coming towards them, shadowed by a trotting Mr Farrell and a grim-faced William Hancock.

"I don't care. He was my baby brother and you slit his throat as if he were a pig. For that we'll kill you; someday we'll gut you until you squeal with pain."

"I think not," Minister Walker said. "And I'll not countenance such threats." He had to stand on his toes to eyeball Philip, but eyeball him he did, with William Hancock hanging over his shoulder. "The next time I see you anywhere close to Mr Graham, I'll have you put under lock and key. Now go! Go, I said," he repeated, when neither of the Burleys moved.

Philip swept the minister a mocking bow and straightened

up to catch Matthew's eyes. "Please convey my regards to your oh so charming wife, Graham. I'm sure I'll have the pleasure of meeting her again." He snickered but beat a hasty retreat when Matthew made as if to throw himself at him.

Minister Walker grabbed hold of Matthew's coat and stood watching the brothers skulk away before turning to study Matthew.

"It would seem, Brother Matthew, that you've made lifelong enemies of them."

Matthew just nodded.

"Don't tell Alex," he said to William as they walked up the incline towards the Hancock home together.

"Why not?"

"It'll make her more afraid than there is need for her to be." It sufficed that he was, grappling with the daunting task of getting them home safely now that the Burleys were here. He straightened his spine and clenched his fists, thereby achieving some control over his trembling limbs. Mayhap he should hire an escort.

"Hmm," William said, but promised nonetheless.

Chapter 45

"Hard night?" Alex asked without a whit of compassion the morning after Dominic's execution. She was still angry with him for having chosen to spend last night with male companions rather than her.

Matthew groaned and grabbed at her pillow to pull it over his eyes. "Don't yell," he croaked. "My head hurts something awful."

"So it was." She poked him and one bloodshot eye flew open to glare at her.

"Aye," he managed to say, looking at her as if he hoped she'd disappear and leave him in peace.

"Where?" she asked, picking up his coat which she found crumpled in a corner. She shook it out, frowning down at a stain on the light grey fabric. "We're supposed to be in church in some hours, and you only have this one coat."

He mumbled something indistinct in reply and rolled over on his side, turning a stiff and unwelcoming back in her direction.

Alex sniffed at the lapels and wrinkled her nose at the overpowering stench of cheap and stale perfume. "Mrs Malone's?" She flipped him over on his back. "I've told you I don't want you to go there."

"That is not for you to decide." He licked his cracked lips and rubbed a hand through his thick, tousled hair. He actually looked quite endearing in a rough sort of way – if it hadn't been for how he stank of beer.

"Fine, but I sure hope you kept Mr Beast here under control." She grabbed him a bit too hard between his legs, making him yelp.

He moved swiftly, pinning Alex beneath him. "You hurt me," he said in an aggrieved tone.

"No permanent damage; at least not compared to the damage I'll do you the day I find out you've been with a whore." She shoved at him.

"I haven't." He stared at her through narrow red-rimmed eyes. "I never would."

"Huh."

"You doubt my word?" He leaned close enough to have his nose touch hers.

"No," she said after a heartbeat or two.

"Good."

Three hours later, they exited the inn, making for the meetinghouse. Repeated head ducking in cold water and an egg or two had banished most of Matthew's hangover, even if he squinted at the sun, muttering something about his head being on fire.

"I've contracted two lads," Matthew said.

"Two?" Alex frowned. "Do we really need two?" She curtsied to Minister Walker and mumbled a quick greeting to Mrs Walker, who smiled back before hurrying after her husband.

"One was very cheap, and as I've also bought five cows, we may need some help to drive them home."

"Or we tie them together and lead them," Alex suggested.

"Safety in numbers. There's no knowing who might want to make off with a cow or two in these uncertain times, is there?"

Alex gave him a sharp look. There was something he wasn't telling her. He lifted his hat at yet another acquaintance, waiting while Alex dropped a curtsey before resuming their walk towards the meetinghouse.

"But still..." Alex gnawed at her lip. "So how much do we have left?"

"Excluding the ingots, 260 pounds – and the coins we presently carry on us."

"Which isn't that much," Alex informed him. In her own little pouch clinked ten shillings and some pence coins, while he had three gold guineas, five shillings, two or three half-crowns and a couple of groats – before last night's binge at Mrs Malone's...

"More than most men earn in half a year," he said.

It was strange to sit in the meetinghouse beside Matthew and see the Hancock family walk in with Jacob in their midst. Her son smiled briefly in her direction before hurrying after Betty, sliding down to sit with the Hancocks. One part of Alex wanted to stand up, tell everyone that this boy was hers, not theirs, while the other told her sternly to sit still and behave.

Matthew's hand found hers, and he slipped their clasped hands out of sight beneath her skirts. All through the service he held her, and somewhere halfway through the far too long sermon about the first commandment, Alex understood: this was difficult for him too. She squeezed his hand, and felt him squeeze back. A shared smile, his hazel eyes in hers, and it was no longer quite as unbearable to be leaving Jacob behind.

After the service Alex hugged her son and kissed him on the top of his head. "I love you," she whispered.

Jacob stood stiff in her arms, shifting from foot to foot as he mumbled to her to let him go; what would Betty think? So she did, and Matthew tousled his hair, telling him that he expected Jacob to behave and work diligently on his new master's behalf. Jacob rolled his eyes and held up ink-stained fingers, making Alex laugh.

Saying goodbye to Jacob had momentarily distracted Alex from her suspicions that Matthew was holding something back, but once they were back in their room she turned to him, set her hands at her waist and waited.

"What?" he tried.

"Tell me," she said.

"Tell you what?"

"Come off it. I know something's worrying you, okay?"

He gave her a sheepish look. "I didn't want to frighten you."

"Well, you already have. It has to be pretty bad for you to keep it from me."

Matthew sighed and fiddled with one of the quilts.

"The Burleys, I had the pleasure of running into them yesterday." In a low voice he told her of Philip's threat, and her belly shrank together into a painful bundle of nerves, making it difficult to remain upright.

"We'll just have to go canny," was what she said, seeing him smile at her use of his expression. "It's not as if we're defenceless, is it?"

"Ah no, that we're not. I've bested them a fair number of times already."

Mrs Parson was unperturbed when Alex told her. "I heard already yesterday."

"You did?" It always amazed Alex how Mrs Parson seemed to plug into some sort of invisible network the moment she set foot in a place. In a matter of hours, she'd know everything worth knowing about anyone – including those rather juicy little titbits like did Alex know Minister Walker frequented Mrs Malone's regularly, or that Mr Farrell's headpiece had somehow ended up in Mrs Redit's bed.

"Och aye, and I know for a fact they left this morning."

Oh God; to ambush them on their way home. Alex took a couple of deep breaths.

"On a ship, aye?" Mrs Parson grinned. "The *Regina Anne*, and Captain Miles has promised to see them safe and sound to Jamestown. Kind of him, no? They have family in Virginia, as I hear it."

Alex just stared at her. "You didn't!"

Mrs Parson looked back, the grin replaced by a formidable scowl. "I don't like it when someone threatens my people and neither does Captain Miles. So we did something about it. Yon brothers didn't protest overmuch – but that may have been due to them being trussed up like chickens."

"With you two at our backs, what do we need to worry about?" Alex clasped Mrs Parson's hand hard. "Thank you."

"They'll be back," Mrs Parson said. "They strike me as most persevering."

"Yeah – unfortunately." In an effort to think of something else, Alex sat back, stretched her legs out in front of her and studied her friend. "So, how did things go?"

"Hmm?" Mrs Parson bent her head to her knitting.

"With Captain Miles."

"That is none of your concern, Alex Graham."

No, it probably wasn't. But from the pleased smile on Mrs Parson's face, she suspected they'd gone well.

Matthew listened, stared, and broke out in laughter. And then he surprised everyone by giving Mrs Parson a hug. After this, he went back to the preparations for their homeward journey, telling Alex he wanted to be well on his way before nightfall – he missed his home, and more importantly his bed, because this squeaky and rickety construction left him with a constant backache.

"I can massage it for you tonight," Alex murmured, placing a hand on his lower back. He gave her a green look before ensuring Mrs Parson was comfortably seated on the mule and that Moses' girth was tightened.

"That's a boy!" Alex hissed when their two new servants hove in sight.

"Fourteen, near on fifteen," Matthew agreed.

Alex gave him a disapproving look. "A child, Matthew."

He smiled but didn't say anything, and when the two came to a stop before them, Alex did a double take. Agnes! Well, no, because this gangling boy was taller than Agnes and had a small, tight mouth that had frozen into an expression of bitterness. But the eyes were wide and grey, shaded by long fair lashes, and the hair was thin and so light it was almost white in the May sun – just like Agnes. He smelled. Both of them did – a rank, heavy odour of sweat and onions and dirt. They bowed a greeting to Alex and Mrs Parson, who studied them with interest.

"Angus?" Mrs Parson said, "Angus Wilson?"

Angus gave her a wary look but admitted that aye, that was his name.

"This will please your sister, no?" Mrs Parson crowed, ignoring Matthew's forbidding look.

"My sister?" Angus' eyes flew to Matthew. "Is Agnes serving with you, master?"

"Aye, she is," Matthew said, "but I wasn't planning on telling you, not yet."

"I wanted it to be a surprise," he told Alex later, sounding aggrieved. He was lying on his back while Alex was busy with his thigh, rubbing slow circles over his scar and the surrounding muscles.

"It will be," Alex soothed, "if nothing else for Agnes." Around them hung the darkness of the night, scented and warm, and by the fire Patrick was sitting, his eyes on the surrounding, flickering shadows. "Just off a boat?"

Matthew grunted an agreement and rolled over on his front to allow her hands access to his back. "Some weeks back. Bonded himself over to escape his irate master."

"Why? What did he do?"

"Fell in love with the daughter," Matthew replied with a yawn. "And she with him – or that's what he says." He relaxed under her hands, made a series of contented sounds, and just like that dropped into sleep. Alex smoothed his shirt down, drew the blanket up over them both and curled up close.

She woke early to find him wide awake beside her. At his silent question, she nodded, and they walked further into the forest, barefoot and half-dressed. She could feel the heat in his hand leap into hers, and all of her fizzed with sudden and urgent desire. It almost made her laugh out loud. They were too old to be driven this crazy by each other's touch. But they weren't, and when he stopped under an oak to spread the blanket, she was wet with want for him and all because of the way his fingertips grazed her wrists. She felt her breath hitch in her chest at the brightness of his eyes. They didn't undress; there was no time. She just opened her legs and took him inside.

"Is it safe?" he asked into her hair. She was beyond the point where she cared, because all she could think of was how good it felt when he pounded into her, how big he was, how warm and strong he was, and how heavenly it felt when he nuzzled her neck.

"I'm not sure," she whispered back, "but I swear I'll kill you if you stop right now." She locked her legs around him, ground her pelvis into his, and raised her head to bite his ear.

"Ah," he groaned, "have mercy, woman!"

"I feel like a teenager," she said with a giggle when they walked back towards the clearing. He looked momentarily confused until he recalled what the expression meant.

"You look like one." He stopped to pick leaves out of her hair. His fingers floated deeper into her curls and he drew her close to kiss her, kiss her as he just had loved her, forcefully and yet so tenderly it nearly made her cry.

"My Alex," he said, taking her hand. All around them stood dawn proper, birds sang and hopped, the ground was covered with the red and yellow of columbines but as far as Alex was concerned there was only one thing to feast her eyes on. Her husband smiled, a slow smile that made her insides quiver with renewed desire. His smiled widened.

"Insatiable," he murmured, bending to nip her throat. "And wanton," he added, laughter colouring his voice.

"It takes one to know one, Mr Graham."

"Oh aye, that it does." He presented her with a red columbine and led them back to camp.

With the cows setting the pace, it took them five days to get back home. The sun was setting, and for the last hour or so they'd ridden in silence, Alex half asleep against his chest. Matthew sat thinking back to all the times they'd ridden like this, with her a heavy weight against his heart. The first time he took her to Hillview, she a wild, strange lass that tried so hard not to show how fearful she was of all that was unfamiliar in this new world of hers... All the times coming back from Cumnock, sometimes with her sitting pillion, but mostly like this, because both of them preferred it that way. He buried his nose in her hair and drew in that scent so particularly hers, of crisp apples and newly spliced wood, of sun and salt.

He turned off the bridle path and halted Moses to study his homestead. The western sky was shifting into turquoise; in the meadows grazed his cows and mule. Encircled by whispering forests, his fields were ripening into gold and, halfway up the slope, Alex's kitchen garden was a multitude of green hues. His bairns were everywhere: Ruth and Sarah squealing as they fought over the rope swing, Daniel whittling with an admiring David crouched beside him. Samuel was tottering after a hen, his smock fluttering in the breeze, and there came Ian and Mark, two dark heads bent towards each other in conversation.

"Home," Alex murmured.

Matthew tightened his hold around her and nudged Moses into a walk.

"Aye," he said, "home." And for the first time since he'd left Hillview, he actually meant it. This was home, here was his family, and this was his land.

For a historical note and for more information
about Matthew and Alex, please visit Anna's website at
www.annabelfrage.com

The Graham Saga continues in:

Serpents in the Garden

"Not again," Alex muttered, throwing an irritated glance up the lane.

"Long time since the last one." Mrs Parson shrugged before bustling off to prepare something to drink and eat for their unbidden guests.

Alex made a face. Mrs Parson was right: the impromptu visits from militia troops were, thank heavens, becoming rarer now that some kind of peace had been re-established between colonists and Indians. In Alex's opinion, the men who still rode in militia companies were the scavengers of this world, more out to feather their own nests than to uphold any kind of peace, but the rules of common courtesy prevailed and so Alex stepped into her yard to welcome the dozen or so men who were riding down their lane.

It was years since Alex had laid eyes on Philip Burley, but she knew him immediately. Older, gaunter, but still with that lock of hair that fell forward over his face, giving him an air of mischievousness belied by the coldness of his light grey eyes. He bowed, his mouth curling into an amused smile at what she assumed to be her aghast expression. With an effort, she closed her mouth.

"Did you hope I had died?" he asked, dismounting.

"Yes, but at least I wished you a quick and painless death – you know, falling off your horse and breaking your neck or something."

Philip Burley laughed, eyes doing a quick up and down before returning to her face. "Alas, here I am."

"But looking quite worn round the edges." Alex took in his threadbare coat, his downtrodden boots.

"I don't dress up for riding through the woods."

"No, none of you have, have you?" Alex nodded to the

man who seemed to be in charge, swept her hand towards the bench under the oak. "Beer?"

"And food," the older man said, patting at his rumbling stomach.

"I'll get you some bread and then there's some leftover stew from yesterday."

Philip Burley sniffed the air. "What? No chicken?"

"No, they're meant for our dinner. Besides, they're not done."

"But we can wait." Philip smirked.

No way! She'd rather have a cobra at her feet than him in her yard. "Stew and bread. Take it or leave it." Alex directed herself to the leader.

"We take it," the man said, "however ungraciously offered."

"That's because of him." Alex pointed at Philip. "For some reason, he gives me severe indigestion – it must be the general look of him. Quite repulsive." Not entirely true, as the man exuded some sort of animal magnetism, as graceful and dangerous as a starving panther. Some of Burley's companions broke out in laughter, quickly quenched when he glared at them.

Alex and Mrs Parson served the men, helped by Agnes. For all that they looked dishevelled and stank like hell, the men were relatively polite, taking the time to thank them before falling on their food. Alex retreated indoors, keeping a worried look not only on their guests, but also on the barn and the path beyond.

"He's over on the other side of the river," Mrs Parson said, no doubt to calm her. "He won't be coming in for dinner – you know that. Besides, it's not as if that Burley can do anything at present, is it? However unkempt and wild, I doubt his companions will help him do Matthew harm."

Alex relaxed at the irrefutable logic in this. "At least it's only him. I wonder where his brothers are."

"We know where one of them is: in hell, there to burn in eternal agony." Mrs Parson replenished her pitcher and stepped outside to serve the men some more to drink.

"Yeah, thanks to Matthew."

"Good riddance," Mrs Parson said over her shoulder. "And we both know why, no?"

Alex nodded. Will Burley had died while attempting to kill her Matthew, and for that the remaining Burley brothers intended to make Matthew Graham pay. Alex swallowed, smoothed down her skirts, ensured not one single lock of hair peeped from under her cap, and grabbed the bread basket.

"So many children," the officer who by now had introduced himself as Elijah Carey said. "All yours?"

"No, but most of them are." She was made nervous by the way Philip Burley kept on staring at her girls, in particular at Sarah.

"Not that young anymore," Philip said. "Soon old enough to bed."

"Absolutely not!" Alex bristled.

Philip laughed, tilting his head at her daughters. "I don't agree, Mrs Graham, but then I like them young."

"Burley..." Carey warned with a little sigh. The younger man raised those strange, almost colourless irises in his direction and just stared, nailing his eyes into the officer until Carey muttered something about needing the privy and, with a hasty nod in Alex's direction, disappeared.

"My, my, what have you done to him? Sneaked up on him at night and kicked him in the back? That's how you do it, isn't it? Under cover of the dark..." In a movement so swift Alex had no time to back away, Philip was on her, crowding her against the oak.

"You don't take me seriously, do you, Mrs Graham?" he said, in a voice so low only she could hear him. "Most women – and men for that matter – know better than to taunt me."

"You don't scare me," she said, her knees shivering with her lie.

He looked at her for a long time. "Oh yes, I do, Mrs Graham. Only a fool wouldn't be frightened of me, and that you are not."

Alex shoved at him, creating some space between them.

"I suppose I must take that as a compliment," she said, mentally patting herself on her back for how casual she succeeded in keeping her tone.

Philip Burley laughed, an admiring look in his eyes. "Take it as you will, Mrs Graham. But never commit the mistake of thinking we have forgotten the blood debt your husband owes us. However long it takes, we will have revenge for what he did to our Will."

Alex tried to say something, but her tongue had glued itself to the roof of her mouth, and to her shame she could hear her breathing become ragged, a slight whistling accompanying each inhalation.

"I was right: I do scare you." With an ironic little bow, Philip Burley walked off, and Alex wasn't quite sure how she made it from the tree to her kitchen door.

Lightning Source UK Ltd.
Milton Keynes UK
UKOW02f1215270616

277170UK00002B/22/P